*Something about a tough guy exposing his
soft side made Katya do crazy things.*

The gravitational pull she'd felt toward Cam all through
dinner might have had something to do with it as well.
Whatever it was, she couldn't restrain herself anymore.

She reached out to touch him, and he stood and leaned
in, his hands bracketing her hips. "Haven't we been here
before?" He tipped his head and took her lips.

This was what she'd missed. This closeness with
another person—his fingers, at the nape of her neck, and
knowing, from the change in his breathing, that he was as
caught as she.

Her need whispered to her. *More of this.*

Sweet on You

Don't miss the other titles in this series!

Sweet on You

Laura Drake

Book Three in the Sweet
on a Cowboy Series

FOREVER

NEW YORK   BOSTON

Copyright © 2014 by Laura Drake
Excerpt from *The Sweet Spot* copyright © 2013 by Laura Drake
Excerpt from *Nothing Sweeter* copyright © 2014 by Laura Drake

Forever
Hachette Book Group
237 Park Avenue
New York, NY 10017

www.HachetteBookGroup.com

Printed in the United States of America

First Edition: August 2014
10 9 8 7 6 5 4 3 2 1

OPM

Forever is an imprint of Grand Central Publishing.
The Forever name and logo are trademarks of Hachette Book Group, Inc.

The Hachette Speakers Bureau provides a wide range of authors for speaking events. To find out more, go to www.hachettespeakersbureau.com or call (866) 376-6591.

The publisher is not responsible for websites (or their content) that are not owned by the publisher.

ATTENTION CORPORATIONS AND ORGANIZATIONS:
Most HACHETTE BOOK GROUP books are available
at quantity discounts with bulk purchase for educational,
business, or sales promotional use. For information,
please call or write:

Special Markets Department, Hachette Book Group
237 Park Avenue, New York, NY 10017
Telephone: 1-800-222-6747 Fax: 1-800-477-5925

For Mom and Nancy—
Any good I may do is for you.

The rest is on me.

Acknowledgments

I owe a huge debt of gratitude to those who helped a city girl get it right:

Dee Cornell, PT, ATC, and member of the Justin Boots Sports Medicine Team. That makes her a hero in my book.

Wiley Petersen, retired PBR bull rider, and bull rider coach, for his advice on managing fear.

Then the remarkable health/fitness specialists who helped me get that part right:

To Angel Cipolla—a kick butt physical trainer (as I have good reason to know) and a wonderful resource.

Sarah Kuyper—physical trainer and all-around people person.

Aleida Zendejas, R.N., H.H.P. (Holistic Health Practitioner), she's the whole package.

Also Lauren O'Gorman, Media & Communications Manager for the Honda Center and the Anaheim Ducks, for giving me a tour of the locker room.

To Donna Hopson, my friend, and "lay editor."

I'm ever thankful for my faithful, giving critters: Greg

Henry, Sharla Rae, Jenny Hansen, Orly Konig Lopez, and Fae Rowen, my very own "plot angel"!

And to my published author buds, Susan Squires, Tessa Dare, and Kara Lennox, who routinely talk me off the ledge.

And as always, thanks to super-agent, Nalini Akolekar, and my ever-patient editor, Latoya Smith.

A Note from the Author

I've taken liberty with the PBR event schedule, and their breaks. They also have more medical personnel on hand for events. The Justin Boots Sports Medicine team is an amazing group of professionals looking after the health of rodeo personnel. Learn more about them at: http://justinsports7medicine.com/

Sweet on You

CHAPTER 1

Kandahar Air Field, Afghanistan

Another night of blood and adrenaline.

Katya Smith pulled her shower-wet hair into a bun. The weight of exhaustion tugged at her, but the fine hum of tension running just under her skin warned that she wouldn't sleep.

Yet, beyond that, resting close to her heart, was a firm pillow of satiety. They'd saved two soldiers' lives last night.

Being alone in the small, fake-wood–paneled room of the Quonset hut was an odd occurrence, given her three roommates. But Role 3 hospital inhaled medical personnel. They must be working a shift. The army was so desperate for medics that Katya had been transferred from physical therapy to triage medic two years ago.

She took the few steps to the American flag-draped wall and the small chalkboard beneath it, almost covered in chalk lines. Neat bundles of five, representing men that they'd saved from the enemy. She picked up the chalk, to add her night's conquests, but hesitated. Keeping score against the bad guys only made sense if you were clear that there *was* an actual bad guy.

That's not right. The enemy they fought in the ER wasn't the Afghani insurgents.

It was death.

She brought the chalk down on the board so hard that it broke. She made two marks, one crossing four others—another neat bundle.

Beep beep! The Jeep's horn through the thin walls got her moving. Shouldering her rifle and pack, she opened the door and pushed into the dry blast of Kandahar heat. By the time she had the door locked, her shower had worn off.

Murphy grinned from the seat of the Jeep he'd commandeered—best not to ask where. Last night in the ER, when he'd invited her on a trip to town, she couldn't resist. Most soldiers longed for a taste of home. They cheered when fast-food franchises opened on base. Not Katya. She loved unfamiliar spices and exotic local dishes. She'd even tried the boiled sheep's head a street vendor once offered, finding the flavor of the facial meat fabulous once she got past the staring white eye and the grinning exposed teeth.

She tossed her pack in the Jeep and climbed in, cradling the rifle in her lap. "I don't remember it being this hot last April." She put her hand to her cloth-covered helmet, shifting it to blot the sweat tickle that made her scalp feel as if it was crawling with bugs.

Murphy's cool, green eyes watched her with appreciation. "It's probably just my proximity, ma'am. I have that effect on women."

She knew she shouldn't encourage him, but couldn't help but smile at the combat medic. He looked like a pencil wearing a helmet—all long bones and knobby joints. His helmet covered buzz cut red hair, but even if she hadn't known his surname, the flushed, freckled skin declared him a Celt.

He gunned the engine, yet drove at a sedate pace to keep the dust down until they cleared the security check at the entrance of the base.

She would have loved to be alone for a while, but knew that was impossible. Kandahar was not safe—especially for a solitary female. Even a female second lieutenant.

The wind swirling behind the windshield cooled as well as a fan in hell. Katya looked out at the receding puddles and rapidly parching grass at the side of the road, thanking God for the road the Corps of Engineers had built last year. Spring rain in the desert was beautiful, but it was hell on goat-track roads that morphed from sliding mud pits to foot-deep cement-like ruts overnight.

Eyes on the road, Murphy yelled over the wind, "We could swing by the airport on the way back and watch the planes do touch-and-goes. Not very romantic by normal standards, but it's the finest that this corner of Afghanistan has to offer."

Like everyone, she enjoyed the Nebraskan's down-home, upbeat sense of humor that had lit up the ER since he'd transferred in a month ago. But comments like these made her wonder if the E-4 had a bit of a crush. "Did you miss the lecture about not fraternizing with officers in boot camp, Corporal?"

"I think that must've been the day that the general's daughter and I were—uh, indisposed, ma'am."

She smiled. *Incorrigible.*

He slowed as they rolled into town. The two-story stucco buildings may have been handsome, before the bombing. They passed one with a missing front wall, exposing jagged rooms like broken teeth. Between the damage and the dust, the town looked tired, weary of all it had seen. Murphy parked and they got out. Katya shouldered her pack and rifle, wondering when it had stopped feeling odd, carrying armaments on a shopping trip.

Tourists were an extinct species in a war zone. The shops were shuttered. Still people needed to eat. Intrepid vendors had set up tables in the narrow band between the buildings and the street. Vegetables mostly, sold by men with light, loose clothing and disrespectful eyes. The bright blush of pomegranate skin and green grapes looked incongruous in the sepia scene.

Dusty muslin awnings extended from the buildings, blocking the sun, but didn't help much with the torpid air. She and Murphy joined the shoppers, keeping their rifles slung, but remaining alert. When Murphy bent to examine something on a table, Katya's eyes scanned the crowd.

An hour later, the cloth bag on Katya's shoulder held her treasure—local figs. She found their dusky sweetness cleared her palette after a mess hall dinner. "I'm ready to head back if you are, Murphy."

She glanced at her sweat-slicked companion, looking as if his M16 would overbalance him. He carried a palm-sized hand-sewn stuffed rabbit.

"You know, you may want to tuck that under your pillow at night, or your roommates are going to give you hell."

He lifted the toy to his lips, kissed it, and dropped it into the pocket of his damp shirt. "It's for my new niece. I haven't met her yet, but I'll show you photos when we get back."

They headed for the Jeep. The next block was unpopulated, its bombed-out buildings long abandoned. The light seemed harder here, as if showcasing the damage—throwing it in the onlooker's face. In contrast, the inky black of the narrow alley on her left made Katya shiver, conjuring thoughts of scorpions and snipers. Her skin pricked, but not from sweat. She stepped quickly past.

A boy stepped around the corner a few buildings ahead. He held his forearm, blood dripping between his fingers into the dust. He looked to be nine or so, wearing a traditional long shirt and loose pants, a round pakol cap on his head. He shuffled toward them, tears streaking his dusty face.

Kayta's heart rate shot up, kicking into triage mode. Quickening her pace, scanning the boy for other injuries, she reached into her bag for her ever-present first-aid kit.

Then she hesitated. The boy's eyes darted, his movements jerky with fear.

The gun was in her sweaty hands before she knew she'd unslung it. Sound ceased. She tried to remember when a vehicle last passed.

Murphy rushed past her, his still-slung rifle bouncing, as he reached for his first-aid kit. Alarm sirens of panic echoed through her head. Something was wrong. She snatched at Murphy's arm, but missed.

He reached the boy and leaned over him, blocking her view. Katya took two running steps forward.

The harsh light exploded in a starburst of yellow and red. The sound was deafening as it threw her backward.

Then blessed blackness took her.

• • •

Katya listened. The hushed conversation and echo of hurried squeaky shoes sounded familiar. So was the smell—dust, antiseptic, and the metallic undertone of blood. She shifted her arms, her legs. All there, thank God, but her slight movement woke a hot poker stab in her side and throbbing in the fingers of her right hand.

She lay still in the dark, afraid to open her eyes. Afraid to assume the responsibility, because she sensed, deep in her mind, something lurked that she did not want to know. Opening her eyes would force her—

"Welcome back, Soldier." The deep voice was familiar too.

Katya pulled her eyes open. Major Samuel Thibodaux, her superior officer and lead surgeon at Role 3, leaned over her. She turned her head, disoriented to see her work environs from a reclined angle. Beds in rows, most filled with wounded—white skin, brown skin, no skin.

The major peeled back her eyelid and flashed a penlight in her eye. The light lasered to the back of her brain. She flinched.

"Headache?"

She closed her eyes and nodded.

"Nauseous?"

A brush of air as the sheet was pulled to her hips. He gently prodded her side.

She winced and shook her head, frowning. It was coming. A hulking memory lumbered down the pathways of her brain, moving fast.

"You were downtown. A bomb…"

The rest was drowned out by the sound of a wailing moan. She realized after a beat that it had come from her.

The heat, the sound, the *light*—"Murphy." She opened her eyes.

The major's jaw tightened, pulling his lips into a thin line.

She realized she hadn't stated it as a question. Her stomach muscles pulled taut, to protect her solar plexus from the blow. A memory came forward, burned into her brain. Murphy bringing the toy to his lips, to kiss it. "No. Oh, no." Her legs writhed, trying to find an outlet for the pain, the horror.

The major pressed the plunger on a morphine drip. "We took shrapnel from your side, along with your spleen and a chunk of your liver. You lost the fingernails on your right hand. But you're going to be okay."

A face swam to the surface of her mind. Wispy black hair, huge, dark eyes, full of liquid fear. "The boy." Her voice came out as a thready whisper, fading.

He shook his head. "Suicide bomber."

She rushed to meet the sweet blackness that rose to swallow her.

Cam Cahill coughed up dust. The sun branded his skin through his shirt. He kicked his borrowed gelding to a canter, chasing down another steer, wild from months on the winter slopes.

How could Texas be this hot and dry in April? He tugged the bandana off his nose, where it was doing nothing to block the dust, and settled it around his neck where it would at least keep the sweat from rolling down his back.

Another billow of dust rolled over him as Len Robertson reined up alongside. The old man's hair might be gray and his face as tanned and creased as a burlap sack, but he sat relaxed in the saddle even after ten hours in it. "You know what Phil Sheridan said about Texas, dontcha?"

"Go east, young man?"

"Close." Len smiled, showing the gap between his front teeth. "He said, 'If I owned Texas and Hell, I would rent out Texas and live in Hell.'" The old coot cackled and rode on ahead, his horse kicking up more dust.

He actually enjoys this. Cam reached for his canteen. *Five more miles till the home corrals.* He uncapped the bottle and took a long drink of the hot, metallic-tasting water.

And more of the same, tomorrow. He hadn't expected a stock contractor's life to be glamorous, but the past five days convinced him he could cross this off his short list of careers.

Which left... exactly nothing.

His last season as a rider on the pro bull riding circuit was half over and his future resembled a black hole in space, sucking light, gravity, and all his peace. He capped the water jug and hung the loop over his saddle horn. He should be content. He'd had a great career. The first rider to win back-to-back titles, and he had the belt buckles to prove it. He reined left, to stay upwind of the small herd.

What if the past fifteen years had been the best of his life? Thirty-two was too young to give up and do nothing, even if he had enough money to live on. The drive that pushed him to the top hadn't lessened with the years, even if his reaction times had.

His knee protested when he shifted in the saddle to ease his sore hip. His body was about done.

He'd planned to have a wife and kids by now. He'd planned to settle on his own ranch in Bandera, and live out the rest of his life in peace. But he no longer had a wife, much less kids, and after years of traveling, the thought of holing up in his run-down cabin all alone wasn't a happy one.

What good were gold buckles and old bull riding stories, if you didn't have someone to share them with?

CHAPTER 2

"Sar san, Katya?"

The ancient voice sounded as shaky as the hand resting on Katya's arm. Her grandmother sat swaddled in a blouse and flowing skirt, as if she'd shrunk since putting them on. Anxiety shot through Katya's chest. When had their keystone become so frail?

"Nothing is wrong, Grand. I've come home, that's all." She lightly stroked the tissue-paper skin of her forearm, enveloped in the smell of the herbs Grand had worked with so long they'd become a part of her. Her body may have aged, but the bright sparrow eyes that regarded Katya hadn't dimmed a bit in what they saw.

The dining room table stretched under the window, crowded as always with piles of sorted leaves and packets of ground herbs. Grand's mortar and pestle sat before her, the queen's scepter. She sat in her wing-back chair, with the same green corduroy cushions Katya remembered, the nap worn smooth in places.

"You have no *kintala*." She turned Katya's hand, palm up, studying it.

Quickly, gently, she pulled back her hand.

Grand's bony fingers clamped on her wrist with more strength than Katya would have imagined they possessed. She curled her fingers closed and looked away, not ready for whatever future the old woman would tell.

"My balance is okay, Grand. I've lived out of the country so long it's bound to seem strange, coming home." She tried not to squirm under the intense regard, just as she had as a child. "I want to know how you're doing. Are the aunts taking good care of you?"

"They hover. I am fine." She dismissed the subject with a wave of her hand. "Have you seen your mother?"

"Not yet. I will." All she'd thought of since waking in the hospital was getting here to Chicago, to Grand.

The old eyes glazed for a moment, then cleared. "You will go, yes? You will need her soon."

Need her mother? Oh yes, she'd needed her, many times. Not that her mother had noticed. "Yes, later." Getting along in a foreign land was a skill Katya had learned growing up in her parents' house.

Katya glanced through the antique lace curtains to the street. Her cousins played in the yard of the family's apartment complex, rolling together like a ball of puppies. She'd done the same in her summers as a child. Hundreds of years ago it seemed. Her gorge rose, and with it, the admission she must keep inside. She'd lost more than blood, a few nonvital organs, and good friends over there.

"What happened? You are in pain."

Katya turned again to the woman, just as she always had. "Too much, Grand. Too much suffering. Too much fanaticism. Too much stupidity."

Grand's baggy blouse exposed bird-like bones. Fragile shoulders didn't look strong enough to support her neck, much less Katya's burden.

"I've lost my healing." Her confession fell on the table, a lump of black, oozing offal. A clock ticked in the silence and she could hear her heart, thudding in her chest. Ten minutes with Grand, and she was spilling her guts. She shouldn't be surprised; it had always been so. She dipped her head.

She'd lost a precious gift; her legacy. There could be no penance for such a sin.

Cool fingers stroked her cheek then slipped under her chin, raising it. The love in Grand's wan smile tore open something—a black festering, overlooked in dealing with all the wounds, real and imagined. Katya realized that the balm of absolution in that smile was the reason she'd come.

"Ah Katya. You cannot lose something that is a part of you. It's only gotten covered up." Grand tucked a hank of hair behind her granddaughter's ear, as she had a million times. "You will find it again and more. When you do, remember; gifts sometimes come in strange wrappings."

Katya knew better than to ask what the small smile meant. Grand was a master in the art of the arcane. They sat in the peace of quiet. Katya pulled in the vibrant energy that was her grandmother. She felt like the confused child who'd arrived here, every summer.

There was a lot of love in her parents' house, only most of it didn't involve her. She'd always been the moth outside the window of her parents' love, bumping the glass to get inside. Her parents' relationship seemed smothering to Katya. Unnatural. If that was love, she'd do without.

God knows what delicate negotiations took place between her parents and Grand, to allow Katya to travel from her home in DC to Chicago, but she'd loved those summers.

In the beginning, she'd only attended Grand's lessons to have an excuse to be close, to suck up the loving acceptance like a dry sponge. But once filled, she listened, and found herself pulled in by the art of healing.

Now, with time and distance, she could see that she'd always wanted to be like her grandmother.

Grand believed Katya had empathic powers. Katya knew that wasn't true. She'd just found there were more ways to listen than with her ears. If she paid close attention, even unconscious patients had things to say.

A door closed somewhere, and heels tapped in the hall, getting closer. The apartment door opened and her aunt's frizzy gray-threaded black hair appeared first, followed by her face. The stamp of Gypsy was plain on her aunt's olive skin and cat-slanted dark eyes. She put a finger to her lips, then waved Katya over.

Eyes closed, Grand's head rested against the back of the chair. She breathed evenly in sleep.

Katya stood carefully, leaned over and whispered, "I love you, Puri Daj. Thank you" and walked out.

Katya sat in a chair in her aunt's kitchen. "Beval, she's so frail!"

"That happens when you reach the age of ninety-four." She walked to the stove and clicked the burner under the teakettle. "Why did you feel the need to fight in their war, Katya?"

Her aunt had always been plainspoken, and she hadn't changed a bit.

Katya opened her mouth, then closed it. She used to know the answer. She used to believe in the answer. She'd grown up outside of DC. When Flight 93 went down on 9/11, enlistment seemed to her the only response. But after ten years of patching up the young pawns of the chess match, the answer had faded like invisible ink, leaving her holding blank pages. She shook her head.

"How is your *daj*, Katya?" her aunt whispered, leaning forward.

Her sister, Katya's mother—the outcast. A full Gypsy, Katya's mother was raised there, living communally in the *kumpania*. Katya grew up hearing whispered stories of her mother's wildness, though they were hard to believe, given the staid researcher she'd become.

As a child, her mother had done as she pleased, defying the laws of the family. Yet when she stepped through the doors of high school and slapped eyes on Katya's father, things got serious. He was *gajo*—non-Gypsy. This building must have vibrated with the buzzing of the *famalia*, men and women alike. When she eloped after graduation, in the eyes of the family, Katya's mother had died.

Only Grand kept tenuous contact, and only after Katya was born. Grand must have used magic, because Katya bore the name Grand chose, and from Katya's earliest memory, her summers were Gypsy.

"I haven't seen her yet. Last I heard, she was fine."

Beval's gaze darted around the room, though she knew they were alone. "Well, tell her, when you see her, that—"

A ghostly moan echoed from the hall. It changed, rising in volume and pitch to a banshee's wail.

"Aaaaieeeeeeeeee!"

Katya jerked, and before she could control her body,

she was crouched under the table, sweat popping in her armpits and her heart hammering like the piston of a red-lined engine. She and her aunt froze, staring at each other in horror.

"Help me! Oh God. Katya, help me!"

The too-human pain in the young woman's scream shattered her aunt's immobility. She lurched from her chair and ran out of the apartment door before Katya could crawl out from under the tablecloth. She tried to stand, but the adrenaline surge left her legs rubbery. She fell back to her knees and leaned her forehead on the carpet, for just a moment, until the black spots retreated.

I don't want to go! That wail had told her whatever waited down the hall was horrible. Her muddled brain processed thoughts in half-time. She tried to force her limbs to move. But as in Kandahar, they rebelled. Katya knelt in a quivering ball, exhaling coward breaths into the carpet.

Why me? Why do they call me?

Flashes fired behind her clenched eyelids; gaping wounds, mouths twisted in agony, the dark, fearful eyes of a strange boy.

Move, damn it! Someone needs you! Gritting her teeth, she forced her fingers to relax and felt the nails pop out of the carpet. Her biceps shook, but supported her weight when she pushed herself upright.

Her unwilling feet eventually carried her down the hall. She stood quivering in the doorway to Grand's room, physically unable to force her body across the threshold. Her aunts crouched around the small body in her grandmother's chair. Beval raised her streaming eyes to the doorway, and shook her head.

• • •

In Washington, DC, a week later, Katya dodged students, pulled the door open, and stepped inside. The glass entry of the university chemistry building soared overhead. The huge silver helix of a carbon atom hung from the ceiling, rotating unnoticed by hurrying students. Even the smell was the same—an odd mix of books, chemicals, and sunlight. She should have known that nothing ever changed here. Shouldn't her arms be full of textbooks? Katya hurried down the hall, the soles of her flats slapping. She'd allowed a half hour before her real appointment, and didn't want to be late.

She didn't have to scan the nameplates alongside the doors she passed; her feet led her to the right one. Hand on the knob, she took a deep breath. Somewhere between Chicago and DC she'd gotten mad. The fact that she'd expected the outcome didn't seem to matter. Seething, she turned the knob and opened the door to her parents' lab.

It hadn't changed either. Table-lined walls, an island workstation in the center, all cluttered with sinks and expensive research paraphernalia. To the left, her white-coated parents huddled beside an electron microscope, deep in conversation.

They had changed. Her father stood bent, staring into the eyepiece. He was handsome as ever, but silver glinted in the too long blond hair sweeping from his temples. He'd forgotten to get it cut again. When he glanced up, there were no smile lines at the corners of his eyes, only a deep frown; the price of decades of contemplating the mysteries of science.

"Hello, Katya."

She took a step toward her father, arms open. But he'd

already returned his attention to the world in the microscope lens. She dropped her arms.

Hand on his back, her mother regarded Katya. A
Gypsy in a laboratory, her mother was as paradoxically
beautiful as ever. Perfect olive skin and huge dark eyes,
her lips pulled into a tight line, as if she were embarrassed
by their fullness. Her black curls were harnessed in a tight
French twist.

"Welcome back, Katya." She said it as though they'd
seen each other at breakfast. Her mother traveled the few
steps to bridge the gap between them and opened her arms.

Katya stepped into them and wrapped her own arms
around her mother, enveloped by her scent—a blend of
exotic perfume and the cold alkaline bite of chemicals.
She leaned her head on her mother's shoulder and clung as
emotion washed over her, a strong mix of regret and hollow
longing that swelled her throat, and pricked behind her eyes.

Her mother gave her a brief squeeze and a pat on the
shoulder.

Katya stepped back, as her anger flared. "You couldn't
attend your own mother's funeral? Really, Mom?"

"Show some respect in your tone, Katya." Her father
threw in his signature line, then checked out of the discussion, bending once more over the altar of the microscope.

Katya tried to ignore the pinprick that tightened the
muscles of her chest. She crossed her arms, leaning a hip
against the counter. "Respect. Now there's an interesting
word."

Her mother had a large repertoire of sighs. She
deployed one of her favorites, the long-suffering one.
"What do you think Rom Baro would have done if I'd
shown up? You know him. He'd have used the funeral

as a bully pulpit from which to preach." She pursed her lips and shook her head, once, fast, as if it were a spasm. "I made my decision years ago. I knew then it was irreversible. Just because I hadn't thought ahead to this point doesn't make it any less permanent." She glanced at her husband, then back.

Katya caught a flash of grief in the moment before her haughty mask dropped back in place.

"Remember this when it's time for you to choose, Katya. Reaching for one thing may require letting go of another." She crossed the room to the coffeepot sitting among beakers and test tubes like a hillbilly at a black tie dinner. She pulled out two cups and poured.

Katya said, "I have an appointment in a few minutes."

Her mother doctored them with creamer, just the way they liked them.

Silly me.

When her mother was done stirring, she picked them up. "Are you home for good, then?"

God, I hope not. "I don't know yet. I'll know more after my meeting with Dr. Raleigh." She consulted the clock on the wall over her mother's head. "Which I'm going to be late for if I don't get moving. I'll call you later." She didn't bother interrupting her father's work to say good-bye.

She climbed the stairs, and at the first door on the right she knocked, then opened the door to an empty office. She checked her cell phone for the time. Ten minutes early. She crossed to the padded guest chair, straightened her skirt and sat. She pulled her peasant blouse a bit farther down her shoulders then smiled at her own vanity. Trace Raleigh had been many things to her: instructor, mentor, lover, then finally, and still, her friend. His had been the second number she'd dialed that awful day that Grand died.

She looked around the office that hadn't changed. Textbooks littered every surface, dumbbells cluttered one corner. Resistance bands hung on the wall next to a poster of the human body, stripped of skin, exposing the musculature. Pinned on the bulletin board, front and center in the place of honor, hung the photo. Trace was always in search of a picture that captured the vision of the perfect human body. The photo changed when he discovered a better one—a calf muscle, caught in the act of explosion from a starting block, or the light, shining just so on a sweating bicep. Male bodies or female, it didn't matter. Katya had called it the Hunk of the Month Club.

She closed her eyes, willing herself back to when she last sat in this chair. It didn't work.

She'd planned on a degree in physical therapy, but it was Trace who convinced her to double major. When he suggested she get her athletic trainer degree, she thought he was crazy. Katya had no love of team sports, or organized sports of any kind, for that matter. She'd watched the spoiled darlings of the high school teams strut the halls, broad shoulders set in an angle of arrogant, swaggering entitlement. She wanted nothing to do with them.

Trace had convinced her that the practical aspects of an athletic trainer would complement her skills as a physical therapist. And he'd been right. So she gave up her job at the library for the locker room, wrapping meaty ankles and icing the hallowed knees of every team the university sponsored, for two long years.

She jumped at the sound of the door opening. Dr. Raleigh swept in and kicked the door shut with his heel. When he saw her, he smiled. Everyone could smile, of course. But Trace Raleigh *smiled*. His charisma punched like a blow to the solar plexus. In that moment, in all the world, you knew you were special. Because you were special to *him*.

He had the chiseled features of a Greek Olympian, and his body was sculpted by a lifetime of athletics. The lighter streaks in his golden hair hadn't come from a bottle. She had every reason to know.

He'd wanted the love her parents had, the love she'd never give. Sarah had, and Katya was glad when they married, two years after she enlisted.

His eyes scanned her face. His smile slipped away. "Aw, hon. Come here." He opened his arms.

And she stepped into them. Leaning her head on his hard shoulder, she found more comfort than on her mother's soft one.

"I'm so sorry, Smitty."

Hearing his pet name almost undid her. A cyclic wind swept through her, stirring memories and waking a wailing she was terrified would escape.

She'd managed to stay strong in Chicago. It was expected of her.

What a joke.

Since then, the keening in her chest continued to build, each day adding relentless pressure, until she fairly bulged with it. She lived in fear that if the pressure were loosed, even the tiniest bit, she'd explode like Humpty Dumpty on a hand grenade.

No one would be able to put that mess back together again.

She let go of Trace and eased out of his arms.

He held her elbow and lowered her into the chair. "You

start talking while I get us coffee." He reached across the desk, unearthing two cups from a stack of paper. The pot he lifted looked to be the same one from their days together.

"Well, I told you the facts on the phone." She pulled at a loose thread in the cotton of her skirt.

"Yes, and there's always more than just facts, now, aren't there?" He finished pouring, opened a packet of sweetener, dumped it in one, and handed it to her. He grabbed the other cup and sat. "What are you going to do now?" His gaze was level and patient, as if he were willing to wait forever for her answer.

Time expanded.

Her chest didn't.

She felt a rumble; a warning tremor deep in her gut. It rose, molten and smoking. She put a hand to her mouth, but it was like putting a napkin over a volcano. "I don't know!" The wail broke from her, savage and loud in the small room. "I can't work. I tried in Kandahar. I freaked out. No, really. Freaked. Out." She took a sobbing breath. "They took me off the floor. Relieved me of my duty! Told me that I couldn't come back to work until a shrink cleared me." Her shame came out of her, lurching, shuddering.

Hoping to soothe the goddess of the volcano, she whispered the rest. "I couldn't face the humiliation of a mental exam I wouldn't have passed. But the army is my home. My family. Losing it hurts so bad."

She covered her face. "I have nowhere to go!"

Trace handed her a tissue to wipe the tears running down her face and put a hand on her knee in comfort.

"It's like I feel everything too much. The pain. All the patients' fears and agony. They tear holes in me." She sucked a short breath before taking another. "How does a physical therapist work if she can't be around pain?"

She wanted to put her head between her knees and howl, but she hitched a breath and blew her nose into the tissue. He handed her another.

"I left my life over there, my friends. The army is the only family I've known for eight years. My friend is dead. My grand is dead." She fought the sobs that roiled from her core. "I've lost *everything*!"

With the admission, her chest loosened a bit. For the first time in weeks, she felt able to take in a full breath. She snuffled and honked, cleaning up the aftermath.

She took another slow, measured breath.

Trace patted her knee, but his eyes were laughing. "Well, shit. You *are* a mess."

She snorted a laugh. "God, I sound like an overacting soap opera diva." She sniffed. "Maybe that should be my next career move."

"Geez, let's hope it doesn't come to that." Trace sat back and sipped his coffee. "Let me think a minute..."

Two weeks later

You're presented with an MCL level II tear. What's the treatment?"

The unassuming man who drawled the question didn't look like a doctor, much less a trauma surgeon. He sat sprawled in a chair in the cinderblock office, thumbs tucked in the front pockets of his blue jeans, as he had since he began the interview a gut-wrenching hour ago.

Katya leaned forward, tugging at the too short hem of her skirt that hadn't been too short in the store dressing room. "Acute, sub-acute, or rehab?"

"Acute."

"Ice and elevation, then compression knee brace to stabilize and decrease swelling. Crutches for a week or so."

She'd wondered why she'd been told to report to the First Mariner Arena for an interview with the PBR. She was used to acronyms from the army, but had to research this one. PBR stood for Professional Bull Riding. Sure, she'd heard of rodeos. She'd even watched a John Wayne movie once. But who knew there were men crazy enough to ride bulls for a living, much less people to watch it?

A short fat man passed the doorless office yelling, "We've got forty-five minutes, people!"

Dr. Cody Hanes straightened in his chair and pulled her résumé toward him. "Katya Smith." He hesitated as if she'd made up the common last name. Her family had adopted the English name for tinker, because the Gypsy equivalent, Petulengro, was used only among their people.

"Yes?"

"You are overqualified for this position." He consulted the paper before him. "A licensed physical therapist, a licensed athletic trainer, a combat medic with two tours in Afghanistan." He tossed the sheet on his desk, leaned back in his executive chair, and gave her the twice-over. "And you're applying for a PT job with a rodeo sports medicine team?"

She looked down to where his hands rested on her résumé. Long-fingered, capable, clever, just as she'd expect a surgeon's hands to be. It had been the cowboy hat she didn't expect. She clasped her fingers to stop their fidgeting and forced her gaze to meet his.

"Why should I hire you, Katya Smith?"

"Is it because I'm a woman, Dr. Hanes? Do you have a problem with a woman in the locker room?"

"It's Cody, or Doc Cody. Someone says Dr. Hanes and I look around for my dad." He laced his fingers. "We're an equal opportunity employer, Miss Smith, and you're a professional. Besides, given where you've been, these cowboys have nothing in their pants you haven't seen, except what's in theirs is mostly intact. I'm more worried about you bailing when a better offer comes up."

"I *want* to be a trainer, Doctor."

What if he says no? She'd searched online. Trace checked in with all his contacts. There wasn't much out there that would work for her. This job had come open just last week, probably only still been available because of the constant travel required.

Once she'd gotten over the surprise, she snatched at Trace's idea. It was brilliant, actually. It might be the only way she could go forward. After all, she wouldn't be tempted to empathize with a bunch of coddled athletes. Sure, this job would have been at the bottom of her list two months ago. But she couldn't think of any other position that would allow her to use her skills. Maybe even recover. It was a chance.

Her only chance.

Her fingers were back at it, worrying the edge of an uneven cuticle. She made them stop.

Doc Cody's knitted brows telegraphed the "why" he didn't ask. "You are aware that this job involves extensive travel. You'd be on the road for months at a time."

She smiled at the joke only she would get. Most people didn't recognize her surname as Gypsy. "I've had five TDY assignments in eight years with the army. I'm used to moving around."

"Well, I'm going to get busy here, pretty quick." He lifted his hat from the table, and looking her over, stood. "Have you ever seen a bull riding event?"

She rose, pulling down the skirt of her new black double-breasted interview suit. "Um, no."

He stilled, and his gaze bore into her, probing, unveiling.

She knew this was it, the Omaha Beach of the interview. Her nerves made her blood fizz through her veins like a shaken soda. She held, letting him look. She took a long breath and imagined Grand, grinding at her pestle. Her hands settled, curled at her sides.

Slowly, his look lost its sharp edge. But she knew a butter knife could still cut. She hadn't gained the beachhead yet.

"Well, I'll tell you what. Why don't you stay and watch the event?" He settled the hat on his head. "That'll give you an idea of what you're getting into. When it's over, come on back here and we'll finish this."

She practiced breathing again. "That sounds good." *He wouldn't have me stay if I wasn't still being considered, would he?*

"Great. Follow me."

The echo of her heels tapping down the narrow cinderblock hall competed with men's voices.

The wall to the right opened into a large room. Men dressed like extras in a Western movie applied rosin and pulled on ropes hanging from metal poles in the center of the room. One of them turned to laugh at something another said, and she got a good look at his face. The stringy attempt at a beard didn't hide the pimples on his cheeks.

These are just kids!

The memory of men this young, dressed in a very different uniform of helmets and desert fatigues marched through her mind. A shudder—an echo of agony—ripped down her spine. She gritted her teeth, looked ahead, and hurried her steps to catch up to the doctor's retreating back.

• • •

Katya sat in the second row, observing the spectators filing into the arena, feeling as if she'd traveled back to another time. Or another planet. Men wore cowboy hats, Western dress shirts, jeans, and boots. And belt buckles. Huge, shiny, gut-digging belt buckles.

The women were dressed similarly, but with fashion flourishes: blouses and high-heeled boots in bright colors, dangling silver earrings, and seam-popping blue jeans adorned with belt buckles that were only slightly scaled-down versions of the men's.

Katya stuck out like a penguin in a flock of flamingos.

Raucous country music blared from the ceiling, almost drowning out the beehive hum of the spectators. She moved from her study of this foreign world's fauna to the flora. Hanging above the arena, the JumboTron screen flashed advertisements. The arena floor might be used for hockey or basketball at other times, but now it was covered in dirt, with a row of sideways stalls laid out at the end closest to her.

In the center a round, waist-high platform stood open on the side closest to the stalls. Squinting, she could just make out the cameras poking from its dark interior, and men moving in the shadows. A cowboy on a black-and-white spotted horse ran in a circle at the opposite end, twirling a rope, the fringe of his leather leg coverings bouncing in a happy dance with the horse's every step.

Feeling a looming presence, Katya cowered, then looked up. An older gentleman in a cowboy hat stood beside her seat, hands full of cardboard trays of food.

"Pardon me, miss. I think those are our seats." He tipped his chin to the seats next to her. She turned her knees to allow him to sidestep by.

An older woman followed carrying drinks. "Pardon us, dear." She sidled past and sank into the seat beside Katya. When her husband was settled, she passed him a beer, and he passed her a plate of cheese-covered chips.

A smell of spicy food, hairspray, and flowery perfume wafted over Katya. Her stomach reminded her with a grinding growl that she'd been too nervous to eat lunch.

"Hello, hon." The older woman smiled over at Katya. Neat and proper in her pastel blouse, pink neckerchief, and salon-coiffed silver hair, she looked like a Western June Cleaver. "My name is Maydelle Deacon, and this is my husband, Tom." The man's weathered face was tanned nut brown, but when he lifted his hat to her, his forehead shone white.

She nodded and smiled. "I'm Katya."

The man looked her up and down. "You're not from around here, are you?"

"Tom! You just mind your nachos and watch for Buster." The woman turned back to Katya. "Are you a schoolteacher, dear?"

Katya smoothed a hand over her hair. Maybe she'd gotten carried away with the hairspray, trying to tame her frizz into a businesslike bun. How was she to know when she was called for an interview by the PBR that it would take place in a locker room? She shook her head.

"Oh, well. You look very nice. Don't you let anyone tell you different." Maydelle aimed a death-ray stare at her husband.

The arena went black. The music stopped, mid-note. The crowd fell silent. For a few seconds there was nothing.

Then a deep, strong voice boomed out of the dark.

"Welcome to the toughest sport on earth! My name is JB Denny, and I'll be your announcer for tonight's event. Sit back and get ready because *this* is the *P* (bang!) *B* (bang!) *R (bang!)*!" The arena exploded with flashes of light and what sounded like gunfire.

Katya's knees scraped the cement of the aisle stair where she crouched in a quivering, heart-fluttering ball. She put up a hand to anchor her helmet before realizing she wasn't wearing one. At another crackling explosion, she looked up. A fountain of silver sparkles fell from the ceiling, and a huge flame shot from the arena floor. The flash of heat hit her in the face, and she ducked again.

The crowd roared. Under the sound, anticipation rolled—a living palpable thing that her nerves picked up, thrumming in ancient instinctive harmony.

You're okay. Her heart beat so fast it almost fibrillated. *It's just fireworks.*

She had to get back to her seat before the lights went up. She grabbed the arm of her chair. The crowd around her was on their feet, the lightning flashes illuminating their rapt faces.

Crawling on stinging knees until she got her feet under her, she slid into her seat, eyes front. She didn't want to know how many people stared.

The sparkles died out and the spot shifted to the center of the arena, where a large flag hung from the rafters. "Now would you please remain standing, and remove cover, for the singing of our National Anthem."

Katya scrambled to her feet and with a hand over her slowly quieting heart, she sang with the crowd. Halfway through, the stars and stripes swam in her blurry vision, and when her throat closed she stopped singing.

A prayer followed, asking God to protect the riders, the livestock, and those fighting for freedom throughout the world.

"And now, I'd like to introduce you to the riders. Thirty of the toughest men you'll meet this side of hell." The announcer introduced the cowboys, one by one, and the spotlight caught them as they strode out of a gate between the stalls in front of her. They each lifted their hat, acknowledging the applause.

Katya took deep breaths. She willed her clenched muscles to loosen by focusing on one part of her body at a time: her jaw, her shoulders, her spine. The technique worked, until she got to her legs. She put her hands on her thighs and pressed down, to stop their jittery bouncing.

When cowboys lined both sides of the arena, the spots were doused, and in the dark the announcer's voice became the only focus. "This kid came up from the Challenger ranks twelve long years ago, to take the National Finals event in Las Vegas. The next year, he captured the world title in a storied season, winning seven individual events, a record not yet duplicated. The next year, he fought back from a career-threatening injury to again take the world title silver buckle. Ladies and gentlemen, our two-time world champion, 'Cool Hand' Cam Cahill!"

Katya squinted as a laser spot hit a cowboy, perched high above the stalls on a platform. Fireworks shot from tubes beside him. The voices of the crowd swelled, the air vibrating with cheers. The cowboy took off his hat, turned, and scanned it over the crowd, in a gesture the soldier in Katya recognized as a salute.

She couldn't see details of his face, only a flash of blond hair when he took off his hat, and a bright white smile. His body, on the other hand, was spotlighted against the blackness behind. Broad shoulders narrowed to slim hips. Muscular arms, big hands. A damned fine specimen of a man.

Whew. No wonder there are so many women in the audience.

"I just love the openings, don't you?" Maydelle settled into her seat with a sigh. "Are you all right, hon?"

Katya colored. The concern in the woman's eyes told Katya the stress of her day was showing. She shot the cuffs of her jacket, brushed her scraped knees, and tucked her dismay behind a fake smile. "I've never seen anything like that."

"Tom, can you believe that? This sweet thing has never been to a bull riding!"

Tom did not look at all surprised, but had apparently learned better than to say so. He patted his wife's hand, gave her an absent smile, then turned his attention to the stalls which now swarmed with cowboys.

Cam took the steps to the catwalk above the chutes slow, to go easy on his knee. Damn, that had been close. His flight had been delayed in Dallas, and he'd barely had time to get taped up before scrambling onto the platform for the opening. He'd have loved to miss that part anyway—he'd always felt like a dancing monkey up there. But some PBR edicts you just didn't mess with.

"You guys can get ready now. They're not going to have to postpone the event after all." Tucker Penny smirked. "The star has arrived."

Cam glared at his best friend and traveling partner. "Yeah, well screw you, Tuck. You ever try to get out of

Dallas in a hailstorm?" When he jerked on his riding glove his shoulder popped, shooting a bolt of hot pain down his arm to the palm of his riding hand. He gritted his teeth, making sure his smile was still in place.

Tucker squatted, stretching his groin. "I've got better sense than to route through Dallas in April. What were you doing there, anyway?"

Cam peeled tape and wrapped it tight around his glove. "Nothing, as it turns out. I'm never going to make it as a stock contractor." He mumbled from between his teeth as he bit the tape and tore it off.

"'Scuse me. Mr. Cahill?"

Cam looked up. The kid standing in front of him looked like he should still have hay in his hair. He couldn't be over seventeen, with red hair, a mess of freckles, and an earnest look.

"I'm Buster Deacon, and um…I just wanted to tell you…" The Adam's apple that bobbed as he swallowed was so big it looked painful. "I grew up watching you ride. And um…I just wanted to say…" Red spread up the kid's neck, staining his face. He rolled his eyes and huffed out an exasperated breath. "Well, it's an honor for me to be here, riding with you." He ducked his head, hiding behind his hat brim and walked away, fast.

Tucker burst out a laugh. "Sheeit, grandpa, can you tell me what it was like back when you rode that T-rex to the buzzer?"

"Do the math Tuck. It's about right, cuz that kid can't be over twelve." He squatted, watching out for his spurs, and started his stretching routine. The same one he'd been doing for more years than he wanted to remember. And thanks to his "friends," he wouldn't be able to forget.

• • •

"What's with the clowns?" Katya watched three men in brightly colored baggy outfits, jogging in circles.

"Don't let them hear you call them that. Those are bullfighters, hon. They're there to distract the bull when the rider gets off, so he doesn't get hurt."

Katya looked at the size of the animal in the stall, then at the men. "But who distracts the bull from *them*?"

Maydelle's tinkling laugh wasn't much of an answer.

The first cowboy straddled what Maydelle had called a "chute," and lowered himself onto the bull's back. Through the slats in the fence she could see the dark-skinned cowboy settle the rope just behind the animal's shoulders. He handed the end to another man who pulled it taut. The rider ran his hand up and down the rope, then slipped his hand into a small rawhide handle, canted slightly to the side of the bull's spine. His friend pulled on the end of the rope, over and over, until it was as tight as he could get it, then he gave it to the rider, who wrapped it around his hand.

The bull reared, pawing at the fence slats, trying to climb out. The cowboys leaning in backed up in a hurry. One grabbed the vest the rider wore to keep him from sliding off.

Katya scrabbled back in her seat. The bull was no more than twelve feet away. What if it got out? Could it jump the six-foot wall into the stands?

The bull stopped fighting and settled back into the stall. The rider pounded on his hand to lock his fingers closed, scooted up until he was practically sitting on his fist, leaned forward, stuck out his chin, and nodded his head.

The two men outside the chute pulled the gate open

wide and fast, then scrambled out of the way. The small, mud-colored bull lunged out of the chute, kicking so high with his back legs that he seemed to be standing upright on his front feet. Tied to the bull, the cowboy was jerked down, and his feet whipped up behind him. The bull threw its head up, and caught the rider's chin coming down.

The rider's head bounced, and from his disjointed rag-doll movements, Katya knew the kid was out cold. She slapped a hand over her eyes and watched from between her fingers. No one had told the bull that the ride was over. It spun in a circle, the rider's hand still caught in the rope.

The clowns—bullfighters—stepped in. Two of them danced around the animal's hooves and horns, while the other caught the tail of the rope on the way by and pulled it free. The rider spun off, to land in a crumpled pile in the dirt. One bullfighter stood over him in a protective stance, watching the bull.

The rider with the lasso rode in, roped the bull, and dragged him from the arena.

Dr. Cody and two other men ran into the arena and huddled around the fallen cowboy.

A waiting bull kicked the metal chute and it echoed in the silent building.

Tom murmured, "He's lucky Fire Ant isn't a mean 'un."

Katya's heart slammed her ribs. How could this kid have lowered himself onto that bull, knowing this was a possible outcome?

Money. Fame. The thought calmed her. *Remember, they're spoiled athletes, just crazier than the ones in college.*

The announcer urged everyone to remain calm while Doc Cody and his staff assessed the situation.

The cowboy's boot twitched.

In thirty seconds, they had the kid sitting up, and in thirty more, they'd helped him to his feet. The crowd gave him a standing ovation. The cowboy wobbled to the exit gate, a man on each elbow, one holding a red-stained wad of cotton to his chin. Before leaving, the rider stopped, turned, took his hat off and waved to the crowd.

The crowd roared.

Katya shook her head.

"Our son is up next. This is his first top-level event, and I'm as jumpy as a bit-up bull at fly time."

Mouth agape, Katya turned to Maydelle's nervous smile. "Your *son* does this? How can you allow it?"

"Allow it? Are you kidding? He got the nickname Buster because he was mutton-busting by the time he was four. We haven't been able to keep him off the rough stock since."

Four? Katya had no idea what mutton-busting entailed, but it didn't sound safe. "How can you stand to watch him do this?" She was disconnected from the rodeo athletes and could barely watch. To have your son on a bull? Katya shuddered.

"This is all he's ever wanted." Maydelle's smile stumbled, then righted itself. "What kind of mother would I be if I stood in the way of my son's dreams, just because I'm afraid?"

Katya studied the older woman, realizing that under all that percale and makeup there was a lot of steel.

Tom cupped his hands around his mouth and yelled, "Buck 'im, Buster! Come on, son, you can do this!"

Maydelle grabbed her husband's, then Katya's hand in a death grip, her gaze focused on the second chute. Katya squeezed the woman's hand, in self-defense as much as support. The massive black bull filled the chute to bursting, a baseball bat–sized horn poking out the slats. The skinny rider wore a helmet with a metal wire face shield that didn't look nearly sturdy enough.

At his nod, the men swung the gate. The black bull swiveled its massive head, and realizing it was free, lunged out of the chute. Buster thrust one hand in the air and hung on as the bull turned into a spin, lunging and bucking.

The crowd yelled encouragement; the cowboys on the back of the chute screamed instructions. Tom didn't yell, but leapt to his feet, leaning this way and that, as if trying to help his son balance. Maydelle sat frozen in her seat, a look of hopeful anguish on her face.

Head down, the kid shifted his feet and hips to stay in the middle of the tornado.

A buzzer sounded. Buster reached down and grabbed the end of the rope and pulled it free of his hand. The bullfighters stepped in close to the spinning animal. One tapped it between the horns, another grabbed at the tail.

Katya held breath in her seized lungs, her muscles locked tight. The bull kicked, and Buster was thrown over the bull's head. He landed on his feet, but the bull brought its head around and the horn hit the cowboy's forearm before he was off, running for the fence.

The bull quit bucking and the bullfighters backed away. The animal looked around with distain, then sauntered out of the open gate.

Buster whipped off the helmet with one hand, and threw it in the air. He leapt on the fence in front of Katya, so close she could see every one of his hundreds of freckles, and his orange-red hair. He hooted, and pumped a fist in the air, holding the other hand against his thigh. Tom and Maydelle rushed past Katya and down the one step to their son. Maydelle hugged him close and Tom slapped his back.

The announcer's voice drowned out the cheering crowd. "Well, folks, welcome Buster Deacon to the big leagues. How about...eighty-six and a half points!"

His parents let Buster go and he dropped back into the arena, cradling his injured forearm in his other hand. The bullfighters pounded his back and smacked him on the head as the crowd stood cheering.

Tom and Maydelle slid past her to their seats.

"What about his arm?"

Tom said, "Oh, he's fine. It's not his riding arm."

Maydelle genuflected, her lips moving in silent prayer. *Couldn't the kid have taken up a tamer sport, like rugby?*

An hour and many rides later, Katya looked down to see a fine tremor in her hands. She clasped them between her knees in an effort to make them stop. One ride to go.

No one says you have to stay for it.

The drama and emotions of the day were getting to her. All she wanted now was a hot bath and bed. Or maybe just a bed. She stood and said good-bye to the Deacons.

Butterflies brushed the lining of her stomach. She tightened her muscles to squelch them and marched the arena steps to go win that job.

CHAPTER 4

"You'll get 'em tomorrow, Cam." Pete, one of the bull-fighters, offered Cam his rope and a commiserating pat on the back.

"Yeah, I let that one get away from me." He limped from the arena to a parting-gift smattering of applause. The TV camera followed him, recording every painful step. He ducked under the catwalk to retrieve his dress hat and ditch the documentary.

Damn sneaky bull. He'd started the ride in perfect shape. He'd stayed up on his rope for El Patron's signature droppy leap from the gate. He'd even made the first sharp corner and settled into spurring on the spin—big money chops to impress the judges. But the danged bull switched leads and turned the other way, leaving him behind, sliding him off his rope before slinging him face-first in the dirt at seven and a half seconds.

He leaned over in the shadows and collected himself, massaging his sore knee. Hell, who was he trying to kid? Two years ago that bull could've turned itself inside out and wouldn't have had a shot at bucking him off.

Face it. Your reflexes are going. Thirty-two may not be considered old in most sports, but in the PBR, it was ancient. The last rider closest to Cam's age retired last year. Getting in shape for this season had about killed him, and his knee was keeping him up nights. Doc Cody was bugging to let him repair Cam's rotator cuff, but what would normally be a two-month layoff would be the end of Cam's career, and he knew it.

That's why he'd gone to Dallas. In December, the weekend he'd spent at the for-sale ranch of a retiring stock contractor had been a welcome vacation. But a full week of trailing cattle and training young bulls was...

Boring.

He wanted to be on bulls, not trailing them. After years of competing, he'd be trailering stock to the events. Instead of riding, he'd be flanking the bull. Left in the chute watching, while a young kid did what Cam was dying to do.

He spanked the dust from his chaps, and taking care not to twist his knee, picked up his hat, slapped it on his head, and walked from under the metal catwalk. The cameraman was gone, moved on to a more successful ride. Cam put his head down and walked the tunnel that led to a hot shower and ice for his sore parts.

Damn, he really wanted to stay on with the PBR after retiring. This was home. He didn't know much else. But he didn't have the voice or the personality for color commentary, and marketing was something he did when he ran out of groceries.

What the hell are you going to do?

He really thought that ranch would be the ticket. Now he was back where he started, and the clock was ticking, counting down the days to the end of his career.

"Shit!" He hurled his bull rope as hard as he could down the hallway. A bolt of agony shot through his shoulder. The dented cowbell clanked as it hit, then skittered away. "Goddamn, sonofaBITCH!" He squatted, clutching his shoulder, gritting his teeth.

Click. Click. Click.

The tapping of high heels penetrated his fog of pissed and pain.

"Well. Excuse *me*." A woman's stick-up-the-butt tone came from behind him. A slim pair of ankles in stylish heels walked within a foot of his face. He turned his head to watch her walk past—a heart-shaped butt in a tight skirt, swiveling in a precision march, dismissal clear in the ramrod line of her back and the set of her shoulders.

"Pardon me, ma'am."

She shot a haughty glare over her shoulder, looking down her nose at him. He caught a quick glimpse of glossy black hair pulling loose from a schoolmarm's bun, smooth olive skin, and huge eyes the vivid green of moss in a windmill tank, before she snapped her face forward and motored on.

His knee barely protested when he stood. *Nothing like a good-looking woman to grease a man's moving parts.*

Katya's heels echoed as she entered the white tiled hallway. The long, emotional day left her wilted, feeling as if she'd worn this suit for days. And she still had to nail this job. She rolled her shoulders. This next hour would be the crossroads of her future.

Buck up, soldier. She straightened her spine, tightened her core muscles, and marched.

She turned the corner of the white tiled hallway. Her step faltered. A cowboy strode ahead of her, head down, spurs jingling. What Maydelle had called chaps hugged his slightly bowed legs, fringes bouncing. She hadn't seen a cowboy from the back before. Wide bands of smooth leather curved from between his thighs to cup his butt, creating a frame for a perfect picture. Not that the jeans were tight. They were a working man's jeans, used and dusty. Which made them all the sexier.

Wowzer.

He held the vest the riders wore in one hand and a rope in the other, a bell on the end dragging behind. The bright red Western shirt he wore tightly tucked at his small waist widened to broad shoulders, his blond hair was cut short beneath the dark brown hat.

Nice. A muscle under her ribs fluttered. Walking behind men in those chaps would be a sweet perk of this job.

He hurled the rope in a sudden vicious burst. The bell clanged and echoed as it hit the wall.

"Shit!" The cowboy squatted, clutching his shoulder and swearing like a drill sergeant.

She almost stopped, to see if she could help. When he rolled his shoulder, she knew he hadn't dislocated it.

Dr. Cody was waiting. If she didn't nail this job, she'd never be able to help anyone.

He swore viciously.

"Well. Excuse *me.*"

Figures. No matter how studly they may look, star athletes were at heart tantrum-throwing toddlers. She had two years of locker room stories to prove it. New sport, same infantile behavior.

"Pardon me, ma'am."

He sounded sincere, but she glanced back, just to be sure.

God save the world from baby-faced men. Washed, blue-sky eyes with sun-squint lines at their corners, a strong jaw, and full lips. Lips, that as she watched, quirked as his eyes took a long, slow trip up her legs.

She faced forward so fast her neck popped. *Why do the good-looking ones just have to be assholes?*

She stopped at the training room, took a deep breath, and pulled open Door Number Two.

Riders in various states of undress lay on upholstered tables, or sat in chairs, talking while waiting their turn. A short, pudgy medic in a Western hat moved between them like a ponderous bee.

Leaning over a reclined cowboy, Doc Cody squinted in the glare of a spot lamp, suturing the kid's chin. He glanced at her over his cheater glasses, then back. "Well, Ms. Smith, what did you think of the toughest sport on dirt?" He tied off a stitch and cut the thread.

"It was..." She realized the cowboys watched her closely, as they had since she stepped in. She searched for a politically correct, yet accurate answer. "Overwhelming."

Doc Cody chuckled. "Hey, Dusty!"

The flushed, round-faced medic looked up from the ankle he was wrapping. "Yeah, Doc?"

"Grab me another couple packets of 9-0 sutures from the bag in the truck, will you? Keys are in the office."

The tech ran his hand over the pressure bandage. "You bet, boss." He hustled out of the room.

Doc Cody skewered the kid's chin again with the curved needle. "We're kind of swamped at the moment. Would you mind helping out? I'll be done here in just a few."

"S-s-sure." Quite aware that this was a test, Katya pushed down the butterflies and crossed to a sink in the corner to wash her hands. What if she froze again? She remembered the last time. The shame of her meltdown, when she tried to resume her duties in the ER in Kandahar. She winced as the brush bit into the cuticle, and lightened up a bit. No reason to think that would happen. After all, this wasn't like dealing with war wounds. She'd be working on a bunch of overpaid camera hogs. She dried her shaking hands, girded her loins, and got to work.

After an hour of probing, kneading, and stretching muscles, her hands had fallen into remembered rhythm. Champagne bubbles of happiness rose into her throat. God, it felt good to work again. She needn't have worried that cowboys wouldn't respect a woman in the locker room. She hadn't been ma'am'd this much in the army. And here, Katya held no rank.

She'd stopped looking at faces, focusing instead on injured body parts in an attempt to triage the worst injuries first.

She'd settled a kid in shorts in the whirlpool tub to treat a strained calf muscle, and turned to see a flash of red hair, Adam's apple, and lots of teeth. Buster Deacon sat next in line, forearm cradled in his lap, a huge grin covering most of his face.

The cowboy beside him teased, "Tomorrow night we'll get you a bull you don't have to put a quarter in, kid."

When she patted the table in front of her, Buster stood

and crossed the room to her. "Doc says it's just a bone bruise."

She eyed the deep purple lump. *Ouch*. She opened the refrigerator and pulled out a cool pack. "That was some ride."

"You saw it?" he asked in a shy, tell-me voice.

"I was sitting beside your parents. They're awfully proud of you." She molded the pack to the freckled muscular forearm then wrapped an elastic bandage around it to hold it in place. "I thought your dad's buttons were going to pop."

Red spread up Buster's spindly neck to his face. He ducked his head. "Thank you kindly, ma'am."

Smiling, she turned to her next patient.

Oh.

She felt like she'd bumped her forehead into an invisible wall. A naked chest filled her vision. No, not just any chest. A *perfect* chest.

Six-pack abs, bracketed by ribs and impressive lats. The pecs and deltoids were so pronounced there was a valley between them. Prominent veins snaked down to bulging forearms.

Trace needs a photo of this for his next Hunk of the Month.

No hair marred the smooth skin or covered brown, pebbled nipples.

Whew. Her fingers flexed. She'd love to massage those muscles. Her blood rushed to her crotch and her face, leaving the rest of her body dry. Then she'd let him massage some of hers.

Oh, very professional. You're working, Katya! In all her years in locker rooms, she'd never forgotten that before. She looked up to the baby face and washed blue eyes of the hissy-fit cowboy she'd seen in the hall.

His lips quirked. Again.

She spun to the refrigerator, hoping to find aplomb nestled in with the ice packs. She turned, a bag of ice in one hand, the other on her hip. "You need ice for your head, right?"

His lips fell into a grim line. "No. My shoulder."

"Oh, yes, that's right." She placed the pack on his shoulder, molding it to the curve of muscle.

Doc Cody's voice came from behind her. "Cam, are you ready to let me take care of that tear yet?"

"Nope. You can put me back together at the end of the season, Doc. I'm going for the volume discount."

The Doctor snorted. "Let's just hope there's enough left by then to work with." Fingers tapped her shoulder. "Let's finish our conversation from earlier, Miss Smith."

"Please. Call me Katya." Turning to follow him out of the room, she could've sworn she heard a snicker behind her.

Back in the tiny office, Doc Cody plopped into the chair, pulled off his glasses, and rubbed the bridge of his nose. "We're a man short, as you can see. Thank you for your help today."

"I haven't worked since I got out of the army. It felt great."

"We need someone soon, no doubt about it." His direct gaze trapped hers. "But make no mistake. The PBR is a family, and it's my job to see that these men get superlative care."

"I understand, sir." She sat at parade rest and forced her hands to still in her lap. *You don't have to say a thing about it.*

He just watched her. She knew he was reviewing everything he'd seen her do in the treatment room. Judging.

She tried not to fidget, biting the inside of her lip to keep the words in.

It didn't work. "In the spirit of full disclosure, sir, I have to tell you." Her throat clicked when she swallowed. "In Kandahar, there was a bomb. I was close. I was injured."

He frowned. Out of sympathy, or concern for her ability, she had no way of knowing. All she could do was spit out the rest. "I have healed physically, but I have some residual . . . PTSD, I guess you'd call it."

She remembered the medics, rushing into the arena to help a downed rider, and imagined herself doing it. An acid gut-bomb exploded in her stomach. "I'm working through it. However, in the short term, I'm not going to be of much help in the arena." She shut up, and waited for his verdict, jaw set, chest tight, hoping she hadn't just blown her last chance.

Still, it wouldn't have felt right, not telling him.

His gaze sharpened. "Everyone has to take a turn manning a stretcher when needed."

Well, you've done your best. She'd go ho—back to her parents' house. The taste of disappointment was as bitter at the back of her throat. Holding her shoulders back seemed a monumental effort.

If she couldn't even get a job like this, how would she ever heal enough to get back to the army?

When Doc Cody cleared his throat she realized he'd been studying her the whole time. "Thank you, for your service to our country."

She nodded, once, more a spasm than acknowledgment. *And as a lovely parting gift, we won't charge you for your seat at the event today. Thanks for—*

"I'm torn." He scrubbed his palm over his face. The sandpaper sound of his beard shadow rasped in the silence. "I believe in hiring vets, and the PBR is a huge supporter of our troops. Hell, the army was one of our sponsors in the past." He tapped his fingers on her résumé. "And you're a good candidate. The best of the ten I've interviewed. But I cannot put the safety of these men in the hands of someone who would fail them."

"I *can* do the job, sir." At least she thought she could. "All I'd ask for is just a bit of leeway—to not deal with emergent trauma in the arena—at least in the beginning." She held his gaze, but the effort cost her. "I promise, sir. You wouldn't be sorry if you hired me."

He lifted the first page of her résumé and scanned the second. "I guess we could leave you out of the rotation, at least in the beginning."

I'd have to be hired to be in the rotation. A smile started in her brain, and shot to her lips. *It's a start.* The beginning of a journey out of the dark maze she'd woken to, that day in Kandahar.

"But." The qualifier dropped between them like a live grenade. "If I see any evidence that you can't handle this—you show any hesitation in a crisis—you're out. No discussion." Doc Cody dropped his forearms on the desk and leaned forward. "Understood?"

She closed her eyes, put down her doubts, and gathered what meager courage she had left. "Yes, sir."

He extended a hand. "Providing your references check out, I'll offer you the job, Ms. Smith."

Her chest deflated with the released breath she hadn't

known she held. She smiled. "I'd like very much to take it, Doctor. If you'll call me Katya." She ran her damp hand down her skirt then shook on it. "If I could ask just one more favor?"

"What is it?" He stood.

"I'd appreciate it if my military service could stay between you and me." She felt the blood pool in her hanging fingertips, and the nail beds on her right hand throbbed. "I'd rather not answer questions about it just yet."

He settled his cowboy hat on his head. "Your past is your business. No one will learn it from me."

Taking care not to use his sore side, Cam shouldered open the back-door shortcut to the parking lot. Tucker and a few of the riders had tried to talk him into a drink at the bar, but he'd been there, done that many years' worth. All he wanted was a good steak and some TV before bed.

You're even starting to act like an old man. Next thing you know, you'll be wearing pants around your armpits and growing hair out your ears.

The halogen lamps created artificial daylight on the pavement just beyond the overhang of the loading area. He walked the ramp, his gaze locking on a curvy silhouette. The girl in the business suit leaned against the wall ahead, talking on the phone. Her delighted voice came to him, amplified by the overhang.

"I know, isn't it wonderful, Trace? I have you to thank for this job."

Cam scanned her slim figure, outlined against the light. Damn, she was easy on the eyes. Something about her capable touch in the treatment room and her focused attention for her patients, wrapped in that bombshell body did something to his insides. Something soft.

Hired, huh? The riders would be getting stomped, even if only to have her treat them. Maybe there actually might be a perk to getting older. He spent a lot of time in the treatment room.

He slowed his steps, waiting for her to finish her call. Maybe she'd like to share a steak.

"Are you kidding? You know athletes, they're all the same. You should have seen this guy today, throwing things and pitching a fit like a tired two-year-old."

Face burning, he walked past her, tipping his hat. "Pardon me, *ma'am*." Only his mama's manners kept him from the term he'd wanted to use.

Damn. Why do the good-looking ones have *to be assholes?*

CHAPTER 5

She never would have guessed Montana would be the gateway to her future. But then, there wasn't much about the past three months she would have guessed. Three hours before her first day on the new job, Katya stood before the hotel bathroom mirror in her underwear, deciding what to do with her hair. Black crimps floated around her face like Medusa's snakes. She wasn't doing the bun thing again and risk being mistaken for a schoolteacher, but this style would frighten small children. She pulled a super-duty elastic from her camo ditty bag and banded the riot into a ponytail, as thick around as her wrist. Not stylish, but it would keep the hair out of her face.

"You're not out to impress. You're *working*, Katya." Beneath her reflection's huge grin, nerves and trepidation simmered. Tonight she stood at the edge of the long road back to her career, her healing and to her army family. She glanced at her watch. The squad in Kandahar would be heading to bed right about now. Those who weren't standing night duty, anyway. She wrapped her fingers around the dog tags on a long chain around her neck. She knew she shouldn't still be wearing them, but the familiar weight resting between her breasts helped soothe the hollow ache beneath them.

I'll be back soon.

Her expression in the mirror looked familiar for the first time in weeks. She looked like a soldier; determined, tough, and ready.

I will.

A few steps from the bathroom, her suitcase lay open on the bed. A fake Indian pottery lamp illuminated the cream, orange, and brown striped wallpaper and the framed landscape print above the bed. Billings, Montana, might be miles from Washington in both distance and culture, but the chain motel rooms were the same. Maybe that would be a comfort, seeing how they'd be her home for a while. *God willing, a short while.* Home was wherever the army stationed her, because her family was there.

She stepped into a full-gored royal blue cotton skirt. Gypsy clothes made her feel closer to Grand, and today she needed any help her mentor might channel from beyond. She'd love to wear her off-shoulder blouses and bangle earrings, but they'd be too different from the denim uniforms she'd seen last weekend. Instead, she shrugged into a white fitted, collared shirt and stepped into flats.

She took a deep breath, anticipation zinging across her nerves. "Stay with me, Grand, I'm going in."

An hour later, freezing wind bit into her legs when she stepped from the cab into the almost empty arena parking lot. She'd arrived early, wanting to find her way around before the cowboys showed up.

She squinted at the gunmetal gray clouds that seemed to rest on the roof of the arena, hoping they weren't an omen. The wind snatched away her remaining wisps of warmth. She wrapped her light jacket tight around her ribs. Who knew Montana could be this cold in April? She paid the cabbie, then trotted to the glass doors spilling light into the overcast afternoon.

The door was locked.

Crap!

The arctic wind howled around the corner of the huge building to blast her, snatching her breath, tearing her eyes. Her desert-thin blood raced through her in a hopeless, frantic attempt to keep warm. She whipped her head right, then left, thinking that a wrong choice would find her dead, flash-frozen, like Jack Nicholson in that Stephen King movie. Hearing a diesel engine to the left, she jogged that way.

Around the corner, halfway down the block-long building, cargo doors stood open, idling semis lined up before it. She cupped her hands over her ears to keep them from breaking off and stomped toward the doors on frozen feet.

She ignored the odd looks from the men in winter coats, scarves, and hats, and scooted in ahead of a backing cattle truck. Just ducking out of the tundra wind felt like heaven, but she didn't stop until she was well into the building, surrounded by a maze of pipe fence. There she stopped, bent over, and sucked the comparatively warm air into her hoar-frosted lungs.

"Are you okay, miss?"

A pair of scuffed cowboy boots stepped into her view. She looked up. Jeans, a bulky suede and fuzzy jacket, craggy face, and dark hair topped by a cowboy hat. The collar of a garish pink shirt peeked from the top of his coat, spoiling his young Marlboro Man look.

"I may live, thanks." She straightened. Several enclosures behind the man sported hot pink bows that matched his shirt. "Could you tell me where I'd find the riders' locker room?"

Katya followed the man's directions, wending her way through the maze of pipe fence. What the heck was she going to say?

Mr. Cahill, I apologize for the conversation you overheard. I was only... Only what? Rude? Unprofessional?

Yeah, that. God, she'd been mortified.

And that was before she'd found the pictures of the baby-faced hardass while researching the PBR on the internet. Two-time world champion. Million-dollar cowboy. He'd almost single-handedly put the sport on the map. Cameron "Cool Hand" Cahill was the poster-boy for the PBR.

And she'd called him a spoiled two-year-old, almost to his face.

She bit the inside of her lip. Within an hour of nailing the job that would get her back to her real life, she'd managed to insult the guy with the influence to get her fired. She hadn't meant to be mean. It had been a long, tense, confusing day, leaving her feeling like she'd fallen down Alice's rabbit hole. Babbling to Trace was like reaching her foot down to touch the ground, testing that there was still somewhere she belonged.

Only there wasn't. The army's mental fitness test was like a slamming cell door, barring her from her home. She had never fit in her parents' world of white wine and science. Chicago felt empty without Grand. She'd only said it to make herself feel better.

God, what an idiot. It took a small person to feel superior by putting someone else down.

The maze of fence spit her out behind the chutes. She squared her shoulders and walked a long tiled hallway not much different than the one last week. Best to just apologize, then ask if they could start over. After all, they didn't have to like each other to work together.

The short heavyset medic from last weekend was alone when she walked in the training room.

"Oh good, you're here early." He huffed, lifting equipment from huge battered plastic totes. "I'm glad of the help. We need to get ready before the first cowboys show up." He straightened, swiped his hand on his jeans, and extended it. "I'm Dusty Bonner, by the way."

"I'm Katya." She shook his still damp hand. Sweat shone on his mottled face. "Are you okay? Maybe you should sit down and order me around for a bit."

A blush filled in the mottled spots, turning his pudgy face a shade of ripe tomato. "Nah, I'm okay." He pointed to a row of coolers lined up in the corner. "Can you finish moving the cool packs? I've got to get out the exercise bike and fire up the stim machine."

A half hour later, the room was ready and the first patients had begun to wander in through the wide opening to the locker room. Dusty was icing an elbow, and she finished taping a cowboy's sprained knee.

Boom! The metal door to the arena hall hit the wall.

Katya flinched and ducked.

She glanced up in time to see the door fly back from the wall. She straightened.

"I've returned, to save you all from fat-fingered, medi-ocre care." A guy stood in the doorway, hands on hips like a superhero. With his black wavy hair, broad face, and lantern jaw, he looked like Clark Kent. But rather than tights and a streaming cape, he wore ivory cowboy boots, skintight jeans, and a Western shirt that hugged his chest in a perfect custom fit. "Well, Dusty, I see you haven't managed to kill anyone. Yet."

An imperious ice-blue gaze stopped on her. "Ah, and who is this?"

Dusty fumbled the pressure bandage he'd been hold-ing. It fell, hit the floor, and unrolled. He scrambled to retrieve it, dropping it again. "Edward Enwright, meet Katya. Katya Smith."

He crossed the room and caught her hand.

"I am smitten." His deep southern drawl dripped like sun-warmed honey. His eyes never left hers as he lifted her hand to his mouth, turned it over, and kissed her palm.

That broke her immobility. She snatched her hand away and thrust it behind her back. Her heart pounded blood to her cheeks. She stood shocked by his unprofes-sionalism as much as his presumption. "I was working."

The warmth of his charm flicked off with the flash of a burned-out lightbulb. His patrician features went cold. He looked over her head at Dusty. "Who is she here for?" With a shrug of his shoulders, he slouched out of his courtly demeanor. "She doesn't look like a buckle bunny." He walked to the long counter, set down his gym bag, and unzipped it.

Buckle bunny?

The cowboys in the room found fascinating details on the floor, and on the ceiling.

She shot a glance to Dusty, who looked away fast.

Dusty smoothed the cowboy's knee wrap, then taped it in place. "Edward's our third athletic trainer; our joint guy."

Doc Cody strode into the room. "Afternoon, everyone." He tossed his cowboy hat on a massage table and crossed to the sink to wash his hands. "Hello, Katya. Welcome to the sports medicine team. Have you met the other members?"

She looked away from Edward's raised eyebrows and tight, disapproving lips. "I have. Thank you, sir."

Cam Cahill walked through the wide opening that led to the locker room, bare-chested, shirt in hand. "Howdy, everybody." His gaze flicked past Katya as if she didn't exist.

Edward patted the padded table next to him. "Let's get that shoulder ready, Cam." He reached for the wand of the TENS machine.

"Hold up a minute." Doc Cody dried his hands. "Stimulation hasn't been giving him much relief. Let's see if a massage will do a better job of loosening the joint."

"Okay, I'm good with that." Edward put down the wand and stepped to Cam's side.

The doctor dropped the towel on the edge of the sink. "Katya is our new deep tissue expert. I have it on good authority that she has magic hands. Why don't you let her handle that?"

The cowboys hung on every word like housewives watching a Friday soap opera. Her face felt like it would burst into flame. *Oh, Trace is dead meat.* He must have blabbed her college nickname when Doc Cody called him for a reference.

"Magic hands, huh?" It sounded dirty, coming out of Edward's mouth. "It looks like this is your lucky day, Cam." He stepped away from the table.

If Doc Cody noticed the sarcasm, he ignored it. "Why don't you finish taping Mario's knee, Edward?" He walked to a skinny kid seated near the door, missing Edward's frown. "Okay Jesse, let's check that concussion and see if you can ride."

Katya snapped to attention. She strode to where her bag rested on the counter beside the table. This was it. The moment she'd both dreaded and yearned for; the first test of her ability. Well, Lord knows, Cam Cahill's perfect chest should help distract her. And maybe she'd get a chance to apologize. She was relieved to see that, though her resolve shook, her hands did not.

From her bag, she pulled out the big gun—Grand's gypsy oil. Katya had tweaked the recipe, doctoring it with frankincense, finding that the exotic scent relaxed the patient. She poured a teaspoonful in her palm to warm it before lifting her hand to her nose. Right now, she could use a little relaxation. Stepping to the table, she closed her eyes, shutting out the man lying on it, the cowboys, and her fear.

Massage had always been her favorite art. Done correctly, it was more instinct than knowledge. Katya didn't massage; her hands and spirit did. She'd step away in her head, allowing something more knowing to flow into her hands.

She took a deep breath through her nose and blew it out slowly. She pictured Grand at her dining table, grinding herbs. When the fresh spicy smell filled her head and she could almost see the curtains billowing at

Grand's window, Katya rubbed her palms together and touched Cam.

Her fingers got acquainted with skin first, sliding over the smooth suppleness, warming it. When the oil coated the entire shoulder, her fingers sought deeper, exploring the sheathed muscle beneath, testing, pinching, rolling, as if it were bread dough under her fingertips. Muscles were an athlete's building blocks, and the tools of their trade. Her fingers worshipped them, slow and strong. The muscle responded, trusting her, opening, releasing its tautness.

When the muscle lay loose and pliable, her fingers delved deeper, to the tendons and connective tissue. There, they located the damage, close to the bone. The tendons were rigid and strained, tired from guarding the shoulder against pain and more injury. Gently, firmly, her fingers stroked the tendon's length, thanking them for their vigilance, but letting them know it was safe to let go. They lay down before her, stretching and relaxing.

Katya smiled at his moan. Cam lay, eyes closed, completely relaxed. She doubted he even knew he'd made a sound. His features in repose lost the hard look of a man; Katya saw what his mother must have seen, looking down on her sleeping little boy. She couldn't help her soft smile. Vulnerability in a grown man was rare. She felt the surprise of delight, as if she'd come upon a deer grazing in a glen.

As if sensing her regard, his eyes opened. Blue-sky eyes with starbursts of white fractures radiating from the iris. His brows came together in a frown. A mask fell over his features. "Thank you." He rolled his shoulder.

She wouldn't find a better time than this. "Mr. Cahill, I want to apologize for my behavior last week. It was unprofessional and mean-spirited. I only hope—"

He tensed and sat up. He located his shirt at the bottom of the table and shrugged into it. "It doesn't matter." He hopped off the table and strode to the locker room.

But his tone told her it did.

Four hours later Cam sat with Tucker at a booth of the chain restaurant next to their hotel.

"Well, I gotta admit, you were sticky tonight, partner." Tucker shoveled syrup-smeared blueberry pancakes in his mouth. "Too bad the bull wasn't much. You're gonna need a good draw tomorrow to make it to the short round."

Cam hadn't wanted the fake eggs or the dry toast. But his vest had been getting tight lately, and it probably wasn't shrinking. He finished chewing the dry wad and swallowed. "Damn, Tuck, didn't your mother teach you not to talk with your mouth full?"

"I only worry about that stuff when there are women around." Tuck picked up a piece of bacon and ate half of it in one bite.

"Obviously." Cam remembered three years ago when he was that age. He could eat three servings of all-you-can-eat pancakes, and never have it show. He took a sip of coffee and eyed his friend's dinner. "You're sitting pretty for tomorrow though. An eighty-eight gets you second pick in the draft."

Tucker looked up from his plate for the first time since the waitress set it in front of him. "When are you going to cut the crap and tell me what you decided? You selling out?"

Cam and Tucker came from the same hometown, so it was natural they'd travel together when Tucker made the circuit. They'd become good friends and had gone partners together, five years ago, buying land for a ranch outside Bandera, Texas. That was before Tuck met Nancy. They'd married and settled on that land in the modern ranch house snugged up against the road, and produced Randy, Cam's two-year-old godson.

"Nah. Looks like you and Nancy are stuck with a third wheel for a while yet."

Tucker grinned. "Damned glad to hear it."

"You just want a babysitter nearby so you and Nancy can go dancing."

"Hell, yeah." Tucker loaded his fork again. "Besides, if it weren't for him and me, you'd never have any company up at the Monastery."

"Yeah, well, screw you too." After playing "Cool Hand" on the road, Cam wanted a place to get away, so he took the old log cabin up in the woods, as far from the road as the property line would allow.

He'd always been a loner. So why had the prospect of settling down on the ranch started to feel like a prison sentence?

"I don't know why our plan of running a cow-calf operation won't work."

"I followed cow tails for a week, outside Dallas. Got my fill." He eyed Tuck's last pancake like a stray hound.

Tuck cut into it and raised it to his mouth, golden syrup dripping. "So? Whatcha gonna do?"

The past week, his anger had dissipated. A desperate fog of pending defeat replaced it. "Damned if I know, partner."

One day closer to Kandahar. Her first day outlasted, Katya closed the menu and gave her order for eggs and toast to the waitress. When Dusty invited her to dinner, she'd accepted. She couldn't afford a coworker friend nosing around her past, but any tips that would help her navigate her new job, she'd accept gladly. "I appreciate anything you can tell me, Dusty. I feel like I'm in a foreign country. I don't speak the language."

Dusty took off his hat and laid it on the seat beside him. "I'd be glad to help in any way I can." A receding hairline exposed his large forehead, shining white and vulnerable above the hat line, in sharp contrast to the ruddy complexion below it. He flipped open the menu before him. "I'm just glad to have some help in the training room." His eyes widened. "I didn't mean to sound like you're working for me. I just meant—"

She smiled. Dusty was younger than his hairline made him look. "No offense taken. I know what you meant." She set aside her menu. "What's a buckle bunny?"

His mouth opened then closed. A flush spread into his sparse hairline. "Um." His eyes searched the room for an escape route. "I guess you could call it a bull rider groupie."

She'd suspected as much. "What is the deal with this Edward guy? He acts professional around Doc Cody, but underneath..."

"He's not too bad." Dusty read the dessert menu in the display clip as if it held the key to his future. "He's one of the best orthopedic therapists in the country. I'm trying to learn from him."

"Well, he may be all that but he must've slept through his course in Manners 101."

"He always takes arena duty, so when you're not assigned there, you'll get a break from him. He tends to come on strong."

That was an understatement.

Aside from that idiot, she'd been on edge all evening, worried how she'd react if a cowboy was hurt badly. Tonight had been lucky, only strains and sprains. If all her days here were like this one, she could do this job.

If she was going to connect with Dusty, a little polite conversation was in order. "So where is home for you?"

"Luckenbach, Texas. You know, with Waylon and Willie and the boys."

"You live with a bunch of guys?"

"Not hardly. I've got five sisters." He chuckled. "It's a song."

"Oh. Did you grow up on a farm?"

"A ranch. Dad used to run cattle, but a few years ago he got tired of the low beef prices and got into exotics—ostrich, emus, and llamas."

"There's a market for that?"

"Oh yeah, there's a good one for the birds. The llamas? They're pretty useless, but my sisters think they're cute, so Dad indulges them. Mom is considering raising chickens for their saddles." He took a sip of water.

"What the heck would ride a chicken?"

Dusty choked, mid-swallow. He grabbed his napkin and coughed into it, eyes streaming.

"Are you okay?" Alarm jerked Katya upright, her hands clutching the edge of the table. "Do you need the Heimlich?"

When he pulled the napkin away from his face, she realized he was laughing.

When he could, he gasped out, "You are a funny lady. She'd sell the saddle feathers to fly fishermen, to tie flies." He wiped his eyes. "You are obviously *not* from around here. Where is home for you?"

"Back East. Nowhere special." She glanced around for a subject change. Across the room, a man stood from a table, in conversation with another. Cam Cahill, her unfinished business. He'd been abrupt this afternoon, not accepting her apology. She hadn't expected much else. He was a top level athlete, after all.

Before you accuse someone else, take a look at yourself, Puri Chikni.

The voice in her head was Grand's. Hot shame flooded her face.

She'd try once more. That way she'd have a clear conscience. And maybe repair the damage with the highprofile cowboy. She pressed a hand to the dog tags nestled in her bra. She *needed* this job. "Dusty, could you excuse me for just a moment?"

"Sure thing."

She wrestled her way out of the low booth and walked across the room toward him. Even in clothes, he looked amazing. When he smiled it dazzled her, even though it was aimed at his friend.

"I'll be right back, Tuck."

He turned, took three steps, and almost walked into her. "Oh, pardon me, ma'—" She knew the nanosecond he recognized her. His face tightened, pulling his mouth into a thin line, and his brows into a frown. "Oh. It's you."

Her stomach hopped like it was full of crickets. She stood at attention, braced to take her medicine. "Mr. Cahill, I just wanted you to know that my apology is sincere. You and I got off on the wrong foot. Can't we please start over?" Her tone sounded perfect, contrite, but not cringing.

He sighed and glanced around, as if checking to

be sure they wouldn't be overheard. His gaze, when it returned, struck like a cudgel. "Look, lady. I don't know why you'd take a job tending a bunch of people you obviously think so little of. I don't even want to know. But I'm telling you now, those people are my friends. My family." He stood, chest out, jaw clenched, a pit bull at a junkyard fence. "If you don't give them respect, and the best care possible, you'll be out so fast that your first clue will be the door slamming behind you."

She squirmed, skewered on the needle of his scorn.

His eyes watched her, as if gauging how deeply his words had sunk. He nodded, once. "Apology accepted. Excuse me, please." He stepped around her and walked away.

She should feel relieved. If he accepted her apology, he probably wouldn't report her behavior to Dr. Cody. But watching him stride away, she had to admit that she'd been hoping for one of those smiles.

CHAPTER 6

Katya emptied what had to be the seventy-fifth bag of half-melted ice into the training room sink and dropped the plastic bag in the trash can next to it. The last day of her first full weekend working, and the muscles in her hands and forearms felt like overtenderized meat. She rolled her shoulders. Her trapezius was a band of sheet metal.

Working her muscles back into shape was the best way. Too bad it was also the most painful.

"Okay, Pete, why don't you grab a shower, then we'll let our newest member put those magic hands to work on that thigh."

Before she had met Edward, she hadn't known a sweet Georgia drawl could be condescending. Their last patient gave her a shy smile, slid off the table, and limped to the door, then pushed through it. Looked like they had a break until the end of the final round. She'd learned that almost all the cowboys stayed to watch after they rode, cheering on their friends.

Doc Cody and Dusty had taken first responder duty, waiting at the out gate of the arena in case they were needed. She didn't want to think about the ambulance pulled up to the back doors for the same purpose.

All afternoon Edward had passed her every cowboy needing a massage. At first she hadn't minded; this was something she could handle. But even if her muscles were in shape, no one could massage for five hours. What was this, petty punishment? For what? Being a woman in a man's territory? For her daring to be as skilled as a man? She didn't know this guy's problem, but she didn't take this job to be his domestic.

Between dealing with this asshole, offending an influential rider, not understanding the sport, the vocabulary, or cowboy culture, this job was turning out to be a lot harder than the lucrative hiatus she'd signed up for. The treatment room was a minefield and what she didn't know could blow up in her face. Cam Cahill appeared in her mind, smiling that sexy smile. She'd already detonated that mine. So why did she still look for him every time a cowboy walked into the treatment room?

But the waiting was harder. Waiting for a rider with serious trauma to be carried through the door. Waiting to see how she'd react. Waiting for failure. As time passed, tension built in the nerves in her spine, pulling her muscles tight, as if to protect her vital organs. She turned on the water in the sink, letting it run warm, down her fingers.

A huff of warm air brushed her ear.

"You are very pretty. You know it too, don't you?" the voice whispered, soft, close, creepy.

Shit! She flinched, ducking away, her hands flying,

showering crystal drops over them both. Her heart stumbled, then double-timed, a hammer against her ribs. She whipped her head around to see Edward looming in her personal space.

His leering eyes flicked over her face. His eyebrows lifted. "Did I frighten you?"

Irritation oozed into the cracks in her armor. She now officially hated that accent. *I need this job. I need this job.* She snatched a paper towel from the dispenser over the sink and stepped away. "Yes. You did. Don't do it again."

Their next patient pushed through the door from the arena, cradling his elbow.

God, it felt good to get two rode to the whistle.

The audience was still cheering when Cam closed the latch to the arena gate, noting that his shoulder allowed the long reach without protest. The new therapist might have personality issues, but she was flat-out *good* at massage. Made a man wonder what else those hands would be good at. She was exotically beautiful. So what? Candi had taught him that was just window-dressing without a sweet disposition.

But she did apologize, and it seemed sincere.

The girl behind the chutes, Lisa Bentley, stuck a microphone in his face, the cameraman recording over her shoulder. "So, do you think your eighty-nine is going to hold up the rest of the short-go, Cam?"

He took a deep breath, trying not to sound winded, knowing he did. "I can only make the best of the bull under me. I'll worry about the next when they run him under me." He tossed his bull rope over the top of the pipe fence and tied it off.

"You've been inconsistent of late, Cam. What do you attribute that to?"

He got a start on the tape holding his riding glove and unwound it. He wanted to bat the mic away. Instead, he forced a smile. "These are the best bulls in the world, Lisa. Sometimes they have a good round, sometimes we do." He pulled off his glove and tucked it into a coil in his rope. "If you'll excuse me, Tucker's up next." He turned his back and took the stairs to the catwalk, while Lisa recited his recent stats for the camera.

Cam knew obsessing about his riding percentage was a self-fulfilling prophecy. You started second-guessing yourself, and went to fixing things that weren't even broke. Before you knew it, you'd ridden yourself into a slump. Well, screw that. He'd learned over the years to keep his mind as loose as his body. It had been a good weekend, and he'd settle for that. With only two riders to go, he couldn't do worse than third.

He wound through the riders, bull contractors, and TV crew on the catwalk, to the rear of the chute. Tuck lowered himself on the back of the polled brindle bull, Gnarly.

Troy Barber put a forearm around Tucker's chest, spotting him in case Gnarly lived up to his name. If the bull acted up, Tuck could end up with his face smashed into the only slightly padded front of the chute, where a judge perched, watching. Cam said, "Don't forget, Tuck. He's gonna take a long jump first. Stay up on your rope."

When Tucker handed Cam the tail of the rope, he stepped up on the slat and pulled the rope taut. When the rope was as tight as Cam's back could get it, he handed the rope back to Tuck, who took a wrap, laying it just so in his palm, then threaded it between his baby and ring finger. He folded his fingers over the rope and pounded them closed.

Cam raised his voice over the chatter of the announcer and the voice of the crowd. "He could turn either way, Tuck. Mind that second gear."

Tucker scooted up to his rope, taking care to keep his spurs away from the bull. Gnarly was touchy, and the chute was small. Best way to get hurt was with a fractious bull in the chute.

Cam leaned over and caught his friend's eye. "And he's mean, so when you're off, haul ass."

His face hard and focused, Tucker leaned forward and nodded. "Let's go."

The chute man unlatched the gate. The other tugged on the rope, pulling it wide. Gnarly, spotting his escape, lunged into the arena.

The ride was textbook. When Gnarly settled into the spin, Tucker was with him. When he sped up, Tucker did the same, making it look easy.

Cam bent at the waist, as if to help Tuck keep balance. "Keep moving!"

The cowboys leaned over the back of the chutes, bellowing encouragement. The crowd cheered.

The buzzer sounded. Gnarly, veteran that he was, slowed his spin. The bullfighters moved in to distract him. Tucker jerked the tail of his rope to free his hand then stepped off.

But Gnarly was having none of the bullfighters. He knew which of the humans had been on his back. He thundered after Tuck, who sprinted for the fence.

A bull will beat a man in a foot race any day. Tucker was ten feet from the fence when the bull lowered his head to hook him. Gnarly didn't know he didn't have horns. His head hit Tucker under his butt, scooping him off his feet, launching him at the fence. When he hit, he scrambled for purchase, then climbed to safety. The bull stopped at the fence and, fun over, trotted for the exit gate.

The crowd cheered. The announcer yelled to be heard over the noise, "The scores are coming in...well, Billings, how about ninety and a half points!"

Tuck let out a rebel yell, snatched his hat from his head and threw it away, up into the stands. Strobe lights flashed, and confetti shot from tubes on either end of the chutes, a multicolored snowfall fluttering into the arena.

Tucker hopped from the fence and met the bullfighters halfway to the gate. They handed him his rope, pounding congratulations on his back. Cheers followed Tucker to the gate. Grinning, he unlatched it, turned and waved to the crowd, who roared their approval.

Cam tried to push through the crowd of riders on the catwalk, but gave it up. Things would clear out soon. The last ride was coming up.

"Ladies and gentlemen, if I can direct your attention to chute number three, for the last ride of the night." The tension in the announcer's voice hushed the audience. "This is Buster Deacon's first weekend in the big leagues and he's already proved he belongs here. He's your current leader." The crowd settled into their seats, all eyes on the chute where the carrot-haired cowboy prepped his rope. "He's also shown he's not intimidated by the bright lights. He may look like a kid, but that cowboy stepped up and picked the rankest bull in the pen, and the baddest bucker currently on the PBR, Big Sleep."

The JumboTron over the arena displayed a close-up of

Buster, Adam's apple bobbing, face covered in so many freckles that he looked like he had a tan. But a muscle jumped in his jaw as he wrapped his hand, jammed his hat on his head, leaned forward, and nodded.

The black Brahma shot from the chute. Buster was ready, up off his pockets, on his rope. The bull leapt into the air and came down almost vertical on his front feet, a move that had pulled more than one rider down into a collision with his head. Buster laid back, knees braced on the bull's shoulders. When the back hooves touched down, he was forward again, toes out, gripping with his spurs, ready for the next jump.

Big Sleep lunged once more before turning away from Buster's hand, bucking into a spin. The crowd was on their feet, roaring. Buster was so far forward on the jump, the bull almost hit him in the chin as he reared. Buster corrected and as the bull spun, spurred with his outside leg. The cowboys slapped the chute slats and screamed advice, which was drowned by the roar of the crowd.

Cam watched, the smile spreading on his face seeping down into his bones. He knew how that felt—balanced in the eye of the cyclone—everything was slow and easy, so focused that the crowd noise was just a blur. It was only you and the bull, so perfectly connected it felt like you were dancing.

When the buzzer sounded, Buster popped his rope from his hand and without a bobble, stepped off. The bullfighters ran in, but they weren't needed. Big Sleep knew the gig. He stopped bucking at the buzzer, lifted his head, snorted, and sauntered from the arena.

Buster took off his hat, got on one knee in the dirt, and put his head down for a moment of prayer. Then he was on his feet, pumping his fists in the air. The arena shook with the roar of the crowd. Wiley, the arena clown, ran over to bump chests and give him a high five.

The announcer's voice yelled over the noise. "People, you're looking at the only cowboy this year that's made eight seconds on that bull."

Buster watched the replay on the JumboTron, looking happily stunned.

"Okay, are you ready to welcome the newest member of the ninety-point club? The judges scored that ride NINETY-TWO POINTS!"

The confetti flew again, spirals floating down onto Buster's upraised arms. The crowd roared. Buster literally skipped from the arena.

Five minutes later, Cam followed Tuck through the doorway from the treatment room to watch the celebration in the locker room.

"Dang, kid, you can ride more than a sheep, after all! Nobody can say that bull had an off day." Mario shook the kid's hand.

Buster looked like his grin was a permanent fixture.

"Great ride, Deacon." Cam recognized the gleam in Tuck's eye. He was up to something.

"Thanks, y'all." Buster unbuckled his chaps then pulled open his locker. Wads of opened disposable diapers spilled out onto the floor.

"Uh, something you want to tell us, kid?" Tuck said in a deadpan tone.

Buster only stood there, a look of horrified incredulity on his red face.

The cowboys fell out laughing.

"I knew you were young, but damn!" Tucker slapped his thigh, cracking up.

Cam yelled across the room, "Maybe so, Tuck, but that kid in diapers just beat the snot outta you!"

Tucker fired back, "Hell, kid, save those Pampers, cuz Grandpa over there's gonna need them next!"

Cam shook his head, and caught movement to his left. The new therapist stood, arms crossed in the doorway, watching with a wistful smile. He'd never seen her smile before. It relaxed the tight lines of her face, making it rounder. Softer. Even more beautiful. But why wistful? Did she have a redheaded little brother at home?

She turned, and walked away.

None of your business, Cahill. He waded through the other riders to his locker.

But he wondered about that sadness, just the same.

An hour later, the weekend was over. The crowd had filed out and the arena echoed with the sound of the road crew disassembling the chutes, and the noise of the Bobcats scraping up the dirt. Katya, equipment bag over her shoulder, once again navigated the pipe corral maze. She flipped her phone closed and rubbed the cramp between her thumb and forefinger. The taxi wouldn't be here for a half hour.

As stressful and confusing as the weekend had been, at least it had given her purpose. The weekdays between events stretched ahead of her, barren as the Montana winter landscape. She knew from experience that the worst thing for her was idleness. Memories and loneliness would wash over her, rolling her in churning emotions, leaving her unsure of the way to the surface. Days later, the undertow would release her and she'd struggle back, weakened, covered in a salty film of guilt.

Why had Murphy died and she survived? The army chaplain told her it was God's will. The army psychiatrist said it was chance. She knew what Grand would say. That she had an unfulfilled purpose.

Katya knew that to heal, she'd have to find her own answer.

She mentally shook herself. Wallowing in self-pity was not helping. She stopped, put her hands in her jacket pockets, and leaned against the fence watching the men load the bulls onto trucks.

"Damn. That's all we need."

The Marlboro Man with the pink shirt and a navy down vest leaned against the fence opposite her watching a small, gray spotted bull limp around the pen. A long-legged redhead wearing the same uniform leaned next to him. "He'll be okay, Max. We'll get him home and have the vet take a look."

Katya watched the bull pace. Sure, it was an animal, but she could tell from his stride... "It's his hip."

The couple turned to her. "Are you a vet?" the man asked.

She walked the few steps across the aisle. "No. I'm a physical therapist and licensed athletic trainer." She smiled. "For people." She watched the bull. "But you can tell. Watch the leg joints as he moves. They're not stiff, see?"

"She's right." The woman stuck out her hand. "I'm Bree Jameson, and this is my husband, Max."

"I'm Katya." She shook hands then pointed to the bull. "If that were a man, I'd suggest heat and massage. Maybe your vet—"

"I'm worried about trailering him home, limping like

that. We came a long way, and it'll be hard on him, trying to favor that leg." Max pushed his hat back on his head. "I've heard of horse therapists doing massage. Why not a bull?"

They looked at her. So did the bull.

Max said, "Katya, meet Beetle Bailey, son of the PBR Champion bull Fire Ant."

She backed away, hands up. "Oh no, I don't know the physiology or the pressure points." She watched the bull out of the corner of her eye. "I don't know large animals."

Max ducked under the pipe rail. "Oh heck, Bailey's a lover." He walked up to the bull, hand outstretched. The bull licked his palm. "See?"

Every day she dealt with the results of bull encounters. She was smarter than a man. "There's no way I'm going in that pen."

"You don't have to." Max put his hand under the bull's cheek and led him to the fence, then pushed his side until he stood parallel to it.

Bree patted the mottled flank through the fence. "Not all bucking bulls are mean. We put my two-year-old up on Bailey and lead her around the paddock." She looked at Katya. "Look, I know we're putting you on the spot. I'm sorry about that. And maybe you can't help. But would it hurt to try?"

Katya swallowed and glanced to the parking lot . . . still no taxi. A muscle in her stomach jumped. The bull's huge soft brown eye watched her.

If it turned out she couldn't do the sports medicine job, maybe she'd have a fallback position. Bulls might be easier to understand than men.

"Katya Smith, bull therapist. It kinda has a ring to it."

Before she could change her mind, she stepped onto the lowest bar and hoisted herself up. Leaning over the top pole, she tentatively ran a hand down the animal's back. The bull stood quietly. *This is just a patient, like any other. Well, a hairier one, but still . . .*

She closed her eyes, to focus her concentration on the data her fingers transmitted. The muscle was much larger than she was used to, of course, and tighter. She felt between the hip bone and the spine, on both sides, to gauge any differences. *There!* Near the back of the hip on the inside. A muscle was tighter. She dug into it, and the animal started. So did she, jerking back, she straightened fast, grabbing the fence to keep from falling.

"Easy, Bailey." Max rubbed the beast's forehead, then nodded to her when the bull calmed.

She went back to the tight spot, slower this time, digging her fingers into the core of the muscle, holding them there until the muscle gave up and loosened. She massaged it and it loosened more. After ten minutes, she moved up the muscle to the tendon. It was inflamed, larger than the other side. "If this were a man, I'd ice him." She patted the bull's flank and hopped down. "Try walking him now. The tendon is swollen, but maybe the massage helped."

Max led the bull out. He walked around the pen, his limp much improved.

"You're a wiz!" Bree clapped her hands.

Katya rubbed her throbbing forearm. "And I thought cowboys had hard bodies."

At the sound of a car horn, she looked up to see her taxi idling outside the huge roll-up door. "I've got to go."

"Wait, at least let us buy you dinner," Bree said.

"I can't. I've got a plane to catch."

"Well, let me pay you something then." Max ducked under the pole fence.

"You don't owe me anything. I'm glad to help."

Max reached for his back pocket. "No, I insist. This is really going to help him ride easy on the way home."

Katya could see they weren't going to let it go. She considered a moment. She'd already stepped on one IED in the treatment room minefield. She needed reconnaissance to avoid others.

She had questions about this world and asking the cowboys was out. If she got to know them more, she'd risk caring about Cam—er, them.

And she couldn't afford to get close to anyone she worked with. They'd want to know things. Things she wasn't talking about with anyone.

"Maybe there is a way you could help me. See, I'm a city girl. I don't know anything about bull riding, or cowboys, or country music, or...*anything*."

Bree laughed. "Believe it or not, I can relate. I'd be glad to fill you in. Will you be at the event in Denver next weekend? We could get together then."

When in Rome, I should at least understand why the soldiers wear those cute little leather skirts.

CHAPTER 7

Cam tightened the hydraulic line on the old Deere, then rolled out from under it.

"You sure you got it tight enough?" His dad leaned down, one hand on the grille, considering checking the work, Cam was sure.

"Dad, relax. I've only wrenched on this workhorse for the past twenty years. I know it better than a woman's body." He sat up.

His dad's high color wasn't from bending over. "No need to be graphic, Son." He pulled the rag from his back pocket and wiped his hands.

Cam's knee wobbled when he tried to stand. He grunted and grabbed the bumper to take off some strain.

"When you gonna announce your retirement?" His father's face might be wrinkled as a tote sack, but there was nothing wrong with his eyes.

Cam took the rag his dad offered and scrubbed his hands. "When I've got something to step off onto." He'd known when he decided to stop at the farm on his way to the Pueblo event, that this conversation was coming. But if he'd come this close to home and gone on past, his mother would have skinned him.

"You know there's always room for you here."

Cam looked out over the flat, golden fields, acknowledging the lie with a nod. His sister Carrie's husband had taken over most of the day-to-day farming. Dad groused, but Cam thought that he secretly enjoyed it, especially the "supervising" part. "I know, and I appreciate that, Dad. But I think if I settled one place after all these years on the road, I'd end up chasing chickens like that crazy old Bo."

His dad shook his head. "That dog sure did vex your mother." He clapped a hand on Cam's shoulder. "Let's get to dinner before she turns that vexation on us."

In the mudroom, they stepped into the smell of roasting meat. Cam's mouth watered. It seemed Mom was treating him to his favorite, pot roast. They washed their hands at the sink, then took turns pulling their boots off at the bootjack. His dad stepped into the misshapen leather slippers that had stood by the back door since Cam could remember, then led the way to the kitchen, slippers slapping the tile floor. Cam padded after in his socked feet.

"Well, put up the Tupperware, Cass, they're gonna eat after all." His mother walked a pan from the stove to the sink, gray hair frizzing from the bun at her neck. His three sisters flitted around her like worker bees around the queen, carrying plates and pouring drinks.

"Wouldn't miss the best supper on the planet, now, would I?" Cam pulled a deep breath of home through his nose and held it. Too bad the smell alone couldn't take him back to the days when this home was his. A knife of homesickness slid between his ribs, hitting near his heart.

Chrys, the youngest imp, looked him up and down. "Doesn't look to me like you've been skipping meals. Do the bulls groan when you set on 'em?"

"Nope. They're just proud for the opportunity." He poked a finger in her ribs as she passed him, carrying a crock on a plate.

She squealed and jumped, sloshing gravy.

His mother didn't even look up. "You two, quit messing around. Cam, you get to the table and stop pestering."

"Yes'm."

Chrys scooted ahead. "Let me go first. I don't want to be behind you when you get stuck in the doorway."

When he pushed the door open for her, she stuck out her tongue then sashayed through. He wondered if she'd gotten a lecture yet about those tight jeans. No wonder his mom's hair was frizzled.

Carrie's husband, Dan, was already seated. Dad sat in his spot at the head of the table, Dan to his right, Cam's seat, growing up. After a pause, Cam walked around the table, to sit at Dad's left.

The women filed in, hands full. His mom, then Cassia, Carissa, and Chrysanthemum. Thank God dad put his foot down about naming a boy after a flower.

The afternoon sun turned the walls of the dining room gold and settled on the lace tablecloth Mom only brought out for company.

Once they'd all settled, he grasped Carrie's and his dad's hands as they bowed their heads for his dad's quick, heartfelt prayer. Then everyone dug in, all talking at once.

Cam ate slowly, taking in pot roast and the comfort of home in big savoring bites.

"Betsy's sorrel is coming right along. I think if I can get him fast enough to win, she'll recommend me to her friends." When Carrie retired from barrel racing, she'd put her experience to good use, training horses. She'd fallen in love with Dan, a team roper at a rodeo.

"Mom, if old 'PBR Confidential' over there was home more, he could help you." Chrys had nicknamed him that years ago. But why use ten words when two would do?

She turned to him. "Did you know Mom was thinking of keeping bees?"

Cam chuckled. "That's 'cause she's already got experience raising little stinging bugs like you, squirt." He glanced down the table. His mother looked tired. More than he remembered from last time he was here. "Why don't you get the stuff, Mom? I'll set you up when I'm home on break in June."

She frowned. "That's your time to heal up, Cam. You don't need to be toting around bee housing."

Dan broke in. "I'll be happy to do that for you, Mom."

Stung, Cam focused on his plate. He'd moved out and been on the road for years now. He knew life here went on without him. So why did that hurt all of a sudden?

Well, I've got stuff that needs doing at home anyway.

Two hours later, in his old room, which now doubled as a sewing room, Cam tossed his clothes in his carryall.

"When are you going to come home and stay for a couple of days?" Carrie leaned on the door frame.

"I don't know, exactly. Why?" He folded his sweats and laid them on top of the pile.

"Well, you remember Lucy Powers? I think she was a year behind you in school."

"You mean the Powers' that own the gas station on County Road Eleven?"

"Yeah. Anyway, she's a friend of mine. She's had a rough time of it the past year. Her husband, you know Ty Randall? No, you wouldn't, he grew up outside Loveland. Anyway, they divorced last winter, and—"

"Not happening." Now, where was that baseball cap?

"She's a barrel racer and really sweet."

He sighed. "Dang it, Carrie, you do this every time I walk in the door and I ain't interested."

"Not every woman who hangs around the rodeo is like Candi, Cam." She crossed her arms over her chest. Her eyes went soft. "But you're never going to know that if you don't open yourself up to meet a couple of them."

"Well, I'm relieved to hear that, Sis. I'll be happy to take your word on it." The burn from Candi's heat had cured him of his rodeo chick habit. For good.

He must've left the cap hanging in the mudroom.

"You're going to retire soon. Please tell me you're not going to hole up in that log cabin of yours and start building a moat."

He zipped the carryall. "That's a great idea. A moat will look better than that razor-wire fence I had planned. Thanks." Smiling, he brushed by her to the hall. "Now, if you're done dispensing sisterly advice, can we go? I don't want to miss my plane."

Katya merged the rented Chevy onto I-25 South. She now understood why the state's plates read "Big Sky." The winter-hibernating land seemed only a table for the bowl of the blue sky to rest on. The road stood empty before her, the rolling land stretching to the edge of the earth.

Nothing like being an ant on the landscape to put your problems in perspective.

She'd gotten to the airport on time. But at a glimpse of desert camos in a crowd ahead, she had to drop out of the flow of people and bend over to breathe, rubbing the hollow pain in her chest.

She'd flown, of course, coming home from Afghanistan. She'd flown to Grand in Chicago, and then to DC.

I must be getting worse.

The thought of walking into that tiny tube and being strapped in, sealed in...she couldn't make herself do it. Passing the car rental desk had given her an idea.

She slid the window down a crack. The biting cold that swirled in smelled of arctic caverns—stony, timeless, silent. Katya pulled the emptiness into her lungs and exhaled. Empty was good.

Glancing at the time display on the dash, she did the math. Her Afghan team would be mid-shift about now. The matinee of memories started up.

Her first day back to work, she'd been first to arrive at the camo-filled stretcher the orderlies ran through the doors. Rules of triage dictated she catalog wounds and deal with the most dire first. Instead, she made the mistake of looking at his face. Brush cut hair—blond rather than red—but familiar freckles scattered across his nose.

She stood rooted, hands halted midair. Eyes closed, his mouth pulled to a grimace of pain. Sweat dampened her armpits. When she put her hands to his chest, her stomach flipped. Her heart banged like a tank laboring uphill. She tried to focus on his body, dripping blood onto the tile. In spite of the clawed panic that slashed at her, she tried.

Then he opened his eyes. Green eyes full of confusion and pain. A bolt of fear slammed into her chest, pushing her back.

"Help. Me." His bloody hand snatched her wrist and instinctively she jerked it away, turning her head just in time.

The scuff-marked gray tile tilted.

Her knees hit the floor.

She couldn't hear past the roar in her ears, but felt the vibration of boots under her bloody hands. Through the black edge of her vision, she saw a forest of camo trees, before the black bled into everything.

The bump of a pothole brought her back with a start. The empty road rolled under her tires. Katya shuddered, and checked the rearview mirror. Empty was good.

And yet, empty wasn't working either. Sure, she'd avoided the claustrophobia of the flying tube, but even in Big Sky Country the landscape was crowded with memories. No matter how fast she drove, they hovered on the horizon like heat shimmered on a hot day.

How could she get past something that never left? Her future sat waiting for her return, but how long would it wait?

The cold had scoured a hollow place in her chest. For a time she listened to the wind howling there, then closed the window.

Doc Cody had warned Cam that it was going to take more to prep this year: more time, more massage, more ibuprofen. He dry-swallowed two white pills then walked into the training room of the Denver Coliseum.

Dusty stood, checking medical supplies in a huge soft-sided carryall, and Cam glimpsed the new girl's very nice rear, poking out from behind the refrigerator door. The stir below his waist surprised him. He'd easily kept the promise he'd made to himself after the breakup with Candi. So what was it about Katya that changed that? Even her name was foreign on his tongue. Was it Russian? In a way, he was keeping his vow. This woman was about as far from a rodeo groupie as was possible.

"Am I too early?" His voice echoed in the painted cinderblock room. Katya's head popped up. She closed the fridge door, straightened, and walked toward him. She was wearing another of those bright full skirts, all the color swirling with the sway of her hips. The contrast against the mannish tailored shirt sent mixed messages. Her face was foreign: high, slanted cheekbones, smooth tawny skin, and big, green eyes. Exotic.

With personality issues. She doesn't think much of us. Don't forget that.

"Hello, Cam. You ready to get started?" She stepped beside the table and patted the padded surface.

Since his right shoulder was too tight to get his T-shirt over his head, he used his left to peel it off. She helped him, her fingers grazing his back, trailing lines of heat. She didn't seem to notice. When she leaned in, he caught the scent of the exotic oils she used on her skin.

Potent stuff.

Her eyes moved over him in a professional perusal of his body, her face a mask of detached concentration. Doc Cody and other sports medicine employees had done that a million times. Why did it seem, all of a sudden... personal?

He made the mistake of leaning on his bad leg when he raised his butt cheek on the table and his knee wobbled. Wincing, he grabbed the edge with his right hand.

Her brows pulled together. He swung his feet up and lay back.

"Do you mind if I check out your knee first?"

"Be my guest."

She pulled his sweats up over his knee. Her touch was light, but sure. "You've got some arthritis. Have you had arthroscopic surgery for cartilage tears?"

"Twice. I blew it out seven years ago—ACL, MCL, PCL."

This time, she winced. Her fingers ran down the back of his knee, testing, prodding. "Are you doing exercises to tighten the tendons?"

"Yeah. Doc Cody gave me some."

"There's not much there that massage will help. But the tiniest bit of swelling will make the instability worse. Let's ice it."

She was back in a moment, wrapping a towel around his knee, then sliding a cold pack under his leg, and settling one on top. The cold was a shock at first, but then felt good. Or maybe it was her hands on his body that generated the heat.

"I'm sure Doc Cody told you that you're going to need a replacement somewhere down the line."

"Maybe so, but not this season."

"Are you taking something for the pain?"

"Ibuprofen."

"I'm sure if you ask, he'd prescribe—"

He opened his eyes. "Nope."

She grumbled under her breath, something about stubborn men, then got to the part he'd been looking forward to. Those hands on his chest.

She poured oil into her palms, rubbing them together to warm it. As he'd seen her do before, she raised her hands to her face, and breathed in. There was nothing sexual in her demeanor, but her enjoyment was private, sensual.

Not that it mattered. He was here to get ready to ride. And she was the best they had, the best he'd had. He closed his eyes, anticipating. He now understood the nickname, Magic Hands. Her fingers seemed to know right where the pain hid, deep.

The rhythmic massage warmed the joint and he sighed, relaxing. If his body trusted her, he did. For this, anyway. He'd learned the hard way not to trust anything else to a good-looking woman. He was close to snoring by the time she finished.

"Okay, cowboy. You're good." She patted his shoulder before reaching for the alcohol and a cloth.

"I'll leave the oil on there, if it's okay with you." He liked the exotic smell on his skin. It reminded his shoulder of her hands, relaxing it. Maybe it was only in his head, but he'd take comfort where he could find it.

The sun came out in her delighted smile. "Smart man. The aromatics will prolong the benefit. I just thought that a big bad cowboy wouldn't want—"

"I want what works to help me ride. That's it." He slid off the table and tested his shoulder. "Thank you, ma'am. That helped." The shoulder now allowed shrugging into his T-shirt unaided.

"You're very welcome. Good luck today."

He looked up, but her attention was already on her

next patient waiting. He headed for the locker room to get dressed, stung at her impersonal dismissal. From the drift of his thoughts lately his head wasn't far behind his body's reaction to her. Maybe he'd think about revising that vow.

You'd better focus on your ride, Cahill.

CHAPTER 8

By some evil twist of fate, Doc Cody asked Dusty to work the arena with him. That left her with Edward. All night. Lucky for her, he seemed in a good mood, chatting up the cowboys before the event and whistling between tasks. Good thing too, because she had enough to worry about.

She overheard the riders talking. Two events without a bad wreck was apparently remarkable. She pushed down the butterflies bumping the walls of her stomach. That meant they were overdue. Her ears stayed perked for every muffled roar of the crowd. And even more for the silence that followed a wreck.

You're a professional, Katya. You studied for five years and you've been in the field for seven. You know how to do your job.

True enough. But could she do it under pressure?

She splashed alcohol on a washcloth and wiped down a treatment table. They'd have a lull until the first injured rider showed up.

"Everyone who can walk goes to a bar after the event."

She spun around. This time, Edward didn't loom. He stood a few steps behind her.

His eyes, sliding away, told her he'd been checking out her butt.

"You know, to blow off steam." He slouched, thumbs in the pockets of his jeans, a car salesman's smile on his handsome face.

Why did his sexy smile give her the willies, when Cam's had the opposite effect?

"I'd be proud if you'd allow me to escort you, Smitty. We could dance."

"My *name* is Katya." Only people she loved could call her by her army nickname. The muscles in her forearms already throbbed with the beat of her heart. No way she'd be up for a night of dancing, even if she did want to go with Edward.

Which she didn't.

She swiped the back of her hand over her sweaty forehead. She was a hot mess. When she dropped her hands to her sides, air puffed from her collar into her face. Make that a hot, smelly mess. "Thank you. But all I want after this is a rest."

"I'll give you time to get a shower. You'll perk up. I'll see that you enjoy yourself."

What an arrogant ass. "I don't date people I work with, Edward. So, again thank you, but I'll have to decline." She forced her lips to a smile.

The movie-star twinkle in his eye winked out. When he scowled, his bottom lip protruded just a bit. "Suit yourself, kitty cat." He spun on his heel and stalked away.

What kind of karma plopped me in a job full of two-year-olds masquerading as grown men?

Silence. Her muscles snapped to attention, reacting to what her ears didn't hear. An arena full of people, by definition, could not be silent. Unless . . . *shit!* She shot a frantic look around the room. Everything was in place. The echo of shuffling feet came from the hallway.

She shouted to Edward, "Incoming!" She tried to force her feet to move to the door. They wouldn't. Horrific photos of ER trauma flashed in her brain, interspersed with useless snippets of procedures. *P-R-I-C-E—protection, rest, ice, compression, elevation.*

Still, nothing would help her deal with the tremor in her hands or her shaking guts.

The door swung in, pushed by Doc Cody's back. The stretcher followed, with Dusty on the trailing end. The bright yellow cervical collar flashed in the lights as they carried the backboard by. The rider's head was strapped in place between two foam blocks. They laid the stretcher gently on the table. She couldn't recognize the cowboy's blood-splashed face.

Move, goddamn it, they need you! She managed one step. No more.

Edward sifted through the medical supply bag. "What do you need?"

Doc Cody's movements were unhurried. He leaned over the stretcher and flashed a penlight in the cowboy's eyes. "He's out. Let's clean him up, see what we've got. Katya, get some ice on him, to try to get a handle on the swelling." His voice was calm, almost slow.

Dusty glanced up at her. His eyes widened. Seeing that she wasn't moving, he hustled to the refrigerator for ice.

She stood, limbs shaking as if she were seizing,

swallowing the bile that surged into her throat. *You need this job. Move, dammit!*

"His nose is broken." Edward gently sponged the blood. "Maybe more."

"Armando. Come on, son. Wake up, now." Doc scrubbed a knuckle over the injured man's sternum.

Two riders came in the door. They stood, hats in hand, heads bowed. Were they praying?

Uniformed ambulance drivers shouldered through the door. "Do you want transport?"

Doc Cody didn't look up. "Give him a minute. I think he's coming around."

Dusty laid a small bag of ice across the rider's nose.

She saw the cowboy's arm twitch. He moaned.

This is not Kandahar. You don't know this guy. He's just a bull rider. Her hands stilled. Her feet moved. She walked to the refrigerator and pulled out two bags of ice.

"Armando, do you know where you are?" At Doc Cody's slow, relaxed voice, the tension in the room came down a notch.

"Dember."

A collective sigh went around the room. Katya put the ice bags on the sink.

"Where does it hurt?"

"Crap, I broke my node, din' I?"

"Don't worry. We'll make you as pretty as new."

"Id dat the best oo can do?"

The onlookers' chuckles broke the tension. Katya returned to the fridge.

Doc Cody looked up at the ambulance attendants. "I think we're okay, for now anyway. But don't go far, boys."

Doc addressed Edward and Dusty. "You guys had better get back to the arena, in case you're needed."

Dusty shot her a worried look, then followed Edward out the door.

The two praying cowboys stopped staring at her, donned their hats, and slipped out the door to the hall.

Oh, I am so fired.

Doc Cody pulled the ice bag from the cowboy's face. "Okay, Armando, you know the drill."

"Yeah, Doc."

"One . . . two—"

Crunch.

Doc pinched the bridge of the rider's nose, holding a washcloth to stem the blood. He looked up. "I think we have enough ice, Katya."

She looked at the teetering pile of bags on the counter.

"Could you hand me some cotton plugs out of that bag, please?"

The pulse pounding blood to her face was proof that you couldn't actually die of embarrassment. She dug through the bag and double-checked the package before stepping to the table. She handed it over, relieved to see that, though her stomach quaked, her hands were steady.

Doc crammed the plugs into the cowboy's nose. "Do you remember what happened?"

"He pulled me down on hid head."

"He sure did. Good thing you didn't hit anything important. You could have hurt yourself." Doc spoke in his calm-a-spooked-horse voice, his hands running over the cowboy's neck, checking his skull, his facial bones. "Does anything else hurt?"

"No. Cad I get up now?"

"Why don't you just relax for a few, then we'll see."

"Katya, will you remove the C-support?" He walked to the locked cabinet that he'd stocked with drugs earlier.

She stepped up and pulled the Velcro strips that anchored the cowboy's head to the backboard. "Do you feel dizzy?" She gently lay the ice bag over the bridge of his nose and swollen eyes. He was going to have legendary shiners tomorrow.

"No, ma'ab."

Leaving the cervical collar in place, she removed the blocks, then ripped apart the Velcro that bound his arms and legs to the backboard.

Doc Cody was back with two pills and a plastic cup of water. "Elevate his neck and shoulders please."

When that was done and the cowboy was resting comfortably, Doc Cody tipped his chin, indicating that she should follow him.

She didn't have long to wait in purgatory; he only walked to the other side of the room. Still, it was enough time for her to think about what job she'd apply for next. Nothing came to mind.

He turned and assessed her, much the way he had the cowboy on the table. "At ease, soldier."

Her spine popped as she forced it to curve. "Old habits. Sorry." She took a deep breath.

The doc continued his study. "You know, these men deal with fear every time they get on a bull. You keep your eyes open you could learn something from them."

He straightened and stepped past her.

She stood, stupid with surprise. Did she still have a job? "Doc?"

He turned. "Eddie Rickenbacker was the first World

War One flying ace. He said, 'Courage is doing what you're afraid to do. There can be no courage unless you're scared.'"

"I froze—"

"Yeah, you did. But then you did something. You're good at your job. For right now, that's enough. Keep working at it."

Relief, like a tropical breeze, blew over her freeze-dried spirit.

She'd dodged a bullet today.

But for how long? Her ears perked, listening for the silence that would signal the next wreck.

CHAPTER 9

Katya surveyed the weathered plank walls of the rustic restaurant. She'd planned on spending the last evening of the weekend in her hotel room, tucked in with the TV and takeout. But when she'd run into Max and Bree on her way out of the arena, they invited her for dinner. She didn't want to miss the opportunity to get her questions answered, so she asked them to pick her up after she'd showered and changed.

Bree said, "I love your outfit. I could never pull off that style, but it looks so natural on you."

Katya decided on full Gypsy regalia tonight for courage. Her coin cascade earrings swung as she glanced down to her black suede slouch boots, turquoise broomstick skirt, full-sleeved white blouse, and fitted tapestry vest.

Bracelets tinkled as she raised her hand to tuck hair behind her ear. "It's me. What can I say?"

Katya only picked at her salad. Today's failure weighed on her stomach, as well as her mind.

"I tried to tell you not to order a salad at a steakhouse, girl." Bree pointed her fork at the chicken breast in front of her. "Do you want some of this?"

Her stomach rolled. Katya tried to twist her wince into a smile. "No, thanks, I'm good."

Max eyed her over his cooked-to-leather steak. "You're not one of those veeegan people, are you?"

"Evolve a bit here, dear. If she's a vegetarian, that's her business."

"Hon, I only—"

"You can relax, Max. I'm an omnivore." Katya's smile eased to a more natural version. She enjoyed watching the couple spark off each other, but bone-tired hovered not far away, waiting to pounce. She pushed her plate to the side. "Do you mind if I keep asking you dumb questions?"

"Have at it." Max took a pull on his beer.

"Do the spurs hurt the bull?"

Max chuckled. "Do you have any idea of what a good bucking bull is worth?"

She shook her head.

"I've had offers of over a million for Beetle Bailey and I'm not selling. Between his event earnings and semen sales, I'm going to make a lot more than that in the long run. Even if I didn't care about the animal, which I do, do you think I'd allow an investment like that to be abused?"

She swallowed. *I massaged a million dollars on the hoof?*

Bree spoke up. "A bull's skin is ten times thicker than ours. Spurs don't hurt him more than a stiff loofah hurts you. The rowels—that's the part at the end that spins— are regulated by the PBR to be sure they can't injure the bull. The cowboys use their spurs to hang on and to impress the judges that they're in a strong enough position to afford to take their leg off the bull."

"What about that strap around his . . . back parts?"

Max swallowed a bite of steak. "That's a flank strap. It's just an irritant. It makes them kick out their back legs, to try to get rid of it. If you didn't use it, the bull would still buck but he might not kick." He demonstrated with his hand, showing the angle of a bull on his front hooves. "That's what helps keep a rider on his rope.

"In spite of old wives' tales, it goes nowhere near the bull's ba—reproductive parts. No contractor would risk injuring a future sire." He picked up the sweating beer bottle. "In your job I'm sure you've seen that a two-thousand-pound bull can hurt a cowboy a lot worse than the other way round." He took a swig.

"That's another thing. Why do some of the riders wear helmets and others wear only cowboy hats?"

Bree frowned. "Some of them value what's inside their heads more than others."

"Now, Bree, don't get on your soapbox. It's a personal preference, Katya, and a hot topic on the circuit. Old-school cowboys grew up riding without a helmet. They didn't exist then. They see it as a distraction that restricts their vision."

Katya couldn't imagine a football player taking the field without a helmet and they only got run over by humans. "Why doesn't the PBR simply require it?"

Max shrugged. "It's the cowboy way. Grit it out, take whatever the bull dishes."

Bree said, "It's going to be a moot point once the old guys retire. The high school and youth rodeos all require kids to wear helmets, so as they come up the ranks, it'll be a habit for them."

Katya's guts squirmed, remembering Armando, lying unconscious on the exam table, covered in blood. "I hope that happens soon."

Crash!

Katya flinched, ducked, and covered.

"It's just the band, hon." Bree reached out, but didn't touch. "They're in the bar, through that doorway." She waved a hand behind her.

The twang of a steel guitar followed the crash of cymbals.

Katya lowered her arms. The band swung into a rolling country beat. The wall vibrated with the bass.

Bree wiggled in her seat and cocked her head at her husband. "We're going to dance, right, love?" She had to raise her voice to be heard.

The cowboy gave his wife a look that would melt plastic. "You bet we are."

Katya pushed her chair back. "I'm going to catch a cab. I'll see you in Tucson."

Bree stood. "Oh, no you don't. No better place to learn cowboy culture than in a country bar." She grabbed Katya's hand. "Max, honey, will you take care of the bill? I'm going to show this Yankee the lay of the land."

"Be happy to, darlin'." Max donned his hat and reached for his back pocket. "You ladies save me a dance now, you hear?"

"Bree, I've had a rough day—"

"That's okay, Cinderella, we'll have you home before your coach turns into a pumpkin, don't you worry."

It was easier just to go along. She'd have one drink,

observe the local fauna, then call a cab. End of fairytale. She allowed herself to be towed along to the arched doorway to the bar.

Bree released her wrist when they stepped inside the low-lighted room. The long mirrored bar was familiar, as were the round wooden tables crowding the floor. Other than that, it didn't look anything like the trendy bars back east.

Near the door to the street, men's neckties hung stapled to the ceiling. A sign on the wall served notice that ties worn in would be cut off and kept as trophies. Sawdust and peanut hulls littered the floor. Past the generous, spot-lighted dance floor, the band played. The men resembled the fans at the events: razor-creased jeans, cowboy hats, and huge belt buckles. The drums advertised the band's name, Goat Rodeo.

She leaned over to shout in Bree's ear. "They have rodeos with goats? Surely they're too small to ride."

Bree laughed for a long time. When she got herself under control, she yelled back, "Hon, that's country for a screwup. Like a snafu."

"Oh. Who knew?"

"Only everyone west of the Mississippi." She patted Katya's hand. "No worry. We'll have you talking country in no time. You'll be 'ya'lling' with the best of them."

The band finished strong. The crowd noise that replaced it didn't lower the decibels much. Bree eyed the few remaining empty tables, then grabbed Katya's hand. They wended their way to the last one, standing front and center at the edge of the dance floor.

Katya recognized a few of the bull riders at the tables they passed.

"Hey, look, boys, it's Magic Hands!"

Katya glared, searching for the source. Tucker Penny sat at a tiny table against the wall with Cam Cahill. Tucker raised his beer in salute. "How you doin' tonight, ladies?"

Seeing no malice in his open grin, Katya waved before glancing to his sour-faced partner. A bit of malice there, maybe. She and Bree pulled out chairs and sat.

"Max will be here with drinks in just a minute, I'm sure." Bree waved to a cowboy at the next table. "Hey, Brody, nice ride today. How's Suzie?"

Katya was only half listening to Bree's conversation when she felt a tap on her shoulder.

One of the bull riders at the next table leaned in and shouted in her ear. "Katya, what should I do for a strained hamstring?"

"Why didn't you come see me after the event?"

"Too crowded. It's not bad, I just strained it on the getaway."

She shouted back, "Well, you should've come in. It's too late for ice, but tonight take a hot bath. Do you have any liniment?"

He nodded.

"Rub that in good. When you get to Tucson, you come see me. Early. I'll give you a deep tissue massage, and then I have a great poultice that should help."

"I will. Thank you, ma'am."

The band started up, cutting off any attempt at conversation.

Across the table of bull riders, a young kid who looked vaguely familiar put his hand over his heart and yelled, "Katya, I have a pain, right here. I think the only treatment is a dance. With you."

The cowboys laughed.

"As ugly as you are, you're gonna die before she dances with you, bud."

"If you're dying, call an ambulance. Your moaning is giving me a pain in the butt."

Katya smiled, gave the cowboys a shooing wave, and turned back to the table. Max had arrived with three mugs of light-colored beer.

Katya didn't drink often, but when she did she was a white wine girl. Beer tasted so heavy... and dusky. Oh well, in small quantities it was known to settle an upset stomach. She thanked Max and took a sip. Cold, with a light, earthy bite. Not as bad as she'd remembered.

Two beers later, Katya tapped her toes to the beat, watching Bree and Max dance. She'd never seen dancing like this. The couples made a big circle that rotated as they spun around the dance floor. No clinging and grinding here. Love and lust were reduced to smiles and tender looks. Not that the sexual tension was any less for the distance. In a less-is-more way, it was even sexier. Anticipation charged the air. Katya shifted in her seat.

"Would you like to dance?"

One more cowboy stood beside her, beer in hand. She would like to. But there was no way she was doing a dance she'd never seen, with a partner she didn't know, in front of a room full of cowboys she would see at work tomorrow. "Thanks so much, but no, thank you." She gave him a parting smile, and he wandered away. When the song ended, Bree and Max returned, hands clasped.

Sighing, Katya stood, enjoying the fuzzy buzz that had numbed her sore muscles and calmed her mind. Worries would be there tomorrow. Tonight she had enjoyed herself. "I need to get back to the hotel, and get some sleep. It's been—"

"Oh no, you don't." Bree again reached for Katya's hand. "I've been waiting for the right song. I'm going to teach you to line dance, girlfriend."

Katya tried to retrieve her hand. "I can't dance to this!"

Max sat, put his thumbs in his pockets, and leaned back. "You might as well go along. She's got the bit in her teeth. There'll be no stopping her now."

Ladies in bright clothes flocked to the dance floor, their jewelry flashing in the lights. Only ladies.

It must have been the beer. Katya gave in and followed.

Bree pulled her next to her in a line, facing the crowd, but near the back. "Just watch what everyone else does, and follow them. You'll have the Tush Push down in no time."

"Tush what?"

The band drowned her out. A rollicking song with a strong one-two beat. Katya's heart beat much faster.

Bree shouted the steps as she did them. "Step. Lift your heel. Step. Lift your heel. Shuffle, clap, rock. Back and forth."

The women stepped in unison. Katya did her best to follow, a beat behind.

After three times through, she had it down. Maybe it was her Gypsy blood. Dancing, for her, was as natural as a swan swimming.

Bree laughed, and added a shimmy of her shoulders to the thrust of her hips. "See? Isn't this fun?"

Katya tried the shimmy. It felt good. "Look at me, I'm a cowgirl!"

The women shifted, the front line stepping back, and her line moved to the front. Her eye caught a flash of gold hair next to the wall. Cam Cahill sat leaning back in his chair, legs crossed, watching with an appreciative gleam and a small smile.

When she faltered she looked down, concentrating on the steps. She added the roll of her hips as she turned, as she'd seen Bree do, knowing he watched. This was *fun!*

Cam couldn't stop watching. Katya's turquoise skirt pulled at his attention and the crystals on her vest sparked in the lights. She looked like a Gypsy. So different than the cowgirls that surrounded her—a rare old gold coin in a pile of freshly minted dimes. And her hip thrusts had him sitting up and taking notice. Compact and curvy, her athletic body was fluid, made for dancing.

Made for sin.

"Hey, it's Cool Hand Cam Cahill!" The tiny voice tried for sultry and missed. The blond buckle bunny sidled up, too close.

God, they get younger every year. "Howdy, miss." He fingered the brim of his hat without actually tipping it.

"Buy a lady a drink?" She batted heavily mascaraed eyes, flashed two pert dimples, and teeth so perfect they must've set Daddy's bank account back some.

Dimples like that had about done him in, last time.

"Well, normally, I'd be proud to, but Tuck and I are heading out in just a few. Maybe next time." As the girl moved on to a rider at the next table, Cam craned his neck to catch a glimpse of turquoise, but the song had ended.

"Fancy that trainer, do you?" Tucker leered over his beer bottle.

"Not hardly." He drained his beer. "That girl's wound more than finger tight."

"Maybe so, but wouldn't you like some of that torque on your threads, partner?"

"Only on my shoulder. And if I tell Nancy you were looking at another woman, she'll flat strip your threads, Tuck."

He sought her out in the crowd. She leaned forward, arms on the table, hand in her hair. When Bree said something to her, she threw her head back and laughed, exposing her long elegant throat. What would it be like to bury his hands in all that hair? To kiss the hollow at the base of that neck, to pull in the exotic scent of her skin?

He looked away, shifted in his chair, giving him some room in his jeans and considered his next step.

And realizing that step would land him back in the dance.

Out of breath from the dance and laughter, Katya and Bree strutted back to the table.

"You're a great dancer, a natural!" Bree fell into the chair.

"I could get into that line dancing thing, I'll tell you that." She reached for her beer and took a long swig, finishing it off. She snatched her purse from the back of the chair. "But I really need to get back to the hotel. I've got a long day tomorrow." She raised her hand at Max, in a policeman's "Stop." "Do *not* get up. I'm getting a taxi, and I'm not listening to arguments. You two have a good time. I'll see you down the road."

Max shifted in his chair, but Bree put a hand on his arm. "We really enjoyed tonight with you, Katya. We'll do it again, soon."

"Thank you so much for dinner and the lessons." She waved and walked away, picking her way through the crowded tables. Just short of the door, a feeling of being watched crawled over her. She glanced up.

Resplendent in a bloodred shirt with white roses on the yoke, Edward perched on the stool closest to the wall, glaring at her like a vulture on a branch. He raised his glass in a mock salute. He didn't smile. Malevolence rolled off him so strong that his eyes glittered with it. A warning hiss and tail rattle sounded in her mind.

She looked longingly at the door, but forced herself to walk over.

He took a swig of beer.

"Edward, I hadn't planned on coming. I ran into Bree and Max Jameson, and they insisted—"

"You're saying that like I'd care." His disdainful glance started at her hair, and ended at her shoes.

Well, she'd tried. She cut her eyes away, hit the access bar of the door, and walked into the chilly night. She was too tired and too happy to deal with him tonight. She'd explain in Tucson.

CHAPTER 10

The next Friday afternoon, Katya was first to the training room. She'd again chosen to drive to the venue in Tucson, avoiding the claustrophobia of the plane. She found she enjoyed seeing the country and the freedom of the open road. Still, this solution cut both ways. With so much time on her hands, her mind hopscotched between memories of Kandahar and worry for her future.

What if she couldn't resolve her problems quickly enough to keep this job? She touched the outline of her dog tags, cradled between her breasts. What if she couldn't pass the fitness for duty test to rejoin her unit? Idle time left her brain chasing nose-to-tail thoughts, which always ended in a spiral. A downward spiral.

Well, none of that was going to help her do her job today. She dropped her duffel in a corner and walked to the sink to wash her hands.

"Mr. Cahill, are you entering events at rodeos during the two-month break?" Buster's high-pitched voice carried from the open doorway of the riders' locker room.

"Yeah."

"Which ones?"

"Haven't looked at it yet."

"How do you decide? There are some big purses in the Northwest, but it costs a lot to get there. I'm not sure—"

She heard the clash of metal as a locker slammed shut. "Listen, kid. I'm not here to wipe your nose. Figure it out."

Cam strode into the therapy room wearing untied tennis shoes, cutoff sweats, and...nothing else. As he walked toward her, she watched his ropy calves flex, noted the corded muscles of his shoulders and arms. The short blond hair, baby face, and blue-sky eyes—Cam Cahill was killer-cute. She should be used to the fact by now. But the smile he'd given her last night was a far cry from today's pinched lips.

And proof that the good-looking ones *did* have to be assholes.

Buster was sweet, star-struck, and respectful. He was only trying to figure out the big-league ropes. Much the same as she was. Her chest filled with the rarified air of indignation. She felt a serious huff coming on.

Cam lifted a hip onto the training table, dropped a forearm on his muscled thigh, and leaned in. "Hello, Katya."

"Hello, Mr. Cahill. Lie down, please." She snatched the generic, off-the-shelf oil from her duffel. She didn't warm it in her hands first, just squirted it on the skin of his shoulder, and started the massage.

"Did you have a good trip out here?" His eyes swept her face and the corner of his mouth lifted.

The twerp was trying to flirt with her! "Well, I managed to figure it out."

"What's that supposed to mean?"

"Do you enjoy stepping on puppies, too?"

"Huh?"

His look was all innocence. Either he was a great actor, or he really didn't get it. Neither prospect cooled the slow burn in her chest that worked its way up, tightening the cords of her neck and the muscle in her jaw. Noticing his jaw tighten, she relaxed her hands a bit. "Why were you so mean to Buster? He's only trying to learn."

His eyes changed. Hard, dark, and sharp. "Look, I'm fully aware of what you think of us, Miss—"

"Oh no, you don't. It's not 'us,' only you." Luckily, her hands could work independent of her brain.

"You should leave stuff you know nothing about to those who do." The hard words barely escaped through the firm line of his mouth.

"Oh, really? And how am I supposed to learn? Ask questions of veterans like you? That worked so well for Buster." She lifted his arm, checking the range of motion of the shoulder. Not there yet. "Apparently you were born knowing this stuff. No one ever helped you on your way up, I'm sure." That one zinged home. She saw it in the flick of his glance toward the ceiling.

"I just wonder." She leaned over him, catching his gaze. "Buster won the last event, and you weren't in the top ten. Could it be that you're a little jealous?"

He sat up so fast his head almost collided with hers. Still, somehow he managed not to look at her. "I'm done."

Hell. When would she learn when to shut up? She'd

been in the right too, right up to the last zinger. That was just mean. Why did this guy get under her skin so easily?

When Cam hopped from the table, his knee wobbled. He grabbed the edge in a white knuckled grip. He shrugged off her hand on his arm, straightened, and limped back to the locker room without a backward glance.

Four hours later, Katya sat folding towels in a closet-sized room separated from the training room by a swinging door. It was worth the niggling claustrophobia to be alone with her thoughts for a few minutes.

Thank God the event tonight had been . . . uneventful.

Except for the very real possibility of a trauma case at every event, she was enjoying this job. The cowboys were beginning to trust her. One had even agreed to try her heat-drawing poultice. He wouldn't be sorry, Grand's cure worked better than ice. She hoped this was only a beginning. She had ideas. Holistic healing could really help some injuries she'd treated, avoiding the need for meds and their unwanted side effects. She grabbed the next towel in the pile.

The cowboys' polite deference was nice too. They acted as if they respected her as a professional, as well as a woman. She found it a welcome change from the macho, one-of-the-guys treatment that was the best she'd come to expect of every sports team she'd worked with in the past.

Then there was Mr. Big Man Cahill. She huffed a lock of hair out of her eyes. Maybe she'd gone a bit too far accusing him of jealousy. But she'd been so *mad*. Well, she wasn't apologizing this time. He had so much knowledge he could pass on to the young riders. What would it hurt? He wasn't going to be able to use his secrets much longer anyway. She felt badly that he was nearing the end of his career, but it happened to every athlete eventually. He had the opportunity to go out an ambassador, instead of a...weenie.

Then there was Edward. She'd tried to talk to him when, as usual, he'd arrived late. He looked down at her as if she were gum on his custom cowboy boot.

She sighed. Men and their egos. It seemed she'd done nothing but step on the fragile little things since she took this job. Which was odd, because, God knows, she had experience tiptoeing around egos. She'd have to wait to approach Edward when no one else was around. After all, she had a perfectly good explanation.

The door swung open, and as though her thought drew him, Edward walked in. He wasn't much bigger than she was, yet when the door closed, he took up a lot of space. And too much air. Her breath came faster.

"You think you're better than me." Softly spoken words, but the close walls amplified their sharp tips.

His smile deformed his movie-star looks. His lips curled back from unfriendly teeth—a dog's warning, before it bit. She'd thought Cam's eyes had been mean, earlier. She now realized he'd only been irked. Edward's narrowed ice-blue eyes glittered with silver, like razor blades in a bathtub.

His steady gaze made her want to flinch, though she had nothing to feel guilty about. She sat up straight, refusing to look away.

Mad dogs sense fear.

"Don't be ridiculous. I was trying to explain earlier.

Bree and Max owed me dinner and I needed to ask them some questions. I had no idea we'd end up—"

"I've met women like you." He crossed his arms and leaned his weight on his left leg, effectively blocking the doorway.

Was it intentional? The walls, close before, edged closer. Her pile-driver heartbeat bounced off them.

"You tease, with all that wild hair and big innocent eyes. With that sweet ass, twitching when you walk. You know men's eyes follow you. You play games." His voice slid to a whisper. "You like games? We can play."

"That's enough!" A surge of anger and indignation melted her fear. "I do no such thing. Ever." Adrenaline poured into her blood and she shot to her feet.

Big mistake. It put his hate-filled face inches from hers. There was no room. Her lungs worked, trying to find oxygen in air thick with antipathy.

"You're a bitch. A stone cold, cock-teasing bitch."

His whispered hiss sent shivers skittering over her skin. Her eyes flicked to the door.

"You going to yell? Scream for some big he-man to come save your nonexistent virtue? What a freaking joke."

Spittle flew from his lips. She recoiled in disgust.

His face contorted to a hate mask, he lunged, grabbing her shoulder with so much force her shirt ripped.

Her dog tags clinked. They reminded her of what surprise and his hulking intimidation had made her forget.

You're a soldier.

Panic drained down her legs and out her feet as if her body were a bucket with a hole in the bottom. It left exposed a solid bedrock of *knowing*.

A smile rose from her chest to break on her lips. It felt righteous. "I'd only yell if I needed help."

Cam was the last cowboy through the door to the treatment room after the event. Some guys trooped through to the locker room, while others stood around rehashing their rides. He dropped into the first empty seat and lifted his right boot across his left knee.

Figures. The odor told him he had stepped in what he'd suspected he had.

Well, didn't that just top it off, a visual and olfactory representative of his ride tonight. Or lack thereof.

Dammit. He knew what was wrong. He was thinking too much, letting his head get in the way of what his body knew how to do. And the more he tried to not think about it, the more he did. As the buck-offs mounted, the more he tried to fix it.

Buster walked by on his way to the locker room. God, the kid looked about fifteen. Cam snorted. Shoot, the kid couldn't be much older than that. He remembered those days—the whirlwind new world of the tour, running, big-eyed and stumbling, trying to figure it all out. He ignored the needle of conscience in his gut.

Katya didn't get it. He wasn't jealous. Oh, he'd had help, sure. But Buster had to earn it. The veterans had been just as hard on him until he'd proved he took riding seriously.

Coddling doesn't make a cowboy. Adversity does.

BANG!

A door slammed open, hit the wall, then bounced back, striking the body that fell through it. Cowboys scattered. Cam jumped to his feet.

Whap! The head hit the tile floor last. Cam recognized

the upside-down face of the trainer, Edward, out for the count, a lump already rising on his temple.

"What the—"

Bam!

The door slammed open again. Katya walked through it. Her blouse was torn at the shoulder, the top two buttons ripped off. Jagged red scratches marred her pale skin from collarbone to the upper slope of her breast.

But she didn't seem to notice that, or the slack-jawed cowboys. She stood over the body at Cam's feet.

"That'll teach you to mess with the U.S. Military." She stepped over Edward's inert legs. "Hooyah, Asshole." Head up, she strode to the hallway door.

She sounded like a girl.

She walked like a soldier.

She looked like a Valkyrie.

When the door closed behind her, the cowboys expelled their held breath.

Tuck came through the locker room doorway. "Damn."

Another whistled low. "I heard one punch."

"You son of a bitch," Cam said to the unconscious man at his feet.

Doc Cody stepped forward. "Cam, when this piece of trash wakes up, tell him for me, he's fired. I'll check on Katya."

"Too happy to, Doc." Cam bit out the words.

Doc lifted someone's shirt from the back of a chair and walked to the hall door, then turned, hand on the knob. "Oh, and Cam? Let's be sure that the last punch he feels is from a woman."

Cam glanced at the faces around the room.

This could get ugly. "Yessir. I'll see to it."

Doc Cody walked out. Dusty, the only remaining conscious trainer, opened a melting ice bag and poured the cold water on Edward's face.

He woke sputtering, to a ring of riders' faces over him. "Wha—what happened?"

"A woman just kicked your sorry ass, dude," one of the faces said.

"Yeah and with one punch."

"You're fired," Cam said.

Edward wiped ice water off his face, moaning when he touched his damaged temple. "I've been assaulted. I'm pressing charges. And you can't fire me, Cahill."

"You're right. I can't. Doc Cody asked me to pass on the good news." Cam's foot itched to kick in this guy's ribs. But he knew if he did, the cowboys would be on Edward in a heartbeat. Doc Cody was depending on him. "You're free to press charges. Course, then it'll be in the public record that you assaulted a woman. And that she took you out." He touched the toe of his boot, gentle, to Edward's shoulder.

"Oh, and if you do, you can be pretty sure every man in this room will be by to pay you a visit."

Nods all around. The silence proved scarier than the threat. After all, Edward didn't know Doc's warning to Cam pretty much forbade any violence.

"Stand back and let me up, damn you."

Cam straightened, not offering the jerk his hand. "Show's over, men. Let this weasel slink back to his hole." He waited while the cowboys walked to the locker room. Dusty crossed to the sink to dump the ice bag.

Cam stepped over Edward, making sure the bottom of his smelly boot smeared Edward's pristine white shirt.

• • •

Katya passed two bends in the hallway before the mad bled away, taking her energy with it. She stopped and leaned against a tile wall, sliding down to sit with her throbbing hand cradled in her lap. When she leaned forward and touched her head to her knees, her hair fell around her in a curtain. Somewhere in the melee she had lost her hair clip.

This job was gone for sure, now. Regardless of the provocation, you can't punch out a coworker and expect to stay employed. But that was only the top problem on the shit heap. She took this job to get better and she was getting worse.

What is wrong with me? She clamped down her muscles to squeeze out the shakes. Being Stateside was changing her; making her soft. For a few minutes in that room, she'd acted like a victim.

Leaning her head on her knees, she tried to harness the wants that pushed up from the deep corner of her brain, where she'd stuffed them. She wanted to be home, in Kandahar. She wanted to talk to Trace.

Most of all, she wanted Grand. The hole in the world where Grand used to be expanded, opening a huge hollow cavern in her chest. Putting a hand over the ache, she rocked, straining to remember the old, scratchy voice falling on her like a balm.

Boot heel clicks echoed, getting closer. Doc Cody came around the corner.

She dashed her fingers across her cheeks and scrambled to her feet, yanking at her torn shirt to cover her bare shoulder. "I'm sorry, sir. I didn't—"

"You've nothing to be sorry for." Taking care not to

touch her, he settled a blue shirt with sponsor names running down the sleeves over her shoulders. "Edward was an outstanding therapist. It's my fault for not realizing he was a lousy human being." He stepped away. "You don't have to worry about him. He'll be gone for good by the time you go back in."

Wow. She hadn't expected that. Back East, she'd have had to go to the labor board to try to keep her job. *Thank God and old-fashioned values for that.* Edward was one witness that she wouldn't have to face. But the rest remained. She clutched the lapels of the borrowed shirt in her fist, wishing the rest of her was so easily held together.

"That's the good news." He blew out a sigh. "The bad news is that we're now short a trainer. Until I can get one hired, you're going to have to take your turn, standing first responder duty at the out gate."

Panic shot through her like electricity down a wire. If she hadn't been so busy feeling sorry for herself, she'd have seen this wall before she walked into it.

That didn't happen to trained army officers. Was she losing that, too?

The sympathy in his brown eyes hardened like a chocolate glaze on ice cream. "Are you able to do that, Katya?"

Hadn't she always known it would come to this? It was time to take the next step even if it was off a cliff.

She stood straight, grateful for the wall at her back. "I won't let you down, sir." She'd have believed it more if her voice hadn't cracked at the end.

Doc's hesitation proved that he might not believe it either.

She cleared her throat. "Sir." Authority echoed off the cinderblock walls.

"Good. Now, let's go take a look at that hand."

She followed him down the hall, sleeves of the borrowed shirt drooping over her fingers, hoping she hadn't just overpromised.

And praying she wouldn't underdeliver.

CHAPTER 11

Cam leaned, ankles crossed, against the cement wall of the arena, waiting. The wall radiated retained heat of the day, but the impending desert night pushed a cool breeze against his face. The Tucson sunset reminded him of home, the huge orange ball of sun and a band of gold-orange stretching on the horizon.

This sure hadn't been your normal day on the PBR Tour. He chuckled, wondering what Edward thought of those magic hands now.

Army. He'd recognized the battle cry. Probably a medic. How had Katya landed here, on the Tour?

After seeing her today, he sure wanted to find out.

He remembered his ex-wife's heavy eye makeup, red lips, and hair teased up, looking like she'd just fallen out of a man's bed. He'd learned the hard way that Candi didn't like the real thing mussing up that look.

The vision of Katya standing in the doorway, proud, primitive, and pissed had burned onto the backs of his eyes. Every time he closed them, he saw her.

Now *there's* a woman. Maybe it was time to update his type.

The door slammed open and Katya walked out, head down, wearing a flowing white skirt and an army green T-shirt that showed off the long, strong muscles of her arms. She set off in long strides, her backpack bouncing.

"Smitty."

She turned, jaw tight, surprise in her eyes. "Only someone who loves me gets to call me that; my name is Katya. What are you doing here?"

"Waiting for you."

She rolled her eyes to the sky, as if irritated with God. "Well, here I am. If you want something, you'll have to talk walking. I want to get to the hotel and a shower."

He pushed off from the wall, jiggling his knee to get it to work.

"You don't take pain meds." She stood watching, hip cocked, arms crossed.

"How do you know that?"

"Because I have eyes." She had her "mother voice" on. "If you took them, you wouldn't be in pain every time I see you."

"It's not bad." He tested his knee on the walk over to her. It decided to cooperate. "You were going to walk to the hotel alone?"

"You don't think I'm capable?" She managed to look down her nose at him, even though he was taller.

He grinned. "Hon, after today, I'd pity the dude who tried to mug you." He fell in beside her.

She marched more than walked. "I wish you'd let me brew you some dandelion-ginger tea. It has wonderful inflammation- and pain-reducing qualities, with none of the side effects of drugs."

"I'm good."

Her nose went higher. "Suit yourself."

"You were army."

A frown softened her hard profile. She huffed out a sigh.

"You're not the only one with eyes."

She motored on, clearly trying to leave the subject behind.

He should let it drop, but he'd found out today that there was a lot more to the new therapist than exotic eyes and a smoking bod. He wanted to know how much more. "Where were you stationed?"

"That's not relevant. Did you want to discuss something current?" Her voice could have etched glass.

Hmm. Sore spot. "Look, I know what it's like, having people poking at you, wanting to know intimate details of your life. I won't go there if you don't want to." He laid a hand on her forearm. That stopped her. "I just want you to know that if you want to talk, I have ears, as well as eyes."

She squinted at him, assessing. "Thanks."

At the exit to the parking lot, he followed her when she turned left. Only an occasional car passed as they walked in silence on the edge of the road. The sun had dropped to a white-hot sliver at the horizon. In the light breeze, the wild oats at the side of the road rustled a sigh of relief.

"I do have questions, if you wouldn't mind answering." For the first time tonight, she sounded like a woman, rather than a soldier.

He didn't like talking about himself. They had that much in common. He would be taking a chance, but he had a feeling he wouldn't learn more about her without a little quid pro quo. "Okaaay."

"Why do the riders wear chaps? Do they help you stay on the bull?"

That question he hadn't expected. "Nope. They're more a tradition. Working cowboys wore them to protect their legs from brush. Nowadays, they're more for the flash. You know, they look good during a ride."

"What's a 'head hunter'?"

"It's a bull that's looking for a target on the get-off. Why all these questions?"

"Because I want to know. You guys speak a different language. I talked to the Jamesons and they helped a lot, but they're not riders. I have some of the terminology, but I don't have a framework to hang it on."

The tension between his shoulders eased. These questions he could handle. He could talk bull riding all day. "Ask away."

She looked at him out of the corner of her eye. "Anything?"

"Look, if a two-thousand-pound bull doesn't scare me, I think I can handle a couple of questions from a Yankee."

Her face was intent, two tiny lines formed between her brows, telling him that this question mattered. "How do you do it? Ride I mean."

"Well, it helps to be really brave. Or really stupid." He hadn't really thought about the why of it in years. He took a moment, watching the advancing dusk. "When you're raised around cattle, you're not as afraid of them as you'd think. This was all I ever wanted to do from the time I was old enough to ride mutton. There's something about testing yourself against nature—to see how you measure up."

"Too much testosterone then."

"More like adrenaline. Like the song says, 'Sometimes I think I get off on the pain.'"

Her green eyes urged him to dig deeper than glib.

"Actually, it's a lot bigger than me. We carry on a tradition—a link between the past and the future. Being a cowboy is an honest, good way of life. It shouldn't die." Damn, now he was babbling like a lovesick calf. He shut up.

They turned in at the parking lot of the hotel just as the neon sign out front flashed on.

"But how can you do it? Get on, knowing that every ride could be the one that kills you?"

He shoved his hands in his pockets and watched the pavement passing under his boots. "By being more afraid of the day I can't do it anymore." He rushed on, before she could say something he was sure he didn't want to hear. "Hell, this way of life isn't something somebody can tell you."

"I guess." She shrugged out of the straps and pulled a key from the pocket of her backpack.

He didn't want her to go. He didn't want to wait two weeks to see her again. God, the waning light loved her face, making her look soft, almost vulnerable. He slowed his steps. "I can show you."

She threw her head up. "Show me what?"

"Next weekend. We've got a week off, and a bunch of us are riding in a fund-raising event in Stephenville. If you want to know about cowboys, that would give you a good idea. It's on the way to the event in Dallas."

She stopped in front of a long line of rooms on one wing of the hotel. "I don't think that's a good idea."

Her first questions had been the Katya he knew: clinical, professional, and factual. The last revealed a deeper interest right before she shut down. Why was she so determined to keep her distance?

He tipped his hat. "Suit yourself. But if you're going to ask questions, you'd better be ready for the answers."

The following Saturday, Katya squinted into the low sun, searching for a sign to tell her where the heck she was. She'd turned off the main road miles ago and all she'd seen since was ranchland, cattle, and mesquite.

She'd been intrigued by the fund-raiser ad. It was to be held not far from Fort Worth, in Stephenville. Dubbed "The Cowboy Capital of the World," the list of local cowboys read like a "Who's Who" of bull riding. She half expected to have to flash a champion's buckle to gain entrance at the outskirts of town.

But she'd taken up the challenge Cam had thrown, only partially to get answers to her bull-riding questions. Other questions had popped up after talking to him that day. Questions she couldn't ask. Like, who is Cam Cahill, really? The tantrum-throwing toddler? "Cool Hand" Cam Cahill taciturn champion bull rider? The hard-ass puppy-pounder? Or the almost sweet guy she'd met last weekend?

Those questions bugged her a lot more than the bull-riding ones.

"Ah, civilization!" She slowed at a clapboard, hand-lettered sign announcing the "Rowdy Rhodes Invitational BBQ and Bull Riding." A pole-fenced outdoor arena, complete with bucking chutes and bleachers, lay on the right side of the road. But the party was clearly on the left. Rows of pickups stood parked in a field and she could see the crowd farther out.

She carefully pulled her rental car off the road, bumping over crop stubble to an empty slot beside a huge, mud-spattered truck with dualies and a cattle guard bumper.

Stepping from the car, she smoothed her layered emerald skirt, making sure the ruffled neckline of her muslin blouse wasn't dipping below decency. She ran her palms over her pulled-back hair to smooth flyaways. Tucking her shyness away where it wouldn't show, she threaded through the trucks to the crowd.

Half-barrel barbecues belched smoke and mouth-watering smells of roasting meat. Kids darted every-where and blankets lay like a huge patchwork quilt in the shade of an oak tree.

"Magic hands!" Tucker Penny crossed the grass to her, soda bottle in one hand, loaded plate in the other. "Cahill owes me twenty bucks. I told him you'd show."

Not sure how to react to that bit of news, she only half smiled.

Tucker looked around. "He was just here..."

"Don't bother yourself. I'm going to wander around a bit."

"Be sure to grab some food. The beef was raised on this land. It's amazing."

"Thanks." On her way to the food tables, she waved to several of the riders she recognized, surprised to see that, even young as they were, many had wives and children. She picked up a plate and utensils, eyeing the platters of meat. They looked wonderful, and smelled better, but the thought of eating a cow that had been grazing where she was standing...she grabbed a hot dog instead, picked up a cup of iced tea and looked for a place to sit.

There were one or two tight slots at the crowded picnic tables, but sitting that close to people sent claustrophobia skittering over her skin on spider legs. Instead, she walked to where a crowd of cowboys stood in a circle, under a tree.

She took a bite of her hot dog, watching a young man in a wheelchair at the center. He looked like the other cowboys down to the gut-digging belt buckle, except for the leg that stretched straight out, strapped in a brace, ankle to hip.

An onlooker said, "That's crap, Rowdy! I was there. You slapped that bull four seconds into the ride!"

The guy's blue eyes twinkled when he smiled. "Yeah, but it's only illegal if the judges see it." He winked, and the cowboys laughed.

"When I'm back next season, I'm picking Bone Dancer, first chance I get. I don't see why none of you wimps have been able to cover him. He's honest; has the same trip every time."

Another rider spoke up. "That bull brings the goods. I made it one jump out the gate on him. Pulled me down on his horns."

Rowdy took a glass of tea from a pretty woman who Katya guessed was his wife. "Thank you, darlin'. Sanders, if you'd brace your knees when he goes vertical—"

"That was a bad wreck," a deep voice whispered next to her ear.

She started, tea sloshing over her hand. Cam stood beside her, watching Rowdy. She chalked up her rapid heartbeat to surprise. "What happened?" she whispered back.

Cam touched her elbow and led her away. "Bulls that don't buck hard are more dangerous than rank ones. A good bucker will throw you out of the way. If you come off a slow one, you're gonna fall right under his hooves."

She didn't want to hear the rest of the story and yet she couldn't stop herself from asking, "Is that what happened?"

"Rowdy'd have been okay, but his spur hung in the rope. He was underneath and the bull kept spinning over him, helicoptering his knee." He winced, and sucked air through his teeth. "Seemed like it went on forever. The bullfighters tried to get the bull off him. By the time they managed to cut the rope, about the only thing holding Rowdy's leg together was the skin." He took her empty plate from her and tossed it in a trash can.

The ground tilted, and her stomach staged a hot-dog rebellion. "No more." Dizzy, she bent over.

"Oh, shit, I'm sorry." His steadying hand clamped around her upper arm. "Are you okay? I thought, you being in sports medicine, it wouldn't bother you."

When her stomach settled a bit, she straightened to his worried frown. "I'm fine." She dropped her dog tags back into the neck of her blouse.

Cam noticed. His gaze followed them, lingering on what she realized was her overexposed cleavage. She yanked her collar up. No problem with blood flow now; her face felt swollen with it. She tugged on the hem of her blouse, trying to ignore the warm band around her upper arm where his hand rested.

"You sure?"

At her nod, he let go, but stayed close when they resumed their stroll. It seemed the sweet guy had shown up today. She so liked that guy. Too bad he wasn't around more often. "Rowdy said he was coming back on tour next year. Unfortunately, he doesn't look like he'll walk again, much less ride."

"Oh, he'll walk again. Ride? We'll see. I wouldn't bet against him." When she wobbled on the uneven ground, his hand found her elbow again, steadying her. "Maybe he's got a better line open to God than the doctors do."

They passed the oak tree, where women stood, folding blankets and packing up belongings. They skirted a woman who crouched, trying to wipe a struggling toddler's face.

"Rowdy was adamant. How can he be so sure?"

Cam looked at the ground. "Because, until he has something to step off onto, he needs to believe he can still do this."

Is he talking about Rowdy? Their gazes locked, but then he flushed, and looked away.

"Rowdy's a fighter. He'll do okay."

They reached the lip of the depression at the side of the road. She felt Cam's hand at her back, and his other took hers. She flinched away.

His hat shaded his face, but his white teeth gleamed when he smiled. He kept her hand. "Where are you from that a gentleman doesn't help a lady over a bar ditch?"

His smile was contagious. "Where I'm from they don't have bar ditches." It would take a stronger woman than she was to resist country-boy manners. Not to mention his charm.

She remembered working with the football team,

where her sex was ignored to the point that players strutted naked in front of her. Both as a trainer and a soldier,
she'd struggled with the balance, as a professional and a
woman.

Dare she hope that here she could have both?

She squeezed Cam's hand as they trotted down the
incline, then back up the other side. The road was deserted,
but he held her hand all the way across anyway.

"I'll have to leave you now. I've got to get ready to
ride."

She noticed he was only an inch or so taller than she
was. "Do you guys need medical support? I could—"

"We've got it covered. Today you're a guest. Just enjoy
yourself, Smitty."

The tops of her ears burned. Only a man who held her
heart had the right to call her that. "Please, not Kitty, not
Smitty. It's Katya."

Cam squinted at her. The question in his eyes told her
he'd seen too much. Again. "Noted. I'll catch up with you
after the bucking, okay?"

She nodded. He walked toward the business end of the
arena, where cowboys were congregating. Disappointment pricked her happy mood, deflating it just a little.

A guest. Not "my guest."

She appreciated the contents of Cam's snug Levi's as
he walked away. *Get a grip, Katya.* And yet she couldn't
deny the rush of warmth, like a wine buzz through her
body.

A gallon pickle jar, half full of money, sat on a TV tray
beside the bleachers, a "Hello my name is" label stuck to
the side. "For Rowdy" was written in red marker. Katya
looked around to be sure no one was close, then reached

in her purse, pulled out a hundred-dollar bill and stuffed it in the wide-mouth top.

In spite of his bravado, he probably needed it a lot more than she did.

The stands were filling as families crossed the road from the barbecue.

"Katya!"

Bree waved from the top of the stands. Katya climbed the ten risers to sit beside her new friend. "I didn't know you'd be here."

The sun glinted in Bree's chestnut hair. "We were running late and I had to help Max unload the bulls."

"You didn't get to eat?"

"I'm good, I've got peanuts." She lifted a bag of unshelled nuts from the metal slat at her feet. "Want some?"

Happiness settled on Katya's shoulders like a silk wrap. Light, rare, and special. Just for now, she wouldn't rather be anywhere in the world than sitting down on a warm Texas evening, shelling peanuts, and watching a rodeo event. And looking forward to the cowboy who promised to be waiting at the end of it. "I'd love some."

Bree chatted about home and her daughter as they watched the cowboys at the end of the arena donning chaps and rosining ropes. The rider prep at events was serious business, but the mood here was different; the men moved slow and relaxed, teasing and laughing together.

Katya tipped her chin at the chutes. "I don't get it. They're risking their necks and their careers in an event that doesn't count." She selected a peanut and split the shell with her thumbnail. "Why don't they just mail Rowdy a check?"

"Because, city girl, this is where these guys come from. They learned to ride in arenas like this." Bree watched the men, a wistful smile on her lips. "The PBR is what they do for money. This they do for love—the love of the sport, and the camaraderie. They're helping Rowdy tonight, but next time it could be any of them." She leaned her forearms on her knees. "Rowdy's too proud to take charity. They all are. But getting together for a meal and a bucking? That's family."

Bree was right. The stress of competition and glitz of a televised PBR event masked what lay deeper. She could see they were a family of sorts, like her unit in Kandahar.

Yet once more, here she sat, on the outside, watching. "Yeah, I can see that."

She hated the wistfulness in her voice.

You're doing what you can to get back there. For now, that has to be enough.

"Ah, there's the man of the hour now." Bree pointed. Rowdy's wife wheeled him to the end of the arena, next to the bucking chutes. She locked the wheelchair in place then squatted beside it, looking up into Rowdy's face. She said something that made him smile and he cupped her cheeks, bringing her face to his for a kiss.

A bubble of lonely filled Katya's chest, pressing on her lungs, her heart.

When a few men walked up, Rowdy's wife stood, and turned to go. Katya saw Rowdy's lingering caress on the inside thigh of her Wranglers. "How do the wives do it, knowing that when their husbands leave for work they could come back broken, or worse?"

Rowdy's wife walked to the stands, putting an extra wiggle in her hips, checking over her shoulder to be sure

Rowdy was enjoying the show. He was. Fine-boned and petite, she didn't look strong enough to bear what must be a smothering burden.

Bree shook her head. "I met Max after his bull riding days, but I imagine the wives handle it like army wives do." She looked at Katya, then quickly away. "Or cops' wives."

News certainly traveled fast here. She worried at the thought of her past being a headline on the PBR hot sheet. It took her mind off worrying that tonight could be the night that Cam got hurt.

They watched the men climb the chutes, preparing the first bull. Bree turned to Katya with a smug smile. "Besides, you think you have a choice in who you fall in love with? Dream on, sister."

The sodium lights on poles around the arena flicked on. A man's voice boomed from a portable mic he held. "Okay, folks, let's get this thing started. First up, the baby on the block, Buster Deacon."

Buster forced his hat down on his head, pushing his ears out vertical, then climbed onto the back of the chute. When he looked up, his face was the color of an overripe tomato.

The announcer laughed. "Ah, Buster, we're just joshing you."

The gate swung open and a sheep bolted into the arena. Katya couldn't help joining in the laughter. The surprise on Buster's face had been priceless.

"Come on now, guys. Run a rank one under that rookie. He may be a kid, but he's been outriding y'all lately."

An hour later, Cam stood behind the empty chutes. He stripped the tape from his glove, getting ready to leave.

His friends did the same, removing spurs, and packing up equipment.

"Nice ride, Cam." A rider stepped around him, duffel in hand.

"Thanks. You'll get 'em next weekend, Brody." Cam unbuckled his chaps. The bull had spun into his hand, first thing out the gate. He'd found the sweet spot, and set to spurring. It had felt so good, so easy.

Yet the glow from his win was snuffed out with the cold-water fact—these bulls were a tier below PBR level. It wasn't long ago he was riding this easy at events.

But not lately. Maybe never again.

"Screw that." He'd had too much fun today to worry about that now. Denial would work for another hour or two. Katya was waiting.

"Could I hop a ride with you to Dallas?" Buster addressed Ben Carter, where he stood against the chutes, using a wire brush on his rope. "I rode out with Armando, but he's staying with friends here tonight."

"Rent a car, kid. I'm not here to wipe your nose."

Buster kept walking. "They won't rent me one until I'm twenty-one."

Cam felt a stab, hearing the worry in Buster's voice. He said good-bye to the guys and walked around the arena to the bleachers, where a few wives waited for their husbands.

And him. He felt a jolt like a low-level shock in his chest. Katya stood, hand on the bleachers, talking to Tuck's wife, Nancy. The wind blew Katya's pretty skirt against her, outlining her dancer's legs

He walked up, a goofy grin he couldn't wipe clean hanging on his face. "Hey, Nancy, Tuck will be here in just a few. He was looking for someone to tie his shoes, last I saw him. Hey, Katya. You ready? I'll walk you to your car." Her welcoming smile did warm things to his insides. He tipped his hat to Nancy and, ignoring her wink, led Katya away.

In the parking lot, they passed a knot of riders. "Can I hitch a ride to Dallas with any of you?" Buster asked, hanging on the edge of the group.

Katya craned her neck to see past the men. "Buster, is that you?"

He walked over, red hair catching the light. "Yes'm."

"I'll give you a ride." She smiled. The same smile she'd just given Cam.

"That would be awesome, Katya. Thanks so much." The kid beamed like she'd bestowed him with knight-hood. "Let me get my stuff."

Oh, hell. He knew Katya had a soft spot for the kid. If Cam objected, they'd end up arguing again. Besides, who was he to say who got in her car? And why hadn't he thought to hitch a ride first? "Take your time, kid."

Buster trotted off.

Katya laughed at Cam's growl and, linking her arm in his, steered him to a white compact with rental plates. "Too late, Cahill. Today I've seen that there's the possibil-ity of a nice guy hiding under all that…"

He took off his hat and fingered the brim. "Asshole. I know."

She laughed again, delighted. Her face shone pale in the lights of the arena, in stark contrast to the dark park-ing lot behind her. In her eyes, light sparked, dancing like moonlight on choppy water. He didn't mean to lean in, but the carefree joy on her face pulled him there.

The smile slid. Her eyes got bigger, the closer he got. Her lips parted, just a bit, and she sucked in a breath. She looked so innocent. So why did he want to pull her into the grass, and have his way with her? Blood abandoned the rest of his body, pounded to his hips, as his Johnson snapped to attention. He slid his hand under her hair to the silken skin of her neck. Her sweet exhale brushed his lips.

"I'm ready!" Buster loped up like a big puppy, his manners about as refined.

Cam swore under his breath.

Katya chuckled, then whispered, "See you in Dallas, cowboy." She gave him a chaste peck on his cheek, and turned to unlock the car.

He watched them pull out, touching his cheek, cursing puppies everywhere.

CHAPTER 12

Blackness hurtled by the car window, broken by only an occasional barnyard sodium lamp. The curved horizon ahead glowed white with the lights of Dallas. Buster's face looked ghostly in the dashboard light.

"Mom isn't really happy about me traveling so much. She's always fretting about me getting hurt. But mostly they're happy that I'm getting to live my dream."

Between Buster's explanations the past hour, and her experience at Rowdy's Invitational today, Katya was beginning to understand. The hype that PBR was one big, extended family wasn't hype at all.

And here she sat, once more on the outside, the hole in her life yawning as vast as the Texas sky in the moonroof.

She didn't belong in DC with her parents. She never had.

She didn't belong in the Medic Corps. Not now, anyway.

And she sure didn't belong here. In a world where macho, testosterone-crazed young men gambled their future for bragging rights and a gaudy belt buckle.

Still, she'd enjoyed Buster's company. He was just as polite, guileless, and as earnest as his red hair and freckles suggested. She could ask him anything. Questions she couldn't ask Cam, who looked too close and saw too much.

"Buster, aren't you afraid? Every time you get on a bull, it could go horribly wrong. How do you manage the fear? Is there some kind of mental exercise you do, or what?"

"No, ma'am. I'm not afraid."

His matter-of-fact tone brought her head around. "Ever?"

He sat sprawled in the seat, elbow resting on the ledge of the closed window, too relaxed to be lying. "No'm."

"You've been injured before, right?"

"Sure. Nothing really bad, thank the good Lord, but I've had my share of doctor's visits and Epsom salt baths, I can tell you that."

If this kid is right, I'm doomed. Maybe courage, once tested and broken, didn't come back. Like a badly burst eardrum, you just learned to live with the loss. After all, she'd yet to see fear in any of the riders. Even Rowdy Rhodes, who'd almost lost his leg, talked of coming back on tour. He hadn't seemed afraid.

That can't be right. Lots of people are afraid, of all kinds of things. "So, you guys are immune to fear. Is it a skill, like riding, that you can learn? Or is it something you're just born with?"

"That's a good question. I couldn't tell you. All I can say is that all I feel before a ride is jumping-outta-my-skin excited."

You had to like Buster and his wide-eyed view of the world.

Unless you're a jaded, bitter old bull rider. "Something else I don't get, Buster. Why are the other riders so mean to you?"

"Oh, they're not mean. That's just part of the deal. You can't expect to walk in and have them hold your hand and sing 'Kumbaya.' You have to earn your place."

"But you did. You earned the points to get to the big leagues."

"No'm. That's just riding. It takes a lot more than points to be a cowboy, and that's what I have to show them." His voice went hard. "What I *will* show them."

The following Thursday, Katya dropped her shopping bags and collapsed on her hotel bed. Another perk of this job was the downtime. Driving to the venues allowed her to see more of the country, and the weekdays between events allowed her time to explore the host cities. This week she'd visited the Dallas Arboretum and Botanical Gardens, the Texas School Book Depository Museum and the Aquarium. Today, she'd hung out at Billy Bob's to watch the mechanical bull riding, and to her slight embarrassment, even bought a T-shirt.

Staying busy helped to push away the clouds of worry at the thought of this weekend's event. But when she sat still, or tried to sleep, black thunderheads obscured her mood. *First responder duty.* It rolled like thunder in her head, getting closer. The hair on her arms stood up, and she scrubbed her palms over them.

"You're going to do fine. You're a soldier. You'll do your job."

But the words rang hollow. She hadn't last time. Or the time before. Or, God knows—

Buzzzzz.

She leapt from lying to standing in one startled move. Her phone vibrated in the pocket of her skirt. She pulled it out and read the text.

Can I call you?

She didn't recognize the number. *Edward?* Her heart slammed the confines of her chest.

"Get a grip, Katya. Edward would hardly ask permission." Just the same, no way she was acknowledging a text from an unknown source.

She walked to the desk and picked up Grand's mortar and pestle, then dug through her bags of herbs. She felt Grand close when working with her tools. She'd grind and talk to Grand in her head. Sometimes her grandmother answered.

Okay, so probably she was talking with her own brain, but it soothed her worries and that was the important thing.

Buzzzzz. She jumped then snatched her phone again.

By the way, this is Cam.

Her heart sped up this time for a different reason. She saved his number into her contact list, then hit speed dial.

"Hi Katya. Did you enjoy your week in town?"

Her traitorous body reacted to his deep, familiar tone, her muscles slackening. "You know you scared the crap out of me, right? Did Doc Cody give you my number?" Annoyance leaked into her words.

"No. Dusty did. He told me he was going to text you about it."

"Well, he—hang on." She took the phone from her ear and scrolled through the texts. Sure enough, she'd missed one from Dusty. She raised the phone back to her ear. "Okay. Sorry. Guess I'm a bit jumpy."

"Well then, you're in luck. Nothing settles jumpy like food. I was just fixin' to head out to my favorite restaurant in Dallas, and I thought of you. Are you up for some adventurous eating?"

For what? A date? Or as a friend, tagging along for dinner? The night of the Invitational, she'd felt his interest, sliding smooth and warm over her skin. If Buster hadn't loped up when he had, she'd already know if those lips were as good at kissing as she'd imagined about ten times since then.

Okay, a hundred times. But she had to know. "Cahill, are you asking me out on a date?" Her boldness crumbled in the onslaught of silence. "Or not?" she squeaked.

His soft chuckle loosened the knot in her stomach. "I forgot. This is the lady full of questions. For clarity, let me reword that." He cleared his throat. "Ms. Smith, would you do me the honor of coming out with me tonight? On a date?"

She ignored her own grin. And the sparkly fountain in her chest. "Well, Mr. Cahill, that depends. It's going to cost you."

"Oh man, everybody has an agenda."

She hadn't realized it was possible to hear an eye roll. "And you don't?"

"Point taken. What's it going to cost me?"

"You have to try my healing tea."

More silence. This guy was good at silence.

"Oh, come on. Buster said he'd try it."

"Good. Then you don't need me."

"No one listens to Buster. The riders look up to you. If you endorsed it, they would try it too."

"Why does it matter so much?"

She sighed. "Because there is a better way. Holistic healing predates modern medicine by several thousand years, and—"

"And you care."

"What? No I don't, I mean, no, I don't mean—" *Shut up, shut up, shut up.* "I'm trying to do my job to the best of my ability, that's all." She blew out a breath.

"Okay."

"Okay? You mean you'll try it?"

"I'll try it, Katya."

"Oh, Cam, thank you. You won't be sorry. This is going to help your pain."

"Maybe you should wait to thank me. You haven't seen the dinner menu."

"Hey, I eat anything."

"I'll remind you of that. Can you be ready in an hour? I'll pick you up."

CHAPTER 13

Katya looked around the restaurant. Surrounded by trees outside, the interior was exposed timber and glass, giving The Wild Side the feel of a hunting lodge in the woods. The fieldstone fireplace with its cheery gas log fire and the trophy animal heads on the wall carried out the theme.

"Well? What do you think?" Cam smiled at her from across the linen-covered table, the dimple in his cheek deepening.

"That gazelle looks pissed. I think he wants his body back." The unblinking stare of the animals on the walls gave her the willies, so she kept her eyes on Cam. Well, maybe that wasn't the only reason. His royal blue Western-cut shirt showed off his washed-blue eyes. The candlelight fractured in them, and she had a hard time looking anywhere else. He'd taken off his hat when he sat down, but it left a mark in his short, hollow-gold hair. She took a sip of her white wine to cool off. God, if he were on the menu, this place would be overrun with women.

He chuckled, and when the waiter walked over with

menus, he held up a hand. "Will you trust me to order?" He gave her a one-sided smile, an eyebrow raised in challenge.

"I guess I'll trust you that far." *Not much farther though.* She had no doubt that smile had separated dozens of women from their panties. *Don't forget, you don't belong here.* Why did she have to keep reminding herself of that lately?

He ordered something called the Hunter's Feast for Two. When the waiter walked away, Cam turned his attention back to her. "You drive a hard bargain, Ms. Smith. It cost me dearly to get you sitting across the table from me. Are you sure you aren't a horse trader on the side?"

She snorted. "I should have warned you, it's in my blood. My great-great grandfather made enough money trading horses to bring his family to America."

"Literally?"

Might as well get it out in the open. In spite of the modern push to accept "cultural diversity," there was still a lot of prejudice against her kind. "I don't just dress Gypsy, Cam. I am Gypsy."

"No kidding?" The touch of his regard settled on her. "I know so little about you. Where did you grow up?"

Well, he'd answered her questions. No harm in answering a few benign ones of his. "In DC. But my summers I spent with my Gypsy family, in Chicago."

"What was that like?"

"It was heaven. I'm an only child. But in Chicago, my huge extended family took me in every summer and folded me into the clan." She smiled, seeing Grand's apartment in her mind. "It was like stepping into another world. Like I lived two different lives."

"When did you join the army?"

"After nine/eleven. A lot of people joined then."

"I wouldn't have guessed you for a soldier, but once I knew it, lots of things made sense. Did you like it?"

"I loved it. In a way, it was like Chicago. Another kind of family. We rely on each other under hard times and stressful circumstances. It forges a strong bond."

"You miss it."

Once again, his eyes made her nervous, seeing too much. "Something happened over there, didn't it?"

"I miss it."

The waiter brought their salads, breaking the pull of his gaze. That gaze made her want to talk, to spill her dark story all over the pristine tablecloth, staining everything.

She lifted her fork. "Tell me about your family. Where are you from?"

They chatted about safe subjects until their meal arrived: a huge platter of unrecognizable meat without a vegetable in sight. Unless fried potatoes qualified.

He looked it over. "I'm torn. I'm afraid if I tell you what's here, you won't eat it, and you'd miss out on some great food. But I don't want to ambush you either. So you tell me. Do you want to know?"

She picked up her fork, stabbed a deep-fried Rocky Mountain oyster, and popped it in her mouth.

His eyes got big. "Wait, that's a—"

"Cow testicle, I know." She licked her lips. "I have to say, it's better than sheep, but not as good as camel." She glanced around for the waiter, then back to him. "Do you think they have hot sauce?"

His eyes got bigger. "I think I'm in love," he breathed.

Katya enjoyed the dinner. She'd had buffalo and venison, of course, but rattlesnake was new to her, and the ostrich. The food was great, but the company was better. They'd laughed through dinner, Cam regaling her with funny stories of his sisters and of being on the road.

The sweet guy was firmly in residence. She'd read the term "dazzled" in books and knew the definition, but she'd never *felt* the word before. When the normally tight-lipped cowboy opened up, he opened all the way, sparking with so much humor, light, and charisma, she wished she'd brought sunglasses. She found the dichotomy of his hard cheekbones, paired with soft, baby-face features, endlessly fascinating.

And he liked her. He showed it in his focused interest when she told a story, or laughed at his. He hadn't physically touched her since they sat down, but his eyes—she'd felt their touch everywhere.

Damn, it's hot in here. She fanned her face with her napkin.

Cam handled the check, then signed an autograph for an older woman who stood beside their table, gushing like a teenage fan girl.

Katya couldn't blame her. After hanging around the sweet guy all night, she was feeling a bit like a fan girl herself.

He finished writing, thanked the lady, then turned those baby blues on Katya. "Are you ready?"

She slipped out from the table and stood. "The question is, are you?"

He settled his hat on his head and took her elbow, leading her to the front door. "For what?"

"My tea, of course." She rubbed her hands together and lowered her voice to spooky. "I'll get you back to my room, and you'll be trapped, my pretty."

He smiled, holding the door for her. His teeth flashed white against his tanned face. She stumbled just a bit, over the doorsill. His arm came around her waist, steadying her.

His breath brushed her ear, making her shiver. "You can trap me in your room anytime you'd like."

Heat shot through her body. She wasn't about to glance down, but she thought maybe her pubic hair had just burst into flame.

Cam waited for Katya to unlock the door to her hotel room. She'd left the light on by the bed, and he looked around as they stepped in. The room was exactly the same as his, except for the rainbow colors shot onto the walls by the silky scarf thrown over the lampshade. It softened the harsh, rubber-stamp room, making it more personal, more intimate, more... Katya.

Not Katya the soldier, or the therapist, but the woman under those that he'd glimpsed tonight. This was the Katya he sensed behind her professional touch: sensual, sensitive, passionate. He was hoping to see more of that woman.

"Have a seat. It'll take me a few minutes to put it together." She moved to the backpack lying on the desk. She dug through it, pulling out sandwich bags of herbs. "Really. Sit, Cam. I promise this won't hurt."

He perched on the edge of the bed. "Cowboys drink coffee, not," he mimed picking up a teacup, his pinkie outstretched "tea."

She turned on the coffeemaker, then poured water from a carafe into the back of it. "Yeah, well, the smart ones will." She dropped leaves from a few baggies into a small porcelain bowl and used a tool of the same material to grind it. "There's no magic here. Prickly ash and comfrey control pain, and the marigold and chamomile help the inflammation."

He studied her profile as, head down, she concentrated on her task. Wisps of hair had pulled loose from the thick ponytail held in place by a complicated woven-wood fastener. Her olive skin glowed in the dim light. Soft and feminine. A deadly combination.

"The World Health Organization estimates that eighty percent of the developing countries use herbal medicine for their primary health care. In the United States and Europe, it's become increasingly popular in recent years, as scientific evidence of its effectiveness mounts."

He winced. "I agreed to take the medicine orally. Do I have to take it verbally, too?"

She glanced at him then laughed. "You look like a little boy waiting to have iodine put on a cut." She poured the steaming hot water into the cup, and set it aside to steep. "Cowboy up, big guy. Did I say that right? Why is it that you're not afraid of a ticked off bull chasing you down, but you're afraid of a cup of tea?"

"I'm not afraid of anything," he said in his "Cool Hand Cam Cahill" voice.

She sat on the edge of the bed. "Really? Are you not afraid of anything?"

Now she was the one who looked like a little kid.

"Afraid? No."

Her face fell, as if she'd been looking for a different answer.

"Of course, I'm not going to say that I don't have a few...concerns."

"About what?"

Time to lighten it up. "Oh, politics, global warming, world peace, you know."

She rose, picked up the coffee mug and handed it to him. "Oh, wait. Don't drink that yet." She rummaged in her backpack, then with a smile, raised a bottle of honey. "You know the song about a spoonful of sugar." She poured a generous dollop of honey in his mug and stirred it with a plastic spoon. "It would be better if you ate the leaves too. But if you don't want to, that's okay."

He took a tiny sip. Warm, sweet, and a bit minty. It was okay. He blew away the steam and took a deeper sip. "I can choke it down."

"Gee, glowing praise. Be sure you drink it all. You should start to feel better in about an hour."

He drained the mug, even managing to swallow most of the tea leaves in the bottom. He stood, and set the mug on the edge of the desk. "There, I took my medicine. Do I get a prize?" He turned and spread his arms. "A good-night kiss, maybe?"

"Well, you were pretty grumpy about it, but if I take into account that you're a big bad bull rider, I guess allowances could be made." Smiling, she stepped into his arms.

Just where he wanted her.

He could see when buyer's remorse hit. Her eyes danced around the room, lighting everywhere but on him. He slid his hands up to cup her cheeks. That got her attention. "It's not a commitment, Katya, it's just a kiss."

When he brought her face to his, her eyelids drifted closed. Still watching, he kissed her, a tentative "hello." But that wasn't enough. The smell of her spicy perfume filled his head, bringing visions of foreign bazaars and dusky, exotic women, dancing in firelight. Something about Katya intrigued him, enticed him closer, made him want to know more.

To want more. He dipped his head to sample her lips again.

This time, she relaxed, her lips opening to him. He closed his eyes, took what she gave, and gave everything he had, his tongue twining with hers. It had been so long. His blood pounded up his neck, behind his eyes, rushing to his crotch. His Johnson throbbed. He stifled a groan. It was everything he could do not to snatch her against him and grind into her. He wanted to back her to the wall, lift her and have her wrap those dancer's legs around him—

Her whimper brought him to. He pulled back. Had he hurt her? Jesus, he'd been so lost in her, he didn't even know. Frank need churned in her smoky eyes, her lips red and swollen from his kisses.

What the hell are you thinking, Cahill? Obviously his Johnson had taken over that duty. *Uh unh. Not going there again.* No more buckle bunnies or one night stands for him. Not that he'd never again consider a relationship, but Katya was too amazing to ruin his chances by rushing things.

The last time he'd rushed, he'd ended up hitched together with Candi. Within six months, she'd wanted out of the ties more than he, slashing her way out with careless claws.

He reached for his hat, and bowed to Katya. "Thank you for coming out with me, Ms. Smith." He put his hat on.

She dropped a quick curtsy, her eyes full of questions. "Thank you for dinner, Cam. I'll see you tomorrow."

He left as fast as he could.

CHAPTER
14

In the locker room the next night, Cam bent to buckle his spur. "The stuff worked. That's all I'm saying. My knee didn't keep me up last night."

"Oh, I hear what you're saying, partner." Tuck held a side lunge, warming up. "You're saying you're drinking her Kool-Aid."

Cam glanced around the crowded, noisy locker room. No one stared, but he sensed ears cocking. "Tuck, pay attention. I drank her *tea*."

"You took her to dinner, then back to her hotel room. Bud, trust me, you're drinking her Kool-Aid."

A few anonymous chuckles came from the cheap seats.

Tuck scratched his chin, considering. "You said she's a Gypsy. You could be in trouble. Maybe she slipped you a love potion." He squinted at Cam. "Just how long did you stay?"

"You'll want to watch your mouth, Hoss. She's a lady."

At his junkyard-dog growl, Tuck's eyebrows shot up. "Oh, it's like that."

Cam stood to buckle his chaps. "Quit standing there with your face hanging out. You'd best focus on your ride, not my love life." He rummaged in his locker for his mouthpiece and slipped it into the pocket of his vest.

He turned around to find that Tuck hadn't moved. Neither had a couple other riders. "What?"

"I'm just trying to get my head around you using 'my' and 'love life' in the same sentence."

"Yeah, well, stranger things can happen. You could actually manage to stay on a bull tonight." He slammed the locker door, ignored the watched feeling crawling on the back of his neck, and walked out.

As he rounded the hallway's last turn, the smell hit him—a heady mixture of animals, people, popcorn, and potential that was bull riding's signature perfume. When he stepped into the area behind the chutes, the sound washed over him; the pounding beat of a country song set to the shifting rise and fall of crowd noise. People streamed from the concourse, down the steps to their seats, hands full of beer and cardboard trays of food.

The familiar mule kick of adrenaline slammed into his chest, and his pulse caught a gear. After almost fifteen years on tour, he still got a buzz. These arenas felt more like home than his cabin in Texas.

The bulls waited. The night lay ahead, a shiny perfect thing.

A tide of emotions rose in him: pride, belonging, anticipation. His glanced at the JumboTron. It flashed the PBR schedule for the remainder of the season.

After this weekend, only four events until the finals.

His shiny mood popped. *It's all slipping away.* The future was hurtling at him. The events were ticking past like white dashes on freeway pavement. Four events until the finals. Six weeks to his last ride. Then what?

A black hole, that's what. His mind toyed with options, but nothing sparked his interest. Desperate, he even considered shoehorning himself back into life with his family on the home place. But he was about as useful there as an ice tray in hell. He shrugged the weight of worry off his shoulders. He had a job to do tonight.

One bull at a time. The mantra had served him well over the years for more than just bull riding. He rounded the corner of the chutes.

Katya stood back to him, looking through the metal slats of the out gate, a folded stretcher in the dirt beside her. Her shoulders hovered near her ears, her back humped like an old crone. Her fingers clutching the gate shone white. From her body language, you'd think Lucifer himself stood in that arena.

Her soft blouse and feminine flowing skirt against the stark utilitarian backdrop looked more out of place than usual. Like a... "Gypsy at a rodeo."

She jumped and whirled, fists coming up, eyes huge and spooked.

Jesus. This girl was more than wound tight; she was terrified. "Katya, it's just me." He talked low and slow, in his horse whisperer voice. "What's wrong?"

"Cam. You scared me." She put a shaking hand to her chest. "How long until the start?"

He stepped beside her. "About twenty minutes." It didn't escape him that she'd ignored his question. "You know, now that you're working the arena, you might want to buy yourself some Wranglers."

Her eyes narrowed.

He smiled. "Don't get me wrong. I surely do appreciate the sight of a lady in a skirt. But this environment is hell on soft clothes." Her white ballet shoes, already stained, sunk in the red dirt.

She looked at her feet, then at him. "You may have a point." The pink in her face was a good change from pasty-white. "No offense, but when I want fashion advice, I won't be consulting a cowboy."

"That's probably wise." He'd give money to know what put the fine tremor in her hands.

Could she be worried about me getting hurt? If he asked, and he was wrong, he'd look like the arrogant ass she'd thought him to be that first day. And yet, he'd still give a bit to know.

He wanted to hold her hands, to rub away the shakes. To stand next to her, to let her know she didn't stand alone.

But this wasn't the time, or the place. "At least it took your mind off whatever's scaring you in that arena." He looked through the slats, to where camera crews were setting up in the round shark's cage in the center. "Maybe sometime you'll tell me what that is." He tipped his hat and walked away, to prep his first bull.

He's right. I've got to calm down. Yeah, like she hadn't thought that eight hundred times since she'd fallen out of her sleepless bed. The cement-mixer in her digestive tract made breakfast out of the question, so she'd gone for a run instead.

Six miles of pavement pounding hadn't helped much, so lunch was out, too. To calm herself, she'd ground up every herb in her stash. When that didn't work, she'd poured the packets of hotel coffee and sugar in her mortar and ground them to dust. Not to drink, just to grind.

Still, her nerves felt like twitching live wires, sparking and spitting.

Finally, time passed, and she escaped the coffin-like hotel room. But it was worse here. She looked out at the arena, imagining herself running in on one end of the stretcher, kneeling in the dirt beside a downed cowboy.

P-R-I-C-E—protection, rest, ice, compression, elevation. Her hands would move with speed and efficiency, stabilizing injuries. Doing her job.

Another vision kept intruding; one where she stood over the cowboy, frozen, while the entire hushed arena watched.

That would be the end of everything: her job, her bank account, her chance to get back to her unit. And her chance to go out with Cam again.

Cam? Where did that come from? Get a grip, soldier.

Realizing her hands were at her mouth, she dropped them to her sides and made herself turn away from the visions in the dirt.

Doc Cody strode through the door from the locker room. She straightened, lifting the corners of her lips. Isn't that what a smile felt like? Well, it would have to do. "Hey, Doc. I've got the stretcher, straps, and braces. And the ER kit is right over there." She pointed. "We're ready."

He tipped his hat back, ignored the equipment, and focused on her instead. "We're going to be fine, Katya. With luck, we won't be needed tonight."

Yeah, like her luck worked that way.

"I'll be up on the chutes." He pointed up the stairs across the gate from her. "I'll be right here if something goes bad."

"Yessir." *Thank God.* She'd pictured him standing next to her all night. Watching. Judging. She let out a breath.

A deep voice boomed over the PA system. "Folks, you might want to find your seats. We're five minutes from showtime."

The cowboys streamed out of the locker room, lining up in front of her gate. She looked down the line, surprised to realize she could put a name to almost all the faces. She didn't see Cam, but halfway down the line, Buster's red hair and huge smile stood out of the crowd. He tipped his hat to her.

She smiled back, a real smile this time, and mouthed, "Good luck."

He winked at her.

The arena went black. The music cut off, mid-note. The crowd fell silent. For a few seconds, there was nothing.

Then, a deep, strong voice boomed out of the dark. "Welcome to the toughest sport on earth. My name is JB Denny, and I'll be your announcer for tonight's event. Sit back and get ready because *this* is the *P* (bang!) *B* (bang!) *R* (bang!)" The arena exploded with flashes of light and what sounded like gunfire.

She was ready this time. The pyrotechnics made her duck, but she just managed not to cover.

The gate swung open and when a spotlight hit her, she scrambled back to a dark corner. The riders were announced, and one by one, they stepped into the blinding light, raising their hats in salute to the crowd as they strode into the arena.

Each received their share of applause, but when Buster stepped out, the applause swelled. He ducked his head and ran into the arena, smile brighter than the spotlight.

She watched from the shadows, proud and happy for

him. And jealous. He ran out to meet the night and all that it could bring, good or bad.

Fearless. He was the poster boy for the slogan. Buster was going to get on a ton of pissed-off, stomp-your-guts-out bull, and he smiled.

All she had to do was pick up the pieces after a ride gone wrong, and she was light-headed with fear.

You are such a wuss.

When cowboys lined both sides of the arena, the spots were doused and the announcer's voice sliced through the dark. "This kid came up from the Challenger ranks twelve years ago, to take the National Final event in Las Vegas. The next season, he captured the world title in a storied season, winning seven individual events, a record still unbroken. The next year, he fought back from a career-threatening injury to again take the world title gold buckle. Ladies and gentlemen, our two-time world champion, 'Cool Hand' Cam Cahill!"

Katya craned her neck. Behind her, on a platform high above the bucking chutes, the spotlight hit Cam. The blast of white light flattened him to a two-dimensional study in light and shadow. He looked bigger than life and badder than bad. His chaps flared, following the slight bow in his legs, up to hug his hips. His huge gold champion's buckle flashed in the lights. When he doffed his hat, the crowd's voice swelled to ear-split level. He looked like a movie star—unknowable, untouchable.

Damn. Every buckle bunny in the place must be squirming in their tight bling jeans. A small thrill shot up the back of Katya's neck.

You've been on a date with that cowboy! Hell, she'd *kissed* him.

She shook herself. *You know that's all carefully staged.* Just the same, she tucked the thrill away, to take out later. The spot went out. The arena lights came up, the cowboys trotted past her and up the steps to the chutes.

A teenage girl entered the arena to sing the National Anthem.

Ten minutes later, it began. In the metal cage closest to her, she watched Jory Hancock lower himself into a chuteful of bull. When the gate swung open, the bull exploded into the arena. Jory sat, hat smashed down, clinging to his rope with one hand, the other in the air.

Katya peered through the metal slats. It was one thing to watch from the stands. Bull riding was different when it happened six feet in front of you. Like the difference between standing in a battlefield with soldiers fighting around you, and watching the news clips on television. This close, the brute power of the animal was real and very personal. She felt the heavy thud of hooves in her chest. Saliva flew in a long arc from its mouth, and when the bull turned into a spin, Katya saw intent in its white-rimmed eyes. It was pissed. If it had its way, someone was going to pay.

Her heart hammered, and her white-knuckled hands grabbing the slats were all that kept her from running for high ground. She was afraid. For Jory, for herself. That bull looked strong enough to burst through the fence, into her face. The crowd screamed encouragement.

These cowboys are insane!

She understood why the bulls were called animal athletes. The bull bucked, muscles bunching, straining to get the rider off his back. Jory sat in the center, spurring with his outside leg, to wow the judges. Smiling.

Yes, she saw it twice as he flashed past. He was smiling.

The buzzer sounded. Jory reached down, jerking the rope out of his hand. The bullfighters stepped closer. The bull kicked out and launched the cowboy, who tried to duck and roll. Except he was too high in the air for that. He came down on his shoulder, his body landing in a heap.

Shit! Katya reached for the strap of the bulky first-aid kit, threw it over her shoulder, then reached for her end of the stretcher. *You can do this. You can.* The world tipped. She swayed, dizzy. *You* have *to.* She shook her head to clear it. Gritting her teeth, she peered through the gate, hand on the slide bar closure.

Jory was on his feet, running for the fence. Grinning. The bullfighters hazed the still bucking bull to the exit.

"Jory gets the best of the bull, to the tune of eighty-seven and a half points!" The announcer's voice boomed. The crowd cheered.

She dropped the stretcher and the bulky kit in a heap at her feet. She sagged against the fence, leaned over, and put her hands on her knees, partially to stop their shaking, partially to clear her head.

That was only the first ride.

The night stretched ahead, ponderous and hulking. She glanced up to see Doc Cody watching her from the catwalk above the chutes. She stood and waved to him, hoping he wouldn't see past her flimsy, facade-smile.

The rides blew by. A little of her tension eked out every time a rider walked or limped out of the arena. Maybe it was just that a body couldn't sustain terror for an indefinite time. Whatever the reason, she was grateful.

She found herself absorbed by the drama on the dirt of the arena.

Seeing past the fear, up close, she could feel the high the riders got from doing this.

Katya let out her held breath when Cam rode his bull to the buzzer, and managed to land on his feet.

The color commentator and cameras were waiting when he stepped through the gate. He straightened his hat, unzipped his padded vest, and strode to them.

The diminutive commentator batted her eyes at the camera. "Cam has been a bit inconsistent of late, but you'd never know it, seeing that ride." She turned to him. "You looked more comfortable up there tonight, Cam, what was the difference?"

"I got a good night's sleep. I feel good." He flashed a quick smile at Katya then focused on the commentator.

A thrill of pride shot through her chest. Grand's tea helped! She'd known it would.

The Cam in front of the cameras looked so different than the Cam she was getting to know. His face was closed, carefully composed. A Cool Hand Cahill mask.

The woman with the mic said, "Well done, Cam. Good luck in the final round." The camera's lights went out. With one more glance at her, Cam climbed the stairs to the catwalk.

When Katya turned back to the gate, the world tilted again. Something was wrong. Her stomach twisted, suddenly, massively hollow, but nauseated at the same time. She felt weak and shaky, her feet light, as if gravity were loosening its hold. A clammy sweat popped on her face and palms.

She took deep breaths, and within a minute, the feeling faded.

The cowboys in the final round were all able to walk to the locker room unaided. Cam led the standings with a ninety-point ride.

JB Denny's voice came over the loudspeakers. "And so we've come, ladies and gentlemen, to the last ride of the night. This teenager burst onto the scene this year and quickly became a fan favorite. A serious contender for Rookie of the Year, Buster Deacon is making his mark on the tour. He's got guts, too. In the bull draft, he reached in and picked the top bull in the pen tonight, Bone Dancer.

"This bull is unridden in fifteen outs. He's smart, he's sneaky. And he's mean."

In the chute, Buster locked his fingers over his rope with a pound of his fist. He pushed his hat down, crossed himself then nodded.

The bull hung his horn on the chute, so his hindquarters swung out first. Once free, he lunged, twisting in midair, too close to the chutes. Buster came off and crashed headfirst into the unforgiving metal. Katya felt the vibration though the slat under her hand.

Seeing the rider on the ground, the beast ignored the bullfighters and charged, running along the fence, trampling the unconscious cowboy.

Katya had shouldered the kit and lifted her end of the stretcher by the time Doc Cody arrived. He hefted his end, and slid aside the lock on the gate. The bull thundered by. When its hindquarters disappeared through the exit, he said, "Let's go." He pushed the gate open.

They ran into the arena. Guts shaking, she didn't have time to think.

When they reached Buster where he lay in the middle of a semicircle of protective bullfighters, Doc Cody knelt beside him. She spread the stretcher open and locked it, trying to avoid the moment when she'd have to look.

"Buster? Buster, can you hear me?" Doc Cody's voice sounded calm.

She looked.

Blood sheeted down his face from a flap-like cut in his scalp, his copper-orange hair wet with it. His eyes had rolled back, the whites pallid as a hard-boiled egg. Red dirt spattered across his face. Or maybe it was freckles, her vision was blurred.

"Come on, son. Wake up now." Doc pulled gauze from the kit and pressed it to Buster's head.

She couldn't breathe, though in the hushed silence, she could hear herself panting. The world tilted and this time, stayed canted. She cocked her head to right her perspective and wiped cold sweat from her upper lip.

"Katya, C-collar and supports." Doc's tinny voice ricocheted inside her head.

Her stomach heaved. *I'm going to throw up. Right here in front of God and everyone.* She swallowed bile and bent, reaching for the cervical blocks. From the end of a long telescope, she saw her hands moving. The periphery of her vision darkened, closing to a small tunnel. Her stomach heaved again.

The light at the end of the tunnel winked out.

Cam saw her go down. Katya's body spun in a boneless, almost graceful pirouette.

Doc Cody saw it too. His head pivoted between his two patients. Cam climbed over the back of the open chute. "Tuck, you get her, I'll help Doc." His voice rang out in the hushed arena.

Tuck didn't have a bum knee. He vaulted easily from the chute and ran to Katya.

Cam wanted to go to her. He wanted to cradle her in his arms, lift her, and carry her back to the treatment room, away from the thousands of prying eyes. He could hardly drag his feet or his attention away from where she lay crumpled in the dirt like an abandoned doll, her face paler than milk.

But Doc Cody would look to him, as the senior rider on the tour, for help in an emergency.

No matter what Cam wanted, the rider had to come first.

He jogged over, pushing into the circle around the downed kid.

He and Doc Cody got Buster's spine stabilized, and eased him onto the stretcher with the help of the bullfighters. Buster was no help, he was out cold.

Weird to see all this looking down, instead of up from the dirt. He was much more familiar with the latter perspective.

Tuck carried Katya's limp body ahead of them and all Cam could do was follow, loyalties torn like a lightning-split tree, his hands full of stretcher handles.

In the treatment room, Doc Cody ordered Tuck to lay Katya on one treatment table, and he and Cam laid the stretcher on the other. "Buster? Buster, can you hear me?" Doc shone a penlight in his eye.

Cam took a step toward the table where Katya lay.

Dusty hovered between the two, stepping one way, then the other.

Doc glanced up. "Dusty, quit dithering. One professional per patient. You help Katya." He focused again on the prone body before him. "Stay with me, Cam, I'm going to need you."

A bark from this unflappable man told Cam everything he didn't want to know about Buster's status.

Doc ran a hand over the teen's skull, then down his limbs. "His shoulder's dislocated. Let's take care of that while he's out." He tore apart the Velcro that restrained the rider's arms. He grasped Buster's hand at a ninety-degree angle, as if he were going to shake hands with him. "Cam, hold his chest so he doesn't move."

The kid was lucky not to be awake for this part. The last time Cam's shoulder had popped out, he'd been all too aware of the agony. He leaned his weight on Buster's chest.

Doc grasped Buster's elbow with his other hand, and lifted.

Pop!

Cam winced. Buster didn't.

"That's that." Doc reattached the Velcro, to hold the arm in place.

A uniformed EMT stuck his head in the door. "You want transport?"

Doc didn't look up, just continued his assessment, lifting the gauze on Buster's forehead. "We'd better. He's not coming around."

The man entered, pulling a rolling collapsible gurney, another attendant on the other end.

"Cam, help shift him, will you?"

Cam helped the second attendant move Buster, while the other EMT stood poised to take notes.

Doc fired off, "He's concussed. I don't feel any skull or facial fractures, but that's for an X-ray to determine. I've reduced a left shoulder dislocation. There's swelling at the distal humerus, but if it's fractured, it's not displaced." He pulled his cell phone from his pocket and held it out to Cam.

Cam glanced to Katya's pale, slack face, then back. He gave Doc a small shake of his head. Doc Cody handed his phone to Tucker. "The Deacons' number is on speed dial. Call them, and tell them that they're transporting him to..."

The EMT looked up from his clipboard. "Baylor Med Center. I think we've got everything we need, Doc."

"I have to see to my other patient then I'll meet you at the ER."

The bystander cowboys cleared the way, letting the gurney through. Tucker walked into the locker room to make the call.

Cam stepped to the table where Katya lay, but aware of his audience, didn't hover. Gone was the tough soldier. She looked like an olive-skinned Sleeping Beauty, her curly black hair framing her face, making it seem paler by comparison.

Dusty had covered her in a blanket. When he laid a wet washcloth on her forehead, she stirred.

CHAPTER 15

Katya opened her eyes to see Dusty standing over her. "Wha—" Her brain processed data like an inchworm. One tiny bit. After. Another. He moved, and the light he'd blocked lasered in, careening around her skull in flashing, throbbing strobes. "What happened?"

"You passed out in the arena." Dusty swiped the blessedly cool cloth over her face.

The arena! She tried to sit up, but Dusty pushed her shoulder down. "Just relax."

"Buster. How is he?"

Doc Cody's face appeared over her. "He's on his way to the hospital. From what I've seen, he should recover."

She remembered blood, in red hair. A handmade stuffed rabbit. Clots of crimson, spattered on concrete, thousands of miles from here. *You failed him.*

Again.

She moaned.

Doc Cody shone a penlight in her eyes.

The memory flashed again with the light, of the

last time someone shone it in her eyes. Her last fail in Kandahar.

He has no choice but to fire you after this.

"Are you dizzy?"

"Not now." Maybe it wasn't as bad as she feared. After all, she'd thought she was going to be fired before. Maybe she was overreacting.

Doc checked her vitals, his face carefully closed, as if she were a stranger. She felt it in his impersonal touch, how he avoided her eyes. *So much for overreacting. You'll be on the street in an hour.*

"Are you in pain anywhere?"

"No. Doc. Listen to me. This was different than last time."

His jaw tightened. Gray eyes darkened in anger. "This has happened before?"

That was the exact wrong thing to say. In her peripheral vision, too-interested riders hung on every word.

None of that mattered now, because if she didn't find an explanation, she'd never see any of them after today.

Think, Katya! She wasn't lying to save her job. This *was* different. Something...

Her brain felt like a weak watch battery, running down. She analyzed her own symptoms, comparing them to diagnoses, discarding them. *Too slow!*

Doc Cody pulled the stethoscope from his ears, folded it, and handed it to Dusty. "You seem to be all right now. I'll call you later. I have to leave."

His distracted expression told her he was already gone.

When she tried to sit up, Dusty held her. She slapped at his hands. "Let me go, goddamn it."

At Doc's nod, Dusty released her.

The room spun when she sat up, but she didn't have time for that. "Doc, I'm telling you, there was something wrong. This wasn't like Kandahar."

He turned away and snatched his jacket from the back of a chair.

"Doc."

He swung back, his eyes flinty.

"Please. I *need* this job." She put a hand to her temple. Something hovered just at the edge of her torpid brain. Not even a thought yet, more an amorphous shape of a thought.

Kintala, Katya. Grand's calm, soft-as-cotton voice touched her mind. *Balance.*

Tumblers clicked with the combination that released her thought. The answer lay before her.

"It's hypoglycemia." Her fingers tightened on the edge of the table. "I know it is. I haven't eaten since..." She stumbled over the memory of dinner with Cam. She shoved it aside. She'd lose that chance, too, if she didn't keep this job. "Last night. It's late afternoon now, right? I felt light-headed, like I was inches off the ground, nauseated and dizzy at the same time. Doc, it's low blood sugar. All the symptoms fit."

Doc Cody shook his head. The planes of his face softened, from anger to regret.

For whatever good that would do. "Please. Just test me. I know the mg/dl will be low."

"I don't have the equipment to check. We'll get you some juice, just in case."

"Does anyone here have a testing kit?" She looked at each cowboy, one by one.

They darted embarrassed glances at each other.

Her stomach, which had been hovering near her lungs, flipped like a weightless astronaut. The world tilted again.

Silence.

"Please?" She hated that she sounded like a scared little girl, but in two minutes, that wouldn't matter either.

Her shoulders slumped. Dammit, she knew she was right, but if she couldn't—

"I have one." The sweetest gruff voice she'd ever heard came from behind her. She hadn't even realized Cam was in the room.

"Hang on." Cam strode past her, his profile hard. No, deadly.

The riders parted, leaving a corridor to his locker.

Not able to see his face, she watched the riders' solemn and twitchy, no one looked at Cam directly, but their body language told her he was the focus of their attention.

Crrrshh! The sound of a flimsy metal door slamming echoed in the silent room.

When Cam walked back, red-faced and looking like he wanted to stomp something, the knot of riders broke up and headed for the locker room, mumbling in quiet undertones.

Cam handed the leather-clad palm-sized kit to Doc Cody.

"Cam."

He turned her way, but his eyes were on the kit in Doc's hands.

"Thank you."

He grunted, and waited.

Her brain spun, trying to process the nuances of emotion floating in the room. She didn't even feel it when

Dusty poked her finger. Her only focus on the meter in Doc's hand.

He touched the test strip to the crimson bubble on the side of her finger.

His eyes widened. "Dusty, I know you have a candy bar stashed around here somewhere. Give it to this woman, or we're going to need another ambulance."

Dusty walked off.

Cam spun on his heel and walked to the locker room.

Doc clasped her shoulders, lowering her to the table. "You rest. When you get some sugar in you, you'll feel better. I've got to get to the hospital." He frowned at her. "I'll see you in Charlotte, next weekend."

She blew out her caught breath. "Yes, sir."

Dusty's face appeared above her again.

"Dusty, you be sure she tests normal before you let her up, hear?" He walked to the door.

"You bet, Doc." He handed her a finger of a Kit Kat.

She took a bite and chewed.

I'm not in the clear, but at least I still have a job.

Thanks to a cowboy sweeter than the chocolate melting on her tongue. She would need to understand the tension that had run between the cowboys like static. Her head felt like a shaken snow globe.

Dusty handed her a bottle of water. She wasn't thirsty, but took it anyway. "What's wrong with all of them?" She tipped the bottle toward the locker room.

Dusty leaned his palms on the edge of the table, and spoke low. "They're cowboys."

That part, she knew. "So?"

He sighed. "They have to appear to be bulletproof. Thanks to the test kit, they now know he's not. You know what kind of injuries they sustain. Have you ever seen one of them show it?"

She remembered Cam's tight jaw, when she knew his knee was hurting. How he avoided pain meds. "But diabetes is genetic!"

"To a cowboy, it is weakness." Dusty shook his head. "You can't reason with a belief system. Cam is a two-time champion, so—"

"So he's got nothing to prove. Everyone knows how tough he is."

Dusty handed her another piece of Kit Kat. "It doesn't have to make sense. It just is."

But an unwanted sliver of her understood, even as she denied it. She'd been a soldier—macho she got.

She knew in Cam's mind, he'd just sacrificed himself for her.

Cam didn't stop. He grabbed his crap from his locker and stomped out, chaps flapping, spurs clinking. He realized when he slammed out into the parking lot in full regalia he might as well have pasted a sign on his back, "Ask me for my autograph." Because every fan still in the parking lot wanted one.

It wasn't in his nature to enjoy being singled out, but his mother would snatch him bald if she ever heard of him being rude. Even so, it took every bit of his self-control to smile for photos and scribble his name on the programs.

He finally made it to his rental car to escape, but had to stop to unbuckle his spurs; he couldn't drive with them on.

When the hell are you going to learn to stop trying to rescue women, Cahill?

He tossed the spurs to the passenger floorboard,

slammed the door, and fired the engine. How much damage had he just done to his reputation in that locker room?

Reputation, bull. You'd need a career to have a reputation. And the four events remaining in the season did not make a career.

"Okay, my legacy then." Out loud, it sounded arrogant. But he wasn't, dammit. He'd sacrificed his body the past fifteen years to get himself to the top and stay there. To have his disease put a black mark on that made him want to pound something. He peeled out of the parking lot and drove. It didn't matter where.

And for what? What was it about big-eyed women, with their bottom lip wobbling, that made him jump into the deep end to save them?

The last time he'd done that, he'd ended up hitched to a female as mean as a she-bear protecting cubs.

Except that Candi had lied about having a cub in the oven. But he'd been so frantic, seeing her bedraggled and dripping mascara, it hadn't even occurred to him to ask for a pregnancy test. He'd done the honorable thing, and married her.

When she told him, tearfully (oh yes, tears were involved), he'd stayed, figuring time would work things out. He didn't make vows lightly.

His snort sounded loud in the closed-in car. And after all that, Candi divorced him. Her sights were set on more elusive prey. He signed the papers when he realized that they were caught in a marriage of mistaken identity; she'd thought she married a star, Cool Hand Cahill, and he'd thought he married a simple country girl, not a social climber.

That experience swore him off damsels in distress. Right up to today.

His cell phone blared the notes of "Dirt Road Anthem." He ignored it.

When it rang again, he hit the speaker button, just to make it stop. "What?"

Tucker's voice sounded tinny. "Hey, Hoss. Wanna grab a beer?"

"No."

"We could just hit a dive where no one would—"

"Thanks, Oprah, but I think I've done enough soul-baring for one day."

"Cam, you know that no one in that room is gonna say a word outside it, right? What happens in the locker room—"

"Yeah, yeah. Thanks, Tuck. Gotta go." He hit End.

Two minutes later, when the phone went off again, he was pulling into the parking lot of the hotel. He snatched it up. "Goddamit, Tuck, I told you. I don't want to talk about it."

"You didn't tell me." Katya's low voice hit him in the chest.

•

Dusty showed her the meter after her second blood sugar test. "See? I'm fine, Dusty. You can stop hovering now." Katya slid off the table.

"I have a Three Musketeers in here somewhere." Dusty dug in his backpack.

"I've had a Kit Kat and a Payday already. I'm going to tip into insulin shock if I eat more candy." She laid a hand on his arm until he stopped digging and looked at her. "Thank you, Dusty. You're a good guy."

His blush seeped into his sparse hairline. "I'm just glad Cam had that blood test kit. If not..."

"Yeah, I know. I owe him a bunch." She patted his arm. "Now, let's get this stuff packed up."

He shook his head. "You're not doing any of this." He raised a hand. "Don't even argue. Doc put me in charge of your care, and I'm telling you to get out of here." He flapped his hands in shooing motions. "Are you sure you're okay to drive? Should I call a cab?"

She backed away. "No. I'm fine. Thank you, Dusty, for being there for me."

"It's what friends do. Go."

She tossed her oils and lotions into her camo backpack and headed for her rental car, thankful for a moment to think. After today, she had a lot to think about. Her brain simmered in a marinade of an acidic funk that she could almost taste. She pushed open the door to the stadium parking lot. The wind almost pulled it from her hands and whipped her hair wild around her face.

Yes, she'd had low blood sugar. Yes, she still had a job.

But as hard as today had been, she was no further ahead. In fact, she'd actually fallen back several notches on her progress timeline. And Doc Cody would now be watching her closely.

Time. Days were passing like windows on a speeding passenger train, while she stood, rooted to the platform. Her army family hadn't been reassigned, but they seemed farther away with every week that passed.

Halfway across the almost empty parking lot, it occurred to her. If her unit wasn't moving, and she was getting farther away, that only left—

Pictures popped into her mind. Of her and Bree dancing to country songs. Of her laughing, chatting up the cowboys in line for a massage. Of Cam, his blue eyes sparking in candlelight, gazing at her as if she held the answer to world peace. Him leaning down, lips hovering over hers, and the wanting, deep in her chest, rising to meet them.

"Oh my God, Katya, you are such an idiot." How could she have settled in here and not have seen it? Her feet moved continuing her journey to the car. To reality.

She *liked* her job.

She *liked* the cowboys.

She *really* liked Cam.

When had they shifted from spoiled athletes to... whatever they were now? She'd stepped over the line she'd drawn through the ashes of her burned-out career without even realizing it.

How was that possible?

Guilt and chocolate didn't mix. Her stomach felt like a washer, stuck in the agitation cycle.

She didn't belong here. She didn't want to be here. She wanted to be with her family, the army. Wherever in the world they were berthed.

"I want that, dammit." But she heard no conviction in the words before the wind whipped them from her. And that frightened her too.

Yet here she stood no closer to a resolution. Today proved nothing. The medical diagnosis was low blood sugar, but she sensed the PTSD still coiled, waiting to strike. What would have happened if she hadn't passed out? Would she have been able to do her job?

She still didn't know. And that was not acceptable.

Time to stop playing around with cowboys and focus on getting herself better.

First, she had unfinished business. She unlocked the

car, opened the door, and fell into the seat. She dug her phone out of her backpack, and hit speed dial.

"Goddamit, Tuck, I told you. I don't want to talk about it." His voice held gravel, no doubt chipped from his flinty cowboy facade today.

That gravel hurt her soft places. It was there because of her. "You didn't tell me."

"Katya." Her name came out a resigned sigh. "Are you all right?"

"I'm fine. I just needed to call and thank you. I know that you put yourself in the line of fire for me today, and—"

"It's nothing. Forget it."

"It's not nothing. I don't know how I'll make it up to you, but—"

"I said it was fine. Let it go."

His clipped words only made her feel worse. He was hurting. "I know it won't help, but won't you let me buy you dinner?"

"No."

"Well, at least let me take you out for coffee or something."

"What part of 'no' is ambiguous here? I need to go."

Irritation sparked, igniting the funk bathing her brain. "What is your problem?" She was trying to be nice, and he'd turned back into the asshole. Again. "Jesus, you macho guys kill me. You're a diabetic. So the hell what?"

"You don't get it."

"Yeah, you're right. I don't. I've worked with men who've had limbs blown off. Burns. Massive trauma. Somehow your fragile ego taking a hit doesn't quite compare." She was on a roll now; the smoking funk blew out of her throat like volcanic ash. "You could be Buster, eighteen years old, and waking up in a hospital, hurt, and all alone." She balanced the phone between her chin and her shoulder, and cranked the ignition. She needed to move. "And I know another redhead who'd have been happy to have that problem. There wasn't enough left of him to bring him home to his parents."

Shut up. Shut up. Just shut the hell up.

"I called to thank you. So thank you. Good-bye." She hit End, tossed the phone into the passenger seat, and peeled out of the parking lot. Better this way. She didn't have time for spoiled cowboys. She had a job to focus on: getting back to her family in Kandahar.

CHAPTER
16

Cam sat on the edge of his hotel bed, staring at the phone. She was right, of course. His problems were non-existent compared to those she'd seen. Not knowing what he was going to do with the rest of his life was messing with his head. And today, she'd made him realize he was behaving like a whiney pansy-ass.

He was a lot more than the shallow asshole he'd been acting like lately. His dad had taught him that you didn't really know a man until you'd seen him tested. It was time to man-up.

His ego smarted from the spanking, and shame burned the back of his eyes. He dropped the phone on the bed and rubbed them. How had he ever thought that woman helpless? Comparing Katya to Candi was like comparing a Doberman to a Chihuahua.

He'd been kidding himself that he knew anything about this woman. Kandahar. She'd been so upset, she'd let it slip in the treatment room today. A war zone.

And all this time, he'd thought she'd spent her tour in

the States, shuffling paper. He didn't know a thing about her, not really. She wouldn't open up to him.

He knew her green eyes, flashing in the red silk draped lamplight. Sexy. And a Gypsy. A healer. A soldier. What else would he find if she really let him peel back the layers of restraint? He didn't know. Still, he *wanted* to.

And he planned to. But first he was going to have to mend some fences.

He stood, gathered scattered clothes and equipment, and crammed them into his luggage. He had a plane to catch.

You're going to have to come up with something good, Hoss. You were an ass, and she's pissed. He slammed the top on his suitcase, without realizing his other fingers were still in it.

"God*damn* it!" He shook out his abused hand.

He had to figure all this out. And he didn't have a lot of time. He grabbed his rope keeper and slammed out the door.

"So, how's the kid doing now?" Trace's voice came from the speaker of Katya's phone, where it lay in the passenger seat.

"I stopped to see him before I left. He's conscious and alert. His parents were there and they were getting ready to release him." She signaled, then pulled around the semi. "He's got a concussion, obviously, a separated shoulder, and tendon strains from the dislocation. Lucky, all things considered."

"And how about you?"

"Well, I still have a job. For now."

"There's a 'but' in there."

The concern in his voice was only one of the reasons she'd called her old mentor. She needed an outside opinion and he knew her convoluted landscape inside and out.

"I'm a mess." She heaved an exasperated sigh. "This job has gotten to me, Trace. What began as a kind of morbid curiosity about these cowboys and their way of life has changed to...I don't know what. You have to admire their guts, even as you question their sanity."

"You're starting to like them." He sounded smug.

"Yes!" The admission came out hot, urgent. "I'm such an idiot! All I had to do was my job. Stay professional. Impersonal. But somewhere along the way, I started to understand them. They're so old-fashioned and well-mannered. They have this crazy sense of values. They can be macho, insensitive assholes, but even though they're exasperating, they can be so danged sweet."

A husky chuckle interrupted her rant. "Sounds like you're talking individual rather than collective, Smitty."

"Yeah, maybe. That was a mistake, too." She tightened her jaw, biting down on the soft little pillow of regret. "All that's over now. I'm concentrating on getting better, so I can return to my unit. I don't have time to play with cowboys."

"Why not?"

"Have you been hitting the Jagermeister? Hello, the goal when you helped me get this job was to heal, to pass my fitness for duty test, and get back to my unit."

"I know. Sometimes plans can change, hon. No law says you have to go back."

She head whipped around to where the phone lay

innocently in the seat. "What's wrong with you? My *family* is in Kandahar."

"And they weren't family before you enlisted. I'm just saying there's more than one kind of family. "

"I have a duty—"

"Yeah, I hear your duty. Smitty, you did eight years in a war zone. You've served your country. Almost gave your life for it. Maybe it's time to let someone else step up." His tone softened. "There's something in your voice when you talk about this job. Something I haven't heard in a long time. It sounds like contentment. Or at least the beginnings of it."

Shocked into silence, she focused on the road rolling under her tires, taking her to the next event in Fayetteville.

"There's more than one way to heal, Smitty. Promise me you'll think about it. Okay?"

She got off the phone without promising anything. She valued Trace's advice, but this? Based on something he heard in her voice? She shook her head.

Preposterous.

Not even in the realm of possibility.

She was not going there.

At the same time though, she couldn't deny the hollow ache that had opened in her chest. She was lonely in a way she hadn't been since she was a little girl. Trace would always be there for her, and she was grateful. But she wanted—needed, more. She needed physical arms to hold her with more than just friendship.

She felt as alone and empty as the landscape rushing past her window. Reaching for the dog tags between her breasts, she clenched them in her fist, which she held against her tug-of-war heart.

Friday night she stood looking up at the Crown Center. She shouldn't feel grateful that this was Dusty's weekend as first responder in the arena. It would delay her knowing if she could function in a crisis. She was grateful just the same.

When she'd forced herself to call Major Thibodaux last Saturday, he'd been very glad to hear from her. Of course, he'd thought she was calling to return to her unit. They were short on medics, again. Still, she couldn't ignore the guilt that sliced through her. She touched the suddenly throbbing scar on her side.

But when he heard why she was calling, he'd greased the wheels, getting her set up with an army psychologist she'd speak with via phone every few days. At least she'd taken a step.

She hunched her shoulders in her pea jacket and headed for the huge roll-up doors that signified the bull entrance. Her first session with Dr. Heinz had been brutal. It was as if he'd known all her buttons, and hadn't been shy about pushing them, one after another, until she ended up, forehead touching the shag carpet of her hotel room, her secrets in a steaming pile in front of her.

Well, he should be good at it. He dealt with survivor's guilt and PTSD every day. Her feet followed the pipe corral maze by rote.

The homework he'd assigned was off the wall.

Act like I'm sixteen again? Work at playing?

Who the heck had time to be sixteen again? She crammed her hands deep into her jacket pockets. He told her that part of her problem was trying to hold too tightly to her emotions trying to control them. She had "too many expectations of herself."

Well, duh. That hadn't begun with her enlistment. You didn't survive growing up in her parents' house, wearing your emotions on your sleeve.

But she'd promised to try. Now she only had to figure out how one went about "playing."

CHAPTER 17

Cam lay on the training table, eyes closed, while Katya worked on his shoulder. Her fingers were competent as always, but something about the massage felt perfunctory. Impersonal. He hadn't realized she'd put so much of herself into these massages until today when she didn't. A thought hit his mind like a wasp's sting. Was that personal touch he'd felt a part of all her massages? Or just his?

He opened his eyes and studied her face. Her lips taut, her eyes cool, shuttered, and professional. And that hurt. "Will you have dinner with me tonight?"

Her look lasered to a hawk's predatory gaze. No cool there now. He tried to ignore the bustle of the treatment room, and the fact that anyone could overhear them. He'd known this wouldn't be easy. This time, he was going to have to put some of himself on the line. In front of an eavesdropping audience. He swallowed. "Because I was an ass, and I'm sorry. Because I want to know you better. Because I've missed you the past week."

Her eyes widened in surprise, then flew to the cowboys waiting in line before returning to him.

He wasn't above blackmail. "You offered to buy me dinner, remember?" Watching the reflection of the war flickering in her eyes, he ignored a pang of guilt. "You're not going to renege, are you?" He tipped a corner of his mouth into what he hoped was his best-ever woman-slaying smile.

She vacillated a moment longer. Then her shoulders lost their crisp line, and she sighed. "I do owe you. I pay my debts." Her chin came up. "But only if I buy."

He wiped the smile off his lips. Now was not the time for smug. "I can possibly live with that."

Following the event, Katya wet her palms under the faucet of her hotel bathroom then ran them over her hair in an attempt to tame the flyaways. Tonight, she could kill two birds with one stone—pay off her debt to Cam and do a little homework at the same time. She'd moved beyond the terminology lately. She wanted to know more about his world and what he thought about it. His dreams, his plans.

Relax. Enjoy yourself like a sixteen-year-old.

The underwear-clad woman in the mirror did not look relaxed. She tried for it, then realized that showing her teeth did not constitute a smile.

She was lying to herself.

She wasn't just killing birds with this date. She *wanted* to get closer to that sweet guy. The hollow place that had opened in her when she'd talked to Trace had become a cavern where a cold wind of loneliness howled. But there could be a price to be paid. She'd have to open up as well.

She practiced her smile in the mirror. Turns out, for a smile to look real, you had to relax. Dr. Heinz would appreciate the irony.

She strode into the room, stood in front of the closet, and chose an off-the-shoulder peasant blouse. It had a Gypsy feel, blousy and sexy, but was Mexican white cotton, with colorful embroidery on the front placket, and down the slit sleeves that tied at the elbow. Slipping it on, she relished the feel of softness sliding over her skin.

Then she pulled out the jeans she'd bought today. Shocked by the huge selection, and not having a clue what to buy, she'd called Bree. On her recommendation, she'd bought a pair of skinny jeans for work, and a pair of what Bree had called "blinged out" ones, with sequins on the pockets. She'd wondered why the salesgirl called them skinny jeans, until she'd worked them up her legs and fastened them.

Taking her new belt from the suitcase, she fastened it loosely over the long blouse, to rest on her hip bones. She had to buy it because the silver conchas had called to her Gypsy soul.

Stepping into her rarely worn, toe-cleavage black heels, she surveyed her look in the full-length mirror on the back of the closet door. Nice.

I hope to God I don't turn my ankle in these things, and if these jeans don't stretch, I'm not going to be able to eat much.

Lifting her jewelry bag, she selected simple thick silver hoop earrings, slid three inches of bangly silver bracelets on her wrist, then checked the mirror again. *Even better.*

A knock sounded at her door. She practiced the relaxed smile in the mirror one more time, then, after a quick glance to be sure there was no underwear lying about, she grabbed her purse, crossed to the door, and opened it.

"Are you read—" Cam's low wolf whistle made her want to slam the door and find something else to wear. "Lord 'a mercy, woman." His gaze traveled from her almost exposed toes to her flyaway hair. He put his hand over his heart. "I know I suggested you buy jeans, but if you wear those to work, the guys aren't going to be able to focus on their rides. They're gonna get stomped."

"Are these not okay?" She looked down and ran her hands over her thighs. "Bree said that—"

"Hon, those are the most okay jeans I've ever had the pleasure to peruse."

She smiled a real smile. For some reason, the minute she'd opened the door, she'd relaxed. She realized she was beginning to trust him.

Time to practice that "carefree sixteen-year-old" thing. She put a hand on her hip. "If my mother had ever met a sweet-talking cowboy, she'd have warned me about them. I'm sure of it."

She stepped out the door and closed it behind her, happy she'd chosen the heels that made her an inch taller than him. She needed all the advantage she could get. Those light blue eyes made her heart hammer, and his cologne was melting her insides. It felt like she'd just drunk a shot of something strong and heady. "Tonight I'm taking you somewhere exotic."

"Bring it on. I'm up for a challenge."

She walked past him to her rental car. He mumbled something she didn't quite catch, but she was sure was suggestive. In a fit of sassy, she strutted a few steps, rolling her hips, giggling at the stifled moan behind her.

Seriously, had she really just giggled? *Not my fault, doctor's orders.*

Besides, it served him right. Let him see what it was like to be off-kilter. God knows, she knew the feeling.

Within a half hour, they were seated on pillows on the floor of what the Internet declared to be the best Indian restaurant in Fayetteville. She could have kissed whoever thought to put spandex in denim.

They had a little alcove to themselves, with candles beside their drinks on the low table, the sultry smell of incense burning somewhere nearby.

"Okay, I'm down here." Cam straightened his bad knee. "But you may need to rent a crane to get me on my feet again."

"Don't worry, I'll help." She watched his face carefully. "Are you hurting anywhere else from your buckoff today?"

He winced. "Only my pride, darlin'." He rolled his neck.

"No, it's more than that. I can tell. Here." She placed another pillow in front of her crossed legs, and patted it. "Come here."

"You worked all day. You don't need to be messing with me."

When she continued to pat, he scooted over. She worked the tense muscles of his shoulders, rolling them in her hands. As if they recognized her, they loosened, and she moved on to the tight muscles of his neck.

After a few minutes, he put his hands over hers. He turned sideways, which put him much too close. Close enough to notice a slight nick on his neck, where he'd gotten too close shaving. She'd never realized that his blond eyebrows were threaded with russet. There was no way she should be able to feel the heat of his skin, but when warmth caressed her face, she knew it was his.

When she would have pulled away, he kept hold of one of her hands. "Would you tell me about Kandahar, Katya?"

Her sharp inhale was loud in the close alcove. Not wanting to meet his steady gaze, she dropped her eyes, to watch his thumb running over her knuckles.

The first thing the army head doc had told her was that it would be good for her to talk—to get the experiences out of her head where they festered and into the light of day. That even made logical sense.

But to talk about Buster—*Buster? Where had that come from?*—Murphy.

She looked up.

Cam hadn't moved. His face was relaxed, his eyes steady and serious. He waited.

She focused inward, listening for the whisper of sacred secrets. There was only the heavy thud of her heart, the soft push of her pulse at the base of her neck, and at the back of her flexed knees.

In spite of Cam being, at times, cold, taciturn, and hard, she also knew he was one who would hold her secrets. She took a deep breath. "At the bazaar, he bought a sweet little stuffed bunny, to send to his baby niece back in South Carolina…"

"Jesus." Cam had wondered if there were more layers to this woman than he knew, but the reality was much more stark and brutal than he'd guessed. It was everything he could do to be still, not to pull her into his arms, tuck her head into his neck and rock her. That bomb had done more than kill a friend; it had imploded her life.

Katya fell silent. She hadn't cried. Hadn't even come close, speaking as if this were the plot to a movie she'd seen. It made what she said more horrifying—her friend's death and her own injuries, inside and out.

The waiter brought their food. The aroma of lamb and curry released them from the story. She pulled her hand away and he shifted his pillow a bit to give her room to eat.

A second waiter brought more small plates of food.

"I ordered a sampler, so you could taste a bit of everything." She must have read his misgivings, because she smiled. "Trust me. You're about to have a memorable experience."

"I already have."

She blushed, then called out names as exotic as their smells: vindaloo, rogan josh, Punjabi curry and flat bread to soak up the sauce.

Turned out, he liked Indian food.

When the table was cleared, Katya ordered them one more drink; something called a *feni*, made from the oil of cashews. She reclined on one elbow on a large pillow while she sipped, her huge green eyes watching him.

He shifted on his pillow. "What?"

"Now you tell me. What's next for you, after this season is over?"

This was the last thing he wanted to talk about. But then, the bomb was probably the last thing she'd wanted to talk about. He remembered the shadows that passed over her face as she'd told her story.

He should have remembered that excavating another's

history always led to digging through your own, exposing the pottery shards and the bones. "You've hit on why I've been such a self-absorbed idiot lately.

"The truth is I don't know what I'm going to do next."

She cocked her head and raised an eyebrow.

He looked down at the silly fragile glass in his big hands. "I've always had this goal to be the best bull rider in the world. Now, I've been there, done that. Got the buckle. Somehow, while I was having fun, fifteen years have gone by." He rubbed a hand over the back of his neck, where worry pulled the muscles tight.

"Maybe I thought I'd just ride off into the sunset or some stupid thing, but I never made plans about what came next. Thanks to the PBR, I've got plenty of money. But what good is that? It won't make me happy. Only the next challenge can do that. Doing something I love is the only reason to drag these battered bones out of bed in the morning. And that's going to end in four weeks' time."

"Surely there are other jobs in the PBR you could do."

He huffed out a breath, and put the empty glass on the low table. "What? Get in front of a camera and talk for a living?"

Her tinkling laugh told him she recognized what a joke that was.

"I've looked into everything I can think of, and none of it appeals to me. The only thing I want to do is ride. And from my stats lately, I have to face the fact that I can't do that anymore."

"I'm sorry, Cam." Her sad eyes pulled him in.

He shook himself. "What is it about you that makes me want to talk?" He smiled to try to make light of it. "I swear, I hang around you long enough, I'm going to end up howling at the moon."

"I hope it doesn't come to that." She glanced around for her purse. "Let's get out of here. I've got some tea back at my place with your name on it."

He waggled his eyebrows at her. "That's a new approach. Most women say they have etchings—" He ducked to avoid her slap.

Katya opened the door and flipped on the light. Warm light from her red scarf over the lampshade blurred the harsh lines of the generic room. Cam stepped in behind her.

"Wow, exact same room as last time."

She dropped the key on the desk. "Nope. Different picture over the bed."

He tossed his hat on the bed and looked closer. In place of the desert print in earth tones hung a mass-produced print of blue-green mountains. "You're right. I stand corrected."

She reached for her camo backpack. "So? You have to admit, Indian food was better than you'd imagined."

He pulled out the desk chair and sat. "It was pretty good. Curry is spicy, kind of like Mexican in a weird way."

She chuckled and pulled out a bag of leaves. "I've never heard it described like that, but I see your point." She counted leaves out of several Baggies and dropped them into the white stone mortar he'd seen last time, and used the pestle to grind them.

"You sure look like a Gypsy doing that."

Her smile was wistful. "My Grand taught me. She was our healer."

"It looks like you've taken up where she left off."

Her head came up, her eyes wary, which explained

faster than words about the prejudice she must have endured over the years.

He put up his hands. "Hey, don't look at me, I'm a convert."

The tight line of lips softened. She dropped the leaves into a hotel coffee mug, turned on the coffeemaker, and poured water into the back. "I appreciate you talking up my remedies with the other riders."

"I didn't do much."

"Oh yes, you did. You must have, because those guys went from looking at me like I was a witch to asking for my advice." She leaned back against the desk, her hands resting at the edge. "Thank you."

He straightened the crease in his jeans. "I care about those guys. I want them to have the best care available. And after drinking that stuff, I can testify that you're the real deal."

CHAPTER 18

Something about a tough guy exposing his soft side made her do crazy things. The gravitational pull she'd felt all through dinner might have had something to do with it as well. Whatever it was, she didn't so much as reach to touch, as she just stopped restraining herself from doing so.

When she put her fingers under his chin to lift it, his whole body followed. He stood and leaned in, his hands bracketing her hips. "Haven't we been here before?" He tipped his head and took her lips.

It was a slow, getting-to-know-you kiss. But she didn't need that. The second his mouth touched hers, she recognized him, as if his lips were as known to her as her own. She ran her tongue along their seam, knowing their shape, their taste. Still, the knowing went deeper.

Though it couldn't really, could it?

When he opened and his tongue greeted hers, the wisp of a question was whipped away. He made a sound, low and dangerous, and stepped between her somehow opened thighs. When he wrapped his arms around her, she settled in.

Oh, this.

This was what she'd missed. This closeness with another person—his fingers at the nape of her neck, and knowing from the change in his breathing that he was as caught as she.

Her need whispered to her. *More of this. More of him.*

When he trailed his lips along the underside of her jaw, she whimpered. When they dipped, finding the deep slit in the embroidery of her blouse, she kicked off her shoes, no longer wanting the advantage.

He'd already taken it anyway.

He lifted her hips, sliding her back so she was sitting on the desk. His mouth. His mouth paid homage to her neck, and she had no choice but to lay her head back, since her muscles would no longer support it. When he sucked at the delicate skin above her collarbone, muscles deep inside her spasmed. She clung to the anchor of his strong shoulders, intoxicated by her senses; his smell, his breathing, his taste. His touch.

"Katya," he whispered the word onto her neck.

She loved that her name sounded foreign on his lips. A delicious shiver ran through her. He raised his head and looked long into her face, as if drinking in what he saw there, before capturing her mouth again.

When his erection bumped against her most intimate place, she realized her legs, wrapped around his hips, had brought him there.

Hot. God, she was hot. She couldn't keep a thought in her head past tearing off his clothes and satisfying her body's demands. Her lips, above and below, felt engorged, every nerve ending on alert.

His hand closed over her breast as his tongue plunged. *More.*

She squirmed against him. He pinched her nipple. She whimpered, and bit his lip.

More.

If she'd pay for this, she'd pay tomorrow.

And tomorrow was a long night away.

She broke the kiss, reached down, grabbed the waist of her shirt and peeled it over her head. She needed his hands on her bare skin, needed to feel his skin under hers. Touching his buttons, she realized they were snaps. They sounded like muted rifle fire as she ripped them open.

She'd seen his chest before, of course. But it was different with soft light playing across its hard planes, painting his skin in a crimson wash. Nestled in his washboard stomach was a thin line of hair she was dying to trace with her tongue.

His fingers brushed her back, and her bra let go. "Katya." His fingers lifted her chin and he looked into her eyes. "Be sure."

He watched as if she was a plump rabbit and he was a hungry wolf. His sky-blue eyes held a man's surety, but also a tentative...awe?

A woman's power surged in her, and to tease them both, she cupped her breasts and lifting, offered them to him. With a moan, he buried his face in her skin.

She twined his hair in her fists as he suckled her. A bolt of electricity shot from her nipples to her crotch. "Please, Cam. Don't make us wait."

He turned, toed out of his boots, kicked them off, and

shucked out of his jeans, even as she stepped out of hers. When he turned back, she exhaled a sigh. His cock was magnificent—high, hard, tight, proud, and sheathed in a condom.

When she looked up, he tipped his chin to the bed, raising an eyebrow in question.

She gave him a slow smile and a shake of her head. A bed was domestic, too tame for the kind of sex her body demanded. She slid one heel on the chair, opening herself to him.

"Oh, sweet Jesus." He breathed, and took the last remaining step to her.

She twined her arms behind his head, and brought him close. *Now, please, now.*

He must have heard her need, because his mouth came down on hers in a crushing kiss as he entered her, deep and hard. Just how she wanted him, needed him.

Her body gave, accommodating him, stretching to a point that should have been painful but wasn't, because she was so ready. She pulled him closer, scratching his back in her haste. He buried himself to the hilt.

Then stopped.

Moremoremore. Her greed made her whimper, and she dug in his buttocks with her heels.

But his will was stronger. His tongue plundered, though his body didn't. The only sign of what that cost him was the shaking in the arms that crushed her to him.

When she thought she couldn't stand it one more second, he began to move.

Slow.

She broke the kiss, to urge him faster until she saw his face.

Eyes closed, he had such a look of fragile rapture that she couldn't bear to break it. She slowed, fascinated by the interplay of soft emotion flickering across his features. He looked like an angel. A wash of tenderness sheeted the hollow spot in her chest, soothing it. Filling it.

Then he opened his eyes, and she was startled, almost frightened by the raw emotion in his gaze. "Smitty... my Gypsy." His hands dropped to her hips. He lifted and plunged into her, fast and hard, his gaze holding hers.

She'd never watched like this or been watched. She melted in the molten heat of his eyes, and their bodies. Her orgasm burst upon her with no warning. It took her spiraling up. Her head fell back, and she moaned in release.

Watching was his undoing too. He pumped, straining with every muscle. Her body milked him, and with a last mighty plunge, he emptied himself as he shouted her name.

Hours later, when Katya shifted to lie on her back, the soft musky scent of their mingled sex drifted up from the sheets. She felt gentled; her mind at ease for the first time in so long she couldn't remember. She wished she could freeze time and stay exactly like this until she couldn't recall reality.

Cam looked as languid as she felt, propped on an elbow, his head in his hand.

She smiled up at him. "So does this make me a buckle bunny?" She ran her fingers over the muscles of his chest, admiring them. "Because I think I'm starting to see the draw."

"Don't ever say that." The steel wool in his tone scratched her peace.

"What?"

His faded blue eyes turned steely. "It's a demeaning term. And it so doesn't describe you." Below his ear, a muscle jumped.

There were years of bitterness in his tone, this was more than a comment on the breakdown of societal mores. "What is it, Cam? What happened to you?"

He looked away. "Oh, it's just another sad old country song."

Yeah, right. From the braided wire muscle under her fingers, it was a lot more than that. She'd read he'd been married before. "Will you tell me about it?"

He took a breath. "I should have known when she sashayed up, winked and introduced herself as, 'Candi with an "i."'' I was Buster's age, and had just started to win at the top events." He studied the wall over her head. "Sure, there were groupies at the local rodeos and Challenger events. But like the bull power, Candi was a big step up in more ways than one."

"She was gorgeous." She held her voice to a "whatever" tone. It wasn't as easy to pull off as it should have been.

"She was legendary." One side of his mouth lifted a tiny bit. She would have missed it if she hadn't been watching so hard.

"Tiny, blond, and shiny as a showroom-floor sports car. Fully loaded." He closed his eyes. "It was more than that. She looked at me like I'd made the world just for her. That's pretty heady stuff for a fresh-off-the-farm boy."

The furrows between his brows deepened. "I kept winning. And she was there, every night. Pretty soon, I was paying expenses to make sure she was there." He opened his eyes. "You see, pain pills aren't the only addiction of bull riders. And she was a drug...the best kind. We'd leave the event and head to the bar to dance and drink until last call. Then we'd go to the hotel, and—" Pink spread up his neck to his cheeks, and he closed his eyes.

"How did it end?" She ran her nails over the hair at the back of his neck, to soothe.

"The fun ended when she came to me crying, saying she was pregnant. I couldn't wait to get her to the altar. Luckily, we were in Vegas, so I didn't have to." He rolled his eyes. "God I was an idiot."

"She lied?"

"Yeah. But that wasn't the worst of it. I forgave her for that. She was so young, and she was insecure. I figured we could go on as we were. Then all that drama got stuck in my head. Riding, which used to be easy, got hard. I started losing. And Candi wasn't hitching her wagon to a loser."

Katya closed her mouth. "She *said* that?"

He looked at her for the first time since he'd begun the story. It wasn't the Cam she knew in those eyes. In them, she glimpsed an artless, heartsick young man.

"Not in person. It was in the note she left on the hotel nightstand."

What a cold-hearted bitch. She smoothed his sideburn with a finger, aching for that young cowboy. How could a woman lie about something so important? To lead him to believe—

Aren't you doing the same thing? A gut-bomb went off in her stomach. *You've got to tell him why you took the PBR job.* If she didn't, after this, it *would* be a lie.

But it would mean exposing herself. That could get her

fired. And she wasn't together enough yet to go back to the army. Worry, which had been lulled to sleep by sex and companionship, surged in her mind. She would be trapped in limbo again—no job, no prospects, and her only family over seven thousand miles away.

I just went to bed with the guy. Brain-blowout sex doesn't mean I'm going to get attached.

Maybe not, but he might. She'd never seen Cam with a woman, and now she understood why. Yet here he was, in her bed. That meant something.

It means more to him than just something.

If I lie, it puts me in the same category as Candi. And he deserves way better than that.

She let her hand fall, allowing herself the comfort of only the backs of her fingers, lying against the velvet skin of his ribs. "I'm going back to the army, Cam. Hopefully after the finals."

His breath came out in a snort. Of course she was. Cam Cahill was only a short stop for women on their way to something better. Apparently it was his fate to stand on the platform, hat in hand, as the train pulled out.

His attraction to this woman was more than sexual. It must be, because he'd never told anyone the details of his marriage that he'd just babbled to Katya. He'd wanted her to know *him*, not "Cool Hand," but the Cam Cahill behind the painted prop. He wanted to know her too; to dive into her mysterious waters and discover what was beneath. He wanted to absorb her into his skin.

But she was leaving. That hurt. "I was right, that first day, when I heard you on the phone. You're using this job."

A bolt of guilt flashed like the flicker of lightning

in her eyes before they went cool, the gray-green of the ocean on a cloudy day. "You have to understand, Cam. I'm a soldier." Her throat clicked when she swallowed. "It's what I do. Since I've come stateside, it's like I left a chunk of myself back there."

The still pink scar that spanned half her waist told him the chunk wasn't just figurative. He had to give her credit for honesty. She held his stare.

"Surely you won't hold service to my country against me?"

That one zinged home. He was sure she meant it to. "Yet you're not there now."

"No." She looked down at her hand.

"Why not?"

She fell back to lie staring up at the ceiling. "I lost my healing." Her voice cracked on the last word, like ice, when hot tea is poured over it. "It tears me up, the soldier's pain. I fall apart. Useless."

The hopelessness in her voice hurt him, even as his lips twisted with the bitter taste of jealousy, for a world she wanted more than his. "I see. But you're fine here, because cowboys don't matter."

She broke her gaze at the ceiling to drill him with a stare. "Given my performance in the arena last weekend, I think that's probably open to debate."

Understanding broke like dawn. She wasn't sure if her passing out was low blood sugar, or her reaction to the trauma. Which means she did care about them. Maybe. He bit his lips to stop a smile before it formed. No doubt he was an awful person for hoping she wasn't healed. At least until he had a fair shot at showing her she could have a place here, with him. Because tonight, during dinner he realized that was what he wanted. Her, in his world.

"Okay. You're leaving. Sometime." He draped his arm across her waist, and pulled her to him. "In the meantime, is there any reason why we can't..." He lowered his head, kissing the slope of her long neck. He felt her skin pebble beneath his lips, and she scooted a few inches away.

But when she looked at him, her eyes were dark with want. "A friend? With benefits? How is that different than a buckle bu—"

He halted her with a kiss. A long, searching kiss, full of questions. When he ended it, her breathing came faster. He whispered against her lips, "How about we don't label it for now? Let's let it be what it is."

Beneath his, her lips stretched in a smile, and her arms came around his neck. "That feels just about right."

He lowered his head, and began the kind of talking he really enjoyed.

The nonverbal kind.

CHAPTER 19

The last day of the event in Charlotte, the sport medicine team worked their way through the waiting line of cowboys. Doc Cody moved from assessing Tucker's hip to his next patient, and Dusty moved in on Tuck with a TENs machine, an electrical nerve stimulation device that helped with pain.

Funny how we've fallen together as a team, almost like Kandahar. Katya's hands moved over Tommy Seaver's thigh. Doc and Dusty had taken her advice to rearrange the room for better workflow; massage near the whirlpool, triage closest to the door, for easy transport. They had their steps choreographed like a dance. She smiled as Dusty waddled by, imagining him in a tutu. Well, an assembly line, then.

Raucous laughter rolled in from the locker room next door. The riders were always rowdy before the event, burning off nerves and high spirits. She had to admit to a bit of that herself. She hadn't seen Cam since he left her room in the early hours of morning. Her face heated, remembering his beard-stubble kisses, while he lingered at her door. They'd have wound up in bed *again* if she hadn't pushed him into the night with orders to get some rest.

She patted Tommy's thigh. "You're ready for prime time, cowboy."

He sat up and swung his legs over the side of the table, pulling down his cut-off sweats. "Thanks, Katya. That feels better. Like the smell, too."

She'd been experimenting, trying out more masculine scents in her oils: sage, sandalwood, patchouli. Her patients now requested her concoctions, rather than the off-the-shelf ones.

"Can you fix me up some of that liniment you made for Jody? He said it really helps his back, and mine is sore after a ride."

Holding back a smile and a secret thrill, she retrieved from her bag a small jar that she'd made, just in case anyone asked. "Here you go. Rub it on before you go to bed. It should help."

"Thanks, Katya."

The door to the hall opened and Buster walked in, gear bag in hand, a bandage covering half his forehead. His other arm rested in a sling attached to a band of Velcro around his chest to stabilize the shoulder.

"Hey, Doc. Hi everybody!" He looked like he'd survived a firefight, but his happy-kid grin hadn't changed.

At the sound of his voice, cowboys in various stages of dress walked in from the locker room, including Cam. His gaze searched the room, until it landed on Katya. When the corners of his mouth lifted in a small, shy smile, her internal furnace kicked on.

Tucker snorted at Buster. "What are *you* doing here?"

"I came to see if Doc Cody would clear me to ride. He says I can't. Not this weekend, anyway. But I'm coming to every event until I can."

Cam shook his head. "Its three weeks to the finals." He nodded at Buster's arm. "That's a three-month recovery time. I know, because I've done it. You need to listen to the doc, kid."

Buster's smile didn't falter. "Doc wouldn't clear me because of the concussion, not this." He flexed the fingers on the anchored arm. "The shoulder won't stop me. I'll just ride with my other hand."

The riders in the doorway burst into laughter. More crowded behind them to see what the joke was.

"You can't ride with your off hand!"

"Yeah, right. That would be like Cy Young winning a game pitching southpaw!"

"You're doing some crazy drugs, dude."

Buster tipped his head back and his jaw got hard. "I can do it."

Tuck said, "Maybe on your momma's milk cows. Not on these rank bulls, you can't."

"I can." Buster's face flushed crimson. "And I will, as soon as the doc clears me."

Cam shook his head. "Dream on, kid."

The riders trailed Cam back to the locker room. Buster took a seat at the end of the line for treatment.

A half hour later, the riders filed out for the opening. Doc and Dusty followed with the emergency kit and the stretcher, leaving Katya and Buster alone.

Katya patted the table. "Looks like it's you and me, big guy. Let's see what some massage can do for that shoulder."

Buster stood, unsnapped his shirt, and walked over, his sunny expression turned stormy. "I can do it, you know. When I was a kid, I got bored with riding the local bulls back home. So, to make it harder, I started riding with my left hand." He eased up on the table, taking care that his boots hung off the end. "It got so I could ride just as well with either one."

Katya removed the neck strap of the sling, pulled his shirt off his freckled shoulder, but left the rest in place, to keep the shoulder secure and relaxed. "If you say it, I believe it." She wanted to give Buster the best. She reached for Grand's special oil. "I can't believe your parents let you come back to ride so soon."

"I have my own money. I'm a grown man."

She guessed from his taut lips that there had been some discussion around the dining room table about this. Probably heated discussion. "Buster, you've got years ahead of you. This doesn't have to be a sprint. Can't it be a marathon? If you let yourself heal—"

"With all due respect, ma'am, it's both. I could have a career-ending injury the next time I get on a bull. I've got to make the most of every single ride, if I want the kind of career Cam had."

She rubbed the oil onto her hands, and ran her hands over his shoulder, front and back, assessing. "You're right. I don't get it."

"All I've ever wanted from the time I was little, was to compete at this level. I'd hang around the chutes at the local events, getting underfoot, just to see the riders close up.

"I'm not letting a stupid shoulder keep me from my dream. My goal this year is to win the Rookie of the Year at the finals, and if I don't make it, it won't be because I'm sitting in the stands."

"Well, if trying has anything to do with it, my money's on you. Let me know if I can help—"

"You can. That's what I wanted to talk to you about." He shifted, and his fingers worried the paper cover on the table.

"What Buster?" *There.* She felt the damage in the deep tendons around the socket. *That* had *to hurt.* But he acted as though he hadn't felt a thing.

"If I'm going to have a chance of making the buzzer, I've got to be in top shape. And I'm not going to be able to get on practice bulls until I'm cleared to ride. And I'm not going home until the season is over. So I was wondering. Would you train me?"

"On the road? There's no equipment. No weights, no machines, nothing." Her hands stilled. "And I haven't trained an athlete since college."

He covered her hand with his good one. His earnest green eyes petitioned her, making arguments he didn't voice. She could see in those eyes how much this meant to him. Those eyes, so much like Murphy's.

"Ma'am. I don't have much money, but I'll pay you. And if it's not enough, if you trust me for it, I'll pay you over time."

She pulled her hand from under his, and grabbed a towel. She couldn't afford to get attached to this world, or anyone in it. "It isn't about money. I wouldn't want payment. It's impossible. I'd need equipment to target muscle groups, and—"

He sat up, still targeting her with those eyes. "You're smart. Doc Cody told me you have two degrees. We could

make do with the stuff at hand. That's how the early riders did it. They worked on ranches, they were strong and
wiry."

This is a crazy idea. But his entreaty pulled at her. He
had no way of knowing that the memory of a face that
looked like his made a stronger argument than words ever
could. She owed that memory, even if it cost her more
than she could afford to lose.

"I don't think this could work." Yet, even as she said
it, her mind picked at the knotty problem. *You have resistance bands, and there are hay bales, and...*

He must have seen her thinking on her face, because
the sun broke in his smile. "You'll do it?"

Hmmm. "I can try. Let me see if I can work something out."

"Oh, Katya, you have no idea what this means. It'll
make the finals possible for me."

She held up a hand. "I'm not promising anything. This
may not work. But call me when you get to Chicago. We'll
see what we can do."

He grabbed her in a one-armed hug. "Thank you."

She hugged him back, wishing she was hugging Murphy, but feeling better about herself than she had in a long
time.

"How are you doing with the homework?" Dr. Heinz's
calm voice came from the speakerphone of Katya's Chicago hotel room Thursday night.

She paced her carpeted confines.

Everything the night of her and Cam's date had simply
flowed. The sharing of their wars; hers in Kandahar, his
with Candi. It seemed so natural to give in to the sultry

pull of him, and sex was more than a culmination of giving in—it brought them close. Her hands jittered over her hair, smoothing it.

Maybe too close.

Cam had been in her head ever since. The sunrise over a fresh-mown Illinois hayfield was the exact shade of his hair. The sky, at its edge, matched his eyes. Those sixteen-year-old's thoughts were embarrassing, but the others were more disturbing.

She wanted to share her nightmares with him. She wanted to tell him her fear. She longed to lean against the solid weight of him and unburden herself.

But she wasn't ready to speak of this. Not to a doctor and not to herself, a tangled mess of emotion writhed deep in her chest.

"Katya? How did it go?"

She took a breath. There'd be no returning to her squad until she got a grip on her problems. It was time to soldier up and swallow her pride. "I've always been an overachiever."

"Well, that sounds promising. Tell me about it."

She wiped her sweaty palms on the legs of her jeans. "I went on a date."

"Young women do that. It's a great first step."

"Yeah, but I kind of skipped steps two, three, and who knows how many others." She plopped on the bed and rested her elbows on her knees. "I *slept* with him." She covered her eyes, as if she could hide behind them. "I've become a buckle bunny."

"A what? I'm not familiar—"

"The semantics don't matter." Braided-wire tension

came with her words. "The point is this 'homework' isn't working."

A rumbling noise that might have been a chuckle came from Dr. Heinz. "On the contrary, I think it's working exceedingly well."

CHAPTER
20

At six a.m. on Friday morning, Katya stood with one foot on the indoor arena pipe corral, watching a bull munch his breakfast. She shivered in the cool air and spandex, but knew that she'd be more than warm soon.

"I'm present and accounted for, ma'am." Buster strode toward her wearing shorts and a sleeveless T-shirt, his arm still in a sling, but the bandage gone from his forehead.

"Good morning, Buster." She straightened and squinted up at him. The stitching was done well, but he'd have a scar. A cog clicked-clunked into place in her mind.

You're helping him get back to a career that could kill him.

"That's nothing that will keep me from riding. Doc Cody won't let me ride today, but I'm ready to work."

"Buster..."

"Yes ma'am?"

This is the life he's chosen. The one he wants more than anything. Who are you to try and talk him out of his dream? You're not God. You don't get to choose.

Something in that thought echoed deep in her mind, like a stone dropped into a dry well. She'd need to think about this, later.

Besides, who knew? Maybe her training would help him stay safe. "You'd better call me Katya. By the end of today, you'll have other names for me, I promise."

She'd arrived an hour ago and had been surprised by what she'd found to work with in the arena, once she looked at things from a training point of view. She had resistance bands, of course, and her own personal hand weights, but she'd also commandeered hay bales, buckets, wooden poles, ropes, and a new truck tire.

"First up, strength training. Have a seat on that bale right there." When he did, she wrestled over a bucket full of dirt and set it at Buster's feet. "You need strength in your forearms and biceps, to pull up on your rope and keep your balance, right?"

Buster nodded.

"Give me fifty bicep curls, then rest a minute and a half, then another set, to start." She lifted her stopwatch. "Ready? Go."

From the look on Buster's face, the first set was easy. By the fourth, his face was scarlet. "Don't forget to breathe."

He grunted as he lowered the bucket for the last time, dropping it with a thump. "Piece of cake, ma'am." A rivulet of sweat rolled down his neck.

"I'm glad to hear that." She lifted the harness she'd fashioned from rope. "We'll alternate strength training with cardio. Heft that tire and follow me. You're going to walk the arena, dragging that truck tire by your waist."

He looked at her, disbelieving.

"Preferably double-time."

An hour later, Buster stood with one ankle in the loop of rope that stretched over a pipe fence, the other end tied to the handle of a bucket of dirt.

"One more set, let's go!" she barked.

His T-shirt was dark with sweat, and hay stuck to his damp, quivering legs. He huffed.

"Come on, cowboy! Do you want that gold buckle or not? *This* is where you earn it!"

He gritted his teeth and began the reps.

"You know a bull rider is nothing without strong groin muscles. Don't pull with your back, tighten your core. Come on, Buster, only ten more."

He finished the last rep with a mighty heave, and the bucket fell, overturning and spilling the heavy, wet dirt.

"Good job." She bent and removed the loop from his ankle. "We're done for the day."

"Thank God." He plopped onto a hay bale. "I don't think I could do one more rep." He paused to catch his breath. "Of anything."

"Does your shoulder hurt?"

He groaned. "That's the only part that doesn't hurt."

"Then it was a perfect workout." She smiled. "Follow me. I'll give you a massage, and we'll get those legs in the whirlpool."

Before she took a step, her breast pocket vibrated. She retrieved her phone and motioned for Buster to take five.

"Hey, cowgirl." Bree's voice chirped. "We just pulled off the interstate. I feel the urge to boogey tonight. Are you up for some dancing after the event?"

"Oh, yeah, I'm there." She thought about Cam's shy smile. "Is it okay if I bring a date?"

"Hon, if you can find a good man, you bring him on. Oh, and I'm bringing you a present, express delivery via a cattle hauler. Don't you get your heart set on a blouse to wear tonight, y'hear?"

After discussing the details, Katya hung up. "You ready for that massage?"

Buster put his hands on his knees. When he stood, she caught his glance, just for a microsecond, long enough to see the loneliness. But his features remained nonchalant, only tightness in his jaw hinted at the strain it took to keep it that way.

There are other ways this rookie could use some help. "Hey, Buster, what are you doing after the bucking tonight?"

Katya read the blinking neon sign in front of the cinderblock building. *Hick's—the best country music in Chicago.*

She smiled. *Probably the only country music in Chicago.* She had to give the town credit though; fans had packed the Allstate arena tonight. A distant rumble of panic echoed from the future. She pushed it to the back of her mind. This was her last weekend off from out-gate duty, and she intended to make the most of it.

Max held the heavy door open, took off his hat, and bowed. "Buster, we're the luckiest hicks in Chicago, getting to escort these gorgeous ladies tonight."

"True thing, sir." Buster waited until the women walked past, then followed.

Just inside the door, a steely-eyed beefcake bouncer looked them over then zeroed in on Buster. "Gonna need to see some ID, sonny."

The walls vibrated with bass. Katya could feel it through her new boots, a siren's call to dance. Her toes tapped as the night's potential fizzed through her.

"I'm nineteen." Buster's Adam's apple bobbed, and even in the dim light she could see his flush.

The bouncer pulled a neon red wristband from a string on his belt. "Gimme your right hand." He fastened it around Buster's proffered wrist. "I hear you took that off, I'm coming after you. You got that?"

"Yessir."

When Max pulled open the blacked-out glass door to the bar itself, a drum riff pressed against Katya's chest. The only light in the room came from the small stage and the spots on the dance floor, leaving this end of the bar in shadows.

Katya couldn't wipe off her smile, even if she wanted to. Bree's present made her feel like a celebrity; a tailored long-sleeved Western blouse in light pink, a trailing pattern of dusky roses and taupe ribbons down the front, contrasting with the hot pink tank peeking from its undone snaps. She wore her concho belt, skinny legged jeans with pocket bling, and her newest purchase, narrow-toed chocolate brown cowgirl boots.

She'd seen them in the store and decided to try them on, only as research. After all, everyone at the events wore them; right down to the toddlers. But they fit her feet as if they were made for her, and they looked so good with the jeans. Besides, the arena dirt was ruining her work shoes.

The boots could be left behind when she shipped overseas.

She followed Bree, anticipation putting a little roll in

her hips. Cam had been held up by his sponsors, but said he'd meet her here.

"Hey, Katya." Tommy Seaver waved from a corner table.

"Magic Hands is in the building!" Jody raised a beer in a bleary salute. Apparently he'd gotten there early, and judging from the number of cans crowding the table, had been busy.

She smiled, waved, and kept going, eyes on the dance floor, the music's tempo in her blood.

An hour later, Cam walked into the raucous bar. The danged appointment had taken forever. It was one part of the job he wasn't going to miss. He felt like a trussed-up Thanksgiving turkey at a photo shoot. The fact that he had a woman call and invite him on a date made the delay worse. The fact that the woman was Katya made it excruciating.

He wove through the tables, tipping his chin in greeting to the riders sprinkled liberally through the crowd. His eye caught on a flash of pink on the dance floor. Katya two-stepped by, held in Buster's one-armed embrace, the other lay Velcroed to his chest. When they turned, she ducked under his upheld arm. The crystals on her pocket flashed.

Like a dental pick on a bad tooth, irritation pricked the surface of his brain. When Katya had invited him out, Buster hadn't been part of the picture Cam imagined.

"Cam. Over here." Max waved from an empty table next to the dance floor.

Squeezing between tables, he fell into the chair opposite.

Max handed him a longneck. "This one has your name on it, and from the looks, it's just in time."

"Past time, thanks." He took a deep swallow, watching Katya dance by. Cam allowed himself a leisurely stroll down those slim legs, to...boots? Katya, in boots? He smiled for the first time tonight. Progress! They'd win her over to the lifestyle yet.

He glanced around as the music seeped into his skin, loosening the tension in his shoulders and the muscles of his jaw. "Where's your wife?"

Max pointed to the swirl of dancers. Bree was attempting to avoid being stepped on by Tuck.

"I'd watch that one. He's slicker'n calf slobbers." Cam took another pull on the bottle.

Max snorted. "I'm not worried about Tuck. All I have to do is threaten to call his wife and he comes to heel pretty quick."

"Yeah, Nancy lets Tuck take his balls with him sometimes, but never on the road. She keeps 'em in a pretty box by the bed."

Max laughed, drained his beer, and signaled a waitress for two more.

The music ended and the band took a break. The dancers wandered to the tables.

He and Max both stood as the ladies approached.

"You made it!" Bree hugged Cam's neck, then walked to the other side of the table to sit with her husband.

"Hi." Light dancing in her eyes, Katya strolled over, with a big smile that he hoped was for him.

Buster followed close on her heels.

Time I gave the kid a lay of the land. Cam snaked his arm around Katya's waist and bent her over his arm. She went stiff and grabbed his neck for balance. With his kiss, he staked his claim. At least, that's how it started.

When she relaxed into him, he forgot everything. Her mouth was sweet and he'd been craving sweet. Her weight in his arms felt just right; he'd missed her. When quiet intruded in their self-contained bubble, he ended the kiss reluctantly. He set her on her feet, and he looked at the blank faces around them. "Sheeit, you never saw a man kiss a lady before?"

The riders stomped the floor, shouting encouragement. Cam smiled, waved them off, and pulled out a chair for Katya, who flushed prettily and dropped into it.

Buster settled in a chair next to Max, looking like a motherless calf.

Cam sat. "I'm buying the next round. Looks like I've got some catching up to do."

Katya took a sip of what looked like a cola. "So, Max, how's my buddy, Beetle Bailey doing?"

Max leaned his chair back on two legs. "You know, you've created a monster. We passed a day spa on the way into town, and Bailey was trying to get me to turn in."

Cam stared at Katya. "You're doing massages on the bulls?"

Buster leaned in. "That's not fair. That gives them an advantage, and they already outweigh us by a ton."

Katya held up a hand. "Settle down, I'm on your side. That was a onetime thing."

Is there anything this girl can't do? He let the conversation flow around him, and took her in. God, she looked good. He leaned close, touched the material of her collar, and whispered, "This is pretty."

The corners of her mouth curled. "Isn't it? Bree bought it for me."

"I love your footwear."

She flipped her jet black curls behind her shoulder. "My old shoes are perfectly fine, but the arena is hard on them."

He saw her swallow and caught a flash of hunted rabbit in her eyes. She had to be worrying about next weekend. It made him want to give her something to take her mind off it, like a star, or maybe the moon.

You've got it bad, Hoss.

To distract his thoughts from turning down that road, he asked her to dance.

They'd just settled in to Lee Roy Parnell's "We All Get Lucky Sometimes," when he felt a tap on his shoulder.

Tuck stood there with his face hanging out. "Come on, Cahill, let me cut in."

Cam would have ignored him and kept moving, but Katya slipped from his arms.

She took Tuck's hand. "I'm game, but stay off the boots, okay?"

They swung away and Cam was left standing alone in the middle of a dance floor full of couples. He wandered to the table.

"Lose your girl?" Max winked at Cam. "Don't worry. I just bribed the band to play a hot, line-dance tune. You know the women love to dance that together . . . and we get a ringside seat."

Cam fell into the chair and finished off his beer. "That's some consolation."

By the time the band quit for the night, he'd managed only one uninterrupted dance with Katya. She seemed a magnet for every lonesome bull rider on the circuit. She said goodnight to her latest partner and strolled back to the table.

He stood. *Ya'll eat your hearts out. I'm taking her home.*

Bree lifted her purse from the back of the chair. "Well, we've got bulls to check on yet."

Max stood and settled his hat on his head. "Cam, I hope you don't draw one of our bulls. I'd like to root for you."

Buster said, "I'd be honored to draw Bailey."

Max cocked his head. "You're not riding tomorrow."

Buster stood tall, and pushed out his chest. "If Doc Cody clears me, I sure am."

Max looked skeptical. Cam took Katya's elbow as she stood. "The kid's dreaming, Max."

"I'll be on somebody's bull tomorrow night. You'll see." Buster shuffled away, shoulders rounded, eyes down.

Glaring at Cam, Katya snatched her elbow away. "Dang it, Cam, why do you have to poke at him?"

"Poke? Who's poking? I'm stating fact."

"This is a good time for us to leave, hon." Bree slung her purse over her shoulder. "I'll see you all tomorrow." Max tipped his hat to Katya and they walked away.

Katya was still glaring at Cam. "What?"

"Can't you see that he looks up to you? You could help him. Since you're retiring, he's no threat to you." She snatched her purse, turned, and walked away.

Dammit, this wasn't how he wanted the evening to end. He grabbed his hat and hustled, touching the small of her back before she opened the door. "Katya, wait."

"Cam Cahill, if you weren't such a stubborn mule, you'd see that your next career is smacking you in the head." She crossed her arms over her chest. "I've been watching. The young riders are all like Buster; kind of

lost, and looking for advice. You have a wealth of knowledge to pass on as a bull riding coach. You just think on
that. I'm giving Buster a ride to the hotel. See you tomorrow." She turned her back on him and stalked out of the
door.

The last thing he saw was a flash of crystaled pockets.

Well, hell. Rather than witness the indignity of Buster
getting into Katya's rental car, he about-faced and headed
for the bar.

Settling in the darkest corner, he slumped on a bar
stool and ordered a shot.

He appreciated that Katya was concerned about his
next career, but a job babysitting snot-nosed newbies?

He'd rather trail bovine butt all over his and Tuck's
ranch. Or shuck his pride and go home and wedge into his
family's pecking order.

But he didn't want to do that either. He tossed back the
tiny glassful of whiskey, wincing when it hit his stomach.
He signaled the bartender for another.

Might as well admit it, he was jealous of Buster. Not
his obvious puppy crush on Katya. Cam envied his young,
unbroken body. His lightning reflexes. And most of all,
Cam coveted the years of bull riding the kid had ahead
of him.

God, what he'd give for one more season.

He rolled his shoulder. It hurt, even with whiskey
lubricant. There wasn't another season in that joint.

If he couldn't ride, wouldn't teaching be the next best
thing? He didn't think so, but he'd roll the idea around for
a while, and see how it felt. Thinking didn't cost anything.

CHAPTER 21

Before dawn the next morning, Katya walked into the arena to find Buster had arrived first. With his bright red hair and baseball cap, he looked like a really tall Little Leaguer. "You ready to work, cowboy?"

His grin reinforced the image. "Doc Cody says I can ride for sure next weekend."

"That's great news!" She dropped her backpack full of hand weights in the dirt, and tipped a chin at his anchored arm. "Not with that hand, I assume."

"Nope, my other one. Doc has a brace I can use that will let me raise my free arm, but only to shoulder height, so it won't pop out of the socket."

To hide her wince, she bent to set up the groin pulley.

"At least it won't slow my getaway like a leg injury would."

She shuddered, remembering his wreck. "Here." When she held the noose out, Buster stepped into it, and she inserted a towel to avoid rope burns. "Okay, you know the drill. Twenty reps." She stepped back to watch his form.

Holding one arm out for balance, he began.

These bull riders led such a crazy life. She still didn't understand it, but she was starting to see why it drew young men: the physicality, the challenge, the lifestyle.

"What is it that you hope to get out of bull riding?"

"A gold buckle." He grunted.

"I figured as much." She crossed her arms over her chest, counting reps in her head. "Is that all?"

First set complete, he caught his breath. "What do you mean?"

"Well, let's say you're lucky enough to stay in one piece long enough to get that buckle. What happens after that?"

"I go get another." He grunted, his lips pulling back from his teeth.

"You're twisting. Keep your core tight."

"No one's ever won the World Championship more than twice in a row." He huffed and started his next set. "God willing, I plan to."

She shook her head. "You mean that all you want from life are a few belt buckles?"

Dots of sweat darkened his shirt. "Not hardly." The bucket thumped at the end of the set.

He leaned over, hands on his knees. "Are you kidding? I've got a full life planned. My parents and I talked about it." He pulled the rope off his ankle. "If I have a long career, by the end, they'll be ready to retire and turn the farm over to me. I plan to start a breeding program for bucking bulls."

"Sounds like a nice life." She handed him a resistance band of the right length. "Bicep curls next."

He sat on a hay bale, stepped on the band, put his elbow on his knee, and pulled his fist to his shoulder.

"And I'm going to have a family with lots of kids."

She counted reps on her fingers. "Any special girl in mind?"

He finished the first set and let his forearm rest on his knee. "Not yet. But I'm sure I'll meet her when the time is right."

Ah, the optimism of youth.

Cam as a young man must have been like Buster, fresh off the farm, dazzled by the big leagues. *This was what he was looking for when Candi reeled him in.* Even when he found out she'd lied, he wanted that dream badly enough to forgive her and try to go on. Katya's heart pinched for that unsophisticated, unsuspecting, big-hearted young man. She rubbed the ache in her chest and her dog tags clinked.

That ache burrowed down, closer to the bone. Her future was seven thousand miles from here. And she had no illusions that Mr. Right was waiting for her, but she was glad she'd told Cam her plans. She couldn't have lived with herself, being just another woman who misled him.

Besides, he's a mature adult now. She bent and dumped the weights out of her backpack. He knew how to shield his heart so he wouldn't get hurt with this relationship, whatever it was.

"That sounds like a great life, Buster. I'll be rooting for you." She untangled the harness she'd rigged for tire-dragging. "You just stay away from those buckle bunnies, okay? I hear they can be lethal."

Cam's stomach growled like distant thunder. The Sunday event was always early, which meant he didn't get lunch. And his whiskey-singed stomach had rebelled at the thought of breakfast. He dropped his gear bag and sat on the bench in front of a locker.

Tucker walked in, equipment bag over his shoulder. "Where'd you go last night? I looked up and you were gone."

Cam grunted, and opened the metal door.

"So, you and Magic Hands..." Tuck dropped onto the bench next to him.

"I'm not talking about that here. If you want to talk later, fine." He muttered, focused on stuffing his bag into the locker, so he wouldn't have to see his partner's face.

"Oh."

When he didn't say more, Cam had to look up.

Tuck's bushy brows pulled together. Cam had known those eyes for fifteen years. They missed nothing. "You sure you know what you're doing, Cam?"

His friend's concern came from experience. Tuck had been the one to help him get back in his right mind, after the Candi tornado. He'd stood by while Cam got on countless practice bulls, coaching him. They only talked about bull riding, but Cam felt his friend's silent, solid support at his back.

Cam pulled his T-shirt over his head and tossed it in the locker. "The only thing I know is bull riding, partner." He stood. "But I realized last night that I may not be too old to learn something new."

He was referring to Katya, not his future career. In his mind, they both fell in the "new stuff" category. He patted Tuck's shoulder to show he appreciated his worry, turned and strode through the door to the treatment room. He'd cooled his heels at the hotel until he couldn't wait any longer to see her, even if she was working.

She stood beside the treatment table in jeans, a rainbow-colored Gypsy blouse, and her new cowgirl boots, wiping her hands on a towel. Jory Hancock lounged on the table, one leg cocked. She said something and the cowboys in line cracked up. Even Doc Cody smiled.

"And you should have seen his face when he realized it wasn't a live grenade!"

They laughed again.

Doc Cody said, "Make room, Jory, rank has its privileges. Older guys get seniority."

A waiting rider said, "Seniority, ha. It just takes old guys longer to get stuff moving."

Cam glared. "Maybe so, but once my stuff gets moving, it'll beat the diaper off you."

The guys' focus turned to joshing the rookie, and Cam stepped to Katya's table.

"Here you go, Jory." She lifted a small jar out of her backpack and handed it to him. "This one I formulated especially for you. It has grapefruit essential oil to help with muscle stiffness in that forearm. If you rub it on your face, it'll help with that acne."

"Thanks, Katya." The kid sprang off the treatment table like that was easy and walked away.

Cam used the excuse of climbing on the table to lean in close, inhaling her exotic scent. "Whatcha got for me?"

She flushed pink, shot a look around the room, and whispered, "I'm not kissing you in the middle—"

"No, I meant, is there one of those little jars in your backpack for me?" He smiled, his eyes on her lips and lowered his voice, "But if you want to kiss me, I'm all for it."

Her eyes narrowed then she smacked his bare shoulder. "Lie down, you big ape. I don't have anything strong enough to fix that swelled head."

He lay back and watched her expression. "Do I owe you yet another apology for last night?"

"You might owe Buster one. I've figured you out." She actually snorted. "You're just a very tall two-year-old."

He raised a fist to his heart. "Now that hurts."

She reached into her bag, a small smile on her full lips. He made himself look away before his body embarrassed him.

She shook a bottle, squirted some great smelling oil on her palms, and rubbed her hands together. His skin tingled, anticipating her touch. "When are you leaving for Medicine Lodge?" The Kansas event would be the last before the two-week prefinals break.

Her strong fingers went to work on his shoulder. "I hadn't really thought about it. Why?"

"Hmmm, that feels good." The tightness in his shoulder loosened. "My flight doesn't leave until morning. I hoped we could have dinner tonight before you leave."

"I don't know. Do you promise to lock up the two-year-old?"

She didn't wear lipstick while working, but her lips were naturally a dusky red, and her hands definitely were not relaxing things below his waist. He whispered, "Oh, babe, I promise—nothing but man." He'd never get tired of watching her blush.

She worked his shoulder with her eyes closed, a look of concentration on her face. It allowed him to study her up close, unobserved. What a brimming handful of a woman. Her lithe body, deep lake-green eyes, and wild hair had entranced him. In bed, she'd shed the mantle of prim professional with her clothing. What remained was a sensual Gypsy: unbound, uninhibited, untamed.

Her passion made him burn.

You lust after her.

But it was more than that. He'd known Katya for more than two months now. He'd had the benefit of these capable hands, doing their job. Seeing her with the cowboys, he could tell that she no longer saw them as spoiled athletes. They mattered. It was clear in her personalized concoctions, her relaxed conversations, her gentle hands. She'd earned a place in the treatment room. Not an easy thing to do for a woman.

Then there was Katya, the battle-tested soldier. He'd watched her struggle with what he now knew to be enough damage to take a good man down.

You admire her.

All true. Still, there was another layer. Leaving her that first night had wrenched something in his chest like a mental ligament tear. He hadn't felt quite himself ever since. As if something was missing. And it was her.

You want her to stay. For good.

He'd woken with those words burned in his mind. Katya couldn't leave. Not until they'd gotten to the bottom of this thing brewing between them. If it wasn't to her what he was beginning to suspect it was to him, he'd let her go. Somehow.

Once he'd opened the rusty door in his mind to possibly consider a new career, it stuck open. He and Katya had agreed not to name their relationship, but without a slot to nestle in, it bumped around in Cam's mind. He kept coming back to that unresolved question. She may not want to name it, but he had to. Dammit, he was too old, too tired for mind games, especially with himself.

You love her.

It wasn't that the knowledge made his guts squirm. It wasn't that he didn't know how she felt.

It just was.

There was no use denying it. It was there, solid as bedrock.

Tonight he'd mention his plans for the two-week break—plans he wanted to be a part of. Plans he hoped to convince her to be a part of.

Thank you God, for a comparatively injury-free event. Katya stood before her hotel mirror, getting ready for her dinner date with Cam. The plan to have two small braids pulling back from her temples and held in a clip at the back of her head had her wishing she had three hands. Her phone buzzed.

Make that four hands.

When she glanced at the number on the display, she dropped her hair and snatched up the phone. "Second Lieutenant Smith." For a moment, all she heard was a long distance hiss, and the frantic beat of her heart.

"Lieutenant Smith. Major Thibodaux."

He didn't have to identify himself; she wasn't likely to forget the gruff voice of the lead surgeon of Role 3 hospital in Kandahar.

"Sir. I have been working with the psychologist you put me in touch with. I'm hoping that in a month, he'll clear me to—"

"Smitty."

He wouldn't use her nickname if it wasn't bad news.

Her knees gave out and she landed on the hard mattress. She put her elbows on her knees and took as deep a breath as her muscles would allow. "Sir."

"There was a bombing. One hit the hospital. We had casualties. Three deaths."

The fist-punch words hit her solar plexus. "No."

He named two surnames she didn't recognize. And one that made her muscles spasm.

"No. Not Carol." One of her roommates from B Hut. "She has two kids. In Missouri." She bit her tongue to stop the high-pitched robot voice. It was scaring her.

"I'm sorry as hell to have to call with bad news, Smitty. But I knew you'd want to know."

"I just talked to her…" A month ago? No. Longer. Acid dumped into her churning stomach. How had she let so much time pass without calling? And now she couldn't.

"I have to go, Smitty. Promise me you'll call that psychologist and talk to him about this."

"I will, sir."

"That's an order, Lieutenant. We need you back as soon as you can get here. But I need you healthy."

"Yes, sir." She hung up and dropped the phone in her shirt pocket, but it fell to the floor. She cradled her head in her hands.

Of course you do. The machine is short three cogs. She slapped a hand over her mouth and ran for the bathroom. She just made it.

After, she lay curled on the cold tile, her brain spinning like a tire in mud.

Here she'd been playing at being sixteen again. Doctor's orders or no, she'd allowed her real calling to drift into the murky past right along with her memory of Murphy. Her stomach heaved again, but there was nothing left in it. She swallowed, breathing shallow until it settled.

While she'd been telling funny war stories to cowboys, men and women were dying. Her friends. Her family. Every. Single. Day. How could she have let herself forget? What kind of person did that?

Her conscience squirmed, trying to get away from itself. Memories unfurled in her mind: rows of bloody broken men, the sound of helicopters bringing more. Always more. Brutal sun on rubble. A stuffed rabbit, scorched and torn.

She crawled out of the bathroom on her hands and knees and onto the bed. She would need to call Dr. Heinz. But the thought of confessing her sin to him made her gorge rise again. It was too raw right now. Too immediate. She'd call tomorrow.

She shivered, feeling as if the cold of the tile had seeped into her bones. Pulling the comforter over her, she rolled to her side, staring out the window into the parking lot. Shame etched words on the prison cell wall in her mind. Disengaged. Dishonor. Deserter.

22

Five o'clock straight up, Cam knocked on Katya's door. The parking lot stood almost empty, since everyone else had headed out of town right after the event. The low sun dipped behind a cloud and a cool wind ruffled his jacket. Sitting in his room for the past half hour, he'd made himself wait; the television on for white noise, possible futures running through his mind. Tonight, he'd see if one of those paths was more than a dead end.

He knocked again. Rustling footsteps then the door opened.

The woman who opened it looked like Katya, if you didn't know her. She wore a flowing Gypsy dress, but no jewelry. Her shoes stained with arena dirt. She wore the same little touch of makeup she always did, but under it, her skin was colorless. It was her eyes that sent alarm jangling along his nerves. There was no spark in them, as if her spirit had been snuffed out.

He reached out a hand. "Katya, what is it?"

"Nothing, I'm fine." She slung her purse over her shoulder and stepped out, dodging his touch.

"You don't lie well, hon. Are you sick?"

"I'm not." Her lips attempted a smile, but her eyes didn't bother. "Really, Cam, I'm fine. I appreciate getting out."

He'd let it go...for now. "What would you like to eat?" He took her elbow and led the way to his rental car. "Know any good Transylvanian restaurants in Chicago?"

"Whatever you'd like is fine."

Normally he wouldn't step foot in one of those salad bar places, but if she wasn't well, lighter fare would be better. He'd seen one on his way to the arena this weekend. "Well then, I'm really walking on the wild side tonight." He opened the door and handed her gently in.

Inside the car was silent on the drive, though his thoughts screamed. He pulled into the parking lot and angled into a slot, leaving the engine running. Katya sat staring unseeing at the cinderblock wall of the House of Lettuce.

Seriously worried now, he hesitated. The engine idled. The wind chased paper around the parking lot. "Katya."

Her start broke her stare. "I'm sorry, were you saying something?"

Katya wasn't behind her eyes; she was somewhere else.

"You're not hungry, are you?"

She gathered her purse from the floorboard. "Don't be silly. Let's go in."

He put his hand over hers on the seat belt catch and shifted the car into reverse. He needed to lose weight anyway.

"Where are you going? You need to eat. Your diabetes—" She frowned at him, and for the first time tonight, he glimpsed his Katya.

He backed out. "Don't worry about me. I had peanuts before I picked you up."

"Where are we going?"

"Does it matter?"

"Not really."

They lapsed back to silence. He drove, not really caring where they went. Driving helped him think and maybe it would calm her enough to talk to him. There was something wrong; and he couldn't fix it until he knew what it was.

What if it's nothing you can fix? God, he hated that voice.

The clouds darkened, partially due to the sun setting behind them, partially due to the rain they held. He flipped on the lights and headed out of town. When the buildings and traffic were left behind and oat stubble fields bordered the road, he could stand the silence no more. "Tell me." He held the wheel in his left hand and took hers with the other. It was cold. "Please don't say, 'I'm fine.' You're not." He glanced from the road, put his hand under her chin, and brought her head around. "I'm worried about you. Don't shut me out, Smitty."

"Don't call me that. I don't deserve it." She looked through the passenger window at the fields, as if wanting could transport her there.

"Will you tell me what happened?"

She drew in a long shaky breath. Her chin went to her chest and she closed her eyes. "I got a phone call. From my superior officer. A bomb hit our hospital. Three casualties. My roommate, my friend, is dead."

He checked the rearview mirror and pulled off the road. When the car stopped, he threw it in park, and shut off the engine. Rain immediately obscured the windshield, fracturing light that bled down the glass. He reached over and gathered her in his arms. Thankfully, she came willingly. "Ah, Katya. I'm sorry." He tucked her head under his chin and stroked her hair.

She didn't cry, just lay her head against his chest and let herself be petted.

Turning, he leaned against the door and pulled her into his lap, her back to his chest. He wrapped his arms around her, her head nestled under his chin.

It could have been her. His arms tightened. He pictured her in cammies, boots and a billed cap, her hair tucked up under it. He knew her. She'd have been in the middle of the action. *If she'd been there, it would have been her.*

When she whimpered and reached for her head, he forced his fist in her hair to loosen. He hugged her close; maybe more for himself than for her. He needed to feel her, to convince himself that she was here, not there. Safe.

He'd hoped that she'd slip into this lifestyle like she slipped into her Western boots—that she'd like walking around in his world and they'd continue their affair. He now saw that, to her, it was much more complicated than that. Here he'd been worried about ending his career, and she'd been trying to get back to one that could end with a body bag.

"What else?"

"That's not enough?" she whispered.

"Why don't you deserve to be called Smitty?"

Her chest hitched; he felt it in his. "Because I let them

down. Murphy, Carol, Lieutenant Thibodaux, all of them." She seemed to shrink in his arms.

"It's not your fault. You can't think this is your fault?"

"But I'm still *here*!" The desperation in her wail slapped the glass and raised the hair on his arms. She slid down on the seat, knees drawn up, her arms wrapped around them.

He pressed his chest to her body, sheltering her, his arms encompassing as much of her as he could reach. He rocked her, humming a broken lullaby as the rain drummed on the roof.

Katya came awake all at once, as if an internal switch had flipped. She opened her eyes to a generic ceiling and a heavy weight across her chest. She realized she was in her bed, naked. With another internal switch-flip, it all came back—the bomb that exploded in Kandahar and the concussion when she got the phone call yesterday. Guilt splashed, staining the morning gray.

I'm calling Dr. Heinz today. I can't go on like this.

Without moving, she scanned her hotel room. The weight on her chest was a blond hair-covered forearm. She looked left. Cam's head lay on the pillow next to her.

She knew her meltdown had alarmed him. Hell, it had alarmed her. It pounced on her fully formed, a dark animal with bad intent and slashing claws. All she could do was huddle down and survive. She remembered Cam singing to her. A solid reality she clung to until blessed oblivion took her.

In sleep, he wore no Cool Hand Cahill mask. He looked like she imagined the innocent bull rider who'd begun his career so many years ago.

Thank God he'd been with her last night when the dark waters of shame closed over her head. She'd floundered, trying to stay afloat in an acid bath of guilt. He'd carried her inside, held her until she'd fallen asleep. Cam Cahill was a kind man. A good man. His tenderness washed through her pain, diluting it. Today she felt as though she'd washed up on the shore.

She leaned over and brushed her lips across his cheek. He didn't open his eyes, but gathered her in his arms, a sound of contentment rumbling in his chest. His toasty warmth and spicy scent enveloped her. She took it in and released it with a sigh.

When he opened his washed blue eyes, the worry in them pierced her. "Feeling better this morning?"

She pushed worry to the back of her mind and ran her nails down his chest. "I'm not sure. Let me check..." She skimmed the skin of his ribs and traced the curve of his hip to where he lay turgid, but not yet hard. His penis jumped under her hand. "I'd say it's getting better by the second."

She lowered her head and kissed him, trying to express her gratitude.

He'd have none of her soft emotion. He seized her lips. His hands came up to cradle her head as he plundered her mouth. Demanding. Taking.

When she grasped his shaft, his moan vibrated against her tongue.

The emotions of last night hung in the room like ozone after a lightning strike. She wanted to get as far from that soul-sucking despair as possible. She didn't want languid. She wanted raw. She wanted it now.

She arched her back, brushing her nipples against his

chest, sending an electric current shooting south. She brushed the velvet skin on the head of his cock against herself. Instead of teasing him, she caught fire.

He sucked the sensitive skin behind her earlobe, and her muscles spasmed. He nibbled his way down her neck, and lower, until his lips met her needy breasts. She moaned when he rolled her nipples between his fingers.

Like a blast of heat, need rose in her, pushing back the dark waters of last night's nightmare, banishing the whimpering victim she'd been. Strength surged from deep within. She remembered what, in her fear, she'd forgotten.

I am a warrior.

She put a hand to his shoulder, pushed, and he fell onto his back. She threw a leg over, caressing his hard length from her ankle to thigh as she slid across him. Twining her fingers with his, she pressed them on the pillow on either side of his head. She needed to be in control.

Her long hair cloaked them from all but their passion.

Holding his gaze, she lowered until he brushed the beginning of her. Legs quivering, she waited, watching him, letting the power build. She lowered her lips within a heartbeat of his. "Do you want me?" She breathed.

"Yes," he ground out.

"Not yet." She arched her back, offering him her breast.

He took it into his mouth and nipped. Her hips bucked, and he entered her, just an inch.

She panted. "You don't fight fair."

His fingers tightened, holding hers captive. "Neither do you."

She slid down him, inch by delicious inch, until she could take no more of him inside. There she hovered, waiting.

He closed his eyes, vibrating with an effort of stillness, sending silken ripples into her, loosening her muscles, allowing her to take more until her pubis bumped his.

He began to move with a slow swell of power that liquefied her core. Her body melted over him in a warm rush. When her arms could no longer hold weight, she sunk to his chest. He captured her lips, and his tongue matched the rhythm of his body, their shared strength stronger, pulling her in, deeper, closer.

She rocked against him, every upward stroke lifting, every downward stroke tormenting. Every ounce of energy poured into him, and his replenishing strength surged back. And she passed it back again. Faster, harder, closer until they fused together, hands, bodies and lips, crying out into each other.

Cam lay with Katya snuggled against his chest. Spent yet energized, he sighed. "Bring on Bone Dancer. I'm ready."

She chuckled. "You may want to give it a few minutes, big guy."

He was half serious. Sex had always been good, but with Katya, it was *amazing*. He struggled with a nebulous thought just outside his grasp. Sex for him had been about taking—he'd always made sure his partner was satisfied, but it had been a journey they traveled together, yet separate.

Sex with Katya was a back and forth sharing he'd never felt before. As if they shared the same journey, he got inside her skin, seeing things through her eyes, and she, his.

Last night, he'd glimpsed the dark in Katya's soul.

This morning, he'd watched her put it aside, grab hold of life, and dig in. The strength that must have taken humbled him. He only got on bulls that wanted to kill him. She walked places that were more dangerous.

Last night was a slap-in-the-face reminder. She intended to go back to the army. The clock was ticking not only on his career, but to the day she'd leave to fly into danger. The day she'd leave him.

He knew it in his head, his heart, in the part of him that lived in her. If it were within his power, she wasn't leaving. Seeing her pain brought out a fierce protectiveness he'd never felt before. He couldn't live with the reality of Katya in harm's way. Not without deploying every weapon in his own personal arsenal.

This is war.

Turning on his side, he propped his head on his hand. He wanted to see her eyes. "What are you doing during the two-week break before the finals?"

She rolled toward him. "I've been so focused on Anaheim, I hadn't really thought much about it." Her mouth turned down. "I guess I'll go see my parents in DC."

He knew she enjoyed the world of the PBR, but she hadn't seen what else his world had to offer. He wanted to touch her, to cradle her cheek. But he didn't want to telegraph how much this meant to him. "How about coming home with me, instead?"

"Home? Where?"

"I'm stopping in Fort Collins at my parents' farm, then home, to Bandera."

She was quiet a moment, then cocked her head and squinted at him. "You want to take me home...to meet your mother?"

Heat pounded up his neck. The tips of his ears burned. "Well, you'll meet her. But I'm not talking a capitalized 'Meet.'" At least he didn't think he was. "My mother would tan me if I didn't pay her a visit on the break. She needs some help with her bees, and Dad—"

"I'm only kidding, Cam. I'd love to go."

Joy burst in his chest, and coursed through him. He felt like he'd just scored a ninety-three-point bull ride. "Sweet."

She sat up, pulling her wild hair into her fist. "Come on, cowboy. We've got time for a shower and breakfast. You didn't eat last night. I'll feed you before you head to the airport." She slid off the bed and stood without shyness, breasts high, skin glowing.

He climbed out of bed. "A shower—now that could be entertaining." He smacked her butt on the way by, and they raced to the bathroom.

CHAPTER
23

Katya lowered the window and Indian summer wind blew in the car, dry, with the scent of fresh hay from the field on her right. On the ten-hour drive to Kansas, she had plenty of time to think, but not the ability. Her thoughts danced from one topic to another, never settling long enough to solve anything. And she still had to call the doctor. A ball of ice formed in her gut, the cold leaching outward. Her skin dimpled and she shivered.

Her memories of this morning with Cam kept intruding. They'd made love in the shower, and the memory of her hands sliding over his muscles, slick with soap, made her stomach jump. She'd explored every curve and angle of him, licking water from his skin. She'd bit his shoulder when he pounded into her—

Stop.

Those thoughts banished, yesterday's memories battered the walls she'd erected to hold them at bay, pounding at her temples.

"Oh, screw it." She turned off at a roadside rest stop.

Talking about it couldn't be worse than dreading talking about it. Could it?

She parked in the almost empty parking lot. Beyond the restrooms a few picnic tables stood lonely in the stark afternoon sun. When she shut down the engine and got out, the wind lifted her hair, blowing it around her face. She strode to the picnic area. Time to soldier up.

When Dr. Heinz came on the line, his tone was somber. "Lieutenant Thibodaux notified me of the accident at Role 3. What are you feeling?"

"Lost." It came out at the end of her sigh. "I used to be so sure, after nine-eleven when I enlisted, and when I reupped. I was protecting my country. I knew who the enemy was." She took a breath. "Now, I'm not even sure I know who *I* am."

"How so?"

She tightened her stomach muscles, to protect her core from the blow to come. "That avenging soldier is still there—the champion of freedom. But there's also a confused, jaded woman who witnessed the gore and bloodshed on both sides, who knows that future zealots are being born even now. That my home is no safer. Is all that sacrifice worth it? What have we really changed out there in the desert?"

The doctor wasn't going to give her the answer. He waited for her to go on.

She'd known when she pulled off the road that it would come to this. She took a deep breath, stepped off her soapbox, and forced the deepest truth past her locked jaw. "And then, there's the traitor, who turned her back on her friends. She let herself be sucked into a world full of bulls, hard men, and cowgirl boots."

She wanted to stop there, but once started, the flow of words wouldn't stop. After all, there was more than enough blame to go around. "And you're not helping. Your idea of therapy is for me to act like a teenager." She snorted. "I'm trying not to get involved here. I'm failing dismally."

"That may have been your goal, but it was never mine."

"What?" The bite of betrayal burned.

"I'm here to help you work through the survivor's guilt and the PTSD that comes with a trauma like you experienced. My job isn't to return a soldier to duty. My job is to *heal* you."

Her eyes filled, but she wasn't sure why.

"You see, the treatment is twofold. The first is through exposure therapy. Certain pictures, smells, or sounds may bring about thoughts and feelings connected with your traumatic event. By confronting and dealing with the fear and anxiety connected with these reminders, you'll learn that it will lessen with time. This, paired with the relaxation techniques we talked about, will help you cope until these feelings fade. And they will fade.

"You know, it's really quite remarkable that you managed to choose the perfect job to confront your fears."

"Yeah, remarkable." She rolled her shoulders, and practiced deep breathing. *Trace has a minor in psychology. I wonder...*

"Victims also have a tendency to isolate themselves. They feel guilt for not preventing the incident they lived through, and they fear the judgment of others. But isolation only escalates the depression and other symptoms. So the best treatment is reengaging. You're doing that. And you're doing it well."

"So what? You're granting me absolution?"

"No, Katya. Only you have the power to grant that."

Something bit into her palm. She looked down to see her hand fisted around the dog tags on the chain around her neck. She dropped them.

"In spite of how you're feeling right now, you're making remarkable progress. I believe you're not far from a breakthrough."

Or a breakdown.

"Now, let's talk once more, about your guilt and Kandahar. Reliving the memories and discussing them out loud will take away their power."

"I'll try." She squeezed her eyes shut. *Why is it that the hardest thing isn't hanging on, but letting go?*

The following Saturday, Cam stood in the parking lot of the Honda Center, phone in one ear, finger in the other. "Mom? Did I lose you?" Traffic on Katella was constant and horns blared on the freeway, a parking lot away.

"Did I just hear my son ask if he could bring a girl-friend to visit?"

He heard his sister's piercing whistle through the phone. "Way to go, PBR Confidential!"

"Mom, you tell Chrys to get it all out now, because if she says anything to Katya, I swear I'll turn the runt over my knee."

"Really?" Her tone said more than he wanted to hear.

His heart pounded like a runaway horse, but spilling his guts would be worth it if he could get his mom's help; she would be a formidable weapon if she were on his side. "I love her, Mom." He closed his eyes, pushing past the embarrassment. "She's not like any woman I've ever met. She's strong and brave and smart and...confused."

"Whew. Let me catch my breath a minute, hon. You'd better start at the beginning."

"Well, she's a physical therapist with the sports medicine team, and..." He went on to tell his mother everything he could about Katya.

A half hour later, Cam showed his badge to the guard at the door and was directed to the locker rooms. Several small rooms opened off a huge cement corridor, but he pulled open doors until he found Doc Cody lounging in the Red Room. It looked like a star's dressing room, complete with a lighted mirror that reflected a red upholstered sofa and chairs.

Cam stepped inside and closed the door behind him. "Well, you're coming up in the world, I see."

Doc looked up from a medical magazine. "You can tell that we're just down the freeway from Hollywood, huh? Next thing you know, the bulls will have their own hairdressers." He put his elbows on his knees. "You're early, Cam. What's on your mind?"

Cam dragged one of the cushy chairs closer and dropped into it. "Do you think Katya has a shot at a career in the PBR?"

Brow furrowed, Doc tossed the medical journal on the coffee table. "She needs to prove she can perform under the pressure of an emergency."

He had to tread a fine line. It wasn't his place to air Katya's plans, or problems, to her boss. "Let's assume she can. Would you want her to stay on? You think she's a good employee, right?"

Doc looked him in the eye. "You want to tell me what's really going on here?"

He shifted in the prissy chair. He hadn't planned

this far ahead. But Doc could be another weapon in his arsenal.

This is a war. What the hell, pride is overrated anyway.

"I'm in love with her." He swallowed. Best say it fast and get it done. "If she stays on tour, I'm hoping she'll get hooked on the job, the way of life, the cowboys." He studied the scar in the leather of his right boot. "Well, not all of them, just me."

Doc fell back against the cushion. "Well. That's some speech."

"I'm serious, Doc."

"I can see that you are. Look, Katya is a wonderful therapist. I hope to keep her on. But it's really up to her."

"I get that, I just wanted your opinion."

Doc picked up the magazine and rolled it in his hands. "If she can't handle the trauma, she could make a living selling those salves she makes. The riders all swear by them."

He clapped Cam on the back and stood. "Now, are you ready to go to work?"

Boom!

Like a starter's pistol, the percussion of the opening pyrotechnics shot adrenaline into Katya's system. Sweat popped on her forehead. She wiped it with shaking fingers. She shot a look around; there was only one other remaining in the training room.

"You'd better get going." Dusty's soft eyes held sympathy, his hands held the trauma kit.

She wiped her hands on her jeans, took it, and tried to smile. "Lions and tigers and bears, oh my!" Thank God this last event before the break was only for one night. She couldn't imagine dreading this two nights in a row.

He touched her shoulder. "You're going to do fine. You care about these guys. When they need you, you'll be there for them. I know you will."

Little did he know that her caring pretty much ensured failure.

He reached in his back pocket, pulled out two candy bars, and tucked them in her shirt pocket. "Besides, like the Duke said, 'Courage is being scared to death, but saddling up anyway.'"

"Well, who am I to dispute a learned philosopher?" She took a deep breath. "Thank you, Dusty. I wouldn't have made it this far without you." She patted his hand, straightened her spine, and marched for the door to finally get the answer to the question that had been hanging over her head for weeks.

At the out gate, she dropped the kit next to the stretcher then moved aside when the riders filed in for the introductions. She searched for a flash of red hair until she remembered Buster was in the audience. Thank God he'd heeded Doc Cody's recommendation that he heal and save himself for the finals. She didn't look for Cam. She knew he would be climbing from the spotlighted platform high above her head.

On his way by, Tuck tipped his hat to her and winked. Had Cam told him she'd be visiting? Or was that just paranoia? The lights came on and Doc Cody gave her a thumbs-up from the catwalk above the bucking chutes.

To keep herself from visualizing a fail more mortifying than her last, she busied herself by checking her equipment.

The next hour and a half passed in a haze of jangled nerves. They'd all been lucky so far; no major injuries.

But the final round is the rank bullpen. Saying a prayer for Cam, she took a cleansing breath and searched within for a speck of calm. *Be with me, Grand.*

During the TV time-out before the last ten riders, she unwrapped the second Kit Kat and ate it. Cam had a good ride in the first round, but the bull wasn't much, so he was in tenth place. He'd be the first to ride in the final round. He'd had good and bad luck in the draw, getting Max and Bree's bull, Beetle Bailey. Good, because Beetle was a sweetie. He wouldn't try to run down Cam on the get off. Bad, because Bailey was a contender for bull of the year—unridden in his last fifteen outs.

Cam would buck out of the chute closest to her gate. Katya watched him straddle the chute. She'd love to capture this scene for Trace's Hunk of the Month Club. Cam's chaps flared at the bottom, making his hips look tiny. His shoulders, set off by his flak jacket, were broad and strong. One sleeve of his bright red shirt was rolled tight against his bulging bicep. But it was the fierce look of concentration that she longed to capture. Under his straw cowboy hat, his face was hard, as if chiseled from quartzite. Except for the muscle working in his jaw. While he tugged his glove tight, his eyes darted, assessing every movement of the bull.

Here is a man.

She stood, elation swelling her chest. She was so damned proud to know this man, who lived life on the only terms he'd accept. His own. He'd set out to accomplish an almost impossible task and through strength, guts, and sheer courage, had done it. Twice.

With that amazing strength of body and mind, he also had a gentleness of spirit. He'd held her, singing her back from a very bad place.

Something else bloomed, rising to fill her head, and her eyes. Love? She brushed her hand over her lashes. It was true. She couldn't deny it. She loved him.

Oh no. She couldn't afford to be in love with him. She was leaving.

But it would be a sweet dream, just the same.

She'd enjoy every minute she had left with him; drink him in, for the long, hot, dry spell awaiting her in the desert halfway around the world. If she'd learned anything the past year, it was to take what blessings fell her way and be glad of them. They would be the glue to sustain her when the bad memories tried to rip her apart.

Cam lowered himself onto the bull and out of her view. Tucker balanced on the slats and pulled Cam's rope, while JB Denny recited Cam's, then Bailey's, accomplishments over the sound system.

Her own fear took a backseat to her fear for him. Strong as he was, he was still only flesh and sinew. She crossed her fingers, stepped to the out gate, and peered through the slats, bouncing on the balls of her feet. She glanced down to be sure the trauma kit was at hand.

The gate swung, and the bull turned right, bucking so close to her she could have tapped its nose. Freeze-frame photos burned into her memory: the bull's white rimmed eye, saliva flying from his mouth as it spun. The fringe on Cam's chaps dancing as he spurred the bull. Intense concentration marked his face as he balanced perfectly, making it look easy.

The crowd was on its feet, roaring. Cam smiled,

reached down with his free hand, grabbed his hat, and tossed it like a Frisbee at Tuck, who hung over the back of the chute, screaming encouragement.

The buzzer went off and the bullfighters moved in to distract the bull. Cam reached down and pulled the tail of his rope. His hand popped out and he was slung, landing on his side. He rolled, then he was up, scrambling for the fence. Bailey trotted to the exit gate like the refined gentleman he was. Cam sprung onto the fence in front of the crowd, pumped both fists into the air, and yelled, the words lost in the roar of the crowd yelling back.

The cameramen ran into the arena, recording Cam grinning ear to ear as he hopped from the fence. The picture was broadcast on the JumboTron, twenty feet high over the center of the arena. Tuck tossed Cam his hat, and he slapped it on his head. "Whooo!" He stabbed a finger at the camera, "That bull *bucked*, y'all!"

JB Denny's voice overrode the din. "Ladies and gentlemen, judges score that a ninety-two-and-a-half-point ride!"

The arena vibrated with the crowd's noise. Cam jogged to the out gate and she scrambled to open it. He turned, tipped his hat to the crowd, then spun and ran out of the arena, cameras following.

Katya stood grinning like a fool. Cam looked like a kid at the county fair, amped up on roller coasters and sugar. Confetti shot from a pipe next to the gate, and fluttered down around them. Red-faced and grinning, Cam snatched her up and spun her in a circle. Joy sparkled up to explode in her head. She threw her head back and laughed. All the while the cameras rolled.

When he put her down, Tuck ran in and pounded him

on the back. "Damn, Grandpa, I didn't know you still had it in you!" The camera lights doused and the men trotted off to position themselves for the next ride. Tuck and Cam climbed the catwalk stairs to watch.

Katya closed and latched the gate, smiling and picking confetti out of her curls. Cam's happiness sang through her—she felt she'd burst from it.

So this is how they feel when they ride.

The announcer's deep voice quieted the crowd. "Next up is Tommy Seaver. He's drawn Bone Dancer, the leader in the bull of the year standings. Tommy's going to have his hands full, during the ride and after. This bull works at living up to his name."

Happiness leaked like water out of the soles of her boots. The worry that replaced it was viscous; it coated her insides and wadded in her throat.

A huge brindled bull with wicked long horns burst into the arena, the helmeted rider tied to his back. The animal took a long jump forward, sitting Tommy back on his pockets. It reared and leapt into the air, coming down almost vertical, jerking Tommy forward. When Bone Dancer came up for its next jump, Tommy's face slammed between the horns. The bull tossed his head, throwing the rider off.

The metal slat bit into her palm. Tommy was out cold. She let go and snatched the trauma kit. The kid landed with a thud in the arena, his body flopping like a discarded rag doll.

One bullfighter stood over the rider, protecting him, while the others engaged the animal long enough for the safety roper on horseback to get a noose over his head and drag Bone Dancer out of the arena.

She shot the bolt on the gate and ran. Doc Cody leapt the stairs and followed on her heels. The crowd was so hushed she heard her heart knock in her chest. She couldn't get a deep breath.

Focus. Focus on the rider.

By the time they got to Tommy, he was moving. Doc Cody knelt next to him and Katya leaned over, hands on knees, trying to get air past the blockage in her throat.

Apparently Tommy came to enough to realize he was in the arena, but not enough to know that the bull had left. He scrambled to get up.

Doc Cody pressed Tommy's shoulders back to the dirt. "You're fine. Just relax." His voice was like long summer days, slow and calm. "Where are you, son?"

"Anaheim."

"You dizzy? Your neck hurt?"

The kid moved his head left a bit, then right. "Nope."

"Okay, let's see if we can get you up."

Katya took one arm. Her chest hitched, but she could only take tiny fluttering breaths. Black spots swirled in her vision. They pulled Tommy upright, and after a few seconds, he stood unaided and pulled off his helmet.

The crowd clapped. Tommy smiled and waved to them.

Her lungs unlocked, and she took a huge gulp of air. The black spots retreated. She took another.

Holding Tommy's elbow, Doc Cody scanned her with a "fitness for duty" look. "Are you all right?"

"Yes. Let's get him out of here."

They led Tommy to the open gate, one on each elbow just in case. The crowd cheered.

I made it. She took another deep breath. *Barely, but I made it.*

There had been no blood. No major trauma. Thank God Tommy wore a helmet and had gotten up quickly. She had no illusions that she was fit for duty.

Still for now, she'd take her blessings where she found them.

CHAPTER 24

The wheels of Katya's suitcase wobbled over the floor of John Wayne Airport. One wheel rolled straight, the other wanted to go to the parking lot. Maybe the crooked one was right. "You're sure it's okay with your family that I barge in on your visit?"

"They can't wait to meet you." Cam's boots clicked on the marble.

She lengthened her stride to keep up, suitcase shimmying behind. Today's nerve-singeing event had been enough to handle for one day, but the day's end was nowhere in sight. The thought of being inhaled into a flying tube made her want to run for the rental car counter. Cam hadn't wanted to waste a minute of the two weeks driving to Colorado, so she'd agreed. She didn't want to be more trouble. She'd be a cuckoo in his family's sparrow's nest as it was.

At the end of the flight, she'd be meeting his parents. It wouldn't be a "Meet the Parents," but still, she wanted to make a good impression. The morning had begun at five a.m., and they'd be arriving in Colorado at ten p.m. She hadn't even gotten on the plane, and she already felt used up, wrinkled, and wrung out.

It would be better for him to spend some time alone with his family. I'll rent a car, and...

And what? Drive to Washington and spend the remainder of the two weeks with her parents? The only bright spot on that trip would be if Trace had a few hours for her. Between the awkward silences and too much time to think, she'd be nuts in one week, much less two.

What if they didn't like her? What if—

"Here's our gate." Still pumped from his win, Cam looked like a kid on his way to Disneyland. He lowered himself to perch on the edge of a seat.

She did a controlled flop into the one next to him.

"Today felt so good; like it used to. If this old body holds up, maybe I can go out on my terms, and win the finals this year." He glanced over. "What's wrong?"

Bad enough he'd seen her meltdown the other night. She was darned if she was admitting to claustrophobia. She rubbed the back of her neck. "I'm just tired, I guess."

He slipped an arm around the back of her chair. "You'll be able to sleep on the plane."

Yeah, like that's going to happen.

She woke when Cam's shoulder slid out from under her head. "The pilot just started his approach for landing."

She snapped upright in her seat, checking to be sure she hadn't drooled on him. When they'd boarded she'd kept her eyes on the aisle carpet, to remain unaware of how close the walls were. Cam's chattering about home had distracted her. Then they'd had a drink to toast his win. She didn't remember much after that. But it wasn't the munchkin-sized drink that had relaxed her to sleep. It was Cam's solid presence at her side. She had no illusions that he could magically keep the plane in the air, or the walls from closing in, yet those things didn't seem to matter so much when he was beside her.

When they stepped off the Jetway, her nerves checked in, picking up right where they left off. She ran a hand over her hair. "Ugh. I've got to try to do something with this mop." *And apply some makeup, and brush my teeth, and—* "I'll be right back." She ducked into the bathroom for some serious mirror time.

Five minutes later, she walked out, feeling marginally human.

Cam pushed away from the wall. He looked like he'd eaten a lemon sandwich.

"What is it?"

"Um. My parents are—" She caught a quick glimpse of his blush before he ducked his head and his hat blocked it. "Old-fashioned, and, well, they're not real open to... unmarried people sleeping together."

He looked so torn, she had to chew her lip not to smile. "I guessed that much." She walked on, saying over her shoulder, "It's better anyway. You're so loud in bed that I couldn't show my face at the breakfast table."

He only grinned and grabbed the handles of their suitcases. "You ready?"

Straightening, she took a deep breath, then nodded, and they walked on.

She needn't have worried about not recognizing his family; a blond girl in a letterman's jacket held a sign over her head: "Welcome to Colorado, Katya!" Complete with big hearts and red lips. The girl was flanked by a small crowd of people. Katya stopped dead.

Cam waved. "There they are!" His hand at the small of her back urged her forward.

Put on your big girl panties, Smith. She swallowed, pasted on a smile, and walked to the people who loved her cowboy.

Cam was consumed by the group. Hugged, kissed, and back-slapped. Laughing, he pulled himself away and reclaimed her hand. "Everyone, this is Katya."

"Hi, Katya," they chorused back.

Her "hi" sounded so mousy she almost twitched her whiskers.

"Okay, stand still, y'all, so I can introduce you." He scrubbed the head of the girl with the sign, mussing her long blond hair. "This is the runt, Chrys." She ducked from under his hand and punched him in the arm.

Katya swallowed the worry that left her throat parched. "Thanks for the sign. I'm overwhelmed." And she was. These people came over fifty miles, late at night, to greet Cam. And to meet her. She ran her hands over her full skirt to absorb the palm sweat, and put out her hand.

The girl stepped forward and gave her a quick hug. "It's the least I could do. You had to put up with PBR Confidential for the whole flight."

Cam moved on. "Next oldest is our bookworm, Cassie." He pulled another blonde from the pack, this one with short hair and glasses. "Cassie got all the brains of the outfit. She's majoring in microbiology at Colorado State."

The girl gave Katya a shy smile and shook her hand. "Hello."

He gestured to a slim blond woman in jeans, a sheep-skin jacket, and a Stetson. A broad-shouldered man stood beside her, arm around her waist. His dark hair and eyes stood out among all the blondes. "This is my oldest sister, Carrie, and her husband, Dan. Aside from running a quarter horse training business, she's our local matchmaker."

Dan tipped his hat with a smile, but Katya felt like a bug under the light of Carrie's frank stare before she stepped forward to take Katya's hand. "Welcome to Colorado."

Welcome maybe, but you'll have to go some distance to win this one over.

"And this," Cam lifted a solid woman with short, steel gray hair off her feet, and spun her in a circle. "Is my mom."

"Cameron Cahill, you put me down this second." The woman's delighted smile overrode her sharp tone.

With a last squeeze, Cam put her down. "Katya Smith, may I introduce you to my mother, Nellie Cahill."

Nellie stepped forward and took both Katya's hands in hers. "Welcome, Katya. I'm so glad you came. Don't worry. You won't be a stranger long with this brood."

"And this is my dad, Roy."

He indicated a slightly stooped, bandy-legged man fingering the brim of a cowboy hat. Roy took only her fingers and shook them gently.

Katya swallowed. "I'm so happy to meet you all. Thank you for allowing me to come."

Nellie beamed at her son. "Any friend of Cam is welcome to stay with us."

Roy said, "Well, it's late, and y'all must be tuckered. Let's head 'em up and move 'em out." He waved his brood toward the revolving doors.

The Cahills had driven in two vehicles. She and Cam rode with his parents and Cassie in a huge Suburban. Dan took the rest in the truck. Cam and his parents chatted, and Katya was grateful to fade into the background and get the lay of the land from their everyday conversation.

An hour later, they drove into the yard of a large farmhouse ablaze with light. Cam handed her out of the car as the truck pulled up behind and disgorged passengers, everyone talking at once. He led her up the stairs to the covered porch that extended the length of the facade. Weathered wooden chairs, braided rugs, and pots of geraniums glowed in the yellow light spilling from the windows. A clutter of muddy footwear lay in a pile by the door.

The rest of the family crowded through the doorway. Nellie held the door for them. "I know you must be tired, so we'll save the tour for tomorrow. Cam, why don't you put Katya in the sewing room, and you can sleep on the pull-out in the family room."

She stepped into a slate-covered foyer. Directly across from them a staircase angled up. To the left, through an arched doorway, she spied a formal dining room, and to the right a study. "I can take the couch—"

"Don't even suggest it. Mom would have my hide." Cam picked up her suitcase, led her to the stairs, and climbed.

At the top, he pointed out the bathroom on the right then led the way down a hall to the last door on the left. A narrow bed covered in a handmade quilt nestled under the window. A long table with a sewing machine took up the wall on the right. A table lamp with a prancing wrought-iron horse supplied the only light.

"Here you go. This was my bedroom, growing up, though you wouldn't know it to look at it now." He caught her in a yawn and smiled. "Off to bed with you." He stepped close and kissed her thoroughly before stepping back. "Sleep well. I'll see you at breakfast." He walked to the door, but then turned. "I really am glad you're here, Katya."

Cam sat with Dan and his dad at the dining room table the next morning, nursing a cup of coffee, when Chrys clattered down the stairs, chattering the whole way. Katya followed, dressed in boots, jeans, and a Western shirt. It must have been a good night's sleep. Her skin glowed, and the light was back in her eyes. Damn, she looked good. "Chrys, you'd better not be telling tales about me."

His sister dropped into the chair opposite him. "There you go, thinking you're the center of the universe, again. See, Katya, what did I tell you?"

"Good morning, everyone." Katya came around the table to stand next to him. "May I help in the kitchen?"

He stood to pull out her chair. His knee wobbled a bit. "You're a guest. No way Mom would let you help."

Frowning at him, she sat. "That knee again. I'll make you some tea tonight."

"Tea? Mr. Bad A—" Chrys shot a glance at her father. "Our Big Bad Bull Rider is drinking tea?"

The swinging doors to the kitchen opened. Cassie, Carrie, and Nellie came in, carrying plates of food. The men stood.

"Cam's drinking tea?" Carrie put a heaping plate of scrambled eggs on the table and sat.

Katya said, "It's just a blend of herbs to help the pain and inflammation in his knee."

Cassie put a plate of hash browns in front of Cam and a plate of toast in front of Katya, then took the seat beside her. "Scientists have proven medicinal herb benefits down to a molecular level."

"Well, I bet the Chinese will be glad to hear that, squirt. They've been using them for thousands of years." Cam held out the chair to his left for his mother, who placed a carafe of coffee in the center of the table and sat. "Katya also makes liniment specifically designed for each rider. They all swear by it."

Katya shot him a grateful look.

Holding a plate of scrambled eggs, Nellie asked, "Where did you learn that, Katya?"

"My grandmother taught me. She was my family's healer."

Carrie cocked her head. "Are you Native American?"

"I'm Romani. Gypsy."

Chrys's fork stopped halfway to her mouth. "Oh, that's way cool. Do you tell fortunes?"

Nellie passed the eggs to Katya. "Young lady, that is rude. And you know better."

When Katya passed the plate on, Nellie said, "All you're having is toast?"

"Yes. I only have toast for breakfast."

"Oh." She set the plate back on the table.

Cam cleared his throat. "Dad, do you want Katya and me to go with you to pick up those parts for the tractor?" Maybe the inquisition would be easier for Katya if he could break it into pieces. He knew better than to think he could stop it entirely. He turned to Katya. "I'll give you a tour of Fort Collins."

His dad reached for his coffee. "That'd be great. There's something else I want to show you downtown."

"Oh, don't take her!" Chrys whined. "I want to show her around the place. We have a new litter of barn kittens."

Do I dare leave her? Chrys may stick her foot in her mouth, but she was well-meaning. On the other hand, Chrys was a country girl, and loved the farm. She'd show it in the best light. He pointed a fork at his sister. "You just want to get her off to talk about clothes and boys. I know you."

Katya touched his arm. "I'll be fine here. I want to see where you grew up and have some girl talk." She winked at Chrys. "Hanging with cowboys is fun, but they just don't get much about the important stuff like clothes and hairstyles."

Well, Chrys would be pretty safe. He'd never have left her alone with Carrie or his mom. His mother sat studying Katya like she was a jigsaw puzzle piece. And his mom loved jigsaws. "Okay, you girls have fun. We'll be back in a couple of hours."

Carrie, who'd eaten almost nothing, stood. "Speaking of pedicures, I've got a horse with a loose shoe. I've got to—"

"I'll do that." Dan stood.

"I'm perfectly capable of pounding a hoof nail."

"I know you are. And I'll take care of it." He shot his wife a long look.

Nose in the air, she carried the dishes to the kitchen.

Hope there's no trouble there.

• • •

Katya sat on a hay bale in the barn, watching Chrys groom her dark brown horse. She'd found Chrys to be open, full of questions, and so anxious to be an adult she could hardly stand it.

She put focus and elbow grease in her brushstrokes. "So. You and Cam. You getting married?"

Katya had forgotten the dark side of gregarious. How to answer? *No, we're just hot for each other?* Not only inappropriate, but untrue. Well, she was hot for him, but there was more. Possibly even a lot more. If they couldn't decide what to call their relationship, how could she hope to explain it to a teenager? "Wow. You just jump in, huh?"

"Hey, how do I know if I don't ask?"

"I guess I see that. And no, we're not getting married. I'm not going to be on the circuit after the finals."

"Well, that won't be a problem. Neither is Cam."

Darned kid and her logic. "I know you're a junior, but what are your plans after high school? Are you going to college?"

Thank God Chrys allowed the subject change. "Cam wasn't kidding when he said that Cassie got most of the brains. I do okay in school, but I don't plan to put my life on hold for four years to study boring stuff."

"So what will you do? Get a job around here?"

She dropped the rubber brush in a bucket and lifted out a metal one. "Not hardly. I'm getting the heck out of here as soon as I have my diploma." She walked to the horse's tail and started working on the snarls. "I'm going to see the world. I'm joining the military. I just have to decide what branch."

"Don't do that." The words shot out like bullets.

Chrys stopped brushing and stared.

The last thing Katya wanted was to discuss her past, or expose the raw meat of her pain.

Yet imagining this sweet girl, in cammies, firing a weapon—being fired upon—imagining Chrys coming home with fewer arms and legs than she left with...Katya grasped the twine holding the bale together to keep from throttling the girl. "I've been in the service. Trust me. The place I got to see wasn't anywhere you'd want to go."

"What happened?"

She held Chrys's stare, though it wasn't easy. "I watched people I love die."

"Oh." Chrys ducked her head and continued brushing. "I'm sorry."

Katya bounced a knee to burn off excess anxiety. "Did you always want to be in the military?"

"Not really. I just want to see things, experience things." She patted the horse's rump, walked to the opposite side, and started on its mane. "Fort Collins and this farm is all I've ever known. I want to see some of the world before I settle down. How do I know if this is best if I've never seen anything else?"

"I wanted that too, when I got out of school. It was right after nine/eleven, so the army seemed like the right way to do it." She sighed. "Looking back now, I wish I'd joined the Peace Corps. I would have gotten to see a lot more." She crossed her arms and thought a moment. "Hey, you know about farming, right? I'll bet there are tons of places in Africa that would need those skills."

Chrys stopped brushing. "Oh, Africa," she said the words like a dieter said "éclair."

"Think about it. You'd be helping people. I bet it would be easier to appreciate your adventure without bullets flying around."

"I kinda like that. Thanks, Katya, I'll Google it." She walked around the horse and dropped the brush in the bucket. "Let me put up Twilight, and we'll go see what everyone else is up to."

While Chrys led her horse clopping out of the barn, Katya sat back to wait. Chrys reminded her a bit of herself at that age. Altruistic. Determined. Naïve.

So why was it okay for you to go over there and not okay for her?

We had 9/11. And I was older.

Yeah, and you knew so much more.

When did I get to be such a smartass?

You hadn't planned on a career in the military either.

Reaching into her back pocket, she pulled out her wallet. She opened it, dug into a deep pocket, and slid out a photo. Her graduation from boot camp.

Trace stood, arm around a slight girl in desert fatigues. Black hair haloed her head in spite of a billed cap. Seeing the shining innocence in that huge grin, she wished she could reach back in time to that lost girl.

More than that, Katya wished she remembered who that girl was. Who was she, if not a soldier?

A Gypsy.

Yes, she'd always be that. But with Grand gone, she no longer belonged in the *kumpania*. Her family was the army. And her family was deployed in Kandahar.

Really? How many do you know there that are still alive?

Shut. Up.

You know there're more kinds of family than just the army. You've seen it the past months. You could be a part of that.

Yeah, and while I dreamed that pretty dream, my friends were dying.

CHAPTER 25

Cam walked into the barn, temporarily blinded by the shift from blazing sun to shadow. "Katya?"

"I'm right here." She materialized as his eyes adjusted, sitting on a hay bale. She leaned against a stall, arms crossed over her chest.

"Chrys told me you were in here." He sat beside her. "You okay? You look pissed."

"I'm fine. I'm just sitting here arguing with myself."

"Anything you want to talk about?"

"It's nothing I even want to think about."

He put up his hands. "I know better than to get in between two arguing women. Did the runt show you around?"

She bumped his shoulder with hers. "Don't you call her a runt. She's a lovely young woman."

"Yeah, I'm kinda fond of her myself, but don't tell her that." He dropped his hat in his lap, crossed an ankle over his knee and slipped an arm behind her back.

She leaned against his shoulder and they sat awhile in silence. She was one of those rare people that wore quiet well.

"What did your dad want to show you?"

"Some land. Apparently there's a farm down the road for sale. He wants me to buy it and settle here."

"How do you feel about that?"

"Oh, I don't know. I've got the place in Bandera. I don't need more to look after."

"Isn't it just a little tempting?" She turned, a soft look in her big eyes. "Your family seems so nice and they obviously love you. Wouldn't you like to be closer to them? Especially when you're not on the road all the time."

"Hang around awhile, hon. They can get overwhelming."

She picked a piece of straw off her jeans. "Have you thought of what it will be like, after the finals?"

Hell, have I thought of anything else?

"After all these years, it must feel kind of like leaving your family."

The future yawned, a black, bottomless chasm. He did not want to talk about this. "They'll still be my friends. We'll stay in touch."

"Have you given any more thought to being a coach?"

"Yeah I have. I'm still thinking." He had the knowledge. He had the skill. What he wasn't sure of was if he had the patience. But if not that, what? His brain fired up the same old songs it had run on for months. His stomach brought the acid to the party. He was so tired of this dance. "Have you ever ridden a tractor?"

She shook her head.

"Well, lady, this may just be your lucky day."

After the dinner dishes were cleared and everyone sat drinking coffee at the dining table, Chrys got out the family photo albums to show Katya while Nellie told stories.

Cam was right. This was my lucky day.

"So I'm frantically looking for Cam and I finally find him standing in the middle of the sheep pen, filthy, his mouth smeared with mud. He tells me he's been eating M&M's which turned out to be sheep droppings!"

Cam dropped his head onto the table as everyone else laughed.

"It's funny now, but at the time I was so worried that I called poison control. They had a good laugh. Said it was one of the most unusual calls they'd ever gotten."

Chrys choked out, "Ugh, Katya, you've kissed those lips! How old were you, Cam, fifteen?"

"Give me a break, I was two. And if you start with the prom story, I'm leaving." He glared at his mother. "I mean it."

Smiling, Katya thumbed through pictures of the Cahills growing up: Cam showing sheep, Carrie barrel racing, Cassie with a blue ribbon from the science fair, Chrys under a tinseled Christmas tree, sans front teeth. She watched the progression of Nellie and Roy from a young couple to parents, aging, graying, smiling. She closed the book.

This is what a full life looks like. A melancholy bubble formed in her chest and she swallowed to keep it in. The army might be family, but it wasn't one that would end in her sitting around a table like this, reminiscing with her children.

Children. She wanted children. A girl like Chrys, so full of life she was bursting with it. A sweet-faced boy, like the towhead in the album.

Another sweet dream.

Dan, his expression sober, tapped a spoon to his coffee

cup. "Now that Cam's home and we're all together, Carrie and I need to talk to you all."

Carrie looked at her hands in her lap and bit her lips.

The table went silent, though Katya could almost hear the crackle in the tense undercurrent.

"Well, spit it out," Roy said, his eyes on his wife. "You're worrying your mother."

Dan took Carrie's hand and his lips twitched. "We're going to have a baby!"

Carrie looked up, a huge smile on her face. "Finally! Can you believe it?"

"Aiiieeee!" Nellie was on her feet, hands over her mouth. Her husband stood, slipping an arm around her shoulder to support her.

Chrys squealed and ran to hug her sister. Cassie stretched an arm across the table to grab Carrie's hand.

They all started talking at once.

Cam stood and strode to pump Dan's hand. "Well it's about time. I was starting to think we'd need to bring in a new bull!" He clapped him on the back.

The melancholy bubble ascended from Katya's chest to her mind. She brushed away a stupid tear then struggled to keep the rest of them in.

Dreams just aren't enough.

Two days later, Cam lounged in a low chair on the front porch, watching the girls play lawn darts. The setting sun reflected the gold in his sisters' hair, in their skin, in the wheat across the road. In contrast, Katya seemed to absorb the light. Wild dark hair framed her exotic face, setting off her dusky skin and almond-shaped eyes.

Bringing Katya home had been a great idea and a bad

one, all at the same time. In spite of her differences, or maybe because of them, the girls took to her. She seemed to enjoy seeing their world and they seemed to genuinely like Katya.

Well, the jury was still out with Carrie, but she'd always been overprotective of those she loved. It would make her a fine mother.

He watched Katya throw a dart and completely miss the plastic ring in the grass. Laughing, she put her hands over her mouth. Chrys, her teammate, shouted encouragement from the sideline.

His chest tightened. The past days, longing had grown to a huge snake in his chest, writhing and wrenching at the peace he'd always found in his childhood home. Its restless movement kept him up nights, walking the fields to a chorus of coyote hunt songs.

He'd brought Katya to show her what was possible: a strong family, a good country life, children. He hadn't realized that seeing her here would make it so much harder for him. He could very easily imagine what a life with her would be like. If she decided to return to the army after this, it would tear him up. Bad.

The screen door flapped, and his mother stepped onto the porch. She lowered herself into the chair next to him. "If your expression is any guide, your thoughts are not happy, my son."

"I'm fine, Grandma, how are you?"

"I'm content. You know, everyone talks about how awful it is to get older. Not me. I love watching my kids turn into amazing adults, marrying, having babies." His mother watched the girls play, a soft smile on her face. "There's a lot to be said for mellowing."

"I'll have to take your word for that."

"You always were my driven one, barely finishing one challenge before jumping into the next."

"It's what I'm good at." He watched Katya contemplating her next throw like an Olympian before a high jump. "But what good is drive, when it won't get you what you want most?"

"Oh, Cam." She reached out and patted his hand on the arm of the chair. "Sometimes instead of hunting down what you want, you have to wait and let it come to you."

He squirmed in his chair, trying to get comfortable. "I don't have that skill!"

"I know." She made a noise like a laugh, except it didn't sound happy. "Once you retire from the circuit, you may find need of all kinds of new skills."

"Great, just when I get something mastered, I have to move on to where I don't know the rules, and have no map to follow."

"From what you've told me, isn't that how Katya was when she started on the circuit?"

"I hadn't thought about it that way. You're right." Katya pumped a fist in the air when she scored a bull's eye. "Only she's a lot braver than I am."

"Sounds like you've found a teacher for some of those skills you're going to need, son."

CHAPTER 26

Katya walked carefully through the uneven grass, trying not to spill a full glass of lemonade. Where had the week gone? Her anxious arrival at the airport felt like months ago, yet they'd be returning there tomorrow for their flight to Texas.

Reaching the fence, she balanced the glass on top and watched Carrie, in the center of the corral, talking to a young girl on a tricolored horse.

Cam's family had taken her in and made her feel so at home that she could actually envision belonging here someday. Someday? Had she really just thought that?

Well, maybe I could.

Maybe had been her word of the week.

Maybe after I get back from Kandahar...

Maybe Cam will wait...

Maybe-he-could-buy-the-farm-next-door-and-have-our-kids'-grandparents-nearby. She thought it fast, as if then it wouldn't count as a real thought.

She shook her head. Dr. Heinz would be proud.

Away from the distraction and worry of her job, her future stepped to the front of her mind. Six months ago, that future was career army. Now, without her realizing it, the past months of pain, emotion, and discovery had scratched like sandpaper, wearing away the hard shell of a soldier. Just this week, she realized she was clinging to a persona that was crumbling away beneath her fingers.

The surprise had been what was revealed beneath. A softer woman. A traditional woman, who wanted nothing more of life than a mate, and some land. And children.

A family.

She still had a duty. After this week, she was clear what that was. She'd enlisted to protect places like this. Ways of life like this. So had Murphy. So had Carol. She owed it to them to finish what they'd all started. Less than two years left on her stint. She'd finish it for them and *maybe* then she could mark "paid" to the heavy chit she'd been carrying in her conscience. There was enough of her old shell remaining to soldier on for that long.

That decision felt right, as if one more tumbler clicked home in the brain-lock she'd fumbled over since the explosion.

Then, maybe she could come home—to a *real* home— with a man, for always. She sighed. Such a pretty dream. It would sustain her in the desert.

"Okay, that's enough for today." Carrie patted the horse's neck. "You two did well. Be sure Bandit is completely cool before you put him up."

When the girl nudged her mount to the gate, Carrie walked to the fence.

Katya held out the glass. "Your mother asked me to bring this out to you. She used vitamin-fortified water."

Carrie rolled her eyes. "If it were up to my husband and my mother, I'd be living in a glass bubble for nine months. How have I managed my whole life without them watching me every second?"

Katya handed her the glass. "I think it's sweet."

"It's just hard to have limitations imposed by others." Carrie took a sip.

Katya watched the tractor growling over the field past the corral. She couldn't see inside the cab, but she knew Cam was driving. "I think you're amazingly lucky."

"I am. My family means more to me than anything." She flipped her long hair over her shoulder and regarded Katya. "Can we talk?"

Here we go. She'd known from the first night at the airport this was coming. She straightened. "Somehow I don't think I could keep you from it."

"I know you think I don't like you, but you're wrong. I can see you and Cam are good together." She glanced across the fields. "My brother is different now. There's easiness around his eyes and a bit of slack in his jaw that I've never seen there. It's as if he's easier in his own skin." Her pale eyebrows pulled together.

The muscles in Katya's core snapped taut. *There's a "but" coming.*

"But know this." Carrie handed over her half-full glass and ducked under the fence slat. When she straightened, she stood in Katya's personal space. "My brother is a swan...he mates for life." She retrieved her glass. "Do not mess with him if you're not serious."

Mate? She put up her hands as if to ward off Carrie's impression. "Hang on a minute—"

"Oh, I'm sure he told you that you coming home with

him wasn't a big deal." She pulled her gloves off, one finger at a time. "I'm sure he was convincing and you had no reason to doubt him." She looked up, and squinted as the sun came from behind a cloud. "But you're the first woman he's ever brought home to us." ·

What? He'd been so nonchalant. Said it wasn't a "Meet the Parents." Could she have completely mistaken his intent? Hot blood thundered up her neck to flood her face. "Candi—"

"Oh, he brought her here. *After* they were married. That was the first we knew of her." She glanced to where the tractor made its way down a furrowed hill. "That told us a lot about their relationship. It was no surprise to me when he told us she was pregnant. Or later, when it turned out she wasn't." She turned back and studied Katya for a long moment. "Has he told you yet?"

This conversation was getting weirder by the minute. Katya's heartbeat tripped, then double-timed. "Told me what?"

"That he's in love with you, of course."

"You've misunderstood. We've agreed to keep things light." Her words sped up. "We both have things to do, places to be."

"I don't know what you're afraid of, or why you need to lie to yourself. I guess that's none of my business." She rattled the ice cubes in the glass. "But my brother is. He was a total mess for a year after that bi—after Candi. And he didn't even love her." Her eyes slitted, though the sun had ducked behind another cloud. "You'd just better not hurt my brother." She spun on her heel, head down, and strode for the house.

Hands clenched at her sides, Katya watched her go.

Carrie obviously had forgotten that her brother was all grown up and able to make adult decisions. She snorted. *He was the one who didn't want to put a name to the relationship. That pretty much says it all, right there.*

Shows what Carrie knows. She hasn't seen Cam in months. She's remembering the Cam she knew, growing up. You know the man better.

Still. He'd never brought a girlfriend home? She leaned on the fence watching the tractor, feeling as though she'd walked into a stun grenade.

Katya's sleep was a tangled mess of haunting faces, cowboys, and desert sun. The last was the worst; Chrys lay broken, splashed in camouflage and crimson beside a peddler's table.

When she opened her eyes, the dark images fled to the shadows of the cozy room revealed in the stark sodium light of the yard. She threw on some clothes, ran a brush through her hair, then tiptoed downstairs. In the family room, a white sheet outlined Cam's sleeping form. She stepped to the bedside, picked up the quilt that he'd kicked to the floor and carefully laid it over him. His peaceful expression tugged at her. She wanted to crawl under the covers and snuggle next to him; to share some of that peace. Only the thought of his mother finding her there kept her feet moving to the kitchen.

She pushed open the door. The soft light over the stove illuminated the country kitchen. Photos covered the fridge, alongside clippings from the local newspaper. The wall clock with a rooster on it ticked off the seconds.

Small eddies of peace stirred in this house, like a whisper against her skin. As if the rooms had absorbed the love over the years and now breathed it out, like plants released oxygen at night. Though it was warm, Katya crossed her arms over her chest and shivered. Much as she longed to absorb that softness, she couldn't afford to. Little enough remained of the solder as it was.

She pulled two plastic Baggies of tea out of her back pocket. The first was for Cam's knee. She'd brew it for him to have with breakfast. The second was for her.

The kettle was just boiling when Cam's mother pushed through the door. "Good morning. You're up early." She tightened the belt on her cotton robe and walked to the refrigerator.

"Good morning, Nellie. Would you like a cup of my tea?"

"I'd love to try this remedy that Cam swears by." She took out a creamer of milk and set it on the table.

"You won't need the one I make for Cam. I have a better one for earlier risers."

"Great. What's in it?"

"Raspberry leaf, nettles, alfalfa, and peppermint. It's a fortifying pick me up to start the day."

They sat at the table in the kitchen nook surrounded by the dark panes of the bay window. Katya inhaled the minty steam coming off her teacup. It brought Grand's comforting presence into the room so strongly she could almost touch her.

"It smells wonderful." Nellie took a sip. "Hmmm."

"My grand made it for me every summer morning of my childhood." A hollow ache bloomed in her chest.

"She was special to you, wasn't she?"

"She was everything to me." Her throat felt thick.

"Are your parents gone?"

"My parents have never really been present. Between

chemistry and each other, there wasn't much room left for anything else." It must be the dreams and missing Grand that had her digging up ancient history. Well, that, and spending time around a close-knit family.

"You know, they say to grow up strong, a child only needs one person who thinks the world of them. It sounds like your grand was that for you."

"She was. I so miss her." She sighed. "I'm grateful to have spent the last week with you all. I envy you."

Nellie's gaze was sharp, but her smile was soft. "After Carrie's announcement, I've been reminded of all my blessings." She sipped her tea, but looked at Katya over the rim. "Now, if Cam would just settle, everything would be right in my world."

"I know he's been worried about what he's going to do when he retires."

"Oh." Nellie's eyebrows went up a notch.

If his mother had been referring to some other kind of settling, Katya wasn't going there. "I think he'd make a great teacher."

She tilted her head. "Do you?"

"If only he weren't so danged stubborn. He'd make a wonderful coach for the young bull riders. I could see him hosting clinics, helping them understand the logistics and pressures of the tour, along with riding tips. He'd be a natural." Her saucer rattled when she set her cup down, too hard. "He believes he doesn't have the patience for it. Yet he's caring with me and has shown so much patience..." She clamped her mouth shut. The heat in her face wasn't from the tea.

"He's always been good with his sisters, too. Chrys thinks of him as her personal superhero."

"You know, I think it's that superhero mentality that's holding him back—as if there's something less manly about helping the young guys." She concentrated on making her jaw muscles relax. "I know that this is a big transition for him, but I hate to see him suffering over something that would be so simple. If he'd just see himself clearly—"

"How much heartache could we save, if only we all saw ourselves clearly." Nellie looked like she would say more, but instead lifted and drained her cup. "Thank you for the tea and the company." She reached across the table to take Katya's hand. "And thank you for caring about my son."

Cam stood on the curb at the airport, arm around Katya, as his parents drove away.

Katya waved to the receding car. "I didn't know families like yours existed outside fifties' TV shows." When his mother's car took the corner at the end of the terminal, Katya turned to him. "Thank you for inviting me, Cam."

He checked one more time to be sure his family was gone then folded her into his arms. She'd have no way of knowing she'd just given him his fondest wish. She'd seen country life and a strong family. The next logical step would have to be her wanting it. "The pleasure was mine, Smitty." He kissed her, long and deep.

At first there was the lightning jolt of sexual tension. He pushed past that, wanting more. He let his longing flow into the kiss, forming a bond. It was a "come to me" kiss, an invitation to share his future.

He felt when she accepted the invitation. He was dizzy with the joy of the possibility until she withdrew. Slowly, maybe even regretfully, but firmly.

Don't push too hard. You'll scare her off. Releasing her, he rested his forehead against hers. Hope and disappointment left a sweet and bitter taste in his mouth. He opened his eyes and pushed the heavy corners of his mouth up. "God, I've missed you. I'm tired of sharing you with my family. You're mine for the next week."

"And you'll be mine." She held up a finger. "But just for the week. Deal?"

One more week to break through her stubbornness and get her to see what he already knew; they needed each other. "Okay."

What if, at the end of the week, it wasn't enough?

Jump off that bridge when you come to it.

He took her hand. "Let's go get started."

CHAPTER 27

Katya ignored the suitcase wheel that wanted to return to the terminal and followed Cam to the long-term parking lot. San Antonio didn't care that it was autumn. Heat waves rose from the asphalt and shimmered above the pavement.

One week.

For one week, she'd leave the past unjudged and the future unforeseen. She was so tired of balancing on the knife edge between what had happened and what could happen, dreading the fall on either side. She was taking a vacation.

It may not last, but dammit, she was going to enjoy every second that it did.

Their boots thumped in cadence and Cam's hand at the small of her back felt just right. That kiss...holy smokes. It lured her like a siren's call. And, oh how she wanted to be lured. To dive into this world with him as if it were warm water, buoying and sustaining her. A week. She had a whole week to wallow in his world. And him.

And then...

Nope. Not going there.

Her lips pulled taut in the smile she had no need to hold in. She raised her face to the sun.

"Here's the old red mare."

Cam stopped by the side of an old ranch truck. Dented, scraped and well-used, the burned-paint hood ended in a rusty cattle guard bumper. He unlocked the driver's side door, opened it, and gestured her in before stooping to heft their suitcases into the bed.

She stepped on the running board, inhaling hot air filled with the scent of dirt, musty leather and hot metal. Scooting across the butt-sprung bench seat, she cranked down the passenger window. Tried to, anyway. It stuck halfway down. An antenna ball with a face in a Dallas Cowboys helmet hung smiling at her from the rearview mirror.

Cam hoisted himself into the cab and hung his cowboy hat on the rifle rack in the back window. He leaned across her, banged his fist on the door panel, then rolled the window down the rest of the way. "Sorry about that. It sticks."

So this was how the slick-packaged world champion really lived. She clicked her seat belt. "I love this truck."

"She's been rode hard and put up wet a time or two, but Cha-Cha gets it done."

"Cha-Cha?" She raised an eyebrow.

"Trucks run better when they know you love them." He rolled his eyes to the roof of the cab, his lips moving in what might have been a prayer as he cranked the engine. It fired up and settled into a jouncing rumble. "See?" He shifted the old column-mounted gear stick into first and eased the truck into the traffic.

She sat back, watching the East Texas hill country flying past. Well, that and Cam's forearm muscles flexing when he shifted. Remembering she was on vacation, she abandoned resistance, unclipped her seat belt, and scooted next to him. He smiled and his arm wrapped around her, though he kept his eyes on the road.

She inhaled the smell of Cam's aftershave and freedom, both sweet and clean. Tucking her feet up under her, she stored this precious memory.

Less than an hour later, they rolled through the picture-postcard town of Bandera. Old stone buildings and wooden storefronts flanked the street. Angled parking spaces crowded with farm trucks and soccer-mom vans fronted the curb. One lone horse stood tied outside the Chicken Coop Bar amid a cluster of Harleys.

Cam took a road that followed what a sign proclaimed to be the Medina River, a slow moving green snake of water shaded by overhanging trees.

He drove with one arm on the window ledge, fingers on the wheel. "I'll warn you, my cabin is a bit rustic. It came with the property and I didn't see the point of building anything else until I retired."

She raised her nose and sniffed, "What, no Jacuzzi?"

"'Fraid not. But I know a quiet bend in the river that's perfect for skinny-dipping." He winked at her.

"Well, I guess there will be a few amenities."

He turned left at a cattle-guarded dirt road. A mailbox stood sentinel beside the wire fence. A blue-steel roofed house sat off to the left, and Cam honked the horn as they rolled by, following a two-tire-track trail deeper into the property.

"That's Tuck and Nancy's place. I'm sure we'll visit

them sometime this week." His arm tightened on her shoulder. His glance held hunger. "But not tonight. Okay?"

She laid a hand on his thigh and made herself stop there. "No, not tonight."

The grass-covered hump between the tracks brushed the underside of the truck. Fat cattle, mouths full of grass, watched the truck pass. The trail led up the side of a hill covered in maples and oaks. When they entered the stand, the light through the canopy filtered pale green and the temperature dropped.

Cam pulled onto a clearing where a small log cabin with chinked walls, tiny windows, and a moss-covered chimney slumbered. The wood-shingled roof canted steeply, angling to a covered porch.

He shut down the engine and turned to her. "Welcome to Casa de Cahill. Such as it is."

Birds chirped and a locust buzzed in long grass. A breeze stirred the trees, and sun and shadows danced together in the dirt.

She took a deep breath of the cool air. Quiet settled over her shoulders like one of Grand's hand-crocheted lap blankets. "I like it here already."

He cocked his head and studied her. "Do you? I worried you wouldn't."

This was a perfect place to hide from everything for a week—even herself. "It's perfect."

"Well, hopefully it's presentable inside. A few days ago I called the lady who does housekeeping for me. She agreed to air it out and put up some supplies."

"Great. I'm starving." She slid across the seat and bounced out of the cab.

When Cam unlocked the cabin door, the ghosts of past log fires assailed her nose. The kitchen area was to the right, with appliances she hadn't seen outside old TV shows. Next to a window overlooking the front porch sat a wooden table with two chairs.

On the left was a large open living room, with a field-stone fireplace flanked by windows. The leather couch and scarred coffee table faced the fireplace. Across the room, a ladder climbed the wall to what appeared to be a sleeping loft, tucked under the slanting timbers.

"The door next to the ladder is to the bathroom." Cam wheeled the suitcases in behind him.

"Well, thank heaven for that." Grateful she wouldn't have to use a latrine, Katya crossed the room and stepped into a large bathroom. It appeared to be the only room that had been remodeled, except for the huge claw-foot tub in the corner. She took care of business, and walked out to find Cam bent over, peering into the squat refrigerator. "What do you want to eat? I could make us some eggs, or—"

"Do you have peanut butter?"

He snorted. "You know me. Do you have to ask?"

They ate PB&J sandwiches in the big iron bedstead in the loft, giggling like kids on a campout. Until Cam leaned to lick a dab of jelly off the corner of her mouth, and her hunger went in a different direction entirely.

She turned her face to catch his lips fully, tasting the sweetness of jelly and Cam. She took her time, reveling in their seclusion and the long afternoon that lay ahead.

He kissed her back in a lazy way. She silently vowed to savor every inch of him. She'd tuck away the sweet memories, for the times when bombs fell.

He opened his arms. "It was a long, lonely week on that sofa bed. Come here."

And she did.

In the middle of the night, Cam opened his eyes, suddenly and fully awake. He listened to her easy breathing beside him, but he couldn't lie still. His slid from between the sheets, pulled on his jeans, padded to the ladder, and climbed down.

He snatched the throw from the back of the couch on his way by. The moonlight bathed the porch in soft white light as he stepped out and gently closed the door behind him. The night was cool, but not cold. He settled the throw around his shoulders and pulled the porch chair away from the wall. He sat, put his bare feet on the railing, and leaned the chair on its back legs.

Crickets serenaded. He inhaled the smell of cool grass and damp growing things. He felt his public persona flaking away like the cheap paint that it was. The peace he always found at home cocooned around him. Next week, at the finals, he'd either go out triumphant, or just go out. Either way, he'd have to start over.

Still, the worry he'd spent over that transition now seemed small. It was only what he did for a living. Katya coming into his life had put a spotlight on his real problem, the gaping hole inside him. No, beside him, where his mate should be. What a team they'd make; him coaching, her training.

How immature his relationship with Candi had been. He'd played the part of macho protector, to her little woman. Whatever Candi's faults, he'd made mistakes too—big ones. He'd never dropped the "Cool Hand" facade with her. Maybe if he had, she would have dropped her guard as well. Or maybe it wasn't a facade with Candi. Maybe it was who she was.

And what does it say when you were married to the woman and you don't know?

Katya had flaws. She was stubborn and was so busy looking over her shoulder at the past that she couldn't see where she was going. Her trajectory would put her in danger.

I need to— His thought smacked into a concrete wall of realization. How was he different from that macho protector who had married Candi? Older, yes, but wiser?

If Katya needed to return to Afghanistan to heal, who was he to tell her she shouldn't? *You can't manipulate her into loving you. Or make her want to stay.*

If he tried, he'd be making the same mistake as before. They could never have a solid relationship, if it were based on that.

Still, the knowledge did nothing to stop the sinkhole in his heart. He had no control. Even on a bull, he at least had some control...of himself. With Katya, he didn't even seem to have that.

Cool air brushed his chest and he pulled the blanket closer. She liked his family. She appeared enchanted with his dumpy cabin. He could only hope that the week ahead would spin a web of tiny, almost imperceptible threads, binding her to him and keep her from returning to the bloody desert.

The screen door creaked. "What are you doing out here?" Her footsteps came up behind him.

He dropped the chair onto all legs. "Just listening to the night." He offered his hand. "Come, I'll show you."

When she stepped to the chair and settled into his lap, he spread the blanket over them both. Her arms circled his waist, and she tucked her head under his chin, against his chest.

How can she not see? She's already home.

The days flew by. Cam took her swimming at a green bend in the river with a rope swing over it. They'd spent the afternoon playing like otters. He took her horseback riding, and showed her how to herd cattle. They'd made love in the woods, in the water, in every corner of the cabin. A tenacious wistfulness tugged her guts. She wished she could stop time and stay in this place with him, for a very long time.

Too soon, the morning of their last full day arrived. And with it, the dread she'd held at bay. But worse. She worried about the finals, gate duty, and returning to the army. She now had more worry to add to the teetering pile. She'd have to tell Cam good-bye, and return to the army

Then she actually had to *do* it.

She slapped mustard on a bologna sandwich, dropped a slice of bread on top, and slid it in a plastic bag. Today Cam was taking her on a tour of the ranch via four-wheeler.

Do not ruin what you have left by being afraid to leave it.

The quiet was shattered by the first notes of "Desperado" blatting from a cell phone. They both jumped.

Cam lifted his phone from the windowsill, where it had been plugged in since they'd arrived. "What?"

Her heart, which had spent the days floating at high altitudes, sank just a bit.

We have one more day! She shoved the sandwiches in a lunch bag along with the apples and Twinkies and carried them to the table. She heard a female voice chirping from the phone.

"Hi, Nancy." Cam rubbed his forehead. "Of course. You go. Don't think about it for a minute. Tell Tuck I'll keep an eye on things here, and we'll see y'all in Vegas."

He hit End. "They wanted us to come down for dinner tonight, but her aunt in Albuquerque wants them to stay awhile on their drive to Vegas, so she and Tuck are heading out tonight."

"I'm sorry, I know you'd like to see them." She draped her arms around his shoulders and bent to give him a peck on the lips. "But I'll admit, I'm selfish. I don't want to share you on our last night."

"Me neither." He stood, and the peck turned into a proper kiss.

She felt breathless by the time he patted her butt and backed away. "Now stop distracting me. I have something I want to show you." He took her hand and she just had time to snatch up their lunch before he led her out the door.

The four-wheeler was loud and the ride was much bumpier than a horse, but clinging to Cam's waist and looking around his broad shoulders were a good trade-off.

They came out of the woods onto a knoll. He shut down the engine, and they sat, taking in the view. The ground ahead sloped down to a wide valley, where a stream ran to meet the river far below. From this vantage point, she could see clear down to the road, past Tuck and Nancy's house. The tree line was a dark green division on either side of a golden meadow flowing to the plain.

"Wow." She threw a leg over and stepped off the machine.

"Yeah. This has always been my favorite spot on the place. I offered it to Tuck first, but Nancy wanted their homestead nearer the road."

The knoll would be large enough for a house with a decent-sized yard. "Oh, can you imagine? You could have a porch, with huge picture windows, overlooking this view." She held up her hands, her fingers touching, forming a picture square. "No, wait." She twisted five degrees to the left. "You need to turn it just a bit, so you get the slope down to the road in the view."

He nodded. "Where would you put the kitchen?"

She glanced around. "Well, I'd want a window on the best view I could get while I'm cooking." She strode twenty feet back and to the right. "If you put a sweet little bay window over the sink, you'd still get a bit of the valley. I'd grow herbs on the sill."

"I'm thinking of a large great room in the front." He pointed to the left. "Huge fireplace, a rough timber mantel, and a trophy elk's head above it."

"Oh, no way." She crossed her arms over her chest. "Oh, gross. No dead animals in the house."

"What? Not even if I shot it? It would be impressive—"

"Nuh-unh. I'm not exactly sure how taxidermy is classified, but it's *not* interior decoration."

"Awww, come on, I'll let you decorate the rest of the house, but I want one trophy."

Okay, if he wanted to play house, she'd play. She narrowed her eyes. "That is so not happening, bub."

"Okay, okay. One story or two?"

"I think two stories, don't you? A loft could look

down onto the great room. Navajo rugs on the walls..."
She glanced over. "Except those are way too expensive.
Maybe some knockoffs."

He put his thumbs in his pockets and puffed out his
chest. "You're talking to a two-time world champion
here."

"Okay, Mr. Moneybags. Real Navajo rugs it is."

"Where's the master bedroom?"

She walked to the left corner of the lot. "Right here."
She could picture it in her mind. "It'd be huge, with lots
of windows." She walked to where the outside wall would
be. "And French doors that open to the backyard." She
mimed pulling the door. "Oh! A hot tub, right there!"

"Come back in the bedroom and close that door. Were
you born in a barn?" He waved her over.

She stepped in, "closing" the door behind her. "All this
planning has got me hungry. I'll grab our lunch."

He snatched her hand on the way by. "I don't know,
that bed looks awful inviting—" He tugged and laughing,
they tumbled, into the grass.

Cam's broad shoulders blocked the sun. He leaned
over and began unwrapping her, as if she were the best
kind of present—slowly, one piece of clothing at a time,
until she lay naked in the grass. His steady gaze made her
feel like she was the first woman, the only woman. There
was no shyness between them, only the heat of the sun, of
their need.

Cam's tender touch brushed the future aside. Tomorrow they'd fly to the finals, and whatever lay ahead for
them both. But for right now, she was content to relish
what she could touch. Cam. Hers, for one more night.

Lulled by the warm sun and his loving, time eased and

slowed. Cam shucked his clothes, then leaned over her, brushing the hair back from her temples. He watched her, his eyes the blue of nightfall. When he came into her long and slow, the only sign of what it cost him was his tiny shiver, when he reached her end.

Fulfillment had always been a pursuit. A rushing climb to the summit, to pause a brief moment, thrilling in the height before sliding down the other side.

This was new.

Cam's deliberate movements brought intense focus to the places they touched, the sliding friction inside her. She struggled to remain as unhurried as he, overcome by the almost painful awareness that time wouldn't always stand still.

Still, he watched her.

She didn't want it to end. Any of it.

In spite of the slow pace, or maybe because of it, she floated up. She bit her lips in an effort to be still. Her orgasm caught her by surprise. It didn't begin, but suddenly, she was there. It exploded in her, opening a hollow deep in her womb. She dug her heels into his buttocks, urging him close, to fill the empty place.

He cradled her face between his broad hands, locking his gaze with hers. "I love you, Katya."

The words broke his iron discipline. He closed his eyes, took her mouth, and with one last solid stroke, filled her.

"And I love you." She lay holding him, aftershocks rocking them both, tears slipping down the sides of her face into the grass.

Oh God, how would she walk away from this?

CHAPTER 28

Cam, we've got to talk."

Katya sat beside him at the airport gate. She smoothed a strand of hair back from her forehead, fiddled with a hoop earring. He bit back a smile. *She's nervous too.*

Yesterday at the homestead site, things changed. He'd felt it. They'd transitioned to a new level. He was over-full, puffed with tenderness, pride, and nerves. They were going to have a great future. He wondered if this was how every guy felt, before he proposed.

They'd had a busy morning, showering, packing, and closing up the house. He wanted to wait for the perfect time to bring up a subject this important. Driving to the airport, he'd rehearsed what he'd say. And what she'd say. And then what he'd say . . .

"You're right. We do have a lot to talk about." He wiped his palms on the legs on his jeans. "But first," he flipped his suitcase on its side and unzipped it. "I've been carrying this around forever, and it's time I gave it to you." He reached in and brought out a creamy felt Stetson, with a thin black leather band studded with stones.

"My woman *has* to own a hat." He handed it to her with a ta-da flourish. "I thought the turquoise would look good with your eyes."

She cradled it in her lap, petting it. Her eyes, when she looked up, were full of old pain. He heard her swallow.

Alarm jangled. "What's wrong?"

"I can't—" She swallowed again. "It's not—" She straightened her shoulders, took a deep breath through her nose and blew out between her teeth. "It is beautiful, Cam. Really. Thank you. I love it." She handed it back. "I can't wear it."

A female voice came over the intercom. "This is the final boarding call for Flight 247 to Las Vegas, at gate number three."

"What? Why not?"

A businessman hurried by, his suitcase rolling over Cam's boot.

"That's our flight." She glanced to the line queuing up at the Jetway and reached for the handle of her suitcase.

"Wait." He grabbed her arm when she would have stood. "Why the hell can't you wear it?"

She sighed so deep that her shoulders slumped. "Cam, as much as I've wanted to be, I'm not a cowgirl." She looked like the words hurt her. "Save it for me. Maybe someday it will fit."

Was this some crisis of self-esteem? Final hour of cold feet? Surely he hadn't mistaken the shift that he'd felt yesterday. He couldn't have. She told him that she loved him. Maybe she didn't understand that the hat was a symbol. He was offering her his world, everything he had.

He took her hand. It was icy. "Hon, there's no test you have to take. You don't need a license to wear a hat. Besides, you've earned it. Not many women can say they've massaged a bucking bull and lived to talk about it." He smiled.

She didn't. She took her hand back and shouldered her purse. "We need to go."

A blade of apprehension sliced through him, and the fullness he'd felt the past day bled out. "What's this really about?" He scanned her face for clues. They loved each other. Surely, that's all that mattered?

Dammit, that's all he'd let matter.

He gritted his teeth, bent, put the hat back in his suitcase, zipped it, and stood.

She rose. "Let's talk on the plane."

His thoughts twisting like a fast spinning bull, he led the way to where a professionally cheery airline attendant stood waiting. He handed her both boarding passes and nodded at her request for him to have a nice flight, even though he was beginning to have doubts. He followed Katya's suitcase down the Jetway.

This had happened fast for her. That's all it was. It would take her some time getting used to the idea of marrying a cowboy. Would her family object because he wasn't Gypsy? The damned hat didn't matter. If she wanted to wear a clown suit and white-face, he'd be proud. Nothing mattered as long as she was next to him. It was time he let her know that.

Normally, he hated bulkhead seats. In this case, it at least gave them the illusion of privacy. He was thankful, too, for the two-seat rows for the long hop to Las Vegas. He stowed the suitcases then took the empty aisle seat.

Ignoring the stewardess demonstrating how to buckle

a seat belt, he twisted to face Katya as best he could. This wasn't how he'd planned to ask, but given her reaction to the hat, he needed to know where he stood. After all, if he were the "wait and see" type, he wouldn't ride bulls for a living. It was time to go all in, lay down all his cards.

"You may not understand what I'm saying here, hon. And maybe now isn't the best time, but," he took her ringless hand and rubbed the base of her ring finger. "I plan to do some shopping in Vegas. For something sparkly. I'm telling you now, so you can tell me what kind you'd like." He added his best smile to his pile of cards.

He studied every flicker of emotion on her face. It didn't take long. His stomach took a drop with no bottom. He'd seen raccoons treed by dogs that looked less cornered than Katya. She darted him a startled wide-eyed look, then away. Her hand slipped from his.

"I'm going back to finish my contract. With the army."

"What?" The angry rumble started low in his gut.

The stewardess stopped her explanation midsentence and stared at him.

He shrugged, and leaned close to Katya's ear. "Why?" His heart joined his stampeding thoughts. "You said yesterday…in the grass. You said—"

"That I loved you."

How could words, so full of life yesterday, sound dead, today?

She tugged at her seat belt and shifted. "I meant it. The past two weeks, you've shown me something I didn't think existed outside of fairy tales. Something I could have." Each word lost momentum. "I want that. All of it. I want you." The hope in her eyes was harder to take than the pain it replaced. "Will you wait for me?"

A deafening roar filled his head, like the crowd noise of the arena. No words, just screaming. It was him. His brain screaming at him that something was terribly, life-threatening, wrong. A bad wreck was coming.

He craved movement—to pace, to run, to pound a wall. Instead, the plane picked up speed, hurtling down the runway. He leaned forward, fighting the grip of centrifugal force. "Why? Why would you go back?" He slammed his open palm on the armrest. "You damn near gave your life over there. That's too much." He fought his panic, his fear that she'd return to him in a body bag. He tried to pull intelligent arguments out of the wreck slamming in his brain.

"I survived. Others didn't. I owe them—"

"You don't owe them shit!"

The stewardess strapped in the jump seat eyed him. He nodded an apology to her, then leaned back in his seat, as the future he'd pictured the past twelve hours receded in a cloud of bull dust. His gut churned and he felt under his seat, not sure where the barf bags were in a bulkhead row.

Katya sat rock-still beside him, eyes focused to drill through the bulkhead wall.

Finally his stomach settled a bit, but not his nerves. "Look, I don't mean to be angry, or mean. I'm sorry your friends aren't home with people they love. But wouldn't they want you to be?"

She looked as miserable as he felt. "Of course they would."

"Then why—"

"I wouldn't be happy. Don't you see? I'd feel guilty, like I was running away, instead of making a stand. I need to at least try to pay back their sacrifice." She looked down at her hands. "To atone. I know it makes no sense to you." Her lips twisted. "But if I didn't try, the guilt would burn through me and bleed into us." She reached to touch his thigh but pulled back her hand before she touched it. "It would ruin me. It would ruin us."

"What about that doc you're talking to? If you stay and work with him, things will get better. I know it may not seem like it, but you won't always feel this way."

"He thinks I'm close to getting my healing back. What I want to do with it, that's up to me." She touched his arm. A light, tentative brush. "Look, Cam, it's not forever. Only eighteen months. Then I'll be back and we'll have the rest of our lives together."

He imagined himself going about his day, not knowing if she were dead, bleeding out into the sand. He imagined getting an impersonal telegram. He imagined his heart being torn from his chest.

He ran a trembling hand through his hair. "And how am I supposed to handle that year and a half?" He tried to control the anger in his voice. Really tried. Really failed. "Do you know how many hours that is? How many minutes?"

The stewardess unbuckled herself and gave him a warning look before disappearing in the kitchen area behind the bulkhead.

Katya sat taller and got that tightness around her lips. He knew he was losing the battle.

"People do it all the time." She shot him a hard look. "All the riders' wives do. Your family does, every time you get on a bull. For fifteen years."

Shit. He'd never thought about how his riding affected others. He'd never had to, since he was always the one riding, never the one worrying on the sidelines. Talk about no control. He shuddered.

"Please, don't do this." He didn't care about pride. Or who heard him. He wasn't too good to beg. "I talked to Doc Cody. You'll have a permanent job on the circuit, when you, uh, solve your issue."

He wanted to hold her. He wanted to get on his knees before her. All he had to rely on was his pathetic verbal skill. And he'd flunked speech class in high school. He had to try. "You *will* solve it. You'll jump in and do your job. Because you're strong. And because, deep down, that's who you are. You're the one who cares."

Her hands fisted in her lap. "Dammit, I'm not leaving you. I'm returning to finish something I started. Something I committed to." The tough soldier dissolved as he watched, revealing the anguished, soul-sick woman beneath. "Cam, I want to stay. I . . . *can't.*"

He sat, watching the shimmer of dust on the horizon that used to be his future. What replaced it was dark. Dark and cold. It was going to be bad regardless, knowing Katya was over there. But knowing his love, his hopeful fiancée, the possible mother of his children was over there, and he was powerless to keep her safe? He had always told her she was braver than he was.

He couldn't handle the uncertainty of a future with her. A lot could happen in eighteen months. Not to him, or how he felt about her. To Katya. How would she feel at the end of her tour?

He drew a shaky breath, realizing he had one more forgotten card—the one up his sleeve—the ultimatum. He wasn't proud to be using it, but he was fresh out of pride.

Besides, it was the truth.

"Look, I'm just a broken-down old bull rider. I don't know much. But one thing a bull rider can't avoid knowing are limits. I know mine. What you're asking is past them." He dug down, to try to find something hard inside himself, to anchor himself to...to keep from unsnapping the frigging seat belt and getting on his knees to beg. "You're asking me to wait. It doesn't matter how bad I want to. I can't."

Katya turned to the window to watch the barren landscape pass under the plane. Something about looking out, knowing there was a world outside this tube calmed the claustrophobia. But that's all it calmed.

He wants to marry you! A small flame of joy started in her core before reality smothered it like a candle flame, to a wisp of smoke. That was just the pretty dream she'd dreamed the past two weeks. That was for other people; ones who didn't carry dead friends on their backs.

Coward that she was, she couldn't stand to see Cam's pain. It didn't matter though; when she closed her eyes, she still saw it burned on the backs of her eyelids. Cam, his blue eyes shiny with anguish, features haggard, looking more his father's age than his own.

This was her fault.

Carrie had laid out plainly what this visit really meant to Cam. She'd even warned Katya what would happen. She should have marched out to that field, right then, and told him.

That was only one of her sins.

Yesterday, she'd actually planned their house with him on that hill. Shame burned like acid, etching deeper, until she squirmed to get away from the knowing. Knowing she loved him. Knowing it for pure selfishness. It had made her feel better at the time, but now it was making him feel worse.

And subconscious ignorance was no excuse.

Tucking her hair behind her ear as a diversion, she ran her fingers under her eyes. It would hurt Cam more in the long run if she stayed and ruined the beautiful thing they'd built together with her past. Her guilt. Her sin.

What is wrong with you? Why can't you put Kandahar behind you?

Cam was right. Carol and Murphy would both want her to be happy.

So why did that make her want to give up living entirely?

Cam couldn't wait for her. She didn't blame him for that. The best she could hope for the next eighteen months was to help some soldiers, and maybe carry out emotional burial duty.

No joy, nothing to look forward to. Maybe she'd get lucky and not come back.

The pitch of the engines changed as the pilot began his approach. She sat up and forced her eyes ahead. All she could do to make it easier for Cam to walk away was to hide her devastation. She took a deep breath and held on to her pain, her remaining strength, and her dog tags.

CHAPTER 29

They'd parted ways at the car rental counter. Cam had halfheartedly offered to drive her to the hotel, but she'd let them both off the hook by renting her own car. Katya paced her luxurious room on the strip, unable to sit still in spite of two cups of calming tea.

The last event of the regular season seemed a lifetime ago. She was having a hard time remembering the riders' faces; imagining walking back into a treatment room full of cowboys and Cam. Buster had already called to verify they'd be training in the morning, so it was time to get her head back in the game.

Which, given her trajectory in life, involved gut-wrenching. She got out the wrench, lifted her phone from her breast pocket, and dialed Dr. Heinz's number.

"Katya. I've been thinking about you. How was your vacation?"

She dropped onto the bed and winced. "Remember that program? 'The thrill of victory, the agony of defeat'? It was like that."

"Tell me about it."

She spilled her guts, filling him in on the past two weeks, laying out the facts, making no excuses.

He was quiet for a few moments. "I know we've spoken about this before. Tell me again. Why is it your fault that Murphy is dead?"

She leapt to her feet. "Jesus, doc. I'm talking about the present, not the past."

"Humor me."

She sighed, then recited, "I saw the kid come around the corner of a building. He was bleeding. Something about him bothered me. I realized he was afraid. I unslung my gun. Murphy pushed past me. I grabbed for him. I missed. He died."

"How was that your fault?" His pushy tone pricked her wounds like a dirty knife slicing a scab. "*You* didn't have a bomb. You tried to pull him back."

"And I failed. What's so hard to understand here?"

"Oh, I see. You must be God." His deep, patient voice ground gravel in the wound.

She resumed pacing. "Of course I'm not." How many times did they have to go over the same tired shit? "I may have complexes, but that's not one of them. Or maybe it is. You're the one with all the diplomas. You tell me."

Deep inhale. "Well, if you didn't have the bomb and you are not God, then why is Murphy's death your fault?"

The bottle of pissed-off she'd kept a lid on all afternoon exploded, the shards shredding her tired, misused heart. "I could have saved him! Don't you see, you overeducated, sanctimonious ass? He was my partner. It was my job to protect him. I didn't. And because I didn't, he's dead."

"Okay, then what about Carol? How was that your

fault, when you weren't even in the same hemisphere at the time?"

He wasn't missing any buttons today. "Not directly. If I'd have been there…"

"She still would have died."

She pinched the bridge of her nose to keep the jackhammer inside her head from breaking through. "I should have caught up to Murphy."

"And you would have died too."

She was so tired; tired of trying, screwing up, and trying again. "Maybe that's what was supposed to happen."

But under that, deep in the bottom of her mind where light couldn't penetrate, was fear. Helpless, paralyzing, curled-in-a-ball-blubbering fear. Every screwup took her down farther into that hellhole. She wondered when she'd reach the place where she wouldn't have the energy to try again.

"Listen to me a moment, Lieutenant. I don't want you to say anything now. Just consider what I've said when we hang up." She heard his chair creak. "The hardest part of survivor's guilt to move past is an unconscious self-sabotage. The survivor feels they don't have the right to success, happiness, or even life, because the ones who died can no longer experience those things."

She dropped on the bed once more, too tired to even be irritated. "Trace, Cam, and now you. Are you trying to convince me not to go back, too?"

"I told you before. My job isn't to get you back to the army. It's to get you back to the living."

Cam paid the man and stepped out of the cab in the almost empty parking lot. The dome of the Thomas and

Mack Center blocked the rising sun. A familiar zing of excitement shot through him. However the next five days turned out, after them he'd never again enter an arena as a bull rider. Wanting to savor the feeling, he took his time strolling toward the building.

Sure, there were some things he wouldn't miss: the buckle bunnies, the cameras, the interviews. But the rest—damn, he'd had fun. He'd miss the challenge, pitting his strength and skill against a ton of pissed-off bovine. He'd miss the men. They'd shared the road, the danger, the friendship. Outsiders thought bull riders were crazy. Well, maybe they were, but they understood each other. He wouldn't be traveling with them next year, but bonds forged like that were strong.

He'd made a promise to himself this morning. This week he wasn't going to look ahead. There'd be time enough next week to sort out his future. This week, he was going to savor his swan song. That's why he'd shown up so early.

He took the steps to the rider's entrance slow, favoring his knee. It was giving him fits again. Today he felt every bad wreck he'd ever had. Was his body missing that tea? Or the Gypsy woman who made it for him?

He may have banished the future from his thoughts, but not Katya. Utter fail.

You'd better learn fast, Hoss. She's in the wind at the end of the week.

That plane ride still stung like a whip's lash. He knew that she had no more control over what she felt, or what she had to do, than he did. Still, he was bitter. Not at her, exactly, but— Why couldn't she just put it down? Her being responsible for her friends' deaths didn't even make logical sense. They were dead. Would saving more lives make up for those who were lost? He'd never been a soldier, but even he knew better than that. Would she even be able to quit at the end of her stint? Maybe she'd re-up, be career army, working on an impossible task like that guy in mythology, pushing a boulder up the hill, only to have it roll back down.

And if he was waiting at the bottom, that boulder would flatten him. He had to move on. Somehow.

The uselessness of it scoured a hollow place in him. Such a waste to snuff out a beautiful future. A beautiful life. For what?

Not your problem. She's leaving. And if you're not careful, your heart will be with her, packed in her duffel.

Much as he wanted to, he couldn't fix things for her. He had to back away.

Had to.

They checked his rider's badge at the door, and wished him luck. Instead of walking to the locker room, he took the twisting, behind-the-scenes corridors to the arena floor. He'd come early today, to steep himself in the atmosphere. Besides, he wanted to check the dirt. If it was good, the bulls had a solid footing, giving them an advantage. If it was bad, they could slip, fall, and splatter you.

He passed a few maintenance people in the corridor, though the arena sat waiting, empty.

Except for Buster and Katya. Buster stretched his bad arm in front of him.

Katya wore tight dirt-swiped jeans, boots, and a camouflage T-shirt proclaiming "Army Strong" across the front. She looked strong. She looked like she had it together. She looked so damned beautiful it made his heart stutter.

Neither seemed aware of him when he slipped into a seat on the bottommost row.

"You've been working hard over the break. That's much better than before."

He dropped his arm. "Yeah, a bit."

"Have you been getting on practice bulls, using your other hand?"

He froze for an instant. "Yeah." He didn't sound sure.

Katya's head came up. "What is it?"

He lifted the hem of his sleeveless T-shirt, and used it to wipe his forehead. His hand shook. "I'm thinking I shouldn't ride."

"Why?" Katya stepped to him, and ran her hand under the brace on his shoulder. "Does that hurt?"

"No."

She slid her hand to the front, bracing her palm against his back. "Does that?"

"No. The brace works great." He rubbed the back of his freckled neck.

She dropped her hands. "Then what is it? You're in the best shape we can get you into, given your injury. If you really can ride with your left hand, there's no reason you shouldn't."

"I don't know. I was thinking maybe I should take the doc's advice and sit this one out."

She looked like she was trying to process data that made no sense. "I don't understand. You told me you wanted to win Rookie of the Year."

He ran the edge of one shoe on the other to scrape off dirt. "I know. But now, I don't know. I'm just—"

"Scared," Cam said.

Both heads jerked up.

"It's just us, kid. You might as well say it out loud." He stood, eased himself over the boards, and dropped into the arena. He forgot and landed on both feet. The knee ground, bone on bone. Katya winced for him. When he could move again, he hobbled over to them. "You've been training him?"

"Well, somebody had to help him." She thrust out her jaw. "And don't you dare start in on him, either. He knows better than anyone whether he should ride or not."

"If his problem were physical, I'd agree." He looked the kid over. Buster couldn't meet his eye. "Say it."

Buster's face went red, his lips pursing like a toddler fixing to throw a tantrum.

"You leave him alone." She tossed hair over her shoulder, then caught Buster's elbow. "Come on, we'll do some stretches to cool you down."

"You can't save a man from facing himself."

Buster shrugged off Katya's hand and stared him down. "Okay. I'm afraid. You happy? You can tell the whole locker room about it."

"Do you think I'd be telling those men something they don't know? Something they don't deal with every weekend?" He shook his head. "This is your first bad injury, isn't it?"

"I've been in wrecks before."

"You couldn't have gotten where you are if you hadn't. This is your first potential season-ending injury." He didn't wait for the answer he already knew. "I've watched you ride. You have amazing athletic ability. You have youth, strength, and a love of the sport." He took a step closer to where Buster stood with his fists clenched. "But the question is do you have the balls?"

"That's enough, dammit." Katya stepped between them.

He glanced past her. "No, it's not. You're not a bull rider, you don't know. After a bad wreck, you have to heal more than your body. The recovery time is to heal your brain to get over the fear, too.

"Course, you know you can get hurt bad every time you straddle a bull. But you lock the fear in a strongbox in your mind, and you go to work. Each ride reinforces the idea that you're invincible. That's good, because it gives you confidence."

He could see the kid's hackles lay down.

"Then the inevitable happens and you get hurt...bad. You have to get back on a bull, remembering what happened last time. You have to stand nose-to-nose with what you've managed to lock away. You can die."

He felt the heat of Katya's intense regard, but he stayed focused on the kid.

"No one would question it if you skipped the finals. In fact, a smart man probably would." He glanced to the empty chutes across the arena, already feeling the ache of missing bull riding. "You only have to decide one thing. You have to ask that guy in the mirror, even knowing you can die, do you love it enough to do it anyway?" He put his hands in his pockets. "Because if walking away won't hurt you more than getting stomped, you're never going to be a champion."

Katya watched Cam hobble away, knowing that the worst of his pain wasn't in his knee. He'd loved riding enough to die for it. And after this week, he'd never do it again. He was giving up more than his livelihood. He was giving up the time of his life.

She'd wanted to know how these men had the courage

to risk everything to ride bulls, thinking maybe she could face down her own fears, if only she understood. Well, Cam had just laid it out, simple and plain. She was going to need more than understanding.

Her feet took a step to follow him, then she made herself stop. Cam was right about something else. No one could help her with this decision. She wanted Cam. Even if she could turn her back on the army, she wouldn't have anything to offer a strong man if she wasn't equally strong. She'd end up a Candi clone, tagging along, hand in his back pocket, wanting something from him he couldn't give, didn't know how to give, because it just wasn't in him.

A golden sliver of hope sliced through the thundercloud over her head.

No one could give her courage if she didn't have it inside herself. The bomb had blown that up, along with her healing. Well, today she had out gate duty, another chance to search for courage and her healing.

Cam's speech had been for Buster, but he'd inadvertently given her something. Something she hadn't known was possible. He made her want to try.

He really would make an inspiring coach. I hope he will.

She made herself turn to Buster. His eyes followed Cam, his choice showing clear in the steel of his eyes, his jaw. Apparently she wasn't the only one inspired by the beat-up hunk of a rider.

She smiled. "Come on, cowboy. If you're getting on a bull in a couple of hours, you're going to need a massage."

Two hours later, Cam flashed his badge to the attendant at the locker room door and was granted admittance.

He'd spent the past two hours sitting at a table surrounded by his sponsor's logos, signing autographs and having his photo taken with fans waiting in a line that snaked down the hallway, disrupting the flow of traffic in the corridor.

Normally this was a chore, but today had been different.

The smell of popcorn, hot dogs, and livestock combined with the familiar scent of his home away from home. The babble of the fans, shouts, and laughter overrode the raucous country music blaring from speakers in the curved hallway circumnavigating the arena. The fans' enthusiasm and the afternoon's potential built until the air fairly crackled.

His normally jaded attitude fell away and he felt like a rookie again, in awe of the big leagues. He was proud to be here. His cheek muscles ached from smiling. Funny that it took the end of his career to make him appreciate it.

As he strode into the busy locker room, the atmosphere smacked him in the face—excitement like in the hall upstairs, only amped with testosterone. The guys stood dressing or prepping their equipment, almost shouting with frenetic tension.

"Hey, Buster, you really going to get on a bull today?" Jody Hancock worked rosin into his rope.

Buster sat bare-chested on the bench before his locker, buckling on his shoulder support. "Yep." His back was covered in freckles, but it was broad and well-muscled. A rider's back.

Tucker slammed his locker closed. "You gotta give the kid credit. He's got stones." He caught Buster's eye. "Good luck today, cowboy."

Buster's smile was bright and goofy. "Thanks, Tuck."

The informal name came off his tongue like he was test-driving it.

"If you ride with your off hand, you are the man, dude," another guy called.

The riders began an argument over Buster's odds.

Tuck walked to where Cam sat. "Sorry we missed ya'll. Nancy's aunt called, and you know how it is. When women are wanting a hen convention, it's safer to just go along." One corner of his mouth lifted. "Besides, I knew you wouldn't be heartbroken to not spend your last night down at my house."

Cam reached into his duffel for his liniment. He wasn't getting into a discussion about this right now. Rehashing the ashes of his love life would get nowhere, and it would kill the sweet adrenaline buzz he had going.

Buster stepped into his field of vision, his hand extended. "Good luck tonight, Cam."

"Thanks, kid." He took it, but when Buster held on, he looked up.

"No, thank *you*, Cam."

In spite of himself, a thrill of pride went through him. "You just needed a reminder of why you do this, that's all." Buster pumped his hand more times than necessary.

Once he extracted his hand, Buster wandered off.

"Well, things have changed, haven't they?" Tuck stood eyeing him.

He unscrewed the cap on the liniment, squeezed out a glob, and slid his hand under the collar of his shirt to rub it on his shoulder. "Seeing how these are my last finals, it's about time, don't you think?" He tipped a chin at the young riders, who stood talking to Buster. "I've just come to realize what I've been too stubborn to see. I'm the old bull in the herd. Younger bulls are taking over the lead. And you know what?" He tossed the liniment back in his duffel and wiped his hand on the back of his jeans. "That's as it should be."

"You're not getting a massage?"

Tuck didn't miss much. "Nah. I think I'll sit behind the chutes and watch the stands fill." He smiled at Tuck's dumbfounded expression. "And if I find a cameraman on the way, I may have something I want to say." He picked up his equipment bag and Thermos, then walked away whistling.

CHAPTER 30

Katya swallowed heavily and set the kit beside her boot at the gate to the arena.

He'd rather go into the finals with his shoulder tight than have me touch him? If that were the case, Dusty could have done his massage. If Cam was stiff, it would delay his reaction time and he'd get hurt. Of all her nightmares about the finals, that one was the worst.

He didn't get his tea. She'd had her Thermos in the training room, waiting to give it to him. She'd even practiced what she'd say: *Thank you for your help with Buster. I know you may be mad at me, but I want you to know that I'm still rooting for you.*

After spending time together every day of the break and every minute of the last week, it felt like she'd had an amputation and kept reaching for the part that was no longer there.

Cahill cold turkey is a bitch.

Her mind kept worrying at the impossible knot of their impasse, looking for a way around it. She hoped Cam wasn't spending any amount of time doing the same or he was going to be distracted and get hurt for sure. Besides, that knot always ended at the brick-wall truth. She had no choice, and neither did Cam.

She also knew that rather than spending hours running over the bombed-out hulk of the past, she should be looking ahead. To the army.

You'd better start focusing on a nearer future than that, like the next two hours' worth.

If she were improving as Dr. Heinz said, wouldn't she feel different? Less afraid? Because she wasn't. Even armed with Cam's advice on dealing with fear, and a full pocket of Dusty's candy bars, her knees had too much give. She stood at the gate, shaking like an overbred Chihuahua.

Peering through the slats, she didn't see many empty seats. Of course, this was the finals. That meant the cowboys would face a full lineup of the toughest bulls in the world. There would be injuries; possibly bad ones. It was ludicrous to pray for a trauma-free night for the riders. But that didn't stop her from looking to the roof of the arena and sending a heartfelt one up anyway. Overhead, the speakers blared out a song about enjoying pain. She winced at the irony. The songwriter obviously never shook in her boots.

The lights went down, and JB Denny's deep, familiar voice filled the arena. "Welcome ya'll, to the World Finals! The toughest riders and the rankest bulls in the world have converged on Las Vegas to prove who is best." The crowd roared. "This isn't the rodeo. The guys in the arena aren't clowns. This is bull riding! This is the P—B—R!"

She put her fingers in her ears, but even knowing the flash-bangs were coming didn't stop her from jumping.

How the hell are you going to handle Kandahar, where incoming aren't choreographed? That shrink is a hack.

The finals and the moment of her truth had begun.

The riders were introduced amid blowtorch flames and percussion. When the spots rose high above the arena floor to introduce the Coolest Hand of them all, she squeezed her eyes shut to keep from looking for him. The world dished out enough painful images. No need to inflict the one of Cam at his finest on herself—what she couldn't have—in Technicolor.

When the lights came up, she checked the equipment one last time, then glanced to where Doc Cody stood on the catwalk above the chutes. He pantomimed eating. She pulled a Butterfinger out of her pocket and showed it to him. When he wagged his finger at her, she sighed, unwrapped the candy bar and took a bite. A sugar-rush was not going to help her nerves, but...

"Cam, can I get a quick interview?" a female voice called.

Katya whipped around; Cam walked down the steps to the chutes, chaps flapping. He didn't limp, but she knew from the line of his jaw that his knee was hurting. *And his Thermos of tea is in the damned training room!*

You could run...

By the time she got back, he'd be lost in the crush of riders on the catwalk. Besides, she knew her duty; she couldn't leave her post.

Lisa Bentley, microphone in hand trailed by a cameraman, waited at the bottom of the stairs.

"You bet. In fact, I've been looking for you."

The woman's look of disbelief morphed to professional perky the second the camera lights came on. "I'm here with two-time world champion Cam Cahill. With all the young guns coming up, what do you think of your chances in the finals this year, Cam?"

"Well, I wouldn't be here if I didn't plan on winning, ma'am. But I'm sure every other man here would tell you the same." His blue eyes looked straight into the camera. "I wanted to let the fans know. This is my last finals. I'm retiring at the end of the week."

A flash-bang went off in Katya's chest. *Ask him what's next for him!*

"Wow, that was sudden. I think we all knew you were coming to the end of your career, but still, that's a shock."

"I guess I just realized it's time to let some of those young guns you talked about have their day."

"Have you thought about what's next for you? Are you planning to remain involved in the sport?"

"Yes, I intend to offer my expertise as a bull riding coach. I'm hoping to be able to pass on some of the knowledge I've learned over the years."

The warm ball of pride that expanded her chest exploded on her face as a grin. He was going to make a great coach. He'd have a good life.

"What made you decide to do this now, Cam?"

He hesitated the span of three heartbeats. "I guess I just realized that I can't grab the good stuff that's next if I'm holding tight to what's already passed. It's time to let go."

The ball in her chest became a blowtorch that burned her heart to cinders. Had he been talking to her?

"Well, we certainly wish you the best of luck, in the finals and in the future. We'll all be rooting for you, Cam."

"Thank you, ma'am." He tipped his hat and, without a glance around, turned to climb the stairs. He did it slower than he had on the way down. His pain hurt her in places massage wouldn't reach.

Katya turned back to the gate.

You should have brought his tea. You knew you'd see him.

She'd been distracted by the last-minute craziness before an event, and her post for the evening. *Idiot.*

She spent the first four rides clinging to the fence slats, willing the riders to stay on. They didn't, but they did manage to scurry to safety.

Tommy Seaver was the fifth and she backed up when he opened the gate and exited the arena to the crowd's applause.

"Good try, Tommy." She looked him over to be sure he was uninjured. "If that bull wouldn't have hipped himself in the gate, you'd have ridden him, sure."

"Thanks, Smitty. I'll get the next one."

"No doubt. Why don't you go have Dusty ice your hand? You don't want it swollen tomorrow." She stepped aside to let him by.

JB Denny's voice pulled her back to the action. "Here's the ride everyone's been waiting for. Buster Deacon was the hot rookie on tour until a bad wreck on Bone Dancer sidelined him six weeks ago."

From where she stood, she could only catch a glimpse of Buster's profile as he lowered himself into the chute. Intently focused, he looked determined. Brave.

"He damaged his shoulder and it should have ended his season right there. But Deacon has stepped up to try to do the impossible. He's going to attempt to ride a finals-caliber bull with his left hand. There's been a lot of speculation on whether he can do it, or if he's plumb crazy. Well folks, we're about to find out. Either way, this cowboy deserves a big round of applause."

The crowd jumped to its feet, their approval shaking the rafters.

"Just to make it tougher, he's drawn Mighty Mouse, a two-time PBR Bull of the Year. The Mouse has been on tour a long time, and he may have lost a step, but I can tell you he's come here to prove that he can still bring the goods. I know, because that's my bull."

Katya wiped her sweaty palms on the pockets of her jeans. All she could see now were the riders around the top of the chute. Cam stood on the side, pulling Buster's rope. His lips moved next to Buster's ear as he handed the rope over. Probably giving advice, though she'd bet the men right beside him couldn't have heard; the crowd's noise was deafening.

Suspense coiled in air gone dense and it was hard to breathe.

She scanned the crowd and found Buster's parents, two rows up in the riders' family section. Tom had his hat off, waving it over his head, yelling. Maydelle stood, hands clasped as if she were praying.

Katya knew when the gate opened because the noise hit the exposed skin of her forearms and face like a concussion grenade. Crossing fingers on both hands, she stepped to the fence and peered through the slats.

The black-and-white spotted bull hit the dirt with a four-hoof thump, then started spinning. Mighty Mouse was small, but made up for it with speed.

Buster never settled. He leaned to the inside, then shifted his hips too far to the outside. The bull went round so fast its spots blurred to gray and Buster was pulled to the inside of the spin.

Muscles taut, Katya twisted right, then left, trying to help him balance. If he fell off to the inside, the bull would be spinning right on top of him.

Even with the pulsing roar of the fans, she could hear the cowboys on the back of the chutes, pounding the metal slats, screaming encouragement.

Buster hung ninety degrees off the bull's side when the buzzer sounded. He let go, but his hand stayed locked in the rope. As the bull spun, the centrifugal force pulled him horizontal, two feet off the ground. The bullfighters did their best to distract Mighty Mouse, but they couldn't get close with Buster's spurs passing their faces every rotation.

Katya grabbed the trauma kit and put her hand on the gate latch. Her lungs heaved, and her heart banged her ribs so hard it hurt.

Please God. Not this redhead. Not again.

God must have heard, because in that instant, Buster's hand popped out of the rope. The force threw him across the arena to land fifteen feet from the bull facedown in the dirt.

In an eye blink, he was up and running for the fence, but he needn't have bothered. The second the rider was off, Mighty Mouse stopped spinning. Staid as a milk cow, tail flicking, he sauntered out of the arena.

"Now how's that for talent, Las Vegas!" JB Denny's voice boomed over the screaming crowd.

Buster hopped on the fence. The brace wouldn't allow

him to raise his bad arm, so he took off his hat and spun it into the crowd. Tom and Maydelle ran to meet him. Tom pumped his hand while Maydelle held her son and cried.

JB had to shout into the mic to be heard. "It may not have been pretty, but it still counts for a score. Buster Deacon bests the bull for eighty-one points!"

The crowd loved him. Katya loved him.

She put a hand over her heart, clenching her dog tags under her thin shirt. "Thank you, God."

Cowboys thundered down the catwalk stairs to meet Buster when he came past her through the gate. They pounded him on the back and shoulders in congratulations, all talking at once. And Cam was right in the middle of the crowd.

She watched the celebration, choking on conflicted emotion. How could a broken heart feel so full?

Thanks to his win in Anaheim, Cam had the last ride of the night. Gripping the fence at the back of the catwalk, he flexed to squat, until his knee crunched with an iron band of pain. He settled for stretching his back instead.

With a clang, the chute to his left opened and the bull and rider lunged out. He was up next. Adrenaline zipped through him. He pictured a blue web of electricity hovering just over his skin, giving him superpowers. Juvenile maybe, but his force-field visualization had worked his entire career. His muscles were stronger. He felt younger. He was invincible.

Cool Hand Cahill was in the building. He'd ride anything they put under him.

He pulled at his riding glove, making sure it was tight.

The buzzer sounded, dumping more adrenaline into his

blood. He took the step to the chute, where his bull waited. He'd drawn Patient Maker, a huge brindled Brahma that had bucked him off in Baltimore.

He climbed and straddled the chute, shaking the slip knot out of the rope he'd put on the bull a few minutes before as it stood in the aisle, waiting to advance. He handed the tail of the rope to Tuck, touched his boot to the bull's back, just so he wouldn't be startled, then lowered himself. The Brahma had a huge hump, making his rope placement farther back than he'd like.

As the bull turned his head to look into the arena he leaned against the back of the chute, trapping Cam's bad knee. He hissed air through his teeth. "Somebody grab the bull stick. This dude is squeezing me." He slipped his mouth guard in, then scrubbed his palm up and down the rope to activate the stickum.

Jody lowered the heavy red plastic two-by-four between the bull's shoulder and the chute, giving Cam a pocket of room.

Tuck stepped onto the chute slat before pulling Cam's rope the standard three times. He bounced the rope off the back of his hand to test it. "One more, Tuck." He pulled again on his glove, then eased it into the handle of his rope, only peripherally aware of the announcer reeling off his accomplishments and the noise of the crowd. When Tuck handed him the rope, he took a wrap around the back of his hand, twisted it, and laid it in his palm.

Tuck leaned over the chute and yelled over the noise. "He's going to take a steep jump out, then duck out from under you. He could go either way, but be sure you're sitting back, or you're going over his head."

Cam closed his fingers over the rope, pounding them closed with his fist.

"And for God's sake, haul ass for the fence, after. This sucker's mean enough to have a squeeze chute in hell."

Cam listened, then pushed all that to the back of his mind. He pushed his hat down on his head, and sidled up on his rope, looking for a good foothold.

This wasn't the bull's first event and it knew when the gate was fixing to open. It lunged forward. Someone grabbed the back of Cam's flak vest to keep him from going face-first into the padded bar at the front of the chute.

His senses sharpened with his focus. He heard the whistle of the short breaths he took in and out of his nose, his heartbeat a trip-hammer in his ears. The muscles of his jaw strained, clamping down on his mouth guard. He focused on the flakes of sawdust in the tuft of hair between the bull's horns. The adrenaline screamed power through his body. This bull didn't have a chance.

The hump seemed massive between his thighs. He felt the bull's muscles tense as he set his feet.

Keep your eyes on his head. Keep your feet moving. Stay up for that first jump.

Run fast.

He took one last gulping breath. "Buck him!"

The gate man clicked the latch. The bull lunged.

CHAPTER
31

Katya waited to hear the crowd roar that would signal the beginning of Cam's ride. She kept her eyes on the sponsor's sign on the opposite end of the arena, even though the writing seemed to swell and shrink with the cadence of her breath. Her knees shook like aspen trunks in the wind. Her hands were their fluttering leaves.

Please, God. One more time. You owe *me.*

She'd gladly bargain. God could take her life right now if he'd keep Cam safe.

She had to look. The crowd erupted as the huge hump-backed bull burst from the chute, bucking like it wanted to kick the lights out. The crowd saw it coming; the arena hushed. The bull reached vertical, then overbalanced. They went over slow, so slow she had time to see the red tissues inside the bull's distended nostrils and the surprise in its white-rimmed eye.

It twisted midair, coming down on its side. Her lungs squeezed to dried raisins. One ton of momentum couldn't stop that fast—it rolled up onto its back—onto Cam. It balanced for a millisecond that took a lifetime, then it rolled on its side and onto its feet.

Cam was out. She saw it in the arc of his arm, when his hand mercifully came out of the rope to fall lifeless onto the dirt. Every muscle snapped taut, Katya slammed the bolt aside and shot into the arena, kit in hand. She didn't know if sound had ceased, her eardrums burst from the pressure in her head, or if her brain no longer registered the deafening noise.

The safety roper galloped up on his horse, throwing his rope on the dazed bull. She dodged the horse, her eyes never leaving the crumpled figure in the middle of the arena.

CamCamCamCam...

When she reached Cam's side, her knees let go. She fell in the dirt beside him. Cam's face shone gray and pasty, but the skin was unbroken. There was something wrong with his jaw; one side canted, off-balance.

Her world tilted, then righted. She ripped open the trauma kit, pulled out a cervical collar, and laid it in the dirt.

Doc Cody jogged up and knelt opposite her. She ran her hands lightly down Cam's body, feeling for breaks. Thank God, no rib fractures. Riders had died when razor-tipped broken ribs pierced soft organs.

"Cam? Can you hear me, son?" Doc's quiet voice sounded loud in the hush.

She reached for Cam's legs. Her hollow gut squirted bile into her throat. His lower leg lay at a ninety-degree angle to the thigh. His knee was gone, totally blown out.

Oh, Cam.

"Let's get him on a backboard," Doc said.

She shifted to Cam's head, becoming aware that the

bullfighters and several cowboys stood in a circle around them. Two of the men set the stretcher in the dirt. She supported Cam's head and neck as Doc slipped the collar under.

She choked out, "Watch his jaw. It's broken."

Doc carefully secured the Velcro straps under his chin. "Bring the board in." Shifting to Cam's leg, he carefully straightened and immobilized it.

Tuck knelt in the dirt next to them with the backboard. She and Doc carefully rolled Cam onto his side and Tuck shoved the board in place, then the stretcher.

Under her hands, Cam's body lay slack and lifeless.

She tore the Velcro straps from the backboard and secured them over Cam's forehead, then his chest. Doc did the same with his hips and legs. She reached for the stretcher handles, but Tuck brushed her aside. Someone else took the foot.

She took Cam's hand, watching his face for any sign of waking.

JB's voice was soft, from the speakers overhead. "Let's not draw conclusions, folks. We'll give you an update on Cam as soon as we have one."

Doc addressed one of the other bystanders. "Go tell the EMTs to fire up the ambulance. We're not going to be able to fix this here."

She squeezed Cam's large, cold hand.

Come back to me.

The entire audience stood clapping. The men hoisted the stretcher and marched to the exit.

Katya sat beside the hospital bed, holding Cam's hand. The only time she'd let go was when they took him to surgery. Was that just yesterday? She laid her other arm on the bed and dropped her head on it.

Cheery morning sun from the world outside poured in the window. Funny, how that world had seemed important yesterday. Today her world began and ended here, in this room. Cam's family was on their way. Doc Cody said he would stop by this morning. The world would intrude again in a few hours, but right now, she was grateful to be alone with Cam.

They'd reattached four tendons in his knee and while they were there, went ahead and replaced the joint. The surgeon told her it looked as though Cam had been walking bone-on-bone for some time. They'd also wired the break in his jaw. But he hadn't yet regained consciousness.

The doctors had said the MRI showed no skull fractures or brain bleeds. He should wake sometime this morning. Even so, from watching all night, her nerves were scraped raw and her eyeballs felt like hard-boiled eggs. She rubbed her forehead on her arm. Tired, yes, but renewed.

She'd done her job. That amazing fact hadn't even hit her until Cam was in surgery and she sat alone in the waiting room. Her healing was back. She felt Grand's gift, a river of calm running through her. It had been missing so long she'd almost forgotten what it felt like.

Doc Heinz had been right; when she'd needed it, it was there.

But that was only part of the seismic shift that began with the wreck yesterday.

She'd spent all night wrestling with her conscience. Murphy had been here with her, and Carol. And a young Afghan boy with fearful eyes. That part was bad.

Grand had said back in Chicago, "You cannot lose

something that is a part of you. It's only gotten covered by things that are not you. You will find it again. And you'll find more, besides. Remember, gifts sometimes come in strange wrappings."

As if she'd been summoned, Grand's papery voice whispered, *Remember your kintala—balance. You were something before you were a soldier. Do you not remember?*

A healer.

That's who she was. Thanks to Grand, it's who she'd always be.

A click sounded in her mind as the last puzzle piece dropped into place.

Cam had said, *You have to ask that guy in the mirror— even knowing you can die, do you love it enough to do it anyway?*

Walking away from Cam would hurt more than getting stomped. It would hurt worse than being haunted by ghosts. Or dying in sand-filled desert wind.

She wasn't God. Things would continue to happen that she had no choice in, or any responsibility for.

It came down to one decision: Hang on to the past, or let it go? Live the remainder of her life in her old world, or embrace the new one?

Which one was she willing to die for?

She lifted her head and looked at Cam. It wasn't even close.

His hand twitched in hers. She'd known he'd wake. Grand had promised.

Welcome back, my cowboy.

Two hours later, Katya opened the door to her hotel room and stepped in, feeling she'd lived a lifetime since she'd last been here. Eyeing the shower with longing, she walked to her medicinal bag. Too bad she didn't have time.

Cam had asked for her tea and his own T-shirt and shorts to wear. She wanted to get back to the hospital before his family got there. She rummaged through her bag until she found the right pouches and tossed them into her backpack.

She walked into the bathroom. "Yikes!" She faced the Medusa in the mirror. "This will *not* do." Grabbing a brush and a scrunchie, she got to work.

Five minutes later, she used the card to open the door to Cam's hotel room. As the minutes had passed, an invisible cord had tightened. She needed to get back to the hospital. To him. Hurrying to his suitcase, she lifted it and laid it on the bed. Trying to remember which shirt he'd asked for, she unzipped it.

Lying atop of the clothes sat Cam's surprise. Her cowgirl hat.

Watching herself in the full-length mirror, she tried it on. Even with her thick hair, it was a perfect fit. It looked right. She took it off and set it on the bed.

She reached under the collar of her Western shirt. Her dog tags clinked when she lifted the chain over her head. These didn't fit anymore.

"I'm not leaving you behind, Murphy. I'm taking you with me. Always." Lifting them to her lips, she kissed them, then tucked them away in a corner of Cam's suitcase. She trusted him to keep them safe.

Then she stood, put on her hat, and followed the tightened cord within her, back to where it ended, at her cowboy.

The Lampasas Star, November 2:

Local Bull Rider Wins PBR Rookie of the Year

Tom and Maydelle Deacon, owners of the Deacon Ranch, traveled to Las Vegas in October to see their son Buster (Tom Junior) compete in the PBR World Finals.

Deacon did his hometown proud, capping off his Rookie of the Year title by riding 3 of the 5 bulls he selected in spite of riding with his off hand due to a shoulder injury.

The future looks bright for our newest local celebrity! If you run into him in town, shake that boy's hand!

The Bandera County Chamber of Commerce Newsletter, February 15:

New Business Report: Cahill Coaching

This week, "Cool Hand" Cam Cahill announced the opening of his new venture, Cahill Coaching. He will offer instruction and lifestyle coaching to aspiring and professional bull riders.

Interviewed at home where he is convalescing after an injury in Las Vegas,

Cahill said, "I've signed several bull riders already, including Buster Deacon, last year's Rookie of the Year. I hope to continue to make a difference and contribute to a sport that has given me so much."

The Bandera Blade, June 23:

Wedding Announcements:
Smith ~ Cahill

Local celebrity Cameron Cahill last Saturday wed Miss Katya Smith in a ceremony that took place on a bluff overlooking the Penny-Cahill Ranch. The bride wore an antique lace gown and an ivory Western hat with trailing veil. The groom wore a black Western tuxedo, hat, and cowboy boots.

Following a honeymoon on their ranch outside Fort Collins, Colorado, the couple will settle here in Bandera, and focus on building their new home, on the same bluff where they exchanged vows.

Charla Rae Denny was
the perfect wife with a perfect
life, married to a champion
bull rider.

But when tragedy strikes,
it's up to Charla to cowboy
up to put her life back
together...

Please see the next page
for an excerpt from

The Sweet Spot.

1

The grief counselor told the group to be grateful for what they had left. After lots of considering, Charla Rae decided she was grateful for the bull semen.

Charla Rae Denny wiped her hands with her apron and stepped back, surveying the shelves of her pantry. This month's *Good Housekeeping* suggested using scraps of linoleum as shelf paper. It had been a bitch-kitty to cut but cost nothing, would be easy to clean, and continued the white-pebbled theme of her kitchen floor. And for a few hours, the project had rescued her weary mind from a hamster-wheel of regret.

The homing beacon in the Valium bottle next to the sink tugged at her insides.

She sipped a glass of water to avoid reaching for it and glanced out the window to the spring-skeletal trees of the backyard.

Her gaze returned to the two-foot-wide stump the way a tongue wanders to a missing tooth. Tentative grass shoots had sprung up to obscure the obscene scar in the soil.

She hadn't thought that an innocent tree could kill a child.

She hadn't thought that an innocent coed could kill a marriage.

And if those pills could kill the thinking, she'd take ten.

At the familiar throaty growl of a Peterbilt turning off the road out front, Char jerked, realizing minutes had passed. She'd been listening for that deep throb for hours. She always did. As the cab and empty cattle hauler swept by the window, she wound her shaking hands in her apron, as if the sturdy cotton would hold her together.

A ranch wife could stretch a pound of hamburger further than anyone, but Daddy's new medication cost the moon, and the bills in the basket beside the computer were piling up like snowdrifts in a blizzard. Hands still shaking, she untied the bibbed apron and pulled it over her head. She'd rather clean bathrooms at the airport than ask her ex for money, but, then, most of her choices these days were like that. Sighing, she walked to the mudroom, shrugged into her spring jacket, yanked open the back door, and stepped into the nippy air.

Jimmy had backed the rig to the corral and left the engine running. He stepped down from the cab to stand, one foot on the running board, looking up into the dim interior, unaware of her approach. After all, the past four months she'd made sure that when he was here, she'd been purposely somewhere else.

He looked different. Her Jimmy, but with an older man superimposed, blurring the strong, familiar lines of the body she knew like her own. The mean midday sun highlighted the deep furrows bracketing his mouth and the brown hair curling from under his cowboy hat glinted with silver. His legs were still long and lean, but a bit of spare tire sheltered his huge oval belt buckle. Jimmy wouldn't go anywhere without his State Champion Bull Rider buckle.

She halted ten feet from the truck, thrust her fists in the pockets of the jacket, and forced words past the ball wedged in her throat. "Jimmy, we need to talk."

His head jerked around, face frozen in guilty shock. He looked like Benje as a toddler, caught misbehaving. Yet another reason she'd avoided him was stamped in the features he'd passed to their son.

He spun back to the cab and mumbled. She followed his line of vision to catch a quick flash of sun on bleached blond hair. Charla stopped, stunned to stillness. She'd doubt her vision if that flash of blond hadn't burned in her mind like a smoking brand.

"You brought her here, Jimmy?" she whispered. "To our—to *my* home?" Oh, sure, she'd known about the Cupcake. The whole town knew. The girl was the straw that had finished off their marriage.

Jimmy slammed the truck door and stood before it like a challenging bull. "That's not Jess, Charla. Jess and I broke up months ago. That's Mitzi, Jess's roommate. And before you get any wrong ideas, I'm taking her to the event to watch her boyfriend ride. That's it."

"Do you think I'm stupid? Lies like that only work once, Jimmy."

He ducked his head, strode the length of the trailer, and busied himself letting down the tailgate. She stalked him, anger advancing with every step.

"Do you have that little respect for me?" The pleading in her voice only made her madder. "James Benton Denny. You *look* at me."

Hands busy, he shot her his I-may-be-wrong-but-I'm-not-admitting-anything look.

Words piled into her throat, and she swallowed. "Aren't you even embarrassed? She could be your daughter, for cripes' sake. People are laughing their heads off—at you—at me." Her traitorous voice cracked.

"Look, I'm telling you the truth, okay?" Jimmy's voice echoed as he climbed into the cattle trailer. "The morning has been a disaster. First, that useless Emilio didn't show, and I had to fire him." The empty metal box amplified his sigh. "I needed to let him go anyway. We're making good money, but now the business has to support two households—" He hesitated, apparently recalling his audience.

"Then we had a flat on that danged retread. I knew better than to buy tires from Baynard's." Eyes down, he scanned the metal floor of the truck bed for anything that could hurt the stock. "I'm seriously late here, Little Bit, can we—"

"Don't you dare call me that!" She charged up the tailgate, her face blazing. "You lost that right two months, two weeks, four days ago."

He trotted by without a word, to the corral. The bulls, who had been watching the proceedings with interest, sauntered to the trailer. Realizing she stood between them and their destination, Char jumped from the tailgate.

Jimmy circled the pen, keeping a wary eye on the bulls, urging them gently toward the gate. "What did you want to talk to me about, Char?"

Slivers of pain shot up her palms. Realizing what she was doing, she relaxed her fingers until her nails popped out of the skin. *God, I'm a fool.* "Never mind."

"I'll be at the event in Abilene for the week."

Char stepped to the side of the corral to hear over the clatter of hooves on the metal tailgate.

"I've deposited the money from the last semen sale into your account, and I'm dropping the bulls off at the vet to have more collected on the return trip. I should be back with them sometime on the twenty-fifth."

After the last bull, Kid Charlemagne, trotted up the ramp, Jimmy hoisted the tailgate and shot the pins into place. His nonchalance stung more than his hubris. *Just another day dealing with the unreasonable ex.* Her odd, out-of-body objectivity kicked in again as Jimmy closed the corral gate. Why shouldn't he brush her off? What was she but an old coffee stain on his Important Life?

He still had a job, two of them, in fact. One, working as an arena announcer for the pro bull riding circuit and the other as a stock contractor, supplying bucking bulls for the events.

Her only job ended the day Benje died.

Jimmy halted in front of her, his gaze sharpening on her face. "You still taking those pills, Little Bit?" His brow creased like it did when he was considering, and the look in his eye softened to...pity? "You've gotta get off those things, Hon. Medicating your life won't make it better."

She wanted to slap the solicitous look off his face. She wanted to run.

Instead, she held her ground, stabbing a finger at the trailer. "Those bulls have nothing on *you* in the balls department. You've got no talking room, Jimmy. Your old life fell apart, so you just threw it away and started a new one. *Your* medication just leans toward blonde and brainless."

Delicious flames licked the inside of her skin, urging her on. "Well, then, you go on and lie in that bed, Jimmy Denny. I don't want to see your face on this property again. Do you hear me?"

Jimmy's mouth dropped. She'd gotten his attention now, all right.

"You can't do that, Char. You may own the semen, but I own the bulls. The land—"

"Is my daddy's. His Alzheimer's hasn't changed that, and I have his power of attorney." The freed flames roared in her ears, and her body shook with righteous crackling heat. "You know very well I can do this, and by God, if you show up here again, I'll call Sheriff Sloan and have you arrested for trespassing."

She crossed her arms over her chest and wished looks really could kill. "Just leave the rig at the vet. I'll pick up the bulls."

"But Char—"

She tipped her chin to the truck cab. "You'd better hurry, Jimmy. Your girlfriend is waiting." Spinning on her heel, Charla stomped stiff-legged to the house, mortification, anger, and fear roiling in her gut.

Giving the door a satisfying slam, she strode to the kitchen, to the fire extinguisher disguised as a prescription bottle.

Aubrey Madison needs to begin a new life.

Starting up a Pro Bull Riding enterprise with an old-fashioned cowboy could be just the ticket she needs—

until her past catches up with her...

Please see the next page for an excerpt from

Nothing Sweeter.

CHAPTER 1

Her "new" life was going be so much better than the last one. Aubrey Madison would make sure of that.

She savored the sight of a solitary saguaro standing sentinel on the flat Arizona landscape. She savored the red-tipped ocotillo branches that waved in the stiff breeze of the Jeep's passing. She even savored the chilled air that swirled in, raising the hair on her body in an exquisite shiver.

God, it's good to be out of prison.

Her face felt odd. Until she realized she was smiling.

Glancing at the gas gauge, she vowed to stop soon, only long enough to get gas and use the restroom. She had to keep putting on distance.

What if it's not possible to outrun your own conscience?

The pull of the road in front of her was as strong as the push from the vision in the rearview mirror.

A weather-beaten Sinclair sign in the distance made up her mind. She took the exit leading to a deserted corrugated building that might have once been painted white.

Pulling to the pump, she killed the ignition and sat a moment, listening to the *tick, tick, tick* of the cooling engine and the wind keening through the power lines. She stepped out, closing her denim jacket against the wind's probing fingers.

A bell over the station door jangled as she opened it, and a black-haired Native-American teen glanced up from behind the register.

Aubrey pulled bills from the pocket of her jeans. "I need to fill it up. Where's the restroom?"

His expression didn't change as his stare crawled over her throat. She fisted her hands to keep them still. When he finally pointed to a dark corner, she almost ran to it.

After solving the most urgent matter, she washed her hands. Her gaze locked on the black-flecked mirror. The ropy scar twisted from behind her ear to the bow of her collarbone, looking like something out of a slasher movie. Shiny. Raw. Angry. She jerked her gaze away, turned the water on full force in the sink, and tried once again to wash away the shame.

In her mind, she saw the sign she'd woken up to in the prison infirmary, hanging on the wall across from her bed.

If you're going through hell, keep going. Winston Churchill

In spite of her mantra, the walls closed in, as they always did. Yanking the door open, she fought to keep from running until she was outdoors, the wind kicking around her once more.

She reached for the gas nozzle, the tightness in her chest easing. When the Feds released her from eight months of perdition, her mother begged her to stay in Phoenix. But Aubrey couldn't get a deep breath there. The suburban ranch house crowded her with memories and worried eyes. This morning she'd packed and escaped.

Holding the lever in chilled hands, waiting for the tank to fill, she turned her back to the wind. *Alone.* She pulled the luxury of the empty landscape into her solitary-starved soul and lifted her face to the sun's tentative warmth, smiling once more. Nothing was sweeter than freedom.

Max Jameson twisted the cowboy hat in his hands and lowered his eyes to the body in the gray satin-lined casket. His father's broad shoulders brushed silk on both sides. His face looked unfamiliar, mostly because it was relaxed. But there was no mistaking the strong jaw and high cheekbones. Max saw them in the mirror every morning.

Just like you to duck out when the going gets tough, old man. His mouth twisted as his father's familiar chuckle echoed in Max's mind. *Leave me holding a sack of rattlesnakes. Lotta help you are.*

No response, which, on several levels, was probably a good thing.

Max scanned the empty viewing room. He dreaded the remainder of the day: the funeral, the cemetery, the reception at the ranch. *"Your dad is reunited with your mother after thirty-five years."* The thought of solicitous friends spouting platitudes was enough to make him bolt for the barn, saddle his horse, and get the hell out of his own life.

He surveyed his father's waxen features. *Yeah, and don't tell me you wouldn't do the same, you old boot.*

"Maxie?"

The singsong cadence in that single word snatched him back to when the man in the casket was a mountain, and a little kid with worshipful eyes dogged Max's footsteps. Only one person on earth dared to call him that.

Strap yourself in, Daddy. It's gonna get bumpy. He turned to face Wyatt.

His younger brother stopped a few steps short of the casket, his gaze dropping to his father. A worried frown marred the angelic face from Max's childhood. Wyatt looked familiar, but different, too. Soft cheeks had hardened to a man's, and his golden locks were gone, shorn short.

Well, the prodigal son returns. No points for bravery maybe, but—

"Did he suffer, Max?" Wyatt's voice wavered, his gaze locked on his father's face.

"Nope. One minute he's pounding in a post for the new fence line. The next, he's on the ground. Gone."

Wyatt's head snapped up, his eyes wide. "Jesus, Max. Do you have to be so cold-blooded?"

So much for the new and improved Max he'd committed to becoming just this morning while lying in bed, probing the scabbed-over edges of the hole in his life. "Kinder and gentler" melted before the blowtorch that was his life lately. "Just telling you what happened. Sugarcoating won't make it any prettier."

A hurting smile twisted Wyatt's mouth. "You sound like him."

Max knew he hadn't meant the words as a compliment. "Let's grab a cup of coffee before the vultures show up." He settled his Sunday Stetson on his head. "You and

I have a bucket of trouble, little brother. And trouble don't wait."

Three weeks later

Crisp, alpine air trumped the heat of the sun. Aubrey steered the top-down Jeep with her knee and swiped wind-whipped hair out of her mouth. The snow-capped Rockies whispered of winter, but brave weeds flowered at the side of the highway. With no set destination the past three weeks, the road had pulled her north. She'd slept in generic hotels and eaten at mom-and-pop diners. The familiar stiffness in her core leached out in the sameness of the days and the anonymity of her role as generic traveler.

A cautious optimism replaced it, along with a niggling of road weariness. When had she last felt excited about the future? College?

A quick look in the rearview mirror told her that her scrunchie had failed. Curly chestnut hair floated around her pale, too-thin face. That and the oversized cheap sunglasses made her look like a So-Cal heiress just out of rehab.

Except for the scar, of course.

She pulled the Dodgers cap from behind the seat and snugged it over the riot to solve two problems—she didn't need more freckles added to her collection.

A city limits sign announced her approach to Steamboat Springs. Her empty stomach growled demands.

Old-fashioned brick-fronted buildings lined the typical Western main street, foreground to a striking snow-capped mountain backdrop. She snagged a parking spot in front of a trendy bar and grill and climbed from the car, her joints creaking.

Noticing a stand of free local papers on the sidewalk, she grabbed one. She tugged open the heavy wooden door of the restaurant to lunch babble and a welcome blast of warm air. High ceilings and a long old-fashioned mahogany bar with a brass foot rail dominated the room. Midafternoon diners occupied the soda fountain–style chairs set around small wooden tables. The smell of onions and grilling beef told her she'd gotten lucky.

She chose a tall seat at the empty bar. The bartender appeared from a back room, a moonlighting college student, unless she missed her guess. "Sorry, ma'am. Didn't realize you'd come in. What can I get you?" He wiped his hands on a damp bar rag.

Ugh. My first "ma'am." Aubrey smoothed her hands over her waist to be sure middle-age spread hadn't begun since she'd gotten dressed that morning. *Everybody looks old to a baby like that.*

She ordered, then opened the newspaper. Designed as bait for cruising tourists, she'd found these local Realtor rags a good source for a quick area overview of the local geography, economy, and demographics.

An earsplitting shriek raised the hair on Aubrey's neck and arms. Her muscles jerked taut and she froze, head scrunched into her shoulders. The scream trailed off to a happy laugh. She spun in her seat.

A young couple sat at a small round table, attention focused on the baby in a high chair between them. The little boy was rapt, watching a small stuffed elephant his father held, his Cupid's-bow mouth open in anticipation. The man shook the toy and the ears flopped.

He swooped down and burrowed it into his son's neck. The baby threw his head back and shrieked again, the pitch rising to dog-whistle range before trailing off in a delighted giggle.

Aubrey felt her mouth stretch in a dumb grin. The peals of laughter were more than carefree; they were total ignorance of care. How long had it been since she'd heard happiness like that? Heard it, hell, had she ever *felt* it? Nobody knew how to party like a baby.

The mother glanced at Aubrey before putting her hand on her husband's arm. "I'm sorry. We forget that what we think is cute can be irritating to others."

A band loosened in Aubrey's chest, releasing a small moth flutter of happiness. "Anyone that finds a baby laugh irritating is dead inside." She smiled at the mother. "Thank you for sharing your joy."

Lighter, she turned back to her research. Turning the page to a marketplace section, she read of lost dogs, goats for sale, litters of kittens, and a burro free to a good home. Aubrey noticed quite a few ranches for sale. She turned to the brief help-wanted section.

WANTED: FULL-TIME STABLEHAND.

ROOM & BOARD INCLUDED. APPLY TO HIGH HEATHER RANCH.

That might be worth looking into. It would be fun to work with horses again. And God knows her new life could use some fun.

The band around her chest ratcheted as the craving for open air danced along her nerves. *I've got to find a way to stop this running.* She glanced out the window to where her Jeep waited, imagining spending the rest of her life as a ghost, driving across the country, never leaving a shadow of an impression on the places she left. Almost as if she never existed at all. A goose-on-a-grave shiver started between her shoulder blades and shot through her body.

Could she stop? Aubrey did a gut check, but her gut just repeated the demand for food. It didn't really matter if she could—she had to.

If I don't stop now, I never will.

She glanced at her faded UCLA T-shirt and sweatpants. Not quite interview couture. The college kid returned with a still-sizzling chunk of beef smothered in cheese. "Here you go, ma'am. Anything else I can get you?"

"This looks great, thanks." Her mouth watered. "Can you tell me—is there a Western-wear store in town?" The kid filled her in as she reveled in her food, taking large bites of yet another meal that didn't come from a prison kitchen.

At the Western Emporium a half hour later, Aubrey stood before a mirror, a shirt in either hand, considering. She'd found the perfect pair of skinny jeans, and the paddock-style lace-up boots she'd tried on went well with them. Good for work, but stylish too.

The tailored shirt on the right was dressy, polished black cotton with pearl snap buttons and white embroidered roses on the yoke. The one in her left was blue windowpane plaid, more a workday shirt. If the High Heather was a dressage barn, she'd know what to buy, but from the merchandise here, odds were against that.

She'd already decided to buy them both, but which one for an interview? The business rule in her previous life dictated dressing one notch above the position. A booster of adrenaline dumped into her bloodstream. This interview would set a whole tone for her new life. In the past week, the shining promise of the open road had soured. It now felt tainted, dark, and off somehow, like a whiff of carrion.

She *had* to get this job.

She changed into the fancy shirt and after a glance-in-the-mirror reminder, selected a package of bandanas on her way to the counter. She handed over her credit card and watched as the clerk ran it through the old-fashioned imprint machine.

She scribbled, *Aubrey Mad—*

Crap. Her fingers spasmed. Heat shot up her neck, making the scar throb. She scratched out her last name and wrote "Tanner" over the bad beginning, then pushed the receipt across the counter. Banks never looked at those things anyway.

THE DISH

Where Authors Give You the Inside Scoop

From the desk of Marilyn Pappano

Dear Reader,

The first time Jessy Lawrence, the heroine of my newest novel, A LOVE TO CALL HER OWN, opened her mouth, I knew she was going to be one of my favorite Tallgrass characters. She's mouthy, brassy, and bold, but underneath the sass, she's keeping a secret or two that threatens her tenuous hold on herself. She loves her friends fiercely with the kind of loyalty I value. Oh, and she's a redhead, too. I can always relate to another "ginger," lol.

I love characters with faults—like me. Characters who do stupid things, good things, bad things, unforgivable things. Characters whose lives haven't been the easiest, but they still show up; they still do their best. They know too well it might not be good enough, but they try, and that's what matters, right?

Jessy is one of those characters in spades—estranged from her family, alone in the world except for the margarita girls, dealing with widowhood, guilt, low self-esteem, and addiction—but she meets her match in Dalton Smith.

I was plotting the first book in the series, A Hero to Come Home To, when it occurred to me that there's a lot of talk about the men who die in war and the wives they leave behind, but people seem not to notice that some of our casualties are women, who also leave behind spouses, fiancés, family whose lives are drastically altered. Seconds behind that thought, an image popped into my head of the margarita club gathered around their table at The Three Amigos, talking their girl talk, when a broad-shouldered, six-foot-plus, smokin' handsome cowboy walked up, Stetson in hand, and quietly announced that his wife had died in the war.

Now, when I started writing the first scene from Dalton's point of view, I knew immediately that scene was never going to happen. Dalton has more grief than just the loss of a wife. He's angry, bitter, has isolated himself, and damn sure isn't going to ask anyone for help. He's not just wounded but broken—my favorite kind of hero.

It's easy to write love stories for perfect characters, or for one who's tortured when the other's not. I tend to gravitate to the challenge of finding the happily-ever-after for two seriously broken people. They deserve love and happiness, but they have to work so hard for it. There are no simple solutions for these people. Jessy finds it hard to get out of bed in the morning; Dalton has reached rock bottom with no one in his life but his horses and cattle. It says a lot about them that they're willing to work, to risk their hearts, to take those scary steps out of their grief and sorrow and guilt and back into their lives.

Oh yeah, and I can't forget to mention my other two favorite characters in A LOVE TO CALL HER OWN: Oz, the handsome Australian shepherd on the cover; and Oliver, a mistreated, distrusting dog of unknown breed.

I love my puppers, both real and fictional, and hope you like them, too.

Happy reading!

Marilyn Pappano

MarilynPappano.net
Twitter @MarilynPappano
Facebook.com/MarilynPappanoFanPage

♥ ♥ ♥ ♥ ♥ ♥ ♥ ♥ ♥ ♥ ♥ ♥ ♥ ♥ ♥ ♥

From the desk of Kristen Ashley

Dear Reader,

In starting to write *Lady Luck*, the book where Chace Keaton was introduced, I was certain Chace was a bad guy. A dirty cop who was complicit in sending a man to jail for a crime he didn't commit.

Color me stunned when Chace showed up at Ty and Lexie's in *Lady Luck* and a totally different character introduced himself to me.

Now, I am often not the white hat–wearing guy type of girl. My boys have to have at least a bit of an edge (and usually way more than a bit).

That's not to say that I don't get drawn in by the boy next door (quite literally, for instance, with Mitch Lawson of *Law Man*). It just always surprises me when I do.

Therefore, it surprised me when Chace drew me in while he was in Lexie and Ty's closet in *Lady Luck*. I knew in that instant that he had to have his own happily-ever-after. And when Faye Goodknight was introduced later in that book, I knew the path to that was going to be a doozy!

Mentally rubbing my hands together with excitement, when I got down to writing BREATHE, I was certain that it was Chace who would sweep me away.

And he did.

But I *adored* writing Faye.

I love writing about complex, flawed characters, watching them build strength from adversity. Or lean on the strength from adversity they've already built in their lives so they can get through dealing with falling in love with a badass, bossy alpha. The exploration of that is always a thing of beauty for me to be involved in.

Faye, however, knew who she was and what she wanted from life. She had a good family. She lived where she wanted to be. She was shy, but that was her nature. She was no pushover. She had a backbone. But that didn't mean she wasn't thoughtful, sensitive, and loving. She had no issues, no hang-ups, or at least nothing major.

And she was a geek girl.

The inspiration for her came from my nieces, both incredibly intelligent, funny, caring and, beautiful—and both total geek girls. I loved the idea of diving into that (being a bit of a geek girl myself), this concept that is considered stereotypically "on the fringe" but is actually an enormous sect of society that is quite proud of their geekdom. And when I published BREATHE, the geek girls came out of the woodwork, loving seeing one of their own land her hot guy.

But also, it was a pleasure seeing Chace, the one who had major issues and hang-ups, find himself sorted out by his geek girl. I loved watching Faye surprise him, hold up the mirror so he could truly see himself, and take the lead into guiding them both into the happily-ever-after they deserved.

This was one of those books of mine where I could have kept writing forever. Just the antics of the kitties Chace gives to his Faye would be worth a chapter!

But alas, I had to let them go.

Luckily, I get to revisit them whenever I want and let fly the warm thoughts I have of the simple, yet extraordinary lives led by a small-town cop and the librarian wife he adores.

♥ ♥ ♥ ♥ ♥ ♥ ♥ ♥ ♥ ♥ ♥ ♥ ♥ ♥ ♥

From the desk of Sandra Hill

Dear Reader,

Many of you have been begging for a new Tante Lulu story.

When I first started writing my Cajun contemporary books back in 2003, I never expected Tante Lulu would touch so many people's hearts and funny bones. Over the years, readers have fallen in love with the wacky old lady (I like to say, Grandma Moses with cleavage). So many of you have said you have a family member just like her; still more have said they wish they did.

Family...that's what my Cajun/Tante Lulu books are all about. And community...the generosity and unconditional love of friends and neighbors. In these turbulent times, isn't that just what we all want?

You should know that SNOW ON THE BAYOU is the ninth book in my Cajun series, which includes: *The Love Potion*; *Tall, Dark, and Cajun*; *The Cajun Cowboy*; *The Red Hot Cajun*; *Pink Jinx*; *Pearl Jinx*; *Wild Jinx*; and *So Into You*. And there are still more Cajun tales to come, I think. Daniel and Aaron LeDeux, and the newly introduced Simone LeDeux. What do you think?

For more information on these and others of my books, visit my website at www.sandrahill.net or my Facebook page at Sandra Hill Author.

As always, I wish you smiles in your reading.

Sandra Hill

♥ ♥ ♥ ♥ ♥ ♥ ♥ ♥ ♥ ♥ ♥ ♥ ♥ ♥ ♥ ♥ ♥

From the desk of Mimi Jean Pamfiloff

Dearest Humans,

It's the end of the world. You're an invisible, seventy-thousand-year-old virgin. The Universe wants to snub out the one person you'd like to hook up with. Discuss.

And while you do so, I'd like to take a moment to thank each of you for taking this Accidental journey with me and my insane deities. We've been to Mayan cenotes, pirate ships, jungle battles, cursed pyramids, vampire showdowns, a snappy leather-daddy bar in San Antonio, New York City, Santa Cruz, Giza, Sedona, and we've even been to a beautiful Spanish vineyard with an incubus. Ah. So many fun places with so many fascinating, misunderstood, wacky gods and other immortals. And let's not forget Minky the unicorn, too!

It has truly been a pleasure putting you through the twisty curves, and I hope you enjoy this final piece of the puzzle as Máax, our invisible, bad-boy deity extraordinaire, is taught one final lesson by one very resilient woman who refuses to allow the Universe to dictate her fate.

Because ultimately we make our own way in this world, Hungry Hungry Hippos playoffs included.

Happy reading!

Mimi

P.S.: Hope you like the surprise ending.

♥ ♥ ♥ ♥ ♥ ♥ ♥ ♥ ♥ ♥ ♥ ♥ ♥ ♥ ♥ ♥

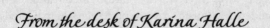

From the desk of Karina Halle

Dear Reader,

Morally ambiguous. Duplicitous. Dangerous.

Those words describe not only the cast of characters in my romantic suspense novel SINS & NEEDLES, book one in the Artists Trilogy, but especially the heroine, Ms. Ellie Watt. Though sinfully sexy and utterly suspenseful, it is Ellie's devious nature and con artist profession that makes SINS & NEEDLES one unique and wild ride.

When I first came up with the idea for SINS & NEEDLES, I wanted to write a book that not only touched on some personal issues of mine (physical scarring, bullying, justification), but dealt with a character little seen in modern literature—the antiheroine. Everywhere you look in books these days you see the bad boy, the criminal, the tattooed heartbreaker and ruthless killer. There are always men in these arguably more interesting roles. Where were all the bad girls? Sure, you could read about women in dubious professions, femme fatales, and cold-hearted killers. But when were they ever the main character? When were they ever a heroine you could also sympathize with?

Ellie Watt is definitely one of the most complex and interesting characters I have ever written, particularly as a heroine. On one hand she has all these terrible qualities; on the other she's just a vulnerable, damaged person trying to survive the only way she knows how. You despise Ellie and yet you can't help but root for her at the same time.

Her love interest, hot tattoo artist and ex-friend Camden McQueen, says it perfectly when he tells her this: "That is what I thought of you, Ellie. Heartless, reckless, selfish, and cruel…Beautiful, sad, wounded, and lost. A freak, a work of art, a liar, and a lover."

Ellie is all those things, making her a walking contradiction but oh, so human. I think Ellie's humanity is what makes her relatable and brings a sense of realism to a novel that's got plenty of hot sex, car chases, gunplay, murder, and cons. No matter what's going on in the story, through all the many twists and turns, you understand her motives and her actions, no matter how skewed they may be.

Of course, it wouldn't be a romance novel without a love interest. What makes SINS & NEEDLES different is that the love interest isn't her foil—Camden McQueen isn't necessarily a "good" man making a clean living. In fact, he may be as damaged as she is—but he does believe that Ellie can change, let go of her past, and find redemption.

That's easier said than done, of course, for a criminal who has never known any better. And it's hard to escape your past when it's literally chasing you, as is the case with Javier Bernal, Ellie's ex-lover whom she conned six years prior. Now a dangerous drug lord, Javier has been hunting Ellie down, wanting to exact revenge for her misdoings. But sometimes revenge comes in a vice and Javier's appearance in the novel reminds Ellie that she can never escape who she really is, that she may not be redeemable.

For a book that's set in the dry, brown desert of southern California, SINS & NEEDLES is painted in shades of gray. There is no real right and wrong in the novel, and the characters, including Ellie, aren't just good or bad. They're just human, just real, just trying to come to terms with their true selves while living in a world that just wants to screw them over.

I hope you enjoy the ride!

♥ ♥ ♥ ♥ ♥ ♥ ♥ ♥ ♥ ♥ ♥ ♥ ♥ ♥ ♥ ♥ ♥ ♥

From the desk of Kristen Callihan

Dear Reader,

The first novels I read belonged to my parents. I was a latchkey kid, so while they were at work, I'd poach their paperbacks. Robert Ludlum, Danielle Steel, Jean M. Auel. I read these authors because my parents did. And it was quite the varied education. I developed a taste for action, adventure, sexy love stories, and historical settings.

But it wasn't until I spent a summer at the beach during high school that I began to pick out books for myself. Of course, being completely ignorant of what I might actually want to read on my own, I helped myself to the beach house's library. The first two books I chose were Mario Puzo's *The Godfather* (yes, I actually read the book before seeing the movie) and Anne Rice's *Interview with the Vampire*.

Those two books taught me about the antihero, that a character could do bad things, make the wrong decisions, and still be compelling. We might still want them to succeed. But why? Maybe because we share in their pain. Or maybe it's because they care, passionately, whether it's the desire for discovering the deeper meaning of life or saving the family business.

In EVERNIGHT, Will Thorne is a bit of an antihero. We meet him attempting to murder the heroine. And he makes no apologies for it, at least not at first. He is also a blood drinker, sensual, wicked, and in love with life and beauty.

Thinking on it now, I realize that the books I've read have, in some shape or form, made me into the author

I am today. So perhaps, instead of the old adage "You are what you eat," it really ought to be: "You are what you read."

[signature]

♥ ♥ ♥ ♥ ♥ ♥ ♥ ♥ ♥ ♥ ♥ ♥ ♥ ♥

From the desk of Laura Drake

Dear Reader,

Hard to believe that SWEET ON YOU is the third book in my Sweet on a Cowboy series set in the world of professional bull riding. The first two, *The Sweet Spot* and *Nothing Sweeter*, involved the life and loves of stock contractors—the ranchers who supply bucking bulls to the circuit. But I couldn't go without writing the story of a bull rider, one of the crazy men who pit themselves against an animal many times stronger and with a much worse attitude.

To introduce you to Katya Smith, the heroine of SWEET ON YOU, I thought I'd share with you her list of life lessons:

1. Remember what your Gypsy grandmother said: Gifts sometimes come in strange wrappings.
2. The good-looking ones aren't *always* assholes.
3. Cowboys aren't the only ones who need a massage. Sometimes bulls do, too.

4. Don't ever forget: You're a soldier. And no one messes with the U.S. military.
5. A goat rodeo has nothing to do with men riding goats.
6. "Courage is being scared to death—and saddling up anyway." —John Wayne
7. Cowgirl hats fit more than just cowgirls.
8. The decision of living in the present or going back to the past is easy once you decide which one you're willing to die for.

I hope you enjoy Katya and Cam's story as much as I enjoyed writing it. And watch for the cameos by JB Denny and Bree and Max Jameson from the first two books!

♥ ♥ ♥ ♥ ♥ ♥ ♥ ♥ ♥ ♥ ♥ ♥ ♥ ♥ ♥

From the desk of Anna Campbell

Dear Reader,

I love books about Mr. Cool, Calm, and Collected finding himself all at sea once he falls in love. Which means I've been champing at the bit to write Camden Rothermere's story in WHAT A DUKE DARES.

The Duke of Sedgemoor is a man who is always in control. He never lets messy emotion get in the way of a rational decision. He's the voice of wisdom. He's the one who sorts things out. He's the one with his finger on the pulse.

And that's just the way he likes it.

Sadly for Cam, once his own pulse starts racing under wayward Penelope Thorne's influence, all traces of composure and detachment evaporate under a blast of sensual heat. Which *isn't* just the way he likes it!

Pen Thorne was such fun to write, too. She's loved Cam since she was a girl, but she's smart enough to know it's hopeless. So what happens when scandal forces them to marry? It's the classic immovable object and irresistible force scenario. Pen is such a vibrant, passionate, headstrong presence that Cam hasn't got a chance. Although he puts up a pretty good fight!

Another part of WHAT A DUKE DARES that I really enjoyed writing was the secondary romance involving Pen's rakish brother Harry and innocent Sophie Fairbrother. There's a real touch of Romeo and Juliet about this couple. I hadn't written two love stories in one book before and the contrasting trajectories throw each relationship into high relief. As a reader, I always like to get two romances for the price of one.

If you'd like to know more about WHAT A DUKE DARES and the other books in the Sons of Sin series— *Seven Nights in a Rogue's Bed*, *Days of Rakes and Roses*, and *A Rake's Midnight Kiss*—please check out my website: http://annacampbell.info/books.html.

Happy reading—and may all your dukes be daring!

Best wishes,

Anna Campbell